W9-CJZ-042

Jane & Michael Stern

FRIENDLY RELATIONS

DAVID OBST BOOKS
Random House   New York

Copyright © 1979 by Jane Stern and Michael Stern
All rights reserved under International and Pan-American Copyright
Conventions. Published in the United States by Random House, Inc.,
New York, and simultaneously in Canada by Random House of Canada
Limited, Toronto.

Library of Congress Cataloging in Publication Data
Stern, Jane.
Friendly relations.
I. Stern, Michael, 1946–   joint author.
II. Title.
PZ4.S8384Fr [PS3569.T3894] 813'.5'4 79-4798
ISBN 0-394-50358-9

Manufactured in the United States of America
24689753
First Edition

To Kathy

Acknowledgments

The authors thank David Obst for the creative energy he has devoted to this book from the beginning.

FRIENDLY
RELATIONS

One

By the time the Washington, D.C., winter had given way to spring, few Americans hadn't heard of Jeffrey Hodge. For this fact there was *Newsweek* to thank as well as its jealous twin, *Time*. The Andrews Sisters of the air, ABC, NBC and CBS, crooned his name into the nation's living rooms as supermarket tabloids trumpeted his impending role as escort to the daughter of the Premier of China.

In Jeffrey Hodge's bedroom there wasn't a trace of his sudden celebrity. Instead, there was only a calendar—a calendar devoid of mark or moment save one square, the center of which was pierced by a feathered dart. It marked the arrival of the Premier and his daughter in the United States. Their visit was to be a historic voyage of international good will, one that had already produced cultural shock waves rivaling crazes from jogging to King Tut. It had become impossible to converse at any cocktail party of note without talking about China. In fact, it was possible to believe that there wasn't an American anywhere who did not anxiously await the arrival of the delegation from Peking. Jeffrey Hodge considered himself a serious committee of one.

He lay motionless, looking out the window, avoiding

the calendar, which nonetheless managed to expose itself to his peripheral vision. The dart was buried deep in tomorrow. He knew too well that this was his last day of aloneness before the Chinese landed in their serious gray jet. He stroked the sides of the fine leather couch on which he lay. He had been chased from bed at noon by his mother's maid, who refused to leave his room until she made the bed. In his pajamas he had trudged heavily across the Oriental carpet and deposited himself on the couch, where he remained, content to lay still for hours, staring, brooding over tomorrow's arrival.

Jeffrey had come to realize that it was not easy to be the son of the Secretary of State. It was not at all easy to be nineteen years old and living at home, having discovered that your whole future has been meticulously planned for you by your parents.

His life had always been painless, enviable to most people. He visited the White House more times in a year than most people went to the movies. He had graduated from kiddie parties there to tea dances to formal dinners, where he and his parents were often seated at the head table with the President. All his life he had been told how promising his future looked and how lucky he was to be Raymond Hodge's son.

Yet, since last summer, when he had set off by himself to hitchhike around the country, Jeffrey had begun to see that there was a world beyond the cloistered society in which he had been raised, and there might be options other than the political path that his family had laid out for him.

To his father's dismay, Jeffrey had dropped out of Princeton and had come home, assuming he would be allowed the time and space to rethink the future that he had never questioned. But the coming of the Chinese and Jeffrey's unexpected reappearance in Washington had provided his father with a new formula to promote the career he had planned for his son. Jeffrey's all-American good looks, complete with thick blond hair and blue eyes that had just begun to crease at the corners, made him the ideal candidate for the job of escort to the Premier's daughter. And as a kind of penance for having left school, Jeffrey reluctantly accepted the assignment.

He had spent the last three months in the office of Lucas Pate, Vice-Chief of the Division of Protocol, listening to minuscule detail concerning his expected behavior in the presence of the seventeen-year-old Chinese girl. Each day his head was filled to bursting with diplomatic homilies, and each night he returned home to hear his father tell him that this was just the beginning, the first step in a lifetime of public servitude.

The Chinese girl had become the focus of Jeffrey's frustration with his assignment. As the weeks passed and the visit drew near, everything about her began to annoy him, even her name. "Chu Li Soong," the official memorandum instructed, "pronounced Chō Lē Soong. Father: Chu Fung-hsi, the Premier of China. Mother: Chu Yumei, deceased." The biographical data that had been heaped upon his desk over the last three months told him she stood five feet, four inches tall, weighed in at an insubstantial 103, and was allergic to wool. Perhaps, he mused, he might rent a flock of sheep to greet her at the airport. She was in her second year at Peking University, she was an honor student in English and a member of the Red Guard.

When her father had left the capital under Madam Chiang Ch'ing's reign in 1976, she had accompanied him to Kwangtung Province, where they were protected from the radicals by General Hsu Shih-yu. She returned to Peking with him the next year. Over the next twelve months, he acceded to power and initiated a program of reconciliation with the West. Like most Chinese youth, Li Soong had been educated that America was the enemy. When David Bromley, the President of the United States, extended his invitation to Chu's family, Li Soong was obligated to accompany her father. But, according to the memoranda, the girl was not positively inclined towards the policy of friendship with America, and from the thousands of pictures he had seen of her Jeffrey knew his role as escort would not be easy. In each picture she stood blank-faced and severe, and in each she was wrapped in a plain gray suit, with two silly-looking braids hanging like limp ropes down her back. Those braids swung like nooses in his dreams.

*

In the late afternoon hours he had heard his family shuffling around downstairs. He had heard them brush past his door repeatedly, but they didn't knock. Through the closed door Jeffrey had heard his mother ask the maid what he was doing in his room for so long, but they had left him alone, and for this he was grateful. The sun had risen and set, and he was still in his pajamas. He was secretly on strike, and he loved the feeling. He wondered if this was what a nervous breakdown was like, never wanting to get dressed. He knew that when the sun rose again, the Day of the Dart would be at hand, and he groaned, turning himself around on the couch so his face was to the soft maroon leather.

His stomach was growling, and somehow that seemed a fitting prelude for the inevitable knock that came at the door. "What?" he grunted listlessly as a cloud of perfume announced the presence of his mother, who had pushed the door open enough to flood the room with light from the hallway. "Hello, Mother," he said inaudibly.

She came closer, touching him ever so slightly with a manicured hand. "Are you feeling ill?" she asked rather formally.

"No, I'm all right."

"I can't hear you, dear," she said.

Jeffrey felt a flash of anger at her insistence. "I said I'm fine." His voice was louder but flat.

"Your father and I think you should get dressed and come down for dinner. It's not healthy for you to be lying like this in the dark. Wash up and get dressed and please come down."

"I'd rather be alone. I'm not hungry," Jeffrey said, but his stomach whined its own plea of contradiction.

"Your father wants you downstairs. He doesn't understand this behavior, and frankly neither do I."

Her perfume seemed to grow stronger as she spoke, and Jeffrey felt weakened by its sweetness, softened by the brush of her cashmere sweater on his arm. Her immaculately groomed blond hair and precise composure only magnified his own feelings of flux and confusion. He pulled himself up into a hunched sit, staring into the shadowy corner of the room. "Why can't you just let me alone, Mother . . . I have things on my mind."

"You're not being fair to your father." She spoke in the tone of voice that is handed out to mothers in the hospital after each delivery. "Really, dear, you have to understand how proud he is of you, and how anxious he is for you to be at your best tomorrow when the eyes of the world will be on you."

"The eyes of the world." Jeffrey repeated the phrase as if it were a court sentence. His mother reached for the light switch, and with a touch banished the shadows. Jeffrey cringed.

"Now, please—get dressed and come down for supper in ten minutes." She closed the door behind her as she left.

Jeffrey Hodge rarely ate dinner at home. It was at the table he most regretted leaving college for the oppressive formality of his parents' dining room. He had once asked his mother if, for a change, it would be possible to extinguish the candles, excuse the servants, and serve the food out of the containers in which it came instead of the silver and Spode receptacles. The look on her face made Jeffrey feel as if he had suggested the family eat their evening meal in the john. Still, he yearned for the one meal that would be served without a white-uniformed maid at his shoulder.

Raymond Hodge, as always, sat at the head of the table. He was half-finished with his fruit cup when Jeffrey finally appeared at the dining room's doorway. He looked up at his son from atop half-frame glasses. The propriety of his banker-gray suit matched the formal table service.

"Hi," the boy said balefully. "Sorry I'm late." He took a seat and laid waste to the grapefruit sections the maid placed in front of him. Jeffrey felt the anxious shift of his mother's eyes from him to his father. He saw her chest ease when Ray Hodge smiled and turned to his son.

"I can understand a little case of nerves. Hell, I have 'em myself, Jeff. After all, the eyes of the world are on us."

Jeffrey's throat tightened. "Yeah, Mom said that already." He had developed a loathing for that phrase. He wondered if in addition to its eyes the world also had ears, lips, armpits. It made him want to throw his fruit cup into the world's prying orb.

"You can bet on one thing, son—the Chinese girl is as nervous as you are."

"You make it sound like I'm getting married," Jeffrey said. "You know, I'm not that important. I'm just a chaperone, for heaven's sake. I mean, her father and all his guys will be here too, not to mention the President and all of you . . ." Jeffrey motioned to his father with his spoon.

"Don't point with the silverware, dear," his mother instructed.

"There's no such thing as 'just a chaperone' for this

one, Jeff. It's the big one. Everything we say to them, every gesture, speech, every place we go is going to re-verb around the world."

Jeffrey's appetite began to vanish.

"You pull this one off, son, and who knows what from there," his father continued, his voice slipping into a lullabye. "You make a name for yourself, and in a few years, when you finish school, you get yourself an ap-pointment, or maybe run for office—"

"I told you, I'm not sure about going back to college," Jeffrey said. "And about politics—"

His mother interrupted. "Going back to college is a subject that will not be discussed anymore. I thought we made that clear enough, Jeffrey. This year is a rest period for you, but as certainly as the sun will rise tomorrow you will be back on campus in the fall."

"Bettina, let's not argue with the boy. Can't you see how nervous he is? Of course he's going back to school in the fall, and he's going to make us damn proud tomor-row, aren't you, son, damn proud?"

Jeffrey felt his features draw into the unpleasant mask he had perfected a long time ago to hide his true feelings from his parents. He stared at a spot on the wallpaper and said nothing. A servant broke his stare. "Thanks, Inez," he said as the serving maid set the gold-rimmed plate before him. "But I'm not at all hungry."

"Just leave it there," his mother directed. "He'll pick at it."

Jeffrey glanced down at a small roasted bird sitting lonely in the gleaming ring of china. Its two tiny drum-sticks were rigid and capped with foolish paper cups.

"Jeffrey," his father said between bites, "have you re-viewed the memoranda Pate sent over here this morn-ing?"

"Yes, sir," Jeffrey lied.

"How about a little quiz. Nothing like a bit of last-minute cramming to make you feel secure on the job."

Jeffrey resisted the pressure building in his stomach. "I don't need any more reviews. I know everything."

"Son, no one in politics knows everything. There is always one last fact to memorize, one last detail to remember."

Jeffrey tried to stem the conversation before it gained too much momentum. "Dad—"

"For instance," Ray Hodge pointed out as he vigorously salted his game hen, "suppose the girl asks you what you think of our trade embargo against Laos?"

"I don't know," Jeffrey shrugged. "I'd tell her I think it should be lifted . . . Aren't the Chinese friends with the Laotians?"

"Wrong!" Ray Hodge thundered in resounding judgment. "They used to be, but ten days ago they severed relations. You see what I mean?"

"I guess I didn't remember that," Jeffrey said, trying to ease his father from the game.

"There can be no wrong guesses in this operation," the man said gravely. "Now, what if she asks you about the birth control program advocated by our government? She might, too. The Chinese are very interested in that sort of thing."

Jeffrey leaned his head on his arm, which was propped on the table. "Uhh . . ." He searched for the right answer. "I'd tell her every men's room has a machine for that purpose," he joked.

His father's jowls grew a beefy red over his white collar.

"Ray, let him eat," Bettina Hodge commanded in an attempt to stave off the outburst she saw coming.

"Excuse me," Jeffrey said as he quickly rose from the table and headed into the hallway.

"Jeffrey!" Ray Hodge's voice rang sharply as Jeffrey hit the first step. "Where are you going?"

"To my room."

"Jeffrey, we have a lot more to go over. Lucas Pate
will be coming for coffee after dinner, and he'll want
to review our position on health care for senior citi-
zens, our grain shipments and trade policies with you
. . . Jeffrey? Come here, I don't like talking to you
through a wall."

But it was too late for Jeffrey to hear. He had grabbed
his old leather jacket from the brass hook in the closet
and raced through the door of the kitchen into the evening air.

He walked ten blocks before he found a direction. His
head was clouded with doubts and angers, and until they
subsided they blinded his path. If his father or Lucas
Pate mentioned "the girl," as Li Soong had come to be
called, one more time, he felt he would scream and bash
them over the head with his mother's candelabrum. He
could not avoid those two awful words, *t-h-e g-i-r-l*. He
saw them looming, Ben Hur style, in crumbling stone,
monumentally huge in his path. He imagined a machine
gun spitting out *the girl* in rapid-fire bullets. He could
feel the seven letters branded into his skin with hot pok-
ers. The more he thought like this, the more he frightened himself; and the more he frightened himself, the
more he found his feet heading for the apartment of his
friend Hazleton Brown.

"Howdy, Hodge," Hazleton drawled as Jeffrey walked
through his unlocked door, then knocked as an after-
thought.

"I had to get away. They were driving me crazy. Can
I hang around?" Jeffrey asked with a politeness that he
rarely used at home.

"Sure, why the hell not?" Hazleton said, downing the
last of a can of Coke, then flinging it in a lazy arc into
a waste basket.

"You get your piece in for tomorrow's paper?" Jeffrey

asked, noticing the cascade of crumpled papers overflowing the reporter's trash can.

"Unh unh," Hazleton said. "I'm heading to the story now. If you had come ten minutes later you would have missed me."

"Oh, yeah, where are you going?"

"A place called the Atomic Bar. It's a hangout for the dock workers who are out on strike. I'm going to play some poker."

"Can I go with you?" Jeffrey asked, his eyes so naked with hope that Hazleton was embarrassed to return the glance.

"Naw, you don't want to come with me, Hodge. Don't you have to be at the air base tomorrow morning to meet—"

Jeffrey interrupted: "Don't say it, please."

"It's gotten to you already? I could have told you—"

"I wish you had. I can't stand it. You have no idea what it's like being with Lucas Pate, my father, all of them. You'd think Jesus and Mary were coming."

"Maybe you'd *better* come along," Hazleton said, his Alabama accent soothing the raw ends of Jeffrey's nerves. "I'll buy ya a beer."

"Thanks," Jeffrey said. "Maybe I can help with the story."

"Sure, kid," Hazleton replied charitably as he headed for the door. "Let's get a move on." Hazleton Brown was the last reporter at the *Post* to want to hang around with the sons and daughters of Washington society. Like most, he regarded them as empty-headed, rich and spoiled. And no one at the paper seemed to understand why he made the exception for Jeffrey Hodge. In fact, he had trouble putting a label on it himself, except that there was a certain turmoil about the kid that he sensed he liked. Perhaps it was the nascent rebellion he saw brewing in the boy against his white-bread upbringing.

He wore jeans while his peers wore J. Press slacks, and he loved to listen to Hazleton's stories about barbeque, truckdrivers, coon dogs, and small-town America. Hazleton sometimes felt like the keyhole through which Jeffrey glimpsed the earthy side of life.

"I really appreciate your letting me come," Jeffrey said as they descended the stairs to the company car parked illegally at the curb. "They're driving me nuts."

"Let's move. I'm late now," Hazleton said, pushing Jeffrey into the passenger seat. "You can cry into your beer at the Atomic. Only one thing—do it softly. It's a blood-bucket tavern."

"Great," Jeffrey said enthusiastically. "My kind of place."

*

As soon as Jeffrey Hodge walked through the doors of the Atomic Bar and Grill, Hazleton Brown sensed that he had made a mistake in bringing his friend. The reporter had worked too hard gaining the strikers' confidence to have Jeffrey jeopardize it. He watched the workers size up the boy. Their eyes flickered over his expensive shoes, his uncalloused hands, the tousled blond curls that had never seen the shears of a buck-fifty barber. Hazleton heard the uncomfortable shuffle of thirty-seven pairs of steel-toed work shoes and down-at-the-heel Florsheims as he and Jeffrey stood just inside the entrance.

As he turned to tell Jeffrey to leave, he was struck by the look of bliss on his young friend's face. He knew the boy was a dilettante of the blue-collar adventure, and the yeasty, sweat-tinged atmosphere of the Atomic Bar and Grill had instantly banished his gloom.

"What a great place," Jeffrey whispered in an awed tone. "It's so . . . so real."

"You *do* remember I'm here on business, Hodge. I can't spend the night messing around with you," the reporter said, regarding Jeffrey's infatuation with amusement.

"I know, I know," Jeffrey said as his eyes drunk in the bar. He stood in the middle of the floor, gawking like a hick at a skyscraper.

"Okay, I'm glad you like it," Hazleton said, pushing Jeffrey ahead of him towards the bar. "Two beers." As the bartender wiped two schooners with a stained apron and held them under the tap, they mounted the barstools. "Now I'm going to buy you a drink, and then I'm going to park you on this stool until I'm finished. All right?"

"Sure, whatever you say," Jeffrey said, reaching for the glass that was placed before him. He took a sip and nudged Hazleton. "How long do you think those eggs have been in that jar for?" he said, pointing to a dozen eggs that floated lazily in pink brine.

Hazleton considered them a moment as he drank too. "Not as long as those wieners." He nodded to a container of embalmed sausages on the bar.

"Eech, do people really eat those?" Jeffrey asked. "Or are they just here for display?"

"Pretty, aren't they?" Hazleton said dryly.

"This is the worst beer," Jeffrey grimaced. "It doesn't even have a head on it."

"That's because it's B.C.P.," Hazleton said. "Hell, I was nursed on this."

"What's B.C.P.?"

"Basic Cat Piss."

Jeffrey burst out laughing, drawing covert looks from the workers.

"Be cool, kid," Hazleton said in a low voice. Jeffrey stifled his hilarity, doing his best to emulate the tough veneer of his friend. Hazleton's street-wise attitude was not the only thing Jeffrey admired about the older man. The reporter moved with a redneck swagger that Jeffrey had never learned in prep school. His life and the excitement of his work were completely different than what had been planned for the son of the Secretary of State. As smart as he was tough, Hazleton Brown was an original, and no one appreciated that as much as Jeffrey Hodge.

"Now, we didn't come here to shoot the breeze," the reporter said as his hand flashed a sign for the bartender to bring another round. "I got a story to get, and you're just along for the ride. Right?"

"Right," Jeffrey nodded enthusiastically. "I won't get in your way. Just go ahead and do what you have to do. I'll sit here and watch."

"That's the ticket. Wait for me to come get you. One more thing: If anyone should strike up a conversation, remember—this isn't the Hasty Pudding Club." Hazleton looked hard at Jeffrey.

"You don't have to worry about me. I've been in lots of bars like this. Tougher ones, too," Jeffrey bragged. "That summer I told you about, when I thumbed my way all around the country . . . I hit some places you couldn't go in without a .44."

Hazleton rolled his eyes. He doubted if Jeffrey would know a .44 from a .22. And if the kid was about to launch into one of his stories about his two-month summer vacation, Hazleton was going to personally heave him out the door. "Well, then, you know just how to sit on this stool and mind your own business." The reporter's voice grew serious. "Those men in the corner. They're my story."

Jeffrey shook his head willingly and let his friend walk across the room to the table of poker players.

Hazleton glanced back over his shoulder to make sure Jeffrey was where he left him, then addressed the seated men. "Remember me, Herzak?" he said to a fleshy bunker of a man who sat closest. "Brown from the *Post*. How about dealing me in?"

*

From behind smoked double-glass portholes, Chu Li Soong, the daughter of the Premier of China, looked out on the iridescent pollution of the Denver skyline. The plane had lifted above the weather, so she could not see the oily diagonals of rain that cascaded down upon the city. It was her eleventh hour on board the mammoth Chinese jet, less than three hours away from its final destination—Washington, D.C.

A copy of the New York *Times* lay on her lap as she leaned back in the velvet seat of the plane. Li Soong had exhausted herself reviewing the American articles about the arrival of her father's delegation. Straining her English vocabulary, she had doggedly translated each piece, then raged to her elderly seatmate, P'eng Hsi.

"Look what they have written, P'eng. They sell kimonos in a store to honor our arrival. Disgusting, decadent culture! They have prepared for our visit for half a year, and they still show no understanding of our people's ideals. They think we still sit idle in ornamental robes!"

Even P'eng Hsi, who had lovingly watched Li Soong grow from a child, was beginning to tire of her endless complaints. He had pulled away from her in his seat, and compressed himself into a tight knot to feign sleep.

Li Soong saw her father watching her from across the aisle on a small couch. "Father, are *you* listening to me? I said there are pages and pages of this newspaper filled with such nonsense!" Li Soong continued her angry recitation.

The Premier stood up and walked to where she sat. He placed his small, dry hand on her shoulder to calm her, and removed the paper from her lap, laying it on the empty seat across from her. He had hoped the extended plane trip might extinguish some of Li Soong's fiery resistance to the visit. But despite the flight's tedium, she still fought against the new principles of friendship that the trip represented. The Premier knew that for five days as guests of the President, he and his daughter would be voluntary captives of capitalist hospitality, and he fretted over his daughter's ability to submit to the regime of protocol that lay ahead.

How young seventeen is, he thought as he regarded Li Soong's windburned cheeks, her smooth-plaited braids anchored with bands of red cloth, the slim stomach that resisted the folds of her somber suit. She seemed half evolved to him, and in her brooding face the Premier could still see the ghost of her childhood, the same sweet mouth and cheeks he used to stroke—now set in petulant adolescent attitudes. She was still his child . . . the braids, the wisps of hair falling exactly as they had when she had slept in his lap on long summer evenings in Szechuan, his first exile from the capital during the Cultural Revolution. But she was becoming someone else, and it made him uncomfortable even to think of it.

The change invariably caught him off guard, and when he saw it he could feel his stomach muscles contract. In the middle of a talk (or fight, as their discussions had increasingly become), a gesture of hers would hurtle him back in time to the memory of Li Soong's mother. In place of the childish features was the face of a woman, the woman he once had loved, and the pain at the transformation made him turn away from his daughter.

Yet he knew he searched for the change. He would match the child to the mother feature by feature. He saw it happen in a transient expression or an attitude she struck. It was unpredictable, and as much as it warmed him to see her emerge from her childhood, the process seemed to be wrenching her from him. The discomfort he felt in Li Soong's presence was added to the long list of other concerns the Premier of China was bringing with him on this visit to America.

"Please, Li Soong, you are tiring us all with your lecturing. Why not try to rest before we land?"

"I have no need to rest," Li Soong said sullenly. "I am not old like you."

"You don't realize how exhausting our schedule will be when we arrive."

"You would prefer I sleepwalk through our visit, so that I do not offend our hosts?" Li Soong pressed her father.

The Premier held his tongue and turned from his daughter towards his advisor, Cheng Wu. He shrugged his shoulders. "She is being impossible," he said quietly to Cheng. "We should not have let her come. She believes that she knows more of international politics than we do. She believes herself to be Chairman Mao's personal reincarnation. Cheng, please speak to her. She doesn't listen to me anymore. Go over the itinerary with her again. Divert her attention."

Cheng Wu stepped over the sleeping P'eng Hsi and deposited himself in the empty seat across from Li Soong. She was staring out the small window at the American military escort planes that had accompanied the Chinese jet since the coast of Oregon. "Li Soong, shall we review the greeting in English again?" he asked.

"I know it, Cheng," she replied brusquely, continuing to stare out at the tiny F-15s that carved their way through the thin atmosphere. From her seat she could see the faces of the American pilots.

"If you know it, let me hear it, please," Cheng insisted. "There must be no errors. The whole world will be watching our arrival."

Li Soong bristled. She knew this fact too well. For months she had studied every aspect of America in her books and with her father's advisers, and she disliked everything they told her. In all her schooling she had learned there were two ways to approach life—the Chinese way and the American way. She had been taught that between the two paths there could be no compromise. Now, to her dismay and confusion, the tables had been turned. Newly opened relations with the West had suddenly thrown everything she had learned into doubt. Her schoolmates, militant as she, chided her for her father's acquiescence to détente.

Li Soong resolved before her young comrades to hold fast to the militant spirit with which she had been raised. She vowed that she would never be a willing dupe of American propaganda. She would return to China with nothing but the unadulterated truth about capitalist society.

"Well?" Cheng Wu startled her from her fascination with the American jets flying alongside the plane.

"They are show-offs, anyway," Li Soong said. "They see me watching and do fancy dives."

"Don't be silly," Cheng said. "They can't possibly see you."

"No?" Li Soong looked disappointed. "I'm not so sure of that."

"Let's get on with the speech, please," Cheng demanded, and Li Soong proceeded to launch into a spiritless but accurate recitation of the short address her father had insisted she give to the Americans upon landing. The adviser complimented her: "Good, very good. Now, if you can remember the rest of your duties as well, we shall have no problems."

Li Soong's eyes narrowed. "What you have insisted I learn is an insult to the Chinese people. We have been taught nothing more than to behave like Americans. You have schooled us how to act as if we enjoy silliness like the American shopping stores and watching baseball players and eating elaborate meals. What we *should* have learned is how to press our hosts into showing us what exists beyond the fancy screens they will erect to block our vision of the true nature of their country—"

Li Soong was only beginning, but Cheng Wu cut her off: "We have gone through this one hundred times. This visit is a mission of diplomatic good will. Now is not the time for your father to press the American leaders. We are here to show them that we are willing to be accessible for future negotiations."

"I do not agree with that," Li Soong insisted.

"This we know," Cheng Wu said wearily. "You have made it most clear." He removed himself from the seat and headed back to join the Premier.

"How is she?" the father asked.

"She is so certain about the outcome of this trip, she has drawn all her conclusions before we land," Cheng Wu said, lighting a cigarette.

The Premier uttered a slight groan. "I'll have one, too," he said.

"Anyway," Cheng continued, "I'm sure she will be fine once we land. We will be with her at all times, and I'm certain she will do nothing to embarrass us."

"I hope you're right," the Premier said, exhaling a cloud of smoke. "One thing I have learned already on this trip—she is indeed my daughter. Her bullheadedness makes it obvious."

Cheng Wu laughed uneasily. "Don't worry, comrade. We will not let her jeopardize the harmony of this visit. We will all watch her. Everyone will be watching her with utmost scrutiny."

"Yes," the Premier agreed. "And that is precisely why I am so worried."

*

A shred of morning sunlight filtered through the small greasy window of the Atomic Bar as the game of five-card stud rolled into its eighth hour. Only hard-core drunks and a tense contingent of men whose last week's pay was on the table remained. Hazleton Brown had managed to milk Otto Herzak and his men for the inside line on their strike, and was preparing to ease himself gracefully out of the game. Throughout the night, he had watched Jeffrey wander around the old bar, drinking beers, moving aimlessly from stool to booth to chair, talking with the barmaids, and occasionally watching the TV that perched over the counter. The boy had been no trouble at all, but as Hazleton considered the best way to extract himself from the game, Hodge suddenly appeared by his side.

"Haz, I gotta get back to the house. I'm gonna leave now."

"Yeah, me too," he said to Jeffrey, then turned to the men at the table. "Fellas, I'm going to call it quits."

"Cut the cards, cut the cards," the dealer said, ignoring the reporter's statement. Hazleton obliged, severing the deck.

"Cut dog got no pups." Herzak laughed as he let go a sulphurous fart.

Hazleton turned to Jeffrey. "Hodge, I gotta stay in for one more hand. Then we'll go. Park yourself on that bench, and we'll be out in a flash."

"I'm tired of waiting," Jeffrey said crankily. "How about dealing me in?" Hazleton could see the boy had had one beer too many and was about to forget the rules he had laid down for the evening.

"Bad idea," the reporter said, laughing him off. "Go on back to the bench and I'll be with ya in a minute."

"Who's he, anyway, yer kid brudda?" Otto Herzak asked.

"Yeah," Hazleton said, passing the question by.

"Deal him in," one of the other men said. "He looks like a heavy roller to me."

"Naw, he can't play for shit," Hazleton said.

"Yes, I can." Jeffrey was by his side again. "I'm a great player. What's the game?"

"Oh, Christ," Hazleton said under his breath, shooting Jeffrey a bullet of a look. Jeffrey was oblivious to it. Hazleton started to get up from the table, but was stopped by a heavy hand on his shoulder, pressing him down. A broken-nosed face pushed towards him.

"We been decent wit you, reporter. Don't get cute wit us."

"Yeah, sure," Hazleton said reluctantly as he gave Jeffrey the nod to join the game. "But just one hand. The kid's got an appointment to get to." He kicked Jeffrey hard under the table with the toe of his cowboy boot.

*

As the phone rang, Bettina Hodge struggled free from the coils of Porthault linen that covered her bed. "My God, what time is it?" She cursed as she tried to locate the phone. "Yes, who is this?" she called into the receiver.

"Bettina, this is Lucas Pate."

"Lucas, what's wrong?" Bettina asked, muffling a morning cough. She noticed light peeking in around the drawn drapes, and realized it was the beginning of the big day.

"It's Jeffrey. He's not here."

"Where?" Bettina said, confused.

"Here, in the office. It's seven A.M. and we had a last-minute briefing scheduled. Has he left yet?"

Bettina Hodge felt the blood stop in her veins. She kicked the form of her sleeping husband with her naked foot as her brain reeled for an answer. "Left . . . of course he left," she stammered. She nudged her bedmate harder, covering the phone's mouthpiece. "Ray," she hissed. "Buzz Jeffrey."

Ray Hodge pressed the intercom twice. When he got no answer, his wife signaled the housekeeper downstairs. "Is my son here?" she asked.

"No, ma'am, I don't believe he came back last night."

The static of the phone line abraded Lucas Pate's ear. He could hear the silent panic on the other end. He waited until the voice of the Secretary of State issued forth, bursting with false assurance.

"Luke, Jeff's been delayed; but he's on his way."

"Ray, what's going on? He wasn't there last night when I came over, and now he's not here this morning. Nothing's up that I shouldn't know about, is it?"

"Pate, would I lie to you? The kid's on his way. Just sit tight." Ray Hodge hung up the phone, looking with horror at his wife.

Bettina read his mind. "He couldn't do this . . . I mean, he wouldn't, would he?" she asked, biting her bottom lip.

"How could a son of mine have so little sense of responsibility?" Raymond Hodge angrily demanded. He plunged his arms into his dressing gown and headed for the bathroom.

"What should we do, Ray?" she called. "Where could he be?"

"I don't know," he shot back. "But if I thought he would pull a stunt like this, I would personally have tied him to the bedpost."

*

The dollars continued to pile up in front of Jeffrey Hodge. Hazleton's back had sprouted a butterfly of nervous sweat. The expressions of the men at the table had gone from casual amusement at the kid's first lucky draw to black anger as their money mounted in front of him.

Herzak was the first to say the word: *"Hustler."* He spit it out like a bad clam. "Lookit his hands, like a goddamned woman's . . . smooth."

Hazleton let the comment float up towards the tin ceiling. To challenge it was to fight.

But the bad wind continued to blow. Jeffrey's luck wouldn't quit.

"As I said when the boy first sat down," Hazleton

spoke with feigned casualness, "he's got to be going. He's late."

The comment was met with four looks that could melt steel.

"You're right. I have to get out of here," Jeffrey said, looking at his watch. "It's nine o'clock. The plane lands in an hour."

"What plane?" one of the men asked suspiciously.

"His mother's," Hazleton interrupted before Jeffrey had a chance to answer.

"His poor old gray-haired mother," Herzak said with a sneer. "She's gonna have to take a taxi, cause your boy's gonna play out a few more hands with a fresh deck."

"I don't have the time," Jeffrey said, starting to rise as he reached out to scoop up the wad of dollars that sat in front of him. A thick, callused hand pinned him by the wrist to the table.

"Hey, that hurts," Jeffrey cried out. "What're you doing?"

Hazleton felt his muscles receive a booster shot of adrenalin. He remained still.

"You ain't goin' nowhere until we get a fresh deck," the dealer broadcast around a stubby cigar butt.

Hazleton cleared his throat. "Why don't we get moving and let the men keep this money as our contribution to their strike fund." The men's tight faces began to ease slightly. At the reporter's suggestion, the situation looked like it might cool.

"That's not fair," Jeffrey interjected.

Hazleton felt an immediate urge to strangle his young friend.

"I won it, fair and square," Jeffrey insisted. The tensions of the long night charged him with emotions that swept away his better judgment.

"Like hell you did," the dealer said, standing up. "I saw you palm that ace before you spread your flush."

"You're crazy," Jeffrey said audaciously. "You're just lousy players. That's my money, and I'm not leaving without it."

Suddenly he felt Hazleton's hand on his shoulder, squeezing through his shirt like a C-clamp. "Hodge, shut the hell up. You have a plane to meet, remember?"

The table fell silent. Each player knew the situation was reaching its outer limit. The stand-off was interrupted by the television set. "Holy shit, look!" Herzak said, pointing to the TV screen over the bar. "Look . . . it's him . . . !" Sharing space with the Secretary of State and the President's family was a picture of the lucky young poker player.

"What the hell?" one of the men wondered out loud as a newscaster announced the boy's name.

"I can't believe the nerve of this little rich bastard," the dealer called out. "He comes in here and hustles us. We outta ram those cards up a place that never sees daylight."

"He ain't walkin out of here with my paycheck, you can believe that."

Jeffrey knew perfectly well what Clint Eastwood would do in a situation like this. He knew all about belting adversaries over the head with barstools and throwing men through plate glass windows . . . at least in the movies. But as the ring of angry workers crowded in towards him he felt his own legs grow numb with fear. Strangely, his mouth seemed to disconnect from his body's cowardice, and as Herzak came towards him he heard his own voice sounding loud and clear. "You're just a lousy loser. Not only that, I've seen trained chimps that play better poker than you."

Hazleton saw the punch coming before Jeffrey's words were out of his mouth. He stepped protectively between Jeffrey and the fist, catching the blow in his left eye. He felt his contact lens detach and sail across the room. Instinctively he returned the blow, his arm sinking into Herzak's flour-sack middle, doubling him over like the Pillsbury Dough Boy with a cramp.

As if a switch had been pressed, the bar broke into a free-for-all. Drunks who had seemed immobile stood up swinging bottles in the air. Ashtrays and dollars, beer glasses and bottles toppled to the ground as the poker table was uprooted. The dealer skidded on a puddle of beer that spread across the floor.

"Go!" Jeffrey heard Hazleton's voice call out as the reporter pushed him towards the door. Flying fists swung blindly behind. "Move it, Hodge," he called as they tumbled together into the bright morning sun.

"You asshole!" Hazleton screamed at Jeffrey as he gunned the engine and peeled away from the curb, leaving at least fifty miles' worth of Goodyear rubber behind. Jeffrey watched his friend's chest rise and fall violently as he gasped for breath. A small trickle of blood dripped onto his knit tie.

"You're bleeding," Jeffrey said, suddenly at a loss for words.

"Give me something . . . there's a napkin down there," Hazleton said in a fury, pointing to an abandoned Kentucky Fried Chicken box that lay on the floor. He pressed the napkin to his nose, driving with his head tilted back. The car swerved and bounced off the curb.

"Can't you see where you're going?"

"No. I lost my goddamned lens. I'm blind."

"Do you want me to drive?"

"No," Hazleton boomed back. "You'll find a way to screw that up too."

"You're really sore about this, aren't you?"

Hazleton responded by leveling his swelling eye at Jeffrey and glaring hard. "You see this mouse? Well, it belongs on your face, buddy, not mine. Why I let you come along I'll never know. You're lucky I didn't carry you out of there in a doggy bag."

"I'm sorry," Jeffrey said, a circle of guilt closing in on him as he spotted the clock on the car's dashboard. "Is that really the right time?"

"I can't see it," Hazleton said, trying to see what was ahead of the car.

"Haz, where are you going?" Jeffrey asked nervously.

"The paper."

"I got to get to the airport. I'm in trouble. I was supposed to be at Pate's office this morning . . . Oh, God, I have to get dressed. They're going to kill me. Drive me home . . . please."

"This isn't a cab," Hazleton said, still angry. He dabbed at his face and checked the napkin.

"You don't understand. I've got forty-five minutes to get to the airport," Jeffrey yelled.

"Believe me, I understand. Why do you think I kept kicking you all morning? Hell, boy, my pet dog is more responsible than you. I think I'll forget about the strike and make you my story—call it "Young Man on His Way Down the Ladder of Success."

Hazleton had tapped Jeffrey's sorest spot—his recurring feelings of being as irresponsible and immature as people whispered he was. "Please, Hazleton, turn the car around. I have to get my suit and get to Andrews."

"And I've got a story to write. I'm not your chauffeur, Hodge."

"Well, then, stop and I'll take a cab."

Hazleton hit the brakes hard, jostling his passenger.

Jeffrey hopped out of the car. He lowered his face to the window. "Haz, I'm really sorry about the fight, I mean that."

The reporter watched him through the slit of his swelling eye. "Ummm," he grunted as he waited for the light to change.

"I'll make it up to you," Jeffrey said.

"Hummph." The light stayed red. Hazleton's fingers drummed the wheel, his rage dropping a few notches.

"Friends?" Jeffrey asked, extending his hand through the window.

"Yeah, sure . . . okay, friends," the man said, accepting the smooth palm.

"Great . . . oh, one more thing," Jeffrey called as the light changed and he felt the car lurch forward.

"What?"

"Can you loan me ten bucks? I left all my money at the bar."

"You never quit, do you, boy," Hazleton groaned. "No shame at all." He fished in his jeans pocket and flipped a bill at Jeffrey. "You might not be a complete washout, after all. You got too much gall."

"Thanks," Jeffrey said as Hazleton mashed the gas pedal and left him in a cloud of blue exhaust.

In the rear view mirror the reporter could see his young friend jogging quickly across the avenue, his arms waving wildly towards a cruising hack. Hazleton couldn't stop the grin that began to spread across his swollen face. He shook his head and flipped on a news station that filled the car with updates on the imminent arrival, and he watched the receding image of Jeffrey Hodge still trying to flag a cab.

*

The Chinese jet shook as the wheels locked for landing. The plane had broken through Washington's cloud cover, revealing to Li Soong a landscape of gold-capped buildings ringed with rainbows of cars. The books and papers the Chinese delegation had reviewed during the long flight were refiled in their cases, the food and drinks returned to the galley.

Li Soong looked the length of the plane. The rows of faces warmed her. Like staunch, simple soldiers, the

Chinese sat in perfect order, dressed alike, tense, yet eager to meet the challenge that lay ahead. The passengers on this trip represented the boundaries of Li Soong's universe: the father, whom she shared with 800 million comrades each day; the old man P'eng Hsi, on whose lap she had slept as a child and whose prerevolutionary hardships served as a talisman for the rest of the group. Seated around Li Soong and her father for the plane's descent were the four select bodyguards responsible for their safety. They were called the Society of the Four Winds, their legendary skills of protection and surreptitious movement as close to magic as Li Soong ever knew.

In each seat was a comrade who shared her ideals and her revolutionary resolve. She loved them all, and as she smoothed her braids and straightened her blouse she renewed the pledge she had made to herself before leaving. She would find a way on this visit to be her people's hero.

The plane gave a surprise kick, and Li Soong started to reach for her father's hand, resting on the arm of the chair beside her. But she held back, her toes curling nervously inside her black slippers.

"Are you afraid?" the Premier asked, leaning closer to his only child.

"No, I am not," Li Soong said tersely as the plane made contact with the American soil.

*

"There he is now," Lucas Pate's assistant said, pointing a finger towards Jeffrey as the boy climbed the ramp, taking three steps at a time. Raymond Hodge had spotted his son too, and pushed his way through the small assembled crowd as the Chinese jet taxied from the end of the runway.

"Just tell me one thing," the Secretary of State said to his son. "Are you all right?"

"Sure," Jeffrey said, gasping for breath as he straightened his starched shirt front.

"Then, don't tell me anything else until we get home, or I'll be hauled to jail for assault." His father's face was deep red as he glared; then he turned on his heel and headed back to his position next to the President in the reception line.

Lucas Pate suddenly filled the space his father had occupied. "We've got approximately five minutes before they deplane. I don't know where you've been, and frankly, Hodge, I don't care. But you're on my territory now, and you damn well better remember everything I have told you about that girl."

Jeffrey's head spun. He had managed to forget the tensions that had driven him to Hazleton to begin with, and it was all starting to avalanche upon him. "I know, I remember," he stammered. "No personal stories, no politics, no jokes, no opinions, no questions about her life," he recited like a nervous puppet.

"All right. Keep that in mind and you'll do fine." Pate steered him to his position on the podium as the jet's door was opened by two Marines.

"But what *do* I talk to her about?" Jeffrey turned to the man one last time.

"The weather," Lucas Pate said through clenched teeth.

As in Michelangelo's image of Creation, the hands of the Premier and the President made an endless journey before they finally touched to an explosion of flashbulbs. Behind them the instruments of the Marine Band shone like molten gold in the sun. The wind whipped the red, white and blue flags and Red Chinese banners.

Jeffrey Hodge watched as a secret service man helped a tiny figure out of the plane. Her gray suit billowed around her slender body in the wind. Her black braids were tossed back over her shoulders. Blinded by her emergence into the sun, the girl reached out a hand to fish for the railing. In the morning light Jeffrey watched her unsure gait and troubled face. He recognized her from his bad dreams. She was Li Soong; Li Soong, alias "the girl"; Li Soong, whose favor he had spent months learning to curry. Never in his life had he disliked the sight of anyone so intensely.

Two

THE PROCESSION of limousines wound through the streets. Americans pushed against barricades, craning to see the visitors, waving their arms, yelling and pushing until the police pushed back at them just as roughly. Li Soong had never seen crowds so undisciplined and chaotic. She stared at the makeup on the Western women's faces, shining incandescently in the noonday sun, their clothes dyed brilliant colors that seemed evolved from dream fevers instead of nature. Signs were hoisted towards the motorcade, and babies lifted above the crowd to drool and cry in Li Soong's direction. Protected by the thick glass of the car, she felt like an exotic fish on display.

When the car finally glided to a halt in front of the Mayflower Hotel, Li Soong and her father were whisked to a waiting elevator, sheltered from onlookers by both American and Chinese security forces. The Premier was escorted to his suite at one end of a cordoned-off floor; Li Soong was deposited at the other end in hers. She sat on the edge of a massive bed as the Premier's security team inspected the perimeter of her room.

"Everything seems to be in fine shape," Hsieh Tsai-tao, leader of the Society of the Four Winds, told her.

"Cheng Wu says he will be here shortly for your final briefing."

Li Soong looked distracted as the man spoke. "How many people were there outside the hotel?" she asked.

"The estimate we were given is two thousand."

"Is that all?" she said.

"Yes, but they were as noisy as ten thousand." The guard smiled.

"What do you think they would have done to us if we had stopped to meet them? Do you think they would have attacked?"

"No, but they might have trampled you unintentionally. Why?" Hsieh asked.

"I'm just curious. When we *do* meet them face to face—"

"You don't have to worry," the bodyguard said with a smile meant to reassure. "It has been arranged so that we will never be in such crowds. All our activities will be sheltered from the masses."

"*All* our activities? You mean there will not be one time when we will meet an American who is not a high official?"

"Excuse me, Li Soong," Hsieh said, "but I must go. Cheng Wu will be in and you can ask him these questions. I will be back for you in three hours, after you have rested."

"Why must you come for me?" Li Soong asked. "I can walk to my father's room when it is time—"

"We prefer you stay in your room," he broke in. "Neither you nor the Premier will walk unescorted. Of course, if you need anything, a guard will be at your door —at all times."

"A guard?"

"Li Soong," he said abruptly, "I must go. I will be back later." The heavy door slammed behind him, leaving Li Soong alone for the first time since her journey began.

In her solitude she regarded the room she occupied—the dense carpet, the weighted drapes. Her ears buzzed with the silence of the air faintly rushing from the floor vents. She rose and moved through the toneless rooms of the suite. She tried to visualize the foreign hands that had prepared the dish of tiny soaps in the bathroom or folded the satin comforter at the end of the bed. The quiet was deathly. Li Soong imagined the room a dying creature, a heavy dragon flapping its ancient wings, breathing its last labored breaths.

She jumped, startled by Cheng Wu, who had entered the room without knocking. "How are you doing in here?" he asked in his usual brusque manner.

"I'm perfectly fine, thank you," Li Soong said, composing herself. "I was just momentarily unnerved by the unnecessary luxuries with which the Americans have surrounded us."

"Yes, they have showed no restraint in their attempts to impress us with their wealth," Cheng said, producing a maroon book and extending it towards Li Soong.

"Don't tell me, Cheng—more facts to review." Li Soong sighed.

Cheng smiled and nodded. "There are a few matters to discuss, and then I will leave you to rest."

"What are they?" Li Soong asked, again sinking down on the edge of the bed. Cheng appeared strangely out of place among the ornate furnishings, and she wondered if she suddenly looked as plain as he.

"Because of security, we will not be going to the department store tomorrow with the President's daughter as planned. We will go after hours, when the customers have left. We will be given a private tour. Also, our hosts have informed me that the trip to the baseball park and the trip to the hospital have been revised so that we may be segregated from any potential danger."

"And what does that mean?" Li Soong asked, fearing

that Hsieh had been right about their complete isolation from the people she had prepared so long to meet.

Cheng Wu confirmed her suspicions. "It means that we will not be able to mix freely with the people of this country, as Mr. Nixon did when he visited us in 1972. The Americans feel that we must be kept away from their own worst enemy—themselves."

Li Soong felt ashamed of the fears she had en route from the airport. To meet the Americans was, after all, why she had come. The idea of a week spent locked in her hotel room and transported in a bulletproof car from one empty building to the next was to her a mockery of the trip's purpose. She slammed the maroon book down on the bed. "Cheng, I refuse to believe my father has accepted these conditions. How can we be expected to see capitalism from a revolutionary perspective if we are treated like privileged royalty?"

"Your father is concerned for your safety, as is the President of the United States. We cannot court danger."

"I demand to see him," Li Soong said. "You must be telling me something quite different than what you told him. I know my father would never have agreed to come here in the first place if he knew these conditions, that we would see nothing."

"Your father has been given an herbal and is now asleep. He is exhausted, as am I, and as you appear to be from your behavior. The Premier was most kind to allow you to accompany him on this trip, and it is your job to follow his wishes—not only as your father, but as the leader of our country."

"Tell my father to speak to the President at once. He must demand to see everything. Millions did not give up their lives in our people's revolution so my father could visit a department store after hours. He is a fool!"

"Never say that, Li Soong!" Cheng Wu snapped at her. "Twice your father has been exiled in his own country because he would not compromise his beliefs. Why do you think Madam Chiang and the Gang of Four ridiculed him in the capital? And why do you think you and he retreated to Kwangtung Province with General Hsu when they seized power?"

Li Soong did not answer his rhetorical questions.

"And why do you suppose your father was welcomed back to Peking the next year? Because, Li Soong, your father's way is the only path by which China can grow strong. He is Premier today because our people know that we must modernize, we must learn from others if we are to grow."

"Even if we forget the directives of Chairman Mao?"

"Even Chairman Mao made mistakes. It is your father who has had the courage to say so. And since the lost decade of the Cultural Revolution, it has become obvious that we can no longer live by dogma and theory, we can no longer live as if the rest of the world does not exist."

"But we cannot simply give up our ideals—"

"Would you have China remain weak and backward for the sake of your theories? You must see that our people need the Leap Outward. They have called upon your father because it is he who has understood all along that the ideals of our revolution must be tried and tempered in the field of practical application. This visit is a crucial step in bringing our country into the world community. It is the only way we will survive. You must do as we tell you."

"I can't."

"You have no choice. When you are Premier," Cheng Wu said with a sardonic bite, "we will do things your way. In the meantime, please rest. We have a long night ahead of us."

Li Soong threw herself the length of the bed, burying her head in her arms. After she heard Cheng close the door behind him, she eased herself from the bed and tiptoed to the door. She cracked it open, but stopped when a massive back came into view. The guard flew to attention, turning to peek in the opening. "Anything wrong?" he inquired.

"No," Li Soong shot back, slamming the door. She trotted over to the small table where a phone sat. She pressed a series of buttons, trying to reach her father's room, reviewing what she would say to him when he answered. She would dazzle him with her revolutionary vigor. He would be proud of her refusal to accept the limitations the Americans had set.

A rude buzzing from the phone rang in her ear, and an inexplicable hostility towards her father began to mount. *I am fooling myself,* Li Soong chastised herself. *If I did reach him, he wouldn't listen anyway. It is* he *who has changed, not me.* He *taught me to be unbending, and now it is he who compromises.* She slammed down the receiver.

Li Soong fought the tears that started to burn the corners of her eyes. *No,* she commanded the emotions that threatened to break over her and wash away her feelings of strength and independence. *No,* she said, like a general whose only war raged within herself. *I do not need him. I am stronger than he is, braver, better . . .* She repeated the litany as she walked the length of the suite, finally leaning against the weight of the damask drapes. She wiped the dampness from her eyes on the sleeve of her suit, and with a deep sigh reached out for the cord that secured the curtains. She pulled the rope, parting the drapes and revealing the kinetic streets below, crowded with the people she felt she would never meet.

*

"Hello, I'm Jeffrey Hodge. I was at the airport to greet you," he said, extending his hand again to Li Soong, who stood stiffly in the reception line beneath the East Room's portrait of Martha Washington. The crystal chandeliers bathed the presidential reception in a golden light, and soldiers in dress uniforms escorted guests who sparkled with expensive jewels.

Li Soong acknowledged Jeffrey without a smile, shaking his hand hard.

He filed down the end of the line, where he was ambushed by the daughter of the junior senator from Arkansas. "Hi, sweetness." Jennifer Clay fluttered in close to Jeffrey. "What do you think of her?" she asked, casting an amused glance at Li Soong.

"Who?" Jeffrey said obstinately.

"Who do you think? You're supposed to be her escort after a fashion, no?"

"I guess," he said. "I haven't said two words to her yet, but I can tell you she won't win the Miss Congeniality award."

"She almost crushed my hand," Jennifer said, holding out a frail limb for Jeffrey's inspection.

"Yeah, I think she tends oxen at home," Jeffrey grumbled, changing the subject. "Hey, Jen, are you going to sit at our table?"

"No, hon." Jennifer giggled. "I sit with my folks. We're not VIPs like you, seated with Rosemary, Robert and the girl, of course."

"Of course," Jeffrey said, wondering how he would get through the meal. Aside from Li Soong, he had to contend with Rosemary Bromley, the President's daughter, and Robert Milne, the Vice-President's son. Since childhood, Rosemary had been Jeffrey's personal nemesis. Her aggressive conformity and empty-headed chitchat represented everything he hated about Washington society. Robert Milne affected an effete sarcasm that Jeffrey found equally unappealing.

Lucas Pate drifted silently alongside Jeffrey like a submarine in the night. "About this morning, Hodge," Pate said, escorting Jeffrey away from Jennifer, "let's wipe

the slate clean. Let bygones be bygones. You've got a job
to do, and when the going gets tough the tough get
going."

Jeffrey was amazed at the number of clichés the man
could string together without a break. "I'll try my best."

"Don't just *try*, Hodge," Pate continued. "You've got
to produce. Remember . . . nothing personal and no
politics, right?"

"Sure, but—"

"But nothing. We picked you in the first place because
you're a bright, good-looking kid. We know you're popu-
lar with the girls. *Use* a little of that charm," Pate said,
poking Jeffrey lasciviously in the arm. "Just don't overdo
it," he added.

The musicians struck the chord announcing dinner,
and to the curlicued strains of a Vivaldi sonata Jeffrey
Hodge walked towards Li Soong as if she was the end of
a gangplank. He offered her his arm, and together they
entered the State Dining Room.

*

Jeffrey and Li Soong eyed each other across the pink
and festive tablecloth. Dark-jacketed waiters strutted by
with silver trays bearing pheasant and kumquats, California champagne and Mao Tai. Rosemary, the President's daughter, sat alongside Jeffrey in a have-a-nice-day
yellow dress. The Vice-President's son slouched in his
chair, toying with silver-tipped chopsticks. Victoria
Banning, the Attorney General's daughter, peered over
thick glasses, her hand nervously patting the bodice of
her formal gown. Jeffrey could see the edge of a falsie
precariously edging its way north.

He forced his eyes back to Li Soong, confronting the
grim face and rigid posture. She returned his stare, running her eyes along his custom-tailored tuxedo, the small
diamond stud piercing his starched shirt front, the carefully tossed blond curls that encircled his head.

Jeffrey realized that no one at the table was talking. It was up to him to break the ice, to see that this terrible representative of the People's Republic of China did not sit there like a toad on a log. He searched his mind for a topic. Her plane ride. No, he rejected it for fear she would think he was snooping about the Chinese Air Force. The hotel. No, it might break security to ask that. The cache of approved subjects vanished as if it had been a mirage. In his panic he began to feel the eyes of the world upon him. He saw the old globe wrinkle up in a loud guffaw, laugh lines cutting deep across continents as it rollicked at what a boob he was. He saw the headline of tomorrow's paper, *"Hodge Says Nothing,"* in seventy-two-point type. His mind reeled as he searched for a way to break the silence.

The President's daughter noticed Jeffrey's face suddenly take on a florid color. The Vice-President's son stopped tapping his chopsticks as he saw Jeffrey lean forward. Jeffrey caught Li Soong's attention and pointedly cleared his throat to speak. "Nice weather we're having," he said with breathless conviction.

Rosemary flushed to match the color of the napery.

Jeffrey felt his own face grow hot as he struggled to retrieve his pride. "I mean it's nice, uh, unusual for it to be so warm now, I mean in April. It's usually a lot cooler in Washington. Is China this cool? I mean warm, too?" His embarrassment blossomed as he stammered.

"It is cool in China this time of year," Li Soong answered bluntly, her attention returning to the glass of water she sipped at.

"Oh," Jeffrey mumbled. "That's nice."

The table was mute, the guests silently prodding their artichokes. The President's daughter blotted her lips with a napkin and tried her own approach. "You know what is the most exciting part of this whole visit for me?" she asked in a rush of false enthusiasm.

"What, Rosemary?" Victoria asked anxiously.

"The little shopping spree we have planned for tomorrow. Li Soong, you're just going to *adore* Garfinckel's. I'm sure they don't have anything like it in China. They simply have the best selection of handbags in the country —anything you can imagine in lizard or suede or, well, anything!"

Li Soong did not reply as Rosemary's fluttering hands finally came to rest on the table's edge.

Jeffrey could see Robert grow visibly nauseous at the conversation. "What possible use would she have for a lizard handbag?" the V.P.'s son said bitchily.

"I don't know, Robert," Rosemary replied with a catty smile, "but I'm sure you could help her figure one out."

Jeffrey saw the situation going into a slow tailspin. Li Soong sat wide-eyed and mystified as the others squabbled around her. To Jeffrey she looked as confused as he felt, but he hesitated to venture another topic.

Victoria tried. "Li Soong, will you buy any American goods to take home with you?"

"No." Li Soong finally spoke in a stony voice that seemed to startle the others. "I have only one interest in visiting the department store, and that is to see how the American worker spends his money."

"Garfinckel's isn't exactly the People's Store," Robert quipped. "The only workers you'll see there are behind the counters or running the elevators."

Rosemary began to giggle, and Victoria found it contagious. The laugh rolled uneasily around the table, excluding Li Soong. Jeffrey watched as she toyed with the food on her plate, her eyes cast down. "That was a joke," he blurted out, feeling somehow responsible for her lack of response.

"Yes," Li Soong said sharply, lifting her eyes to meet his. "I understood it to be so."

"I thought maybe you didn't get it," Jeffrey said awkwardly. "Would you like me to explain?" He tried to turn the conversation around to fit Lucas Pate's laws.

"No, thank you," Li Soong said, her pink cheeks turning bright. "It did not, as you say, 'get lost in the translation.' Rather, to me the ideology was distasteful, and I found nothing to laugh at."

"Oh, wow," Robert said under his breath. *"Pardonnez-moi."*

Jeffrey's worst fears were materializing. Li Soong had transformed from a faceless demon to a flesh-and-blood enemy who was already making his life unbearable. He envisioned the five days of the visit stretching before him like an endless chasm filled with itchy tuxedos, elaborate banquets, and worst of all, the stony face of the girl who sat opposite him. He groaned out loud without realizing it. How he wished he could trade places with Hazleton Brown, with anyone who was free to come and go as they pleased, anyone who did not have to play host to a humorless steel trap who masqueraded as a girl.

"You do have jokes in China, don't you?" Victoria asked Li Soong, trying again to make contact.

"Of course we have jokes," the girl replied. "But they are not at the expense of the downtrodden."

"May we hear one?" Victoria asked.

Li Soong thought a moment, looking around at the assembled faces. "Ah, yes," she said. "This one you will certainly enjoy." To Jeffrey's amazement her face had come alive. "The joke, or as we say in China, *hsiao hua,* concerns a beautiful woman of the Emperor's court who is carried through the streets of Peking on a litter. Of course, this is before liberation. On a street she passes a handsome young man who does not bow his head, but, rather, peers through the rice-paper shades of her cart and sees her lovely face. And the young man is sad because he cannot marry the woman." Li Soong's face shattered with laughter. Her shoulders rocked, her giggle rose to draw amused looks from surrounding tables. But her tablemates stared blankly. There was a long, awful silence.

"You have got to be kidding," Robert moaned. "That belongs on *The Gong Show.* "

"Did you get it?" Victoria whispered to Jeffrey. "I sure didn't."

"Me neither," Rosemary added, forking a large piece of potato into her mouth. "Did you, Bobby?"

"Did it have to do with the woman being in drag?" he suggested.

The rest of the table broke up, now leaving Li Soong on the outside. Feeling the brunt of the responsibility for her discomfort, Jeffrey asked, "What was the point of it? I guess we didn't get it."

Li Soong looked crestfallen. She glanced around the table to see the alien faces looking at her with confusion. She sighed and proceeded with great pains to explain. "It has to do with the difference between the breeding of the young man and the noblewoman. Of course, neither one . . ." The faces around the table revealed no enlightenment. She began again. "You see, you must understand that before my country's great revolution, it was unheard of for a peasant to even look at such a woman, and . . ." But she could tell by the dispassionate looks of the others that her analysis only mired the joke deeper into obscurity. She refused to give up. "As I was saying, the class difference—"

Li Soong was interrupted by a strange chortle. Jeffrey cleared his throat, trying to mask the noise.

"A woman of the upper classes—"

But the chortle grew into a laugh, and it grew until Jeffrey could no longer suppress it. He exploded with hilarity that brought tears to his eyes and rocked him back and forth in his chair.

Li Soong was surprised. Her face softened tentatively.

"I think at least one of you has understood my joke." Her shoulders relaxed and her own laughter joined the howls that were convulsing Jeffrey and drawing stares from the other tables.

But no one truly understood what was causing Jeffrey to explode with uncontrollable mirth. The shudder that came from deep in his chest was a reaction to the joke that had begun six months ago and only now found its punch line. How ridiculous was this banquet, where people gathered to exchange bits of conversation that held absolutely no meaning. Li Soong's joke was a distillation of the absurdity with which Jeffrey had lived for half a year in the Division of Protocol.

Through tears of laughter, Jeffrey looked around the table and saw the others laughing with him, each convulsed by his or her own private joke. Across the room Jeffrey could see his father seated next to the President and Premier. As he lifted the back of his hand to brush the water from his eyes, the President raised a glass in his direction. "To the young," the Chief Executive spoke out, "for they will show us the path." He beamed, and the Premier of China joined him in the toast.

*

"How's it goin', kid?" Hazleton said loudly into the mouthpiece of his office phone.

Jeffrey strained to hear him over the noise at the other end. "Hazleton? Boy, is it good to hear your voice. Where are you?"

"At work. Can't you hear the racket? So how the hell are you?"

"Okay."

"Only okay?" the reporter queried. "They've got you singing for your supper, huh?"

"You said it. Yesterday the ball game, then the zoo, then to the hospital to see some guy have a brain operation. I swear I almost threw up at that one, but she kept right on watching."

"She?" Hazleton asked.

"Li Soong," Jeffrey said. "Boy, is she weird." He could hear Hazleton laugh at the other end.

"What do you mean 'weird'?"

"I mean she never lets her guard down for a minute. Every time I try and talk to her she drags out some smart-ass political statement. I mean, if I say, 'Would you like a stick of gum?' she says, 'Chairman Mao thought gum was the opiate of the bourgeoisie.' What a royal pain!"

"Think she's having a good time?"

"Who knows? It's been three days and I don't think I've seen her smile, and if she's not contradicting me she's bragging about her father and those four guys who are always with us . . . you know, the Society of the Four Winds—her old man's goon squad."

"She thinks they're hot stuff?" Hazleton asked.

"I guess they are, from what I've heard. Anyway, I wouldn't mind at all if they stopped staring at *me*. Between them and Lucas Pate, I feel like my fly's open all the time. Haz, I gotta ask you a question." His voice had turned serious.

"Sure, what's up?"

"When this is over and I have some time, how about letting me join you on one of your road trips? I really have to get away for a while."

"I don't think so," Hazleton said.

"Why not?" Jeffrey asked.

"Look, Jeff, my eye is still black and blue from your little show at the Atomic, and I just spent a hundred bucks for a new contact lens. I can't afford to have you along. You're too expensive."

"That was just an accident. It could have happened to anyone."

"I doubt that," Hazleton said. "Maybe in a few years." He tried putting him off. "Let's think about it awhile."

"Sure," Jeffrey said gloomily. "Hey, how come you called, anyway?" he asked, embarrassed by his friend's rejection of him.

"Well, to be honest, kid, I heard your mother is throwing a private bash for the Chinese this afternoon—no press allowed—and I thought you might be able to sneak me in the back door."

"And that's it?"

"And I wanted to see how you're making out," the reporter added. "Hey, don't get me wrong, we're pals. I just thought you might want to make up for the little beating I took for you the other day by doing me a favor."

"My mother would shoot me if you showed up."

"Aw, come on, you'll think of a way to get me in. Look, I'll tell you what. I promise I'll give what you said some thought. Maybe you can tag along on the next trip. What time is the party?" Hazleton asked.

"Uh, two o'clock," Jeffrey said, the words *tag along* ringing in his ears.

"Okay, see you then. Thanks a lot, kid," Hazleton said, hanging up the phone.

"Goodbye," Jeffrey said after the connection had already been severed. "Thanks for calling."

*

"I find nothing whatsoever wrong with her," the Premier's physician said to Li Soong's anxious father, who was waiting outside her door. "Why don't you go in and speak to her? Perhaps she will tell you what is upsetting her. She will say nothing to me."

The Premier shook his head. "We should not have let her come. She is not ready for the diplomatic rigors of this trip." An aide opened the door of the suite, and the Premier entered. "Cheng Ch'en says he finds nothing wrong with you, Li Soong. Isn't that fine news?" The man looked down to find the girl huddled under a blanket, a pillow half obscuring her face. "Li Soong, I cannot see you with the sheets draped over you. Please sit up. We will talk."

Li Soong grudgingly rose to a sitting position on her bed. Her braids fell askew over her sleeping clothes.

The Premier turned to his bodyguards and aides. "Comrades, would you please leave us alone for a moment." When the door was shut, he turned to his daughter. "Now, what's wrong?" the Premier asked somewhat uncomfortably as he looked into Li Soong's sad face. "I don't believe for a moment that you are ill. Why are you lingering in bed and not dressed for this morning's appointments?"

"I don't want to go," she said almost inaudibly.

"Why not? This day has been especially planned for your enjoyment. Disney World is the President's family's favorite."

Li Soong fell back on the bed, pulling the sheets up over her head.

"I will have none of this nonsense," the Premier said angrily. He pulled at a corner of the blanket. "Stop this at once. I am ashamed of you."

"Leave me alone," the girl cried.

"I will not leave you until you dress yourself for the day's activities. You will not embarrass me before the Americans."

"You can't force me to go," Li Soong said, suddenly sorry to have escalated the fight. She confronted her father's glowering face, and his expression sent a shiver through her. "I'm sorry," she said, her voice dropping. "I . . . I just don't like this Disney World place. It is a place for children. It is an insult to take us there. Instead of such foolishness, I should be seeing how Americans work and where they live."

"While you are at Disney World, I will be meeting with the Congress," the Premier said. "You don't have to worry about your father seeing the foolish part of America. While you are at play, I shall be at work."

"I should be with you, then," Li Soong implored.

"No," her father corrected. "You should be where I decide you shall be."

"Why did you take me along, then? I wish I had stayed home. I am seeing nothing of this country."

"I took you along because I thought you would be an asset in creating a dialogue with the American youth. Obviously, I was wrong. You haven't spoken at all to the President's daughter, or to the young man who joins us daily."

"No," Li Soong said. "There is nothing of interest to speak to them about. I dislike them both. The daughter is simple-minded, and the other, Jeffrey Hodge, speaks only of the weather."

"Perhaps you will not let him talk about anything else. Li Soong, you do not understand the role of a politician, I am afraid. We learn by listening to others."

"Hmmph," Li Soong said, sitting up a bit straighter.

"I want you dressed and ready to go in fifteen minutes. I will tell the guard at your door to come for you then. At that time you will procede as planned to the airport for the plane ride to Disney World. I will see you late this evening when you return, and you will tell me what you have learned from your hosts." The Premier walked closer to his daughter, who had moved to the edge of the bed. He hesitated a moment before he leaned down to kiss the top of her head. "Remember," he said, "it is both our duties to see this country. Our people are waiting anxiously for the information we gather. Let them be as proud of you as I."

The girl watched her father's back disappear through the door as she slowly unbuttoned her nightgown.

*

Li Soong boarded Air Force One and walked towards the presidential cabin. She scanned the plane, looking for an unfamiliar face to provide her with a fresh perspective of America. Instead, there sat Jeffrey Hodge and the President's wife and daughter, not a newcomer in the group except Rosemary's boyfriend, Bert, a handsome jock who resembled a side of beef in a Brooks Brothers jacket. He shook her hand with vigorous abandon, and on his third mispronounciation of her name Li Soong gave up on him.

"Li Soong, sit next to me," Rosemary called out. "Right here." She pointed to a seat between herself and Jeffrey Hodge.

Jeffrey seemed fascinated studying the back of his hand. He looked up and forced a smile. "Hello."

"Hello," Li Soong ventured back, then sat silently as the plane took off and climbed above the clouds.

*

"This is the day we've all been looking forward to the most," Rosemary exclaimed as they passed over the Georgia coast.

"It should certainly be something," Jeffrey acknowledged diplomatically, trying to suppress a memory of a stoned conversation he had had with Hazleton Brown a few weeks before when they fell down laughing at the thought of the Premier in a Mousketeer hat.

"You do know what Disney World is like?" Rosemary asked Li Soong. "I mean, they did explain it to you, didn't they?"

"Yes. It is an amusement park, a place where American families go to vacation."

"Oh, *no,* " Rosemary declared with patriotic outrage. "It's much more than that. Jeffrey, you explain it to her."

"Disney World—America in a nutshell," Jeffrey heard

himself proclaim. It was the title of one of Lucas Pate's memoranda in preparation for the visit.

"Have you been there before?" Li Soong asked him.

"No. I think as a kid I went to the one in California."

"If it is so wonderful, why haven't you gone again?" she asked.

Rosemary took offense. "It is no reflection on Disney World, Li Soong. It's just that Jeffrey likes to go places that no one else would visit."

Li Soong looked at her quizzically. "What do you mean?"

"Surely, Jeffrey, you haven't forgotten to tell her about your crazy adventures? You know, Li Soong, he dropped out of school to hitchhike around the country. Why, Jeffrey Hodge is our own little old home-town version of Grizzly Adams."

Li Soong only half understood Rosemary's teasing, but she straightened up in the seat, her father's admonition about not listening coming back to her. "No, I have not heard of this adventure."

Jeffrey looked pained. He knew Rosemary was playing with him like an addlebrained cat with a mouse. "It's nothing much, Li Soong. Just a summer vacation. I traveled a little bit on my own."

"Come on, Jeffrey, why so shy?" Rosemary prodded him. "Tell her all about the bars and the truckers, the horses you rode and the girls you left crying in their pillows. You certainly never spared the details with any of us."

"Cool it, will you," Jeffrey said to her.

"Is this true?" Li Soong asked. "Did you really see the other side of America?" She was more animated than Jeffrey had seen her since the visit began.

"Sure," he said, starting to relax a little. The idea of the Premier's daughter thinking he was a hard-traveling man appealed to him. She would not call his bluff the way Hazleton did. She wouldn't question the elaborately embellished version of his two-month adventure on the road. "I guess I've roamed around a bit. You see"—he fixed his eyes on Li Soong—"I felt hemmed in, so I took off. Hardly more'n a few dollars in the old pocket, but I thumbed my way across the land, getting rides from truckers who followed that long white line, and even bumming rides on freight trains when I had to. I lived off the land, sleeping under a sweep of stars, and I ate beans out of a rusty tin can." Jeffrey could see her transfixed, and he was falling in love with the images of America that came tumbling out of his own imagination, where fact and fiction had become romantically fused.

"I hit some rough weather in the Oregon woods and had to hole up a while in a roughneck lumber camp where I cut wood for my meals. Then I traveled down to Texas, where I busted wild horses on a ranch. Sure, I had my heart broken a few times, and I got into more than a couple of brawls in redneck bars, but it was all worth it. I should tell you about the fishing boat I worked on up in Maine . . ."

Rosemary cut into Jeffrey's soliloquy with a huge yawn. "Oh, this is getting boring, let's talk about something else," she said, picking a piece of lint off her sweater.

"No, please continue," Li Soong implored.

Rosemary shot her boyfriend a look of disgust. "Li Soong, you don't really want to hear the story of 'Jeffrey Hodge Meets the Yokels,' do you? I'm warning you, it's endless."

Jeffrey grew angry. Rosemary had interrupted him just as he was beginning to elaborate and embellish his two-month vacation more gloriously than ever. To his surprise, Li Soong was proving to be the perfect audience for his tales of glory, and she had no way of knowing about the American Express card and full wallet that had eased him along on his journey.

Just as he was about to continue the saga of his mostly imaginary exploits, Li Soong turned to Rosemary. "You see," she said, "it is not that I am especially interested in hearing one man's opinion, because that is only a subjective view and, as you have pointed out, somewhat tedious. But it is interesting to me to hear how badly one is treated if he ventures out in this country without money or elite protection. Jeffrey's story is a first-hand account of the malevolence of capitalism."

"Hey, wait a minute, Li Soong," Jeffrey said. "Where'd you get the idea I was mistreated? I had a great time!"

"Jeffrey." Li Soong spoke his name directly for the first time. "You have just told us of a trip on which you were beaten up, had to ride in freight trains like an itinerant vagabond, were scorned even by barmaids and could find little to eat. *That* is being badly treated," she declared. "It would never happen in China."

Jeffrey heard Rosemary's boyfriend laughing at his expense, and he stifled an urge to leave his footprint on the big bozo's face. "I can't believe you," he moaned, forgetting his manners as Li Soong's escort. "You turned my words completely around. I *wanted* to ride in trains, I *wanted* to eat out of cans, and everyone knows about those kinds of bars where everyone slugs everyone else after a few beers."

"And that is the fate of the moneyless," Li Soong sighed dramatically, shaking her head. "I saw no one 'slug' anyone over dinner last night, and we were drinking more than beer."

Rosemary and her friend giggled at the remark.

"It is apparent," Li Soong continued, acting as she wished her father would with the Americans, "that you are so deeply entrenched in the prevailing ideology that you cannot see its evils."

"And it is apparent to me," Jeffrey said, "that you don't know what the hell you're talking about. You come over here for a couple of days, you don't see a damn thing except the most sanitized sights—and then ringed by a hundred and fifty guards—and you think you're an expert on this country."

"I have tried to see things without guards, but it is your country's policy not to allow it. You are obviously ashamed of something."

"No matter what you say, you could never see it the way an American does. You wouldn't be able to see the beauty of the Nebraska cornfields on an autumn afternoon, or smell the sage under a Western sky, or feel the salt sting of the ocean in a Maine sou'wester . . ." Jeffrey sounded to himself like a cross between the national anthem and John Wayne. He usually left the patriotism to Rosemary and her family.

"Those are all sights of natural beauty, but have nothing to do with a rotting, dehumanizing system," Li Soong countered.

"But at least we are free to go off and see them, rather than spending twelve hours a day in a factory making some doodad to help the revolution." Jeffrey could tell by Li Soong's face that he had stepped beyond the bounds of the argument. She leaned back in her chair and glared at him. He met her gaze and glared back hard. It was an awful moment, and it seemed to last an eternity.

"Look, everyone, it's Tupperware!" the First Lady cried from across the plane, breaking the tension of the debate. Through the portholes the passengers could see the Kissimmee, Florida, landscape below and the headquarters of Tupperware International. Waving up at them were five hundred tiny figures. They were the Tupperware hostesses and executives, who had created a portrait of the Premier and the President on the ground by arranging ten thousand multicolored snap-top food containers. "Isn't it beautiful?" the First Lady cooed. "It looks just like your father," she called out to Li Soong, who looked more than a little confused.

"What is that?" she asked Rosemary.

"It's Tupperware. You know—to store leftovers," the President's daughter explained. "I guess you don't have that in China yet."

Li Soong snuck a glance at Jeffrey. He met her eyes with a hurt look. The confusion on her face and the silliness of the moment combined to defuse his anger. He shrugged at her and smiled. She returned the smile slowly, and as the airborne contingent circled the plastic portraits once again, Li Soong and Jeffrey held each other's eyes a moment longer.

*

The official delegation drifted through the empty streets of Disney World in a daze as huge-headed mice with human bodies danced in the streets and cartoon voices spoke through hidden speakers. Void of tourists, as the secret service had left it, Disney World was a phantasmagoric ghost town. Li Soong and her Chinese bodyguards sat dumbfounded on the Jungle Boat Ride as mechanical animals snapped at them from below, and they watched in awe as robot presidents walked clumsily across a stage.

Rosemary and her mother were having too good a time to notice the expression on Li Soong's face. In all the planning for the visit, no expert could have calculated the effect of the magic kingdom on a girl who had been raised without fantasy. Only Jeffrey, seated beside her, looked into her eyes and saw the terror of complete diso-rientation into which she had been plunged.

"Oh, great, it's time for the Haunted Mansion," Rose-mary exclaimed as the procession headed under the wrought-iron trellis of the spook house. Jeffrey was pressed in behind Li Soong in the welcome room. A disembodied voice droned supernatural incantations. The lights dimmed and the floor gave way as the underground lever system went into action. The Americans tittered with jaded anticipation, but Li Soong shrieked as they plunged below. Her small hand clutched Jeffrey's arm. He had expected her to follow him from ride to ride, chanting political slogans in his ear, but he had been wrong. Holograms of ghosts flickered through the air, and she turned away in fear. He placed his palm on top of hers, and in the dark she let it lie.

Dim lights gave way to phantoms and skulls and coffins that danced beside their silent carriage. Li Soong could hear the others laugh at the ghostly serenade. She could feel the heat from Jeffrey's body near hers, but she did not turn to look at him as they moved through the electric waters.

She could not take her mind from what he had said on the plane, from the images of another America that lay beyond the restrictions. She still felt her anger, intensified by this unnatural tunnel that the Americans thought of as fun. To block out the spirits that assaulted her from every side, she concentrated on the wheatfields, the cowboys, the churning oceans that Jeffrey had described. Her cheeks grew warm as her shoulder brushed against his tweed jacket in the darkness. She could see his profile looking straight ahead. Was it her imagination that he was sitting closer than before? That his thigh leaned heavily on hers? She could feel his weight, his muscles against hers in the tight seat. She shifted uncomfortably, and the dark tunnel through which they rode seemed endless and smothering.

Under the cries of the animated monsters, Jeffrey swore he could hear his pulse. His hand felt awkward on Li Soong's and he wondered if he should remove it. He could feel her silken braids like heavy water flowing against his arm. He could smell her scent of clean cotton and soap. He wanted to tell her to not be afraid. Her sudden frailty made him feel protective. He searched for a way to begin, to draw her attention from that which disturbed her so, but as the words formed in his mouth, a blinding flash of Florida sunlight signified an end to the shadowy world of the Haunted Mansion.

Three

It was late, so late that the local stations had already offered their video prayers. Hazleton Brown awoke when the light from the refrigerator shot a low-kilowatt beam into his bedroom. He cursed himself for forgetting to lock the door. Extracting himself from bed so as not to disturb Sylvia Charles, the ABC correspondent to the capitol, he padded to the door of the room and eased himself out. He knew no burgler would hit the refrigerator first. It was Jeffrey Hodge, silhouetted in the kitchen doorway.

"Mind if I take some of this?" Jeffrey asked as he bit into a cold chicken leg that Hazleton had long forgotten.

"Help yourself," he said, looking around for a cigarette. "I have someone in there." He motioned towards the bedroom.

"Okay, I know it's late. I couldn't sleep. If you want me to go—"

"Naw, it's okay with me. I wasn't sleeping anyway. Just looking up at the ceiling listening to her breathe."

They turned into the kitchen and sat on the folding chairs that sided a painted wood table. Hazleton pulled a container of orange juice from the refrigerator and poured a glass.

"Who's in the bedroom?"

"Sylvia Charles."

"You mean the one on the tube?" Jeffrey asked.

"Yup."

"She's really great-looking, but isn't she in her forties?"

"I guess so," Hazleton said. "I didn't check her birth certificate. How'd you get here, anyway," he said, changing the subject. "Car or cab?"

"Car. Don't worry, I'll clear out soon. I just wanted to stop in for a—"

"Few minutes," Hazleton interrupted, relieved that Jeffrey's visit was to be brief.

"Yeah."

"So what's up?" He tried to get a fix on Jeffrey's glumness. He sensed the boy had something heavy weighing on his mind.

"Aw, I don't know. Nothing, I guess," Jeffrey said, chewing absentmindedly on the chicken leg.

"You don't come visiting at two A.M. for nothing," Hazleton noted.

"Why not? Maybe I just wanted to talk. Maybe I had a craving for stale poultry."

"I think it's more like you've had it up to here with the Chinese," Hazleton said, running a finger across his unshaven chin. "But that's old news. We both knew that before they came. So what brings you out on this wee-hour constitutional?"

"I don't know," Jeffrey mused. "I can't sleep. Tomorrow's their last day, and I should feel nothing but relieved. Instead, I feel jittery and awful."

"Cumulative," Hazleton declared, lighting up a smoke. "Hey, today was the trip to Disney World, wasn't it? Premier Chu meets Donald Duck. What was that like?"

"On the record or off?"

"Either."

"Well, for one thing, the Premier stayed behind. It was just Li Soong and her bodyguards. And, of course, Rosemary and the rest."

"And did Chairman Mao have any quotations to explain dancing pigs and singing mice?"

"No, but it was awful. I couldn't believe how frightened she got."

"She? You mean Li Soong?" Hazleton questioned. "Frightened? What the hell of?"

"Everything. All the animation and special effects . . . all of it."

"You're kidding." Hazleton laughed. "Shit, maybe we should tell the Pentagon to paint Goofy's picture on the nuke heads. You've found the secret weapon, boy!"

"I don't mean frightened like that. Just disoriented, weirded out," Jeffrey explained. "I sort of felt sorry for her. She's not such a bad kid after all."

"Is this the same Jeffrey Hodge I remember?" Hazleton said, pinching the boy through his sleeve. "The one who was comparing Chu's daughter to Lucrezia Borgia and the bride of Frankenstein?"

"C'mon, you know what I mean," Jeffrey said uncomfortably. "She's just used to reality, facts, sameness. There's nothing like Disney World in China. Anyway, the whole visit with all the bullshit parties and places to go is enough to make anyone crazy. I mean, I don't like her, don't get the wrong idea, I just feel sorry for her, that's all."

"Uh huh," Hazleton said warily. "I'm glad you clarified that or I might have thought you had changed your mind about her. It sounds to me like you've developed more than a diplomatic interest in the girl."

"Are you kidding?" Jeffrey said defensively, depositing the chicken leg next to Hazleton's cigarette in the ashtray, causing the rendered fat to smoke slightly.

"Then why are you here? What's on your mind?"

"Nothing. I just had to get away for a while. I tell you, they've had me under lock and key, not to mention what it's like when I'm trailing around with the Chinese. This is the first time since I brushed my teeth this morning that I haven't had two secret service goons breathing down my neck. I don't know how the Chinese can stand it either. They're not seeing anything—just a lot of empty buildings."

"What do you want our guys to do?" Hazleton asked with a shrug. "Give Chu a dozen tokens and a map of the city? You know, he isn't everybody's favorite Chinaman. We get at least fifteen calls a day at the paper from groups who would like to blow him off the map, and his daughter as well."

"I guess," Jeffrey considered. "But if I had planned the trip I would have shown them something—the real America, the nitty-gritty places that only you and I know about."

Hazleton spit a rain cloud of juice over the table in a clench of uncontrolled laughter. "You and I," he repeated. "That would be one helluva tour. I'd show them poor-white-trash Alabama and you could take them to visitors' day at your old prep school."

Jeffrey felt embarassed as Hazleton tried to control his hilarity. "Hey, you're going to wake her up," Jeffrey said, motioning to the bedroom. "Shhhh."

Jeffrey floundered for words, but Hazleton beat him to it. "I don't mean to laugh at you, kid. It's just that you're about the last person I know who could show anyone the 'real' side of anything. You've been raised in a silk cocoon, my boy."

"Hey, I know a lot more than you think," Jeffrey said. "While you had your ass parked at your typewriter, I was thumbing my way across the country."

"Now, looka here, boy," Hazleton said, leveling his

gaze. "You can lay that diddly squat on everyone else in this town, but not me. You can be a rambler and a gambler all you want with all the little blond debs between here and Chevy Chase, but don't try your act in here, 'cause you won't even get the curtain up."

Jeffrey knew that Hazleton was fully awake now, and was teasing him like a junkyard dog with a tender scrap of meat. "I just wish I could take you to Balmorhea, Texas, with me—then you'd see what I mean."

"Why, what happened in Balmorhea? You ripped your good jeans, and a nice old lady sewed them up for you?"

"It was more like a nice young lady who wanted to rip my jeans off me. The problem was her old man was the ranch foreman, and I had to fight my way out of town."

"He must have run one tough ranch. What do they raise in Balmorhea, bull Chihuahuas? I think you've heard one too many farmer's daughter jokes, Hodge."

"Think anything you want, Hazleton, but that town was the best place on earth, and I'd go back in a minute. That's the kind of place Li Soong and her father should be seeing."

"Okay, Hodge, you still owe me ten bucks. Put it towards a Greyhound ticket and go to Balmorhea—or is that too soft a way for a broncobuster like you to travel? Maybe you could hogtie the Premier's daughter and strap her to the back of a packmule."

"I'm not kidding, man. If you ever get to Balmorhea, just ask around. They'll tell you about me. I really wish you'd go there. You'd see."

"At least maybe there I could catch some shut-eye without people wandering in my door at all hours."

Jeffrey stood up. "Sorry I bothered you. I'll leave." It was impossible to win a fight with Hazleton Brown. He had cornered the market on the rough side of life, and made a career reporting on it. He didn't want to share even a corner of it with Jeffrey.

"Where're you going?" Hazleton asked as the boy headed towards the door. "You got me all woke up, stank up my place with burning chicken, and now you're gone? Here, have some more juice."

Jeffrey knew this was Hazleton's peace offering, and so he sat down again. He needed to talk.

Sylvia Charles emerged from the bedroom, wrapped in a blanket. "Hi, who are you?" she asked, wiping the sleep from her eyes. She recognized Jeffrey before he spoke. "Oh, sure, you're Jeff Hodge. We've certainly been seeing your face a lot lately."

"Yeah, I know," he said almost apologetically.

"Jeffrey's just been telling me his plans to reroute the Premier's visit. He's going to take them to America's real garden spots, places like Podunk, Dogpatch, and Balmorhea, Texas." Hazleton grinned as he drawled the words, leaving Sylvia puzzled and Jeffrey again feeling his ire.

"Like where?" Sylvia said, sitting at the table, letting the blanket drop slightly around her pale, freckled shoulders.

"It's nothing, we were just joking," Jeffrey said, trying to loosen Hazleton's jaw from around his jugular.

"Well, it wouldn't be a bad idea," Sylvia said. "Maybe that way some of us could get near enough to talk to them. You're about the only person I know who's been able to get near them all week. How are you and Li Soong getting along?"

Jeffrey felt the interview coming on. He hadn't fled to Hazleton's apartment to be confronted by another story-seeking reporter, even if this one did sit wrapped in a blanket at the kitchen table. He felt strangely defensive at the mention of Li Soong's name. He stood up. "Thanks for the chicken. I gotta go."

Hazleton walked him to the door, giving his shoulder a friendly squeeze. "Keep your chin up, kid," the re-

porter said. "They'll be gone tomorrow. Then you'll be
back doing what you always do."

"Sure," Jeffrey sighed.

"Bye," Sylvia Charles called to him as the door closed.
Hazleton walked back to her and placed his hands on her
shoulders, stroking the smooth pale skin. "Nice kid," she
said, as he gently kneaded the muscles underneath.
"Looks like the visit is really getting to him."

"Um hm," Hazleton said as he continued his steady
massage. "You know what, babe? Let's not think of that
right now."

*

"We would like you to wear this tonight at the fare-
well banquet. It is a gift from the President's family."
Cheng Wu stood before Li Soong, holding a white silk
dress swathed in a protective wrapper. "And this is to be
worn with it." Cheng extracted a black case from his
pocket and handed it to Li Soong. She opened it as if it
was a velvet clamshell, and looked inside at a rope of
pearls. She then looked intently at Cheng Wu. She could
see his face muscles knot, as if preparing to argue with
her. But she regarded the gifts in silence. "Did you hear
me, Li Soong?" he asked.

"Yes, Cheng, I did," she said quietly.

Cheng looked at her with some puzzlement, then hung
the dress in a closet. "Where shall I leave these pearls?"
he asked. "They are very valuable and you must be careful with them."

"On the dresser, please."

"Are you all right?" Cheng asked. He had girded himself for a battle royal, not expecting her to consent so
easily to the wearing of the Americans' gifts.

"I'm fine," Li Soong said. "Is that all you wanted?"

"No, unfortunately, it is not. We must review some
items for our departure."

"All right," Li Soong said vaguely. Her eyes looked at

her own reflection in the dresser mirror. She ran a silver-backed hairbrush through her waist-length hair.

"I want to go over the speech you will give to the Hsinhua agency when we arrive in Peking. I have a draft of it here."

"Fine," Li Soong said, paying more attention to her hair than to Cheng Wu.

The man could not ignore her uncharacteristic behavior. He felt as if he had entered a lion's den only to find a kitten. "Li Soong, please look at me a moment."

She swung around on the upholstered bench and looked impassively into his face.

"The dress I brought in, the jewels . . . I expected you to put up a fuss about them. You have been raised to despise such symbols of bourgeois wealth. Of all of us, you would be the first to voice your objection to these things. Why do you sit there?"

"Do you prefer me to fight now? You and my father have spent this last week trying to silence me. Well, now I am silent," she said sarcastically, "just as my father's policy of revision and compromise demands."

Cheng Wu detected the resistance in the girl's eyes. "Of course, I do not wish to provoke you, but it is odd," he taunted, "that our great revolutionary has suddenly become so agreeable."

"I am only trying to hurry our journey home," she said haughtily. "I have made my discoveries about America, and I am anxious to pass them on to my comrades."

"Your discoveries?" Cheng said with some amusement. "Perhaps I should hear them. Perhaps your father and I have been listening in all the wrong places."

"Perhaps."

"If these discoveries are so grand, why not tell me first. Are you afraid I will steal your secrets?"

"No," Li Soong said sharply. "They are not as grand as all that. But they are an insight to the workings of this land."

"I am surprised you feel ready to explain the nature of America," Cheng Wu said, suppressing a smile, "since it was you who constantly complained about being allowed to see only the most formalized sights."

"Exactly. That is the point," the girl said, sitting up straighter. "Do you remember the young man who follows us everywhere, Jeffrey Hodge?"

"Yes, the light-haired boy who speaks only of the weather? Of course." Cheng Wu grinned. "The son of the Secretary of State. What of him?"

"Yesterday he told me that he had once tried to set off across America alone. He was rebuffed by the peasants and workers with whom he tried to make friends."

"So?"

"It is clear to me that the ruling class of which he is a part is not free to mix with the working class in America, despite what they tell us. If the Americans had given us the freedom to roam where we wanted, we would have met only closed doors. Don't you see, Cheng, to the American workers politicians are like a monarchy, and they would think of *us* no better than their own rulers. The President could not let us see what we wanted to, because it is closed even to him. The class structure is that rigid. Only one disguised as a laborer or peasant could truly see this country."

Li Soong's declaration was met with a broad grin. "I am glad your passions have been tempered some by your 'discoveries,' " he said in a patronizing tone of voice.

"Not at all. I feel more strongly than ever, Cheng. But I see my job now is to bide my time until we return home and I can tell this to the comrades who wait for me."

Cheng began to leaf through the papers in his hand.

"What is more," Li Soong continued, "this Jeffrey Hodge has suffered only ridicule by his peers. The President's daughter only laughs at him when he tries to convey his experience to the others."

"I'm sure," Cheng said absentmindedly as he finally

located the correct document. "Now, if we have finished with all that, please turn your attention to this speech. It is what you will say to our news agency when we land in Peking, and I want you to begin memorizing it now so that we may review it on the plane tonight."

Li Soong scanned the page Cheng Wu had handed her. "What is this!" she exclaimed.

"I see you were preoccupied. It is the speech that—"

"Yes, I heard," Li Soong interrupted, her coolness falling away. "But this is . . . is . . . nothing but lies. I cannot say this!"

Cheng Wu felt the familiar aggravation with Li Soong return. "It is exactly what you will say, Li Soong. Your father has already approved it."

"But it is totally ridiculous." Li Soong's finger raced down the page. "Here . . . it says I spent an enjoyable five days engaged in meaningful dialogue with American youth, and here"—her finger pointed to the text—"I am to say that the President's daughter and I had a challenging discussion on the role of education. I never said a word to her about any such thing. She was too busy with her boyfriend to be interested in anything else!"

"It is no matter," Cheng Wu said firmly. "Don't you understand, it is only a gesture, a statement of cordiality meant to convey the impression to the people of China and the Americans that the trip was a success."

"A success to whom?" Li Soong yelled. "To hear the truth would make this trip a success. The truth is what our people must hear."

"The truth!" Cheng Wu said with exasperation. "And just who is to be the oracle of this great truth, Li Soong? You? Did you find it at Disney World or the department store? Do you flatter yourself this much?"

His chill words fell heavily on Li Soong's ears. She turned away from his awful cynicism, but he continued to demean her. "You grow increasingly tiresome with this heroic picture you paint of yourself. It would be a relief to us all, and most especially to your father, if you realized exactly the purpose of your presence on this trip."

Suddenly Li Soong saw herself in Cheng's eyes. To him she was like the little speech he wished her to make —a peripheral accouterment to the mechanics of power. Like the string of pearls they expected her to wear, Li Soong was a useless ornament.

She could see Cheng's features in the mirror at her dressing table. He handed down another copy of the speech to replace the one that she had crumpled in her hand. Like a dumb machine dispensing pieces of candy, he refused to acknowledge even her resistance. Li Soong knew at this moment that her anger and protest had been for naught. Cheng Wu and the others would always find a way to make her bend to their will. They would cajole or shame her into doing what they wanted. She had taught the Americans nothing about the true nature of China, and she was expected to bring the same empty gift back to her own people.

"Now, when you have memorized that, I will quiz you. In the meantime, I must return to your father. Is there any message you would like me to give him?" Cheng's manner was again businesslike.

Li Soong did not answer.

"Don't take too long to get to it. We have much to do before we leave. We will be on our way home before this night is over." The sharp crack of the door closing as he left made Li Soong jump.

She lifted her hairbrush from the table and began to run it through her hair in long, lazy strokes. Her eyes unfocused, and her mind spun like a star dislodged from orbit. How could she have been so blind to her limitations? To her impotence and meaninglessness on this trip? To Cheng she appeared a foolish adolescent instead of the righteous soldier she knew she was. And now, there was no time left to convince her father or Cheng Wu that she was a woman to be taken seriously. Tomorrow morning she would be in Peking, face to face with her friends, expected to deliver the insights and truths she had promised them. But she had learned nothing at all during the visit. How could she let her comrades down? How could she let Cheng Wu make her feel so useless? The tears that had been threatening to fall finally tumbled down her face, dampening her hair.

She rocked slowly to comfort herself. The faces and landscapes of the visit flew behind her eyes, and familiar places from home rolled by as if in final review. The special cord that had connected her to her father had frayed so thin that Cheng's slam of the door had ruptured it, and she knew for the first time that she had to make her plans without him. She was on the verge of the most daring step she would ever take. As Mao had instructed long ago, she would *seize the time.*

The movement of the hairbrush slowed and her eyes focused as the wetness left them. Sharing her reflection in the mirror were the piles of documents she was obliged to study; the white silk dress hanging in the closet; the endless array of valises to be packed; and the dull gleam of the pearl necklace resting in its box. She looked at the mute objects with a new sense of detachment, as if they were the brittle remnants of a life she had suddenly shed like an old skin. Her cheeks flooded with color, she felt a rush of energy warm her and a bold independence crowd out her fears. Li Soong looked excitedly at herself in the mirror, and she liked what she saw. It was the image of a girl whose journey was finally about to begin.

*

Jeffrey Hodge awaited the arrival of the Premier and his daughter in the East Room. In the guests who had gathered for this final banquet was a new vivacity. Jeffrey watched the President walk through the crowd, shaking hands with dignitaries and honored guests. His election to a first term in office was predicated on a promise that he would use the newly opened China connection as a means of bettering not only America's position in the balance of world politics, but the domestic economic situation as well. The visit represented the opening up of a market of 800 million consumers to American industry. Tonight, the final night of the Chinese visit, was David Bromley's triumph. "Damn finest thing that's happened since diplomatic relations were resumed," Jeffrey heard the senator from New York tell the ambassador from Guinea. "He's a shoo-in for reelection . . ."

Jeffrey wondered if Li Soong's father would be greeted on the other side of the world with similar praise. Then the Premier appeared at the portal of the East Room. Beside him walked Li Soong, her drab outfit replaced by a delicate sheath of silk. A yard of her blue-black hair shifted unfettered with every step. The clasp of pearls glowed across her collarbones. A stunned semicircle of dignitaries broke into spontaneous applause at the sight of her radiant transformation. Her father smiled at the reaction. He watched his daughter proudly, fully pleased for the first time that she had come with him.

"Doesn't she look lovely tonight," Bettina Hodge said to her son. "I don't see why the Chinese insist on looking so dowdy," she whispered as a postscript.

Jeffrey was amazed but, oddly, not impressed. Somewhere deep inside he responded badly to the new image Li Soong had assumed for this evening. Surrounded by clots of women dressed like his mother, Rosemary, and the wives and daughters of the powerful, Li Soong appeared as yet another detail set and approved by Lucas

Pate. Somehow, Jeffrey missed the familiar gray outfit and the limp braids that swayed as Li Soong talked. It was as if the Chinese had already half-disappeared, and Jeffrey felt the same sadness he had brought to Hazleton's last night.

Raymond Hodge approached his son, throwing a hardy arm around Jeffrey's shoulders, breaking him from his momentary reverie. "My boy," he exhaled a scotch-tinged cloud, "my boy," he said again, to Jeffrey's embarassment, "you did all right after all. And after this evening's over, that's it! Back to the old grind . . . for both of us." He dropped his voice lower. "The next Chinese you see will be when we go to the Golden Dragon for dinner."

"The old grind." Jeffrey repeated the words for lack of anything original to say. His father was a stickler for responses to even the most one-sided proclamation.

"We're about due for a little talk. Your mother's been on my back about the college business again. Tomorrow, when the decks are clear, what say the three of us sit down and plan out your courses for the fall."

Jeffrey nodded unthinkingly, but his father didn't seem to notice.

"But that's tomorrow." Ray Hodge said jovially. "Tonight, let's raise a glass to a job well done."

An unsettled feeling grew stronger as his father spoke. Jeffrey was glad when the string quartet struck the chord that signified the start of the final banquet.

This evening, Jeffrey and Li Soong were seated at separate tables. Jeffrey could see her sitting with her father, and his conversation lagged as he looked towards her across the room.

"She looks a hundred percent better, doesn't she?" one of his tablemates said as Jeffrey pulled back his gaze. He didn't want to be seen looking at her.

"Don't stare, dear. It's impolite," Bettina Hodge said under her breath.

"I'm just looking because I'm glad I'll never have to see her again."

"Why so grumpy?" his mother said, clucking her tongue. "It's all behind you now."

"The way you and Dad keep saying that, it sounds like I'm about to die," Jeffrey blurted out.

"My son is known for his sense of the dramatic," Bettina Hodge said, smiling at the lady to her right.

"That poor girl," the woman said, rekindling the conversation. "What a long trip they have to make this evening. What is it, thirteen hours on the plane? How exhausting!"

Jeffrey's feet grew restless under the table.

"Please," his mother said out of the side of her mouth, "we don't need a dance recital."

But Jeffrey could not dispel his anxiety. He wanted to bust loose once and for all from the slow procession of events of the last six months, and now, with the Chinese only hours away from departure, the life that lay in wait for him seemed unbearable.

"You must be so proud of your son," the lady said to Bettina. "He looked so handsome in all the pictures. And wasn't he a charming escort for the girl! They couldn't have done better." She smiled at Jeffrey, who could see her upper plate wobble as she talked.

"Of course we're proud of him," his father said. "He came through with his colors flying."

The discussion only depressed Jeffrey further. He had at least expected a certain sense of victory in the accomplishment of the duties in which he had been drilled. But instead, as the end grew near, he realized that a wooden dummy could have done as well, probably better. He had been a respectable body of the right age and background, one who could be placed next to Li Soong for the benefit of the press photographers. The Jeffrey Hodge who liked movies but not the opera, who liked dogs but not cats, who swam well but couldn't throw a football, was of no interest to these people. And the more he searched for a role in his life that was his own invention and not his parents', the more unfulfilling his position as escort became.

"Darling, it's your favorite—roast beef. Why aren't you eating?" his mother asked with concern. Then, for the benefit of the rest of the table, she added, "Honestly, whoever said that young men are ravenous eaters certainly never met my son."

Jeffrey cut a triangle of meat from the heavy cut that lay on his plate and placed it in his mouth. He chewed with great effort, grinding the meat with as much concentration as he could; then a swallow, washed down with wine; then another piece of meat, another swallow.

"That's a good boy." His mother patted his knee under the table.

Li Soong cast her gaze out over the guests as they sat before her like a landscape of bright flesh. Encased in brocade and animal fur, these were people who smelled of red meat and car upholstery, not like the workers in the factories and fields that lay half a planet away.

The lights in the dining room dimmed as waiters rushed among the tables bearing baked Alaskas ablaze in cobalt flames. The Americans gasped, their jewels shimmering in the light of the blue fires, their cologne swirling through the room in a low-lying cloud. Li Soong blessed the momentary darkness, for the cakes had temporarily displaced her as the center of attention. She allowed herself to search the room for Jeffrey Hodge. In the dim light she could see the shine of his blond hair, see the whiteness of his dinner shirt. She knew no one could see her watching, no one could look into her mind and see that Jeffrey was at the very center of her plans.

The lights flashed on again, the dinner conversations renewed. Champagne and Mao Tai flowed, the President and Premier exchanged the traditional Chinese toast of *ganbai,* and the majority of the guests were soon dizzy from an overdose of wine and splendid sentiments.

"I believe the rain has let up," the Premier said, leaning towards his daughter. "The skies are parting to welcome us back."

"Why don't we go for a stroll outside," the President suggested. "You haven't seen our gardens at night."

A fine dampness had spread over the grass. The President and First Lady led their Chinese guests towards the Jacqueline Kennedy Herb Garden. The First Lady stooped in her yellow gown to pick a leaf from a small plant. Crushing it between her fingers, she handed it to the Premier's physician. "I believe you use this medicinally, don't you?" she chatted pleasantly.

Ray and Bettina Hodge converged with Cheng Wu as the party leisurely moved through the illuminated walkways. Behind them walked Jeffrey, his eyes straight ahead, focused on Li Soong's back. The Chinese bodyguards flanked the procession, walking with an informal gait, their vigilance eased by the celebratory relief of the White House party. Jeffrey noticed Li Soong drop back slightly as her father and the First Family strode ahead. He quickened his own step, finally matching and meeting hers.

"Hi," he said, catching her attention. She turned to look at him, an uncharacteristic smile on her face. But now that he was by her side, he was not sure why he had been in such a hurry to meet up with her. He started with some uncertainty: "Listen, about yesterday, on the plane... When I said you didn't know what I was talking about, about my trip and all . . . Well, I just wanted to apologize. That was pretty rude of me. Lucas Pate would kill me if he knew what I said. I guess I've been in a bad mood." He felt the words speeding from his mouth, but he could not explain why he felt so eager to engage Li Soong in conversation.

She looked squarely into his face. "I do not think badly of you. I think you are exceptional."

"You do?" Jeffrey said with wonder.

"Yes. I think your adventure into the American countryside was admirable. Perhaps you were right on the plane. Perhaps I did not know what I was speaking about."

"Hey," Jeffrey stammered, "wow, that's really nice of you to say. I mean, what I did wasn't that big of a deal. It was just a two-month vacation."

"It was more courageous than anything else I have heard since I arrived," Li Soong said with certainty.

Jeffrey was astonished. It was hard for him to match the girl who now stood before him in the formal gown —with hair flowing softly down her back and kind words coming from her lips—with the baggy-suited soldier of the previous days. She looked different tonight, but he was sure the changes went beyond the dress and hair. He could see the blood course under her fine skin, the pulse in her neck beating against the rope of pearls. She radiated an energy that held him to the spot as the First Family's contingent walked onwards.

Overhead stretched a great bruise of sky. The tip of the Washington Monument could be seen in the distance, glowing white in the hazy damp air. The city lay beyond the iron gates that encircled them.

"Listen," Jeffrey said as he thought he noticed Li Soong shift her weight to leave, "have you seen the Rose Garden?"

"No. I would like to."

"Great, let's walk over there," Jeffrey said, leading her along the path to where a yellow glow from the Oval Office fell over the thick-cut hedges. The rose bushes were weighted with blooms. Jeffrey and Li Soong stood, isolated from the others, under the arbor, sheltered from the threatening sky.

"Who is it you didn't want to see?" Li Soong surprised Jeffrey with her perceptiveness. He had spotted Hazleton Brown up ahead with a group of the other pressmen.

"Just a reporter I know. He would have bugged you with a lot of questions." The truth was that Jeffrey did not want his friend to ruin Li Soong's image of him as a workingman's hero. He rather enjoyed the idea of her going back home and telling her people of his singularity.

"Thank you for my privacy," she said. "I can believe that half your country are reporters and the other half are secret service men. They spend all their time guarding and tattling on each other."

"That's not far off," Jeffrey said, still surprised by her vivacity. There was an electricity in the air that could not be explained by the oncoming storm. He fidgeted, thinking of what to say next, but she grabbed the opportunity from him.

"About what you said on the plane . . ."

"You *are* mad."

"No, I am not," she insisted. "But I must know if you really did all you said . . . the cowboys, the fishing, the lumber camp . . . all those adventures. Are they true?"

Jeffrey could still feel the sting of Hazleton's laughter from the night before. He scanned a break in the hedge, but he couldn't see the reporter nearby. "Sure," he said softly, "I did all that." *What the hell*, he thought. *She'll be gone in an hour anyway. At least she can bring a good story back home.*

Somehow, the wall between them had vanished. Jeffrey imagined his tuxedo falling away, replaced by leather chaps and a cowboy's guitar. Li Soong was the last person he would have imagined to be his best audience.

"Why did Rosemary make fun of your travels?"

"Because, if you haven't already noticed," Jeffrey said,

"Rosemary is an idiot." His growing bravado had steam-rolled the few remaining diplomatic sprouts.

Li Soong beamed the new smile again. "And you would rather live among the common man than here, in Washington, with all the luxury and formality?"

"I sure would. In a few months, when I have enough money saved up, I plan to take off again," Jeffrey said, surprising even himself. "My parents want me to go back to college, but the best education a person can get is to thumb their way across the country."

"Thumb?" Li Soong asked.

"It's slang for hitchhiking. You know, getting rides with whoever will pick you up."

"I see." She pondered. "And how long would it take to travel that way across America?"

"A few weeks, a month. It depends on what kind of luck you have."

"Why luck?"

"You don't know who's going to pick you up. I mean truckdrivers, teen-agers, old people—they'll stop easier than married couples or middle-aged folks."

"Is that true?" Li Soong asked, her eyes widening.

He nodded. He knew it was true because Hazleton had explained it to him more than once.

"And where do you sleep?"

"Farmhouses, on the ground in a sleeping bag, wher-ever it's warm and dry." Jeffrey's restlessness had chan-neled into a conversation he was thoroughly enjoying.

"If you could go again, where is it that you would head?" the girl asked him, brushing a strand of hair back from her face.

Jeffrey didn't understand why he hadn't noticed how pretty she was before this. "I guess Texas," he said. "Maybe around Balmorhea. It's beautiful down there in the spring. I know the guy who cooks for the rodeo, and I bet the old woman who runs the laundromat would remember me . . . maybe a few others, too." Jeffrey was more and more at ease. "Boy, Li Soong, it's really a shame that you didn't have the time to see what's outside Washington. But I guess even if you did, you could never travel like John Q. Public."

"Who is he?" Li Soong looked confused.

"Like John Doe. It's just a name for anyone you want. Understand?"

"No," the girl said.

"Sort of an anonymous person. Someone whose real identity is unknown. But that's not important. What I mean is that you and your father could never see the real America any more than the President could just go to Peking and hang around."

"Exactly," Li Soong said, her eyes growing more intense. "Jeffrey, do you hear what you are saying?"

"No . . . I mean . . . what?"

"You are saying what I have been trying to tell Cheng Wu and my father, but they wouldn't listen; that it is impossible for either of us, as we are, to see this country. We must go in disguise."

"We?"

"Yes, we. You, because you are brave and have done this before. Because you are not content to assume the role of bourgeois, moneyed heir that your parents want for you, or to go to school to learn a life that has no meaning outside the privileged class. And I shall go because I have come here to see America. It is my duty to go."

"Go where?" Jeffrey said.

"Across America. Like John Q. Public."

Jeffrey stood looking into the girl's shining face. "I don't understand, Li Soong. Is this a joke, like the young man and the beautiful woman? I don't get it."

"It is not a joke. What do you think we have been talking about together, on the plane and now?"

"I don't know. I thought we were just, you know, talking . . ."

She modulated her words like a teacher with a not-too-bright pupil. "I have come here to see America, but no one will show it to me. I think you will. I think you will run away with me. Am I right?"

"Right? Me? Are you crazy?" Jeffrey heard his voice crack.

"I do not think so."

"I can't believe this," Jeffrey said. "How could you even consider doing something like that? Don't you know what you'd be up against? There are Marines and cops at every gate. Everyone would recognize you in ten seconds. And you know, there are dozens of people out there who would like nothing better than to see you and your father sent back home in a box, *dead,* Li Soong!" He was practically screeching. "And, my God, you wouldn't even know how to cross the street in America by yourself."

"Then you will teach me."

"*No,*" Jeffrey said.

"First, it is only hard to break in the White House, not out. Second, people would see us as just another American boy and girl. There are many thousands of Orientals in your country, so I would not be so easily recognized. And because of this, I would be safe from the terrorists of whom you speak."

Jeffrey moaned. "You really mean this, don't you? You're insane. Don't you know the kind of trouble we could get in if anyone even overheard this conversation?"

Li Soong stood still as Jeffrey started to pace along the rose hedges. "Please come here, Jeffrey," she said, holding out her hand. "Listen."

He walked closer to her, his arms in a tight embrace of his own body. "What?"

"Jeffrey, I know how much you want to go with me," she said. "I have watched your face for a week with Rosemary and the others, even your parents. You don't fit here any more than I do. You are of the real world, not of this." She waved a hand towards the sumptuousness of the White House. "You have told me as much yourself. Don't you hear your own words?"

Through the hedges Jeffrey glimpsed Hazleton Brown, Sylvia Charles on his arm as they walked past. Jeffrey flattened himself against the roses so as not to be seen.

"Who is there?" Li Soong asked.

"Shhh," Jeffrey said. "It's somebody I don't want to see." As the words left his mouth, he felt a rush of joy. Hazleton would never believe that he was hiding in the bushes as the Premier of China's daughter propositioned him to run away with her. A grin spread across his face.

"Now what is funny?" Li Soong asked as a raindrop fell on her shoulder. "We don't have much time. Will you go?"

"Yes," Jeffrey heard himself say.

To their mutual surprise, the girl threw her arms around him.

Through the roses Jeffrey could see Hazleton recede into the distance, and the word he spoke froze in his mouth. "I . . . I changed my mind. I mean no," he suddenly said, causing Li Soong to back off.

"You're scared," she challenged.

"No, I'm not. It's just that, unlike you, I am being realistic. Plus I just remembered I don't have my wallet." He dug his hand into his tuxedo pocket and withdrew a few dollars. "See, this is all the money I have."

"That's enough."

"Enough! You couldn't even get a meal at McDonald's with this."

"Then we will not eat at MacDonald's," Li Soong said with precise pronounciation.

He could no longer argue. He felt ashamed of himself, standing before the young girl who was willing to take the risk he never had. He hated himself for fighting so hard against the adventure he had always dreamed of having. Li Soong was offering something he had hoped for and bragged about and chased after. And now he stood, shaking his head, refusing it.

A cloud burst overhead, sending a drenching rain onto both of them, wetting Li Soong's dress, soaking her hair.

She looked deeply into his eyes. Again she held out her hand. "Will you come?" she asked, and there was something in her voice that told Jeffrey the question was being asked a final time.

Jeffrey nodded his head yes, in silence, then took her hand. "Let's go," he said.

The water fell in sheets upon the lawn as the President's guests headed for the shelter of the White House, accompanied by Marine valets who had emerged with black umbrellas.

Jeffrey stripped off his jacket and gave it to Li Soong, who hoisted it above her head like a warrior's shield. They emerged from the garden and ran along the winding drive towards the southwest gate. Chauffeurs sat in parked limousines, bored or asleep, as the rain ricocheted off their windows and down the slick black sides of their cars. In the distance the sound of the city pulsed louder.

Jeffrey looked back. He could see the lights of the TV crews shimmering in the rain, recording the final moments of the visit, searching the crowd for the Premier and his daughter.

At the gate stood two Marines. The couple approached and they snapped to attention. The rain pelted the patent-leather brims of the soldiers' hats as they stepped aside to let the couple pass out onto E Street.

Their footsteps quickened on Ellipse Road as they headed south towards the Washington Monument. They ran into the rush of traffic on Constitution Avenue. The girl's slippers were soaked with the iridescent mix of water and oil that swirled in the street.

A taxicab cruised towards them and Jeffrey flagged it to a halt. Trailing rivulets of water, they sank into the tobacco-stained seats and slammed the door. The cab peeled away.

"Where to, buddy?" asked the driver.

"Texas," the passenger replied.

Four

THE SKY over the White House cracked open, sending celebrants rushing to the shelter of the south portico. Rain drenched and depleted gossamer fabrics, and magnified the diamonds and emeralds that encircled distinguished throats.

The President and the Premier stood surveying the scene from the south porch. "This should blow over in a few minutes," David Bromley said, rocking on his heels. "Our meteorologist says it's just a squall."

The Premier agreed with relief: "Yes, I'm sure it won't affect our flight plan." He was exhausted, and the many glasses he had raised during the after-dinner toasts had numbed him.

The President could see a bedraggled phalanx of photographers and newsmen file in the side door. "There's a hardy group," he said with a half-smile as the reporters dripped water onto the marble floor. "I guess they want their final shots."

"Of course," the Premier said. "But I would be happy to never see the pop of a flashgun again."

The President agreed, turning to an aide. "Let's get everyone assembled. Where are my wife and daughter?"

Rosemary pouted as she approached her father. "Look

at me." Her hairdo had collapsed like a fallen soufflé.

The First Lady took her husband's hand. "We're soaked," she said.

"And where is my child?" the Premier asked, scanning the crowd. "I thought our daughters had gone off together."

"No," Rosemary answered. "I was talking with Bert."

"I think I saw Li Soong heading towards the powder room," the First Lady said, then turned to her daughter. "Darling, please get her."

"All right," Rosemary said, fingering a wet strand of hair. "I better fix myself up too."

"I'm sure Rosemary will bring her out momentarily," the First Lady said cheerily. "The poor thing is probably soaked to the bone and had to dry off."

Ray and Bettina Hodge approached the President's family. "David, you certainly could have ordered better weather for his evening," Bettina said to the President. "We almost got washed away."

"And it seems like my son has disappeared in the flood." Raymond Hodge laughed uneasily. "You haven't seen him, have you?"

"No," the President said. "We have our own little hunt under way."

Rosemary appeared at the portal, her hair restored, but Li Soong was not with her. A worried look flickered across Premier Chu's face. "She's not in there," Rosemary said with a shrug as she drew closer.

The press secretary approached the contingent. "Excuse me, Mr. President, could we get the final portrait?"

"Sure thing," the Chief Executive said with a smile. "Just give us a minute. We're trying to get everyone together."

"Where could she have gone?" the Premier asked in a mildly agitated tone. "Wasn't she behind us on our stroll?"

"I saw her," Rosemary said. "She was sort of lagging behind."

"Get Bettinger over here," the President ordered his aide.

"But you did see her?" the Premier asked, turning to Rosemary.

"Sure I did. I think she was walking with Jeffrey Hodge."

Bettina Hodge tensed with a small current of anxiety.

"Don't worry about a thing," the President said. "She's probably upstairs; but just to make you feel better, this is my top man. He'll get her." He gestured to secret service agent Robin Bettinger, whom he dispatched into the White House.

"Where are my bodyguards?" the Premier asked Cheng Wu, who was now standing by his side. "I want them to join in the search party."

"I would hardly call it a search party." The President chuckled benignly. "This isn't the wilderness."

"I insist," the Premier said humorlessly.

"Whatever you wish," the President conceded. "Hell, I'm sure she'll turn up before your men get to the foot of the stairs."

*

Jeffrey had held his breath as the cab picked up speed, allowing his chest to rise and fall with regularity only as the buildings around the White House faded from view. The cab driver searched for Texas Avenue among the capital's state-named streets, and Jeffrey felt blessed that they had not already been recognized. He turned to Li Soong and saw her silhouette against the pane of glass. "We made it out," he whispered. "We actually made it out."

"Of course," she said with a smug smile. "I told you that would not be a problem."

Jeffrey stifled a yelp of exhilaration that was forming

in his throat, and instead gave himself a verbal pat on the back: "This is without a doubt the most incredible thing anyone I know has ever done."

"You are glad we left?" Li Soong asked. It was obvious he was. "Do you think they know we're gone yet?" Her voice dropped half a note.

Jeffrey nodded, sitting quietly for a moment. "What do you think they will do?" He glanced nervously out the back window of the taxi.

"I imagine they will be very upset," she replied with a hint of a smile on her lips.

"Oh, wow," Jeffrey said, throwing himself back into the brittle leather seat. " 'Upset' is hardly the word for it."

"My father will be especially upset," Li Soong said, drawing her face into a haughty expression. "Probably more so than yours. He would never expect me to accomplish anything this daring."

"Hey, look." Jeffrey defended himself. "Don't kid yourself. My father is going to blow a gut when he realizes what's happened. You don't know how uptight he is about—"

"Yes, but my father will assuredly get his bodyguards, the Society of the Four Winds, to come after us. And your father has no such force at his disposal," Li Soong proclaimed.

"And your mother wears Army boots," Jeffrey mocked in the rising silliness of their debate.

"What?" Li Soong said, trying to understand his retort. "She does what?"

"Forget it," Jeffrey said. "So who are these guys anyway? The Four Winds?"

"They are the ones who followed us everywhere. They have no peers in their proficiency at every level of protection, investigation and defense."

"Defense?"

"Martial arts," Li Soong clarified.

Jeffrey shifted his eyes uncomfortably. "Oh."

"But don't worry about them." Li Soong brightened. "We are much cleverer than they. Look how far we have gotten already."

Jeffrey's gaze fell upon the rapidly ticking meter of the cab. It was already approaching the double-digit mark as downtown Washington became a distant blur in the background.

*

"Something's up," Hazleton Brown whispered to Sylvia Charles. They had watched the President's security men come and go. They had seen the jovial expressions on the faces of the President and Premier vanish.

"What do you think it is?" the newswoman asked.

"Beats hell out of me. And even if I knew, babe"— Hazleton grinned—"most likely I wouldn't tell you."

"Every man for himself?" Sylvia mused.

"Yup," Hazleton agreed. "This side of the bedroom."

They waited restlessly a while longer, but when no official word was forthcoming, Hazleton said, "I'm going to look around, see if I can scout anything up. Want to join me?"

"No, I'll wait. I'm sure it's just the usual bullshit delay. But thanks anyway."

"Anytime," Hazleton said, relieved that she had refused his invitation. He turned away from the other reporters, seeking Jeffrey Hodge, who might be able to provide an explanation for the delay.

*

After forty minutes the President had run out of small talk. The Premier stood with his hands clenched behind his back, staring out over the lawn. Rosemary and her boyfriend exchanged limpid gazes, and the Hodges engaged in conversation with the First Lady.

"Mr. President." Robin Bettinger approached, speaking in a low voice. "May I see you . . . alone?"

The President moved a few steps to the side with his secret service man. He tried to ignore Chu's anxious eyes, which he knew were trained on him.

"I didn't think you would want to hear this next to the Premier, but—"

"Don't tell me you can't find her!" the President said sharply under his breath. "This is ridiculous." Faint anxiety mushroomed into a chill across David Bromley's scalp.

"I don't understand it either, sir. I took Scott and Chadwick with me. We looked outside on the grounds and in each of the rooms. She's just not here."

"Of course she's here, damnit," the President said in a hard whisper. "She has to be here. Where the hell else would she be?" His glance met the agent's, unmentionable possibilities mirrored in each other's eyes. "No." He shook his head. "No, you missed something, that's all. Look in every closet, in the kitchen . . . Christ, I shouldn't be telling you your job. Go and hurry up about it," he ordered, dismissing the agent.

As the President turned, he calculated what he would tell the Premier. He saw the man talking rapidly to the four bodyguards, admonishing them severely. The situation was quickly slipping from his grasp. He moved steadily towards the Chinese with the certitude of step one uses in approaching dangerous animals that must not be allowed to sense fear. He reached out to touch Premier Chu's shoulder, barely able to suppress a tremor. His words were weak. "Don't worry. She's here somewhere. Kids are always . . ." The President's voice trailed off.

His uncertain gaze was now locked by the fixed stare of the Premier of China, whose narrow eyes shone like polished obsidian. The President could see his jaw muscles knot. His mouth barely moved. He spoke two words: "Find her."

*

"Hey, kid," the cabbie called from the front seat, "where is this Texas Avenue anyway? I ain't been drivin' D.C. too long . . . Help me out?"

"Driver." Li Soong spoke up. "We do not wish to go to Texas Avenue. We are going to the state known as Texas."

The driver mashed the brake pedal and swerved towards the curb, pulling to an abrupt halt. He swung his bulk around, hanging an arm thick as a leg of lamb over the back of the seat. "Okay, youse two jokers, cut the monkey business. I got a long night ahead of me. Where ya goin'?"

"Let me talk," Jeffrey said under his breath to Li Soong. He cleared his throat, stalling for time to compose his thoughts. He spoke with forced innocence: "You don't go that far?"

The cabbie shot him a look that could grill cheese. "No, buddy, I don't go that far." He looked hard at the face of his passenger. "Hey, what is this, a fraternity stunt or something? Y'know, you college kids make me sick. I'm tryin' to earn a workingman's living, and what do I get but a couple of clowns looking for kicks."

Li Soong was shocked at the man's anger. She pressed close to Jeffrey to get his attention. "He sees your fancy suit and my dress and pearls." She fingered the clasp. "He does not realize we are like him at heart. Let me explain. We are not college kids." She had piped up before Jeffrey could stop her. "We are common, like you."

"No, no." Jeffrey winced as he saw the man's offended face. "We're college kids, like you said. But, mister, this isn't a prank. We really do have to get as far as you'll take us. How far can you go? How about Purcelleville?"

"Acchh, I shoulda stayed in Rego Park," he muttered

to himself, shaking his head. "What does the wife know about what's a better place to live, anyway." He looked between his two fares and then at the ticking meter. "All right, youse two have wasted enough of my time. I guess I'm stuck witcha. My sticker says I can go into Virginia."

"How far?" Jeffrey asked.

"Purcelleville, huh? Towards Winchester? Okay, I can take youse that far."

"Okay, that's fine," Jeffrey said as he saw a patrol car cruise by. "But let's get going. We're in a hurry."

"Everybody's in a hurry," the cabbie groused. Suddenly he fixed his passengers with a penetrating stare, looking hard at Jeffrey, then at Li Soong, then back at Jeffrey. "You ain't in any kind of trouble? I mean, you didn't pull no heist?"

"Heist?" Jeffrey said, suddenly feeling giddy.

"Yeah—the hurry you're in and whatnot. I saw youse both get edgy when that black-and-white cruised by."

Jeffrey giggled. "No, we're just late. I have to get her home, before . . . uh, before her parents get mad. It's past her curfew."

The cabbie ignored the story. "Y'know, I thought for a minute you looked familiar, like from the post office or the papers, I don't know." He looked at their fancy clothes. "Prom night?" he asked, becoming a little friendlier.

"Yeah," Jeffrey said, whooshing out a long breath. "Prom night."

As the cab picked up speed, Jeffrey felt Li Soong pinch him hard on the arm. "Ow," he said. "Now what's the matter?"

"Why did you lie to him?" she demanded in a low voice. "He should be made aware that we are common people, like him."

"In these clothes? Are you crazy?"

Li Soong looked down at herself, then at Jeffrey. "Of course, you are right. We must get rid of the clothes quickly, so that we are not mistaken for the despised elite."

"That'll be a neat trick," Jeffrey said, his attention again drawn to the cab's meter, where the numbers spun wildly as the cab sped onto the highway. Suddenly, their journey seemed utterly impossible, unimaginable. It was crazy to expect that he could pull off a grand and glorious voyage across the country if he couldn't even figure out a way to pay the man at the end of this short ride. He glanced at Li Soong, who again watched out the open window with an exhilarated expression on her face. *Damn her,* he said angrily to himself. *How could I have let her talk me into this hairbrained exploit?* He thought of his parents, and Lucas Pate, and Hazleton, and what a fool he would feel like to be turned in to the police by a cabbie from Queens. He could imagine them all laughing at his feeble attempt to do something wild and reckless. He wondered if it was too late to turn around. Maybe they could sneak in the gate as they had left. They could say they had gone for a short walk and forgotten the time.

Li Soong turned as Jeffrey gave out with an audible sigh. "What's wrong?" she asked. A stream of moonlight illuminated her full face. Her eyes looked softer than he remembered.

"I guess I'm just worried about, you know . . ." He pointed towards the driver.

"You are?" she said with genuine surprise. "It seems like such a small obstacle. I'm sure you will think of a way to overcome it. After all, you have been in danger far greater than this," she said with a gleam in her eye.

Jeffrey looked hard at the girl. "You really believe what I told you," he said. "I mean, about my travels."

"Of course," she said.

"And you don't have any doubts about this . . . I mean, it's not too late to . . . we could go back."

"Go back?" Li Soong steeled her eyes. "This is just the beginning."

"I just want to be sure you know what you're in for," Jeffrey said, hating his own doubts.

"We will find what no others like us have seen. I will be able to tell my people about the real America. We will find it together."

"All right," Jeffrey said. He liked the idea, and he felt his confidence tentatively return. "I was only testing you. I had to make sure you weren't going to suddenly get scared and want to run back."

"Never," Li Soong declared.

"Okay," Jeffrey said emphatically. "No sweat."

" 'No sweat'? What is that?"

"It means don't worry. It means . . ." Jeffrey hesitated, admiring the determination in her face. "It means we're friends."

"Yes, of course we are friends, and we are comrades on this journey," Li Soong said. "No sweat."

*

The lamps were dim in the Oval Office. The President sat at his desk. Behind his chair, flashlight beams moved through the Rose Garden. Their postures grimly stiff, Raymond Hodge and Sam Agoglia, chief of the FBI, sat in the semidarkness on a couch to the President's right. Opposite them were Cheng Wu, P'eng Hsi and two Chinese aides. Standing to the right and left of the President were Bettinger, secret service agents, two Chinese interpreters and Jake Rosenfeld, the press secretary. Sitting in the armchair facing the President, surrounded by the Society of the Four Winds, was Premier Chu.

The President sat in his shirt-sleeves. He had emptied the last of the coffee from his silver thermos. He looked up as Bettinger began again, for the third time.

"Think back again, if you would, Mr. Premier, to this afternoon. It would be enormously helpful if you could recall anything unusual, anything at all, that she might have said to you. Did she mention anyone suspicious, any phone calls—"

"No, I have told you before, she spoke of nothing unusual. The day proceeded exactly as planned."

"I remember years back"—Agoglia spoke reassuringly —"when Amy Carter locked herself in a linen closet. She pounded for an hour before anyone heard her."

"My daughter is not a little child," the Premier shot out. "She does not lock herself in closets."

"I'm sorry, sir," the man started apologetically, "but…" The Premier glowered at him, his face beaded with sweat. The chief resumed his straight-backed posture. "Did you check all the closets?" he asked softly of an aide standing next to his couch. The aide nodded yes, then shrugged.

The President's grandfather clock struck one A.M. in the silent room. The President spoke. "It is impossible for her to have left the grounds. Impossible."

Agoglia nodded in agreement.

Bettinger repeated the President's word: "Impossible."

Raymond Hodge spoke up. "Our best men—and yours —were watching her. According to the guards at the gates, there was no suspicious activity anywhere along the perimeter of the grounds. My own son was by her side as we strolled—"

"And what of your son's vanishing from sight?" Cheng Wu asked. "Are we the only ones who see a possible connection between that and Li Soong's disappearance?"

Ray Hodge scoffed: "You don't understand my son. Jeffrey is the type of boy who would run home at the earliest opportunity. He dislikes parties, and I am sure the rain provided him with the perfect opportunity to slip away unnoticed."

"Call your house again, please." The President motioned to one of the desk phones.

The room was quiet as Ray Hodge dialed the number. They watched as he shook his head when his wife told him that Jeffrey was still missing. "Look, now, I know my own son," Ray Hodge blurted out as he hung up the phone. "If he's not home, then he's probably at that reporter friend's house, Brown, from the *Post.*"

"Call him," Cheng Wu said.

"No," the President countered abruptly. "The press already knows something is up. Let's not fan the flames, please."

"What have they been told?" Chu asked.

"That your daughter took ill and is resting upstairs; that your departure has been temporarily delayed."

"I don't like that," the Premier said. "I want them to know what has happened—"

"What on earth for?" Jake Rosenfeld interrupted. "That could only escalate the situation further."

The President was visibly sweating. "That's a bad idea, Chu; a bad, bad idea. You don't want the press to pick this up. Believe me, it could only jeopardize your daughter if she . . ." He fumbled for words. "If she's . . . out there."

"Mr. Premier," Bettinger said, coming to the Chief Executive's aid, "if, by remote chance, Li Soong *has* fallen into unfriendly hands, disclosure would only put her in further danger. It could provoke those who might have forcibly . . . detained her."

"You mean kidnapped," Chu spat back.

"It's one chance in a million; almost unthinkable, with the security forces we have had in position. But I assure you, we are leaving no possibility unexplored."

"Your thoroughness is admirable, but dangerously

late," Chu said to Bettinger while looking directly at the President.

The FBI chief spoke up. "We are now waiting to see if we receive any communication—"

"Wait?" Premier Chu stood. *"Wait!"* He punctuated the air with a Chinese curse that made his staff color. "Wait for some bandit to contact us?" he shouted at the President. "I have no intention of waiting. In China we do not let criminals determine the course of action."

"Now, you wait a moment, sir," the President said. "We are hardly sitting by. We are doing everything in our power to find the girl. But we are all agreed that Li Soong is most probably somewhere on the White House grounds, having wandered off—"

"We are certainly not agreed!" the Premier said, turning to his staff. "Are we?" They shook their heads.

The President felt the tension crackle. He forced his voice into its calmest tone and flashed Chu his most earnest expression. "What is it we can do that we are not already doing?" he asked, obscuring the white knuckles of his tight fists under his desk.

The Premier did not respond to the President's question. Instead, he called Cheng Wu close. The adviser bent down and the men conferred in private.

The President stood. "Bettinger, I want an update every fifteen minutes. Agoglia, every bureau chief will be briefed by you, now. Jake, tell the press to go home and come back for a seven o'clock statement. Tell them Li Soong is still resting."

"You are trying to whitewash this crime!" Chu stood and faced the President. "The press must be told the truth."

"The press will *not* be told," the President countered.

A deathly hush fell over the Oval Office as the two leaders backed off from each other like pit-fighting dogs. Chu smelled fear sweat in the room. He watched fingertips tap tables, heard coins rattle in pockets and pencils rap out staccato rhythms on clipboards. He tried to equate his daughter's safety with the ends of power at his command, and her value escalated without end. Her life was measureless in his eyes, greater than any threat he could make to bring her back. He saw President David Bromley shift his eyes uneasily as he lowered himself back into the seat behind his massive desk. The American knew what Li Soong meant to him, and he knew the power Chu had to unleash if her return was not imminent.

*

Washington's lights had given way to an asphalt ribbon of highway. Jeffrey and Li Soong sat close together as the cab rolled on.

The gruff voice from the front seat interrupted the calm: "Pal, I hope you're one big tipper. I'll never get a fare back, that's for sure."

They were approaching Purcelleville, the end of the line. Jeffrey could see the driver's small eyes, like disembodied headlights, glaring back at them in the mirror.

"Whaddaya say we settle up and I'll drop youse at the Seven-Eleven off the next ramp."

Jeffrey stalled: "Maybe you could just take us a couple more miles."

The cab pulled onto the auxiliary road that sided the highway. The driver sensed his passengers' nervousness. "Why don't you gimme thirty-five even, for the meter and the tip."

Jeffrey realized the man wasn't going to stop until the fare was settled. "Please pull over. I'd like to talk to you. I have something to explain," Jeffrey said, hoping for the sudden inspiration of a plausible way out.

The cab continued to cruise along the darkened road. The driver thrust his hand over the back of the seat, palm extended. "Settle up, kid . . . or . . ."

"Or?" Jeffrey dared the word.

"Or you and your girlfriend are gonna get dropped with the nearest cop."

Li Soong gave Jeffrey a desperate look.

Jeffrey searched for an explanation. "I, um, I seem to have left my wallet." He patted his pockets unconvincingly. "Gee, how could I have done a thing like that?"

The driver flipped the door locks down with a master control on the dashboard, and hit the accelerator.

"Where are you taking us?" Li Soong asked.

"Like I told your boyfriend, nobody screws Joe Hollywood outta a fare."

"Joe Hollywood," Jeffrey said with wonder. "Is that really your name?"

"Never mind my name . . . Y'know, I can't believe the nerve of youse—"

"Please, Comrade," Li Soong spoke. "Let me explain."

"Comrade? What kinda name is that?"

"It means friend," Li Soong said.

"Yeah?" the man said sarcastically. "In what language?"

"Try to understand our situation—"

"Shh," Jeffrey said. "You can't tell him."

"Can't tell me what? Hey, youse *are* in trouble, ain't ya?"

"No," Li Soong said sharply. "We are not criminals. We have escaped a desperate situation of oppression. We were political prisoners of sorts—"

"Prisoners?" The man raised his voice. "Don't you try nuttin' funny. I got a tire iron right here."

"Not that kind of prisoner," Jeffrey said. He turned to Li Soong. "You're making it worse. Just shut up and let me explain."

She sat back with a hurt look on her face.

"It's a simple misunderstanding," Jeffrey said. "Please stop driving for a minute and listen."

The driver pulled the car to the side of the deserted access road. "Explain," he said. "And it better be good."

"It's simple," Jeffrey said, making it up as he went along. "We were at a party, a fancy party—"

"A prom," the driver reminded Jeffrey.

"Sort of. Anyway, something happened. We had a fight. We had to get away. And we just took off without our coats, and that's where I left my wallet."

"Jeffrey." Li Soong spoke. "Tell this man we are engaged in trying to understand the problems of the American workers."

"He doesn't care," Jeffrey said. "Be quiet."

"You can tell your girlfriend," the cabbie declared, "that one of the biggest problems of the workers is getting stiffed by rich college kids."

"Yes," Li Soong said, shaking her head seriously. "I will make a note of that."

"Buddy"—the cabbie addressed Jeffrey—"I'll give you a piece of free advice. Your girlfriend has a screw loose. Find yourself a nice American broad."

Li Soong looked shocked.

"Are you married?" Jeffrey asked, eyeing Li Soong's pearls as potential barter.

"I can't believe dis guy. Whattaya, Dr. Joyce Brothers? He screws me outta a fare and then plays marriage counselor!"

"Wait a minute," Jeffrey said. "I thought maybe you would take her necklace instead of the fare. It's worth a lot more than thirty-five dollars."

"Hand it over and I'll see." The cabbie examined the pearls, sliding them along his teeth, fogging them with his breath. "Bee-ootiful," he proclaimed. The locks on the cab doors flipped up.

Jeffrey put a foot out into ankle-deep mud. He withdrew back into the cab, looking from his patent-leather shoe to the man's flannel shirt and tweed cap. "That outfit you're wearing. Is it for sale?"

"This?" the man said, looking down at his raunchy clothes.

"Yeah, that," Jeffrey said. "And if you have anything else to wear—"

"I got my work clothes in the trunk."

"We can't wear this stuff," Jeffrey said to Li Soong, tapping the satin lapel of his tux. "We'll stand out like a couple of penguins. Mister"—he turned back to the cabbie—"I'll let you have this suit and her dress for whatever clothes you've got."

The driver didn't wait to ponder the situation. "You got it, bud. And by the way, I take back what I said about your girlfriend. Youse make a perfect couple—both looney."

Jeffrey and the driver walked around to the trunk, where, piece by piece, they traded clothes until Jeffrey returned to Li Soong wearing the man's baggy pants and work shirt and carrying a sweater and jeans for the girl.

"Here," he said, pushing the clothes through the window. "Change into these."

She emerged moments later with a smile on her face, the cuffs of the jeans rolled into two huge donuts, the man's sweater hanging to her knees. "It looks funny?" she asked Jeffrey.

"All you need is a cigar butt on a toothpick to complete that outfit," he said. "Emmett Kelly, look out."

"Very nice, very nice," they heard the cabbie say as he gathered the dress from the back seat. He waddled towards the driver's seat, his belly bulging through Jeffrey's dress shirt.

"You're not just going to leave us here, are you?" Jeffrey asked, suddenly noticing the empty fields that surrounded them. "Can't you drop us back at the highway so we can hitch a ride?"

"Buster, you're on your own," the cabbie said as he spun away, kicking gravel back at the couple.

Li Soong and Jeffrey stood by the darkened roadside, alone for the first time. An indigo sky stretched overhead, stars filling the empty trails that the storm clouds had left behind. They could hear the interstate far ahead in the distance.

"Now what?" Li Soong turned to Jeffrey in anticipation. "Now what do we do? Where do we go?"

The night air made Jeffrey feel bouyant and unafraid. He looked at her for an extended moment, watching her blue-black hair shift as she spoke.

"Jeffrey?" she asked again.

"Oh." He shook himself out of the haze. "To the highway," he said, offering her his hand, "and then to Balmorhea."

Five

By the time they reached the highway, Jeffrey's formal pumps were caked with mud and Li Soong's slippers had all but disintegrated. "Here we are. Now what?" she asked excitedly as they approached the leveled plane of the interstate.

"Flag down a ride," Jeffrey said. "I'll teach you to hitchhike."

"I know how to stop a car," Li Soong said impatiently. "Watch me."

Headlights approached, the car slowed to look at the couple on the shoulder of the road. Li Soong began to wave her arms wildly, and the car sped away.

"That's all wrong," Jeffrey said. "You scared them off."

"I did? Why?"

"Because you look desperate, like you need a ride too badly . . . It's uncool."

"Uncool?" Li Soong pondered the word. "That's bad."

"Very," Jeffrey said with a glower, "You have to approach these situations with a lot of know-how."

"Then show me," Li Soong said, pulling her shirt tight around her. "It's getting cold."

"Okay, you do like this," Jeffrey said, taking her slim

hand and pulling out the thumb to position it in the classic pose. "Then you stand by the side of the road, look bored, and the cars just can't resist stopping." He smiled and winked knowingly at her. "Here, I'll show you." Jeffrey stood posed dramatically with his thumb out as two cars whizzed past. From a purple sedan, an empty Schlitz can and a catcall came flying their way.

"It's not working," Li Soong said, crestfallen.

"Sure it is," Jeffrey said, refusing to be defeated. "That was just practice."

She looked skeptically at him. "Are you sure this is the correct way?"

"Of course it is. I've done this a million times," he lied. "It never fails."

One hour later Jeffrey and Li Soong stood wearily together in the same spot, thumbs outstretched.

"Something is wrong," Li Soong said gloomily.

"It's this road," Jeffrey countered. "It's so dark no one can see us."

"We have to be far from Washington before word of our escape is out."

"I know, I know," Jeffrey said, starting to get discouraged himself. "Give it a few more minutes. I promise someone will stop."

*

The cab driver hefted his tuxedoed bulk up three flights of stairs to his apartment, where he leaned on the buzzer until his wife answered. "Whatsamatta, you forget your key again?" she said as her eyes looked him up and down. "What the hell is this, New Year's Eve?"

He regained his breath and stepped inside. With a grand gesture he produced Li Soong's string of pearls from his pocket. "Heh?" he said, enticing her by holding them before him.

She eyed the necklace like a beautiful but dangerous snake. She reached out and touched it.

"They're yours," the man said, recognizing her awe. "Take 'em, don't be scared. It's a little present to make up for last night."

"They can't be genyoowine?" she asked, slipping them through her hands, polishing them on her housecoat. "But they sure look it."

"Would I getcha anything but the best?" he asked.

"They must've cost a fortune," she cooed. Suddenly her voice dropped. "You went to the track, didn't you?"

"You don't want 'em?"

She was too fascinated by the jewels to argue. "What's that?" She pointed to the bundle under his arm. "And what's with the monkey suit?"

"Don't worry yourself about me. Look at this," he said, producing Li Soong's dress from the newspaper bundle. "To go with the pearls."

The slip of material unfurled in the wife's hands and she held it up to her formidable form. Her excitement quickly fell away. "Hey, big shot," she said, screwing up her face towards his. "Hold your horses. What is this, a size five?"

"So?" the man said.

"So how many times I gotta tell you, I wear sixteen and a half? Where'd you get this thing, anyway?" She searched for a store label. "There's nothing here," she yelled, turning the custom-made garment inside out.

"I . . . I thought it would fit you," he stammered. "I always see you in my mind as a dainty thing—"

"Like fun you do!" She paced towards him. "I know what this is. It's a costume, a stripper's costume, and the cheap pearls go with it." She threw the dress at him. "Get outta here with your cheesy rag! Get out!"

The cabbie balled the flimsy dress in his hand and angrily descended the steps. He sat in the cab, rage swelling up in his chest until he threw the old heap into gear. With a mighty sound, the seat of his trousers split.

"Damnit to hell!" he cursed, reaching for the starched collar that was digging into his flesh. "Damn this, damn her," he repeated, throwing different parts of the disintegrating tuxedo out the window of the cab. He ran two red lights and hung a right onto River Road. He reached over and rolled down the passenger's side window, heaving Li Soong's dress onto the road, where a passing car laid a set of tread marks across the garment.

*

"Breaker nineteen, breaker nineteen, this is one Devil's Son-in-Law, motorvatin' with his radidio smokin' and a-jokin', searchin' the airwaves for a four-wheel beaver with her ears on, c'mon . . ." The double set of headlights washed over the concrete slab that stretched out in front of the cabover Peterbilt.

The trucker saw two hitchhikers along the darkened shoulder, hung the CB microphone on its hook, and slowed slightly to get a better look. "Could this be my lucky day?" he said to himself as the mighty lights flickered off Jeffrey's blond curls and Li Soong's long black hair. "Two beautiful beavers up ahead . . . oh, Lordy!" He hit the air brakes and the diesel horn at the same time. The truck slowed and the driver flicked on the console stereo in the cab, ricocheting Merle Haggard off the double tuck-and-roll Naugahyde.

"Hop in, ladies," he said as he pushed open the door on the shotgun side of the Pete. "Hop on up into trucker's heaven." As his eyes adjusted to the darkness, his mouth fell. Jeffrey's strong jaw and sideburns caught his attention. "Oh, my Lord," he said. "You're the sorriest-looking excuse for beaver I ever saw, son." His eyes traveled to Li Soong. Her flannel shirt flapped as other semis flew by on the highway. "Well, I'm stopped, so you might as well get your butts on in here. I could use the company. It's lonely out here tonight on the superslab."

Jeffrey boosted Li Soong up the metal steps into the

cab. The driver motioned Jeffrey towards the bunk behind the seats. The truck lurched into gear, and the driver flashed through a triple-H gear pattern until he hit number thirteen and settled into the tall-backed seat.

The scream of the tape cassette, the hum of the tires, the raspy crackle of the CB radio, surrounded Jeffrey and Li Soong in the cab. They looked at each other and at the trucker. Li Soong's eyes locked on the weathered face that hid in the shadows of a silver-banded cowboy hat. In a mostly toothless mouth, a toothpick spun elegant configurations.

"Wow," Jeffrey said to himself in a whisper, leaning forward and poking Li Soong on the arm. "Look at this place." His eyes traveled the circumference of the cab's interior. "It looks like a jungle."

"You like them pelts?" the trucker asked, referring to the wall-to-wall leopard skin that surrounded them.

"I guess so," Jeffrey said with uncertainty.

"How about you, girlie?"

"Are they real?" Li Soong asked.

"Naw, better 'n real. They're fake. I'll tell you something, this truck is one of a kind, and I invented the design myself. In fact, I invented leopard skin," the trucker said proudly.

"I thought leopards invented it," Jeffrey said.

"Don't get smart, boy, or I'll leave you back out on the road where I found you."

"No, please don't. Sorry," Jeffrey said.

The trucker perused them with cool blue eyes. In the beams of oncoming lights Jeffrey and Li Soong could see the deep lines etched under his eyes, a stubble of beard shadowing his gaunt face. "How far you goin'?" he asked.

Jeffrey and Li Soong looked at each other, seeking reassurance in each other's eyes. Li Soong held Jeffrey's gaze, nodding her head as if to banish any doubts either

of them had. "Well, uh, as far as you'll take us," Jeffrey
answered.

"That's no answer, boy," the man said. "I asked how
far you're going. If you got no destination, then that
makes you a bum, and I don't give rides to bums—"

"Wait a minute," Jeffrey interrupted. "We've got a
destination, don't we?" He turned to Li Soong, who
started to smile. "Texas," he said. "We're going to
Texas."

The man startled them both by letting out a piercing
yell. Li Soong jumped and hit her head on the padded
roof. "Well, why didn't you say you were a Texican," the
man said, booming forth with another rebel yell. "That's
my home, too."

"Will you take us that far?" Li Soong asked sheepishly.

"You just try and stop me before we cross over the
Lone Star border," the man said, revealing a vista of
tobacco-stained gums.

"Perfect," Jeffrey said, renewed by their luck.

"Damn!" the trucker hollered enthusiastically. "Let's
put the pedal to the metal and go home!" He took off his
broad-brimmed Stetson and plunked it playfully on Li
Soong's head. They were on their way.

*

It was two A.M. when Hazleton reached his desk at the
Post. Like the other reporters, he had heard the an-
nouncement of Li Soong's malaise and the official White
House proclamation of a delayed Chinese departure.
The changes of plan, together with his friend Jeffrey's
unexpected absence, began to coalesce in the reporter's
mind. He dialed Jeffrey's private number and heard Bettina Hodge anxiously pick up the phone after a single
ring. Hazleton Brown headed for his night editor, feeling as taut as a drawn bow.

"Listen to me, Jimmy," he said, leaning across the
man's cluttered desk. "I got a lead on a story that's so hot

I don't know if I should tell you or the fire department."

The editor looked at him hard. "I figured something big was up for you to show your face in here this time of night. I haven't seen you in about three months. What's cooking?"

"I can't tell you," Hazleton said flatly.

"You can't tell me," the man repeated: "Then good-bye, Mr. Brown, I have a desk full of work to do."

"You'll have to take my word for it, but if this buzz I've got in my head is right, we've got the biggest story since Adam and Eve bit the apple."

"So what do you want here? What is this, twenty questions? Go out and cover it."

"I can't. I need help."

"Help? Hazleton Brown, the lone ranger, needs help?" The editor arched his eyebrows.

"Not that kind of help. I need a good car, better than the piece of shit you gave me, and I need a thousand bucks right away."

"This sounds like a holdup, not a story. I can't give you that kind of cash without knowing where you're heading."

"Sorry," Brown said. "I can't risk leaking this, even to you. Just believe me when I tell you I have this buzz and it's never failed me yet."

"Buzz?" The editor sipped his tea from a Styrofoam cup.

"Yeah . . . it's an itch, but inside; something I can't scratch."

"Spare me the medical report."

"I've had it before every big story I've broken—"

"We all know your track record, Brown, and we're all impressed as hell, but before I empty the kitty for you I have to have at least some idea of what you're up to. I can't tell the boss your head itches! How do I know you haven't got lice, or maybe a mother earthworm is giving birth to quintuplets inside your well-fertilized brain."

"While we're bullshitting, the story's getting further away."

"Why don't you wrap up the Chinese visit, then we'll see—"

"I can't wrap it up, Jimmy. That's what I'm talking about."

The man lifted his head with some interest. "Tell me about it."

"All I can say is, I have good reason to suspect that the Premier's kid isn't sick."

"She's got the grippe. The White House issued a statement last night."

"If she's so sick, where's the President's sawbones? How come he hasn't left his apartment at Columbia Plaza all night?"

The editor sipped his tea. "Go on."

"It's also the first I ever heard of when a simple case of the trots has caused a midnight security meeting."

"Go on." The editor was increasingly interested.

"Agoglia, Robin Bettinger, Dean Anderson, Ray Hodge—they're all still there, Jimmy."

"Go on."

"Will you cut this 'go on' crap?" Hazleton said. "I can't go on until you give me the car and the money. The only thing I can say to you is, I have a pretty fair idea of why that Chinese jet is still on the ground; and what's holding them up is one helluva story."

"Come back at seven and see if the boss will clear it for you."

"You know why you haven't moved up from this office in ten years, Jimmy? You're chicken shit, you got no balls. You're throwing out the biggest story of your career . . ."

The man's jowls quivered. "I've been patient with you, Brown. You can muscle others here, but don't try it on me. It takes more than a twitchy eye or itchy head or whatever goddamned deformity you got to make a good reporter. I've seen other hotshots come and go on this paper. I've seen 'em take one step too far and get canned quicker 'n a sardine."

The two men looked at each other across the desk. Hazleton's foot tapped uncomfortably. He wanted to move fast. "Let's make a deal," he said with strained patience.

"No deals."

"Wait a minute," Hazleton said forcefully. "I'm putting my ass on the line too."

The man's tight fist of a face relaxed slightly.

"If you don't give me the money, I'm going to go out and get this story on my own. And when I get back I'll hold up every paper in town for what I got. If you give me the go sign, it's all yours."

"You mean if I don't okay it you'll quit?" the man said.

Hazleton nodded, keeping a poker face.

"If you come back empty-handed, both our names are shit," the editor said, nervously ripping pieces from his Styrofoam cup.

"Trust me," Hazleton said with reassuring conviction.

"Get out of here," the editor said. "Get your cash voucher on the second floor. And one other thing. I don't want to hear any 'I'm close' bunk. If I don't get the story from you by the end of the week, I'm declaring the car stolen and calling the cops. Fair enough?"

"Not exactly," Hazleton said as he stood.

"Hey," the editor called as Hazleton stepped towards the door.

"Yeah?"

"Just give me a clue so I can cover my ass on this."

Hazleton looked back over his shoulder with a half-grin. "Clues are for kiddie games, Jimmy." He strode through the newsroom and began to softly whistle a tune to himself: *I'm an Old Cowhand from the Rio Grande.*

*

Night bugs splattered against the truck's windshield. Field mice darted between the tires that sang as they spun along the asphalt strip. Li Soong leaned back in the seat as she watched the hypnotic pattern of the road. She was bouyed by the mobile hospitality of the trucker. She had already broken through the veils of protocol and diplomacy that had kept her from the American workers. She had only to leave Washington to discover the secrets of the world that lay beyond.

"You ever ride in a semi before?" the trucker asked his passengers.

"No," Li Soong said at the same moment Jeffrey said "Yes."

"You better make up your minds."

"What is a semi?" Li Soong asked.

"You're sitting in one now. Honey, you got a lot to learn."

"Yes, I do," Li Soong said vigorously. "And you will teach me."

"You haven't heard anything unusual on your two-way radio?" Jeffrey asked with feigned casualness.

"What'd you have in mind?"

"Oh, nothing."

"I got nothing but wall-to-wall smokie reports. They're thick as molasses tonight."

"What is a smokie?" Li Soong asked.

"Po-lice," the man said, breaking the word into two even syllables. Li Soong looked nervously at Jeffrey. "You two aren't on the lam, are you?"

"No," Jeffrey said. "Of course not."

"Don't make no nevermind to me." The man grinned. "I been in trouble too many times myself to point the finger at anyone else."

"What kind of trouble?" Li Soong asked.

"Trucker trouble, mostly. Haulin' without permits, hot loads, breakin' the Sullivan law . . . the usual."

Li Soong understood nothing. "Are those criminal actions?"

"Depends on how you look at it. The way we gearjammers see it, the law just don't want us to make a decent living."

"You mean the police interfere with your work?" Li Soong was fascinated.

"You bet your sweet patooty. Whoever said this is a free country sure as hell never drove a truck. You gotta pay through the nose for every mile you go. Taxes, tolls, state stickers . . . I got a lot of people to support, and I can't make enough money unless I make up a few rules of my own."

"And such oppression is the truckdriver's lot?" Li Soong asked, turning to Jeffrey. "Give me a pencil and paper. I have to take notes."

"A pencil and paper?" the trucker asked. "What is this, *Sixty Minutes?*"

"She's just kidding," Jeffrey said, shaking his head nervously at Li Soong. "Excuse me a minute," he said to the trucker, and pulled Li Soong by one braid towards the sleeper bunk he sat on. "What's the matter with you, Li Soong? You never told me you were going to ask all sorts of stupid questions. People don't like having their lives pried into by strangers."

"Ow," Li Soong said, wrestling her braid back. "You don't understand. It is imperative I find out this information. Why do you think I left with you in the first place?"

Jeffrey's face fell slightly. "I don't know . . . I thought you wanted to see America with me, not act like the Mike Wallace of China."

"Who's he?" she asked, noticing the hurt look on Jeffrey's face.

"It's not important," Jeffrey said. "I'm sorry if I hurt you pulling on your hair."

"No sweat," Li Soong said. "I will be more discreet in my questions."

"Okay, just be cool, or we'll never get to Texas."

"You two must be married, fighting like that," the trucker interrupted.

"Us?" Jeffrey said with surprise. "No, we're not!"

"You don't live together or anything immoral like that?"

"No, we're just friends. I don't think I ever want to get married," Jeffrey declared.

"Don't knock marriage," the trucker said, rounding a curve. "It's great. I oughtta know, I did it enough."

Li Soong's ears perked up. Jeffrey watched her closely, ready to interrupt her again. "How many times have you been married?" she asked.

"Twice."

"Have you been divorced or widowed?"

"That's none of her business," Jeffrey interjected. "You don't have to answer."

"I ain't ashamed of nothing," the trucker said. "I don't believe in divorce. It's immoral. And, knock on wood, I ain't lost a wife yet, neither."

"I don't understand." Now Jeffrey was curious.

"It's simple, boy. I just fell in love with a woman up in Maine, and then when I changed my route a few years later, I fell in love with one down in Georgia. Marrying is the decent thing to do when you want to have kids."

Li Soong's mouth fell open. "You have two wives at the same time? And how many children?"

"Eight," the man said proudly.

"Do your wives know about each other?" Jeffrey asked.

"Nope. Why make 'em jealous? I love 'em all. I'd get me number three if I found the right one."

Li Soong was astonished. She thought of her predictable future back home—the approved marriage in her upper twenties to a right-thinking male counterpart, a correct number of children . . . She had never heard of anything like the trucker's story.

"Don't you want to stay home and watch your children grow up?" Jeffrey asked, remembering his own sedate home life.

"That wouldn't be a bad notion if I didn't have diesel fuel in my blood."

Li Soong tried to fit the pieces together. "Then you are a narcotics addict," she said sagely.

The trucker and Jeffrey laughed. "Just about," the man said. "Driving a rig is almost like a drug. I tried to get off the road. I worked in factories, got a job as a guard in a warehouse, even had a farm for a while, but none of it worked. I'd look out the window and watch the trucks roll by, going in all directions. I'd hear those big old diesel horns calling back and forth to each other. And one night my old lady in Maine rolled over, and I was gone."

From the bunk Jeffrey watched the trucker's face as he drove. His eyes were sharp pinpoints scanning the road. His skin was prematurely old, crisscrossed with lines, dry from the road breezes that blew on it endlessly.

Li Soong imagined her comrades seeing her now, traveling with the kind of person even her father had been kept away from during the official visit. She thought how proud they would be of her courage, how they would come to admire her for going where others were not allowed. She drank up the trucker's tale. It was everything she had wanted.

"I first started driving with my pop. I was about fifteen at the time. He used to haul swinging beef from Amarillo up north to Beer City."

"Beer City?" Li Soong asked, trying to locate it on a mental map of the United States.

"Milwaukee," the trucker decoded for her. "All the

cities got trucker names. Like Boston is Beantown,
Tampa, well, that's Cigar City, L.A. is Shaky City—"

"Because of the earthquakes," Jeffrey interjected.

"You got it," the trucker said.

Li Soong clapped her hands in appreciation. She felt
she was at last being let in on a wonderful secret code
shared by the American workers.

"You like that kind of talk?" the trucker asked, turning
up the volume control of the CB radio. "Why not shoot
the breeze on this here box awhile?"

"That's not a good idea," Jeffrey said cautiously.

"Why not?" Li Soong asked, causing Jeffrey to glare at
her. "My friend thinks we should remain unknown," she
explained to the trucker.

"No one will know who you are. Everybody uses a
handle on the CB."

"A handle?" Li Soong questioned.

"A moniker, a phony name. Like me—I'm the Devil's
Son-in-Law. That way we can talk about the police and
the speed traps and all without anyone knowing who we
are."

"Ahh." Li Soong's eyes lit up. "An assumed identity.
And in this manner the worker protects himself from the
threat of police brutality."

Jeffrey groaned as the trucker looked puzzled.

"Your girlfriend sure has some strange ways of saying
things. You want to get on the horn or not?" the trucker
asked, offering the mike to Jeffrey.

"Okay," he said. The idea sounded like fun. "I need a
handle, though."

"Here's a few I used to use. You're welcome to 'em: the
Dixie Delight, the Bionic Bandit, the Texas Tornado."

"Texas Tornado isn't bad," Jeffrey said, trying on the
name for size. "I think I like that one."

"Then, that's you." The trucker turned to Li Soong.
"How about you? You get the idea?"

"Yes," she said. "I think I have the perfect one: Girl Who Wanders the Land in Search of Green Fields Where Crops Grow Freely."

The trucker was dumbstruck. "Wha . . . ? The girl does what?"

Jeffrey was laughing as Li Soong earnestly tried again. "You do not like that one?" she asked. "Well, how about the Tractor Driver Who Marches with Determination in Search of Justice"?

"Oh, brother, they'd have my hide if I let you on the radio with that one. Say, what's your real name, anyway?"

"Li Soong," she said before Jeffrey could stop her, but there was no recognition in the trucker's face.

"Well, then, we'll call you Li'l Bit. That's close enough."

"Li'l Bit? What does that mean?" the girl asked.

"It means you're tiny and cute," the trucker explained.

"I am?" she asked.

"Sure, why not?" Jeffrey allowed, anxious to try his hand at the radio. "Let me try and call someone."

"Okay, just do like me," the trucker instructed, grabbing the cord from his hand. "It's easy . . . breaker one-nine, breaker one-nine," he warbled in a sorghum-thick accent, "you got one Devil's Son-in-Law here, keepin' the shiny side up and the greasy side down. I'm the undercover lover, that beaver-chasin' trucker, the one all women cheer and all men fear. Can I get a smokie report on that double-nickle superslab, come back."

Jeffrey was dumbfounded. "That's great," he said in awe of the rapid-fire trucker talk. "But I could never talk like that."

"Sure you could. All it takes is practice. By the time we get to Texas, I'll have you both jawin' into this box better than me."

"Oh, Jeffrey." Li Soong turned around in her seat. "Isn't this wonderful!" He couldn't have agreed more.

*

By five A.M. the CB mike had been hung back on its hook and Jeffrey and Li Soong were riding quietly with their host. Their heads spun with new words, signs for towns they had never heard of, and the now-familiar sight of the leopard-bedecked truck that rocketed them closer to their destination. Still too exhilarated to sleep, they watched the countryside rip past the windows of the rig.

Li Soong leaned her face against the glass, looking beyond the wash of the headlights to the black velvet of the Carolina sky. She marveled at how easy their escape had been, how freely the trucker shared his thoughts and painted word pictures of the America that still lay ahead for them.

"I know it sounds crazy," the man said, "but there's something to that saying that the grass is greener some-where else. You always expect the girls to be a little prettier, the scenery a little nicer—just over the next hill."

"Don't you ever want to stay put somewhere?" Jeffrey asked. "Like at home?"

The trucker didn't answer the question. "What brought you two out on the road?" he asked.

"We are going to Texas," Li Soong said. "But no fur-ther. We know when to turn back. We have plans."

"I admire that," the trucker stated. "But once you get that itch to wander, it never leaves. Maybe it's just stay-ing one step ahead of your troubles."

"Maybe," Jeffrey said wearily, lulled by the bounce of the truck.

"There are no troubles that cannot be solved ration-ally," Li Soong declared.

"You're pretty young to be so sure of yourself," the

trucker said, looking at the small figure that sat next to him. "When I was your age, I thought I knew everything too."

Li Soong felt a twinge of discomfort as the man spoke to her. "You sound like my father," she said grumpily.

"Then your father must be a pretty smart bastard." The trucker smiled.

"Not as smart as people think," Li Soong said as Jeffrey cleared his throat to signal an end to the discourse.

"She's a fiery little beaver, ain't she? I bet she keeps you on your toes." The trucker winked back at Jeffrey.

"What is a beaver?" Li Soong asked suspiciously.

"You are," the driver said. "That's CB talk for a girl."

"A beaver." Li Soong rolled the word on her tongue. "Is that good?"

"Sure," the man said. "Beavers are the finest thing on God's earth."

Li Soong thought. "Yes, a beaver is an industrious, diligent animal. I think I like that. I'm proud to be a beaver."

"Fine." The man laughed. " 'Cause in my book, you're a first-rate beaver. Not many gals want to hear truck-driving stories all night."

"And in my book, you are a first-rate truckdriver," Li Soong mimicked him, with admiration.

"You know, if I wasn't twice your age, I'd take you on as wife number three. I bet you'd like that," the man said.

"No— you can't." Jeffrey spoke up instinctively.

"Cool down, son. Just teasing. I know she's yours."

"How far are we from Texas?" Jeffrey asked, hoping for a new course of conversation.

"About a day away. But don't worry. I won't let you get bored. You know, I write songs and make up poems, too. I got a mess of things I made up, stored in my brain."

"Can we hear one?" Li Soong asked.

"Sure. I don't usually say my poems in front of men, but I guess he's all right."

"Yes, he is," Li Soong offered in Jeffrey's defense. "His character is admirable."

"Here's one you'd like," the trucker said.

> *"I met a beautiful lady*
> *All dressed in a silver coat.*
> *She said she felt like wandering,*
> *And would I like to go.*
> *We climbed the highest mountain,*
> *And crossed the rolling sea,*
> *And drove into adventure—*
> *Just this silver lady and me."*

"That's wonderful," Li Soong said. "But who is the lady?"

"Your wife?" Jeffrey guessed.

"Hell, no," the man said. "It's my truck."

*

Jeffrey and Li Soong had dozed while the sun appeared behind the westbound truck. The trucker pulled a long blast on his air horn, causing Jeffrey to wake with a start.

"Where are we? What time is it?"

"It's breakfast time in Caroline," the trucker said. "Time for red-eye gravy, biscuits and grits."

"Great, I'm starving," Jeffrey said, watching Li Soong rub the sleep from her eyes. "Also . . . my bladder is about to burst."

"Son, you pee in my bunk and I'll throw you out of this truck on your keester."

"Look how beautiful it is outside," Li Soong exclaimed, noticing that a soft rural landscape had replaced the commotion of the interstate.

"I got off the highway a ways back when you two nodded out on me. I take this road to avoid a scale they've got set up a few miles down. I got a hot load in the back and no Carolina stickers, neither."

"What's a hot load?" Li Soong asked.

"It's freight you don't have rights to haul. In my case, some unstamped liquor."

"What would happen if you were caught?" Jeffrey asked.

"They'd fine me good, and you could forward my mail to the crowbar hotel. But this here little road is safe—not a smokie in sight."

"Can I roll down the window and breathe the fresh air?" Li Soong asked.

"Sure, but watch out for those branches. Don't stick a hand out or nothing. There's hardly room for this truck on the road."

Li Soong cracked the window open, flooding the cab with a rush of sweet country air. She inhaled deeply and fell back in her seat. "Ahhhh." She breathed loudly. "This is even better than I had imagined—an American worker who is unafraid to talk, a courageous comrade by my side, and the simple beauty of the open fields."

"It sure is different than Washington," Jeffrey agreed, leaning easily against a rolled-up blanket in the sleeper. He took in the passing greenery, the smell of the earth, and imagined the hearty breakfast that lay ahead. He wished Hazleton could see him now. He closed his eyes to savor the moment, feeling a newfound sense of freedom wash over him with the morning air.

In their reveries, neither Jeffrey nor Li Soong noticed the police car that had positioned itself in the road, directly in the path of the bouncing truck.

Six

Secret Service Agent Robin Bettinger excused himself
from the Oval Office at 6:42 A.M., when the tone sounded
twice from his pocket page. He moved across the hall
into the Roosevelt Room, where two field agents stood
alongside a crumpled brown paper bag on a table.

"I think we've got something," agent Donovan said
grimly. "It was found by the Metro cops, and they
figured we should know. It came into Operations ten
minutes ago."

"Good. He's going crazy in there with nothing to go
on. The Chinese are leaning hard," Bettinger said, stepping forward. "What is it?"

"It isn't good," Donovan said, reaching for the bag on
the table. "You better call the chief out here so he can
think of something to tell Chu."

Inside his office, the President was cornered. His men
had read the same reports to the Chinese all night. He
had to move. At 6:46 A.M. the light on his desk phone
blinked. He picked up and his secretary said, "Mr. President, Bettinger wants to see you outside. He has something important."

"Send him in," the President commanded.

"Sir . . . he thinks it would be better—"

"Send him in!" the President said, cutting her off. "Now!" He turned to the assembled group of weary men. "They have something," he said with some relief as Bettinger swung open the oak door.

The agent stood, unspeaking, holding the brown bag in both hands in front of his waist. He forced himself to step towards the desk, with a deliberation and intensity that drew the eyes of all in the room to his motion. He stood next to Premier Chu's chair, across from the President.

"Well?" the President asked. "What have you got?"

Bettinger unfolded the top of the wrinkled bag and turned it over, allowing the contents to fall onto the surface of the desk. As the shredded remnants of Li Soong's silk dress spilled out, the Premier of China rose from his chair with the cry of a wounded animal.

*

"We caught this one hauling a load of illegal liquor in his truck, and these two here won't talk," the deputy said as he shoved Jeffrey and Li Soong closer to the sheriff's desk.

"Won't talk, you say?" the sheriff said, scanning the odd couple who stood handcuffed in front of him. "What identification did you find?"

"Nothing, sir. No papers, no money."

"Vagrancy—South Carolina statutes 447 A, B and F. Refusing to give information to a uniformed officer—statutes 17 and 102. Did they put up a fuss?"

"Yes, sir," the deputy nodded.

The sheriff grinned stiffly. "Resisting arrest—South Carolina penal code 34, paragraphs 4 and 5." He cleared his throat and looked with officious contempt upon his prisoners. "That's enough to hold you here until the Fourth of July—unless you've changed your mind and want to talk."

Jeffrey read the frightened expression on Li Soong's

face. His own hands were shaking so badly that his metal handcuffs chattered like castanets.

"I have no choice but to detain you," the sheriff declared. "Cells one and two," he told the deputy.

"Wait," Jeffrey called out as he felt a hand fall roughly on his elbow.

The deputy looked to the sheriff, whose nod of the head signaled the release of Jeffrey's arm. "Go ahead, boy." The deputy poked him. "Speak your piece."

"You've got to let us go. We didn't do anything. We just hitched a ride with him. We didn't know what he had in his truck."

"Hitchhiking is illegal," the sheriff said in a mechanically flat voice. "Code 478, amendment 4, December 1, 1979."

"Let us go. We won't do it again," Jeffrey pleaded.

"Now," the sheriff proclaimed with a single flourish of the hands, like a symphony conductor about to begin. "Let's back up." He extracted a massively long legal form from the drawer of his desk, and smoothed it on the surface of his blotter. "Now that you have decided to talk, we will begin with the facts." He inserted a pencil into an electric sharpener, laboriously scrutinizing the operation until the point was needle sharp.

As Jeffrey waited he cast his gaze around the small jailhouse that squatted in the center of Thicketty, South Carolina. The dingy cinderblock walls were painted the color of bleached celery, and the whole place smelled like a mildewed sponge. Out-of-date calendars yellowed on the wall, fly tape hung from the ceiling, but the sheriff's desk, in the center of this decrepit place, was a bastion of efficiency. The man himself was so meticulously garbed that each crease of his uniform looked as though it had been edged in stainless steel. His nails were manicured and polished to match the shine of the silver gun that weighted his belt. Jeffrey couldn't help but think how Lucas Pate would have loved him.

"Is this really necessary?" Jeffrey asked as the man touched the tip of the now-adequately-sharpened pencil to his tongue.

"This is not necessary," the sheriff said, stiffening his posture even further. "It is *imperative.*"

"Oh," Jeffrey said glumly.

"We will proceed." The pencil was poised in the air. "First, the girl will answer. We'll start with your names. Last name first, first name last, middle initial inserted between same."

"What?" Li Soong asked in total confusion. "Do something," she implored Jeffrey. "We cannot be detained here." The deputy jostled her hard.

Jeffrey felt a surge of anger and panic. It was trouble enough that he had allowed Li Soong to talk him into this crazy adventure, but what would happen if he let her get hurt? The possibility made his knees weak. "Hold on," he shouted. "Let me speak to her alone."

"No," the sheriff said, getting agitated at the delay. "This is my jail. We will proceed in an orderly fashion."

Jeffrey took a deep breath, glanced at Li Soong, then blurted out: "I have something to confess, then."

"Confess?" the sheriff asked with increased interest as the others fell silent. He straightened his tie, tucking its tail into the space between his shirt buttons.

"It is important you know who we really are—our true identities."

The sheriff picked up his pencil again and adjusted the form. "That is exactly what I want."

"You won't need that when I tell you— It's more for the newspapers than for your files."

"No, don't!" Li Soong cried out. "Tell them you are John Doe, the Texas Tornado, and I am Li'l Bit, the American Beaver."

The deputy holding Li Soong looked at her aghast and began to laugh.

"Shut up!" the sheriff barked, feeling the situation slipping away from him. "John Doe," he mumbled angrily, erasing the smudge he had started to make on the legal form.

"I'm not John Doe," Jeffrey exclaimed. "I'm Jeffrey Hodge." His statement was met by blank eyes. "Jeffrey Hodge, Jeffrey Hodge!" he repeated like a verbal hammer. "Don't you get newspapers down here, or TV?"

"You're an actor?" the sheriff asked. "They're the worst kind of trouble."

"No, you moron," Jeffrey said before he could edit his speech. "I'm the Secretary of State's son. And this is Li Soong! *Li Soong,* the daughter of the Premier of China!"

At this the deputy burst out with a guffaw that doubled him over. He looked at the tattered rags and dirty faces of his captives, and laughed until he lost his breath. "And I'm the King of France," he roared. "And this," he said, pointing to the sheriff, whose face was now tomato red, "this here's the Duke of Paducah."

"Enough!" the sheriff yelled, banging a heavy fist down. "You might think this here's a little no-consequence jailhouse, boy, but you got the wrong number. You don't know it, but you are dealing with a master of modern police science and procedures when you break the law in my town." He stepped from behind his desk, shooting a deadly glance at the deputy, who still tried to suppress the hilarity bubbling up at Jeffrey's confession.

The sheriff grabbed a floral-printed screen that obscured one corner of the office and moved it aside, revealing a sleek metal console and video screen.

"What's that?" Jeffrey asked.

"This," the sheriff said proudly, "is TR-A57. There's not a crime committed or a criminal at large that this little unit don't know about. With this"—he glared at

Jeffrey—"I cross-check your MO and your ID with all local APBs and the FBI in Washington, D.C."

"The FBI?" Jeffrey said. "Why don't you just call them?"

"Not necessary," the man said, flipping a switch and watching the computer's multicolored buttons dance with light. "Ahhh," he moaned. "Beautiful, isn't it? Now, where's that booklet that tells how it works?"

Minutes ticked by. The sheriff finally put down the booklet and began pressing buttons. "One male Caucasian, age approximately twenty, height approximately six feet, hair blond, eyes . . . What color are your eyes?" he called out.

"Purple," Jeffrey said with annoyance.

"Collie, what color are his eyes?" the sheriff demanded, too intrigued with the machine to bother with Jeffrey's remark.

The deputy looked Jeffrey squarely in the face. "Kinda blue," he called back.

"Fine, bring him here. Son, you can lie all you want," the man said to Jeffrey, "but the truth is in your fingertips." He pressed Jeffrey's ten fingers against a glass panel on the console. Jeffrey felt a slight vibration as sensors read his fingerprints. The process was repeated for Li Soong. The sheriff stood back and waited.

"Here she comes!" he called as the machine kicked to life. "Wha . . . ?" he said, his face falling as the words *no data avail* printed across the screen for both suspects. "Nothing," the sheriff said with disappointment.

"Nothing!" Li Soong gasped. "How can that be possible?"

"There is no record of either of you in local, state or federal crime archives." The sheriff brooded. "Damn."

"What do we do with them?" the deputy asked, his laughter replaced by a restless boredom.

"Lock 'em up. The trucker too." The sheriff read-justed himself behind the desk.

*

"What's wrong with him?" Jeffrey asked as the deputy maneuvered him towards a cell. "Is he nuts?"

"Y'all are getting on my nerves," the man said, pushing Jeffrey and Li Soong into separate cells. The trucker was pushed in behind Jeffrey.

As his eyes grew accustomed to the dark of the windowless cell, Jeffrey saw the faces of two men who shared the small space with him and the trucker. He made eye contact with the older black man, about thirty, with a close-cut beard and gold-rimmed glasses. He sat fully clothed on a seatless toilet. He finally addressed Jeffrey: "What you in here for, man?"

"Nothing," Jeffrey replied with panic in his voice, his arms flapping at his side.

"That's funny," the man said from his seat. "Me too." He pointed to the younger man, who sat cross-legged on a cot. "This here's my little brother, Jesse. He didn't do nothin', either. My name's Clarence."

Jeffrey looked at the brother's sullen face and corn-rowed hair. "What do they think you did?" he asked.

"Murder." Clarence spoke with a smile that revealed a gold eyetooth.

"There ain't a man in prison that ever did what they say he did," Jesse said with a shrug.

"But I really didn't do anything," Jeffrey said, falling back against the filthy wall, frightened and nauseous.

"Name's Clyde Anderson," the trucker nodded to the two men. "You can call me the Devil's Son-in-Law. I'm a truckdriver."

The men nodded at him, but they kept their eyes on Jeffrey. "He all right?" Clarence asked. "Looks like he's going to be sick."

"You okay?" the trucker asked him. Jeffrey shook his

head weakly, trying to suck some of the stale air into his lungs to steady himself.

"What's his name?" Clarence asked.

"I told them who I was. I'm Jeffrey Hodge!" He yelled so loud his voice cracked. "I'm the son of the Secretary of State in Washington, D.C."

The two black men looked at each other. Jesse shook his head sadly, then looked at the trucker. "Crazy, huh?"

"Yup," the Devil's Son-in-Law agreed. "Him and the girl too. Both nuts."

*

At 9 A.M. David Bromley excused himself from the Oval Office and entered the semiconcealed door to the left of his desk. There, between the Presidential Study and the Oval Office, was the six-by-nine isolation cubicle called the Telephone Booth. He sat with his head in his hands, trying to clear his mind to form a new and logical agenda that could avert the international crisis that Li Soong's disappearance was rapidly becoming.

A knock on the door jarred the President from his meditation. "Yes?" He snapped open the latch to find Raymond Hodge standing grim-faced outside.

"Something's up, David. They've come to a decision. They want to see you now."

The President reemerged into the sour air of the Oval Office. Standing next to the Premier's chair was an unfamiliar courier. He had been summoned by the Chinese from their waiting jet, and his presence was quickly understood by the American Chief Executive. Cuffed to his wrist was the leather case that contained the transmitter that could signal Peking to launch a military offensive. His presence was, of course, only symbolic, but it was nonetheless a rattle of the Chinese saber that chilled the President.

"Mr. David Bromley," Chu began, clearing the hoarseness from his throat. "It is time to be serious."

"I believe that we have been serious from the beginning, sir," the President countered.

The Premier shot up his hand in a halt sign. "Let me speak, please," he said. The President compressed his lips and let the man continue. "I am aware of all the methods you employ in the search for my daughter. I am also aware of the intense danger she is in."

"Of course. I wouldn't begin to deny that," the President interjected.

"Good," Chu nodded. "Then you will understand what I will say next. My assistant, Mr. Cheng Wu, has convinced me of the necessity of my return to our homeland, despite Li Soong's absence. I have been gone too long already."

"Of course," Bromley said, secretly sighing with relief.

"But"—Chu punctuated his interjection by slamming the desk with an open palm—"but I have one request before we leave."

"I'm listening," the President said.

"Perhaps *request* is the wrong word," Chu said, looking at the man with the valise. "It is a demand. The Society of the Four Winds will stay behind. They will be given free reign to find my daughter."

"It's not necessary," Bromley said. "We have more than enough manpower—"

"May I see you a minute," Ray Hodge interrupted. He practically dragged the President from his chair to a corner, where he was joined by Robin Bettinger. "Tell him what you told me," Hodge said to the secret service agent.

"Sir," Bettinger said, "you can't let these four loose. They're trained, well . . . differently than our men. They employ methods that we would never consider."

"I don't understand. What are you saying?" the President asked.

"They're not just bodyguards, sir. They have been trained to get to their target by going through a wall, not around it. They won't stop at anything to retrieve the girl. Am I making myself clear?"

"I think so," the President said.

"What they are," Raymond Hodge clarified, "is a predatory band of cutthroats. Let them loose and they'll carve a path of destruction across this country like the plague."

"Thank you," the President said. "But he's got my back to the wall." He walked back to his seat across from the Premier. "I'm sorry," he said, "but it is impossible."

Chu continued, ignoring the statement. "They will be given full diplomatic immunity. They will be given access to your internal security codes and lines of communication. You will furnish them with whatever equipment they need—"

The President cut him off. "No way," he said abruptly. He would not be intimidated by Chu's implied threat of nuclear war. It was too drastic a step to take seriously. He would call the Premier's bluff.

" 'No way.' " The Premier considered the words with a strange expression. "I believe, Mr. Bromley, that there are at present many hundreds of American technicians, teachers, cultural leaders and politicians, with their families, visiting China. All expect to return home safely, as did my daughter when we arrived here six days ago."

"And they *will,*" the President asserted as he felt the pulse in his neck beat faster with the threat.

"We hope that will be the case. However, until my daughter is returned safely to me, you can ensure the Americans' safe passage only if you agree to our request."

"Demand," Bromley corrected.

Chu nodded, and sat implacably across from him.

The President turned to meet Ray Hodge's face, white

as parchment. He searched the Secretary of State's expression for a sign of an alternative to submission to the Chinese blackmail. Seeing none, he returned his gaze to the Premier.

"You have agreed?"

The President grimly nodded his head.

At 10 A.M. the four Chinese agents were unleashed.

*

That night Jeffrey lay on his back in the jail cell, listening to the snores of the two black men. In exchange for a wallet full of money, the Devil's Son-in-Law had been released at dusk. Moonlight reflecting from the hall illuminated palmetto bugs scampering up the cinderblock wall. From the other side of the concrete, Jeffrey heard a soft song. He strained his ears and crept closer to the barred door. From the next cell he could hear Li Soong's reedy soprano singing the words to a Chinese song.

"Li Soong?" Jeffrey whispered through the bars. "Is that you?"

The voice stopped its singing. "Jeffrey?" the girl called back. "Can you hear me?"

"Yes," he said, straining to keep his voice low. "Are you all right?"

"Of course," Li Soong said stubbornly, although Jeffrey thought he detected a slight quaver in her voice.

"What were you singing?"

"It is a resistance song. To keep up the spirits in the face of adversity."

"Are you frightened?"

"Are you?" the voice echoed back.

Jeffrey hesitated to answer. He was scared to death, but he didn't want Li Soong to know.

"Are you?" she persisted from behind the wall.

"No," Jeffrey lied. "But we better figure a way out of here before it's too late."

"Too late for what?" Li Soong whispered.

"Didn't you see that sheriff? He's crazy. He's like a little dictator marching around out there in those shiny boots and hat. He could keep us here until we rot. I can't believe he didn't know who we are."

"And you shouldn't have told him," Li Soong said, annoying Jeffrey.

"Li Soong, I don't think you understand what kind of trouble we're in. It's not just a matter of being caught or having to go back. He thinks we're criminals, and nobody is going to find us in this Godforsaken place to let him know otherwise."

"Good. I do not want to go back. This way we can observe the brutal conditions inside an American jail."

"Oh, God," Jeffrey groaned, feeling a wave of panic wash over him. "Please don't say that. Li Soong, we *have* to convince them who we are. We have to get out of here."

"You *are* frightened, aren't you?" she asked.

"Shhh," Jeffrey growled. "Keep your voice down. Yeah, I'm frightened; and you're nuts if you aren't. Believe me, Li Soong, this is dangerous as hell."

There was no answer from the other side of the wall. Jeffrey heard a frail voice singing the lyrics to the song again.

"Hey, Li Soong, answer me. Are you there?"

There was a long silence. Finally, she answered: "You scare me, Jeffrey."

"I didn't mean to. But you have to realize that this place isn't some kind of study lab for you to see the workings of prison life. They can do anything they want to us here."

"What will they do?" she asked in a tiny voice. "I thought all Americans who travel must spend some time in jail. You yourself said that you have been in many."

Jeffrey cursed his prevarications. He knew if his nose had grown with every lie he told Li Soong, it would by now be touching the opposite wall of the cell. "Well, it wasn't exactly the same. I had money with me and an identity they believed. Anyway, it was only for an hour or two."

"And other travelers don't routinely stay in jails?"

"No," Jeffrey said weakly. "They stay in motels."

"I don't feel so well," Li Soong said, slumping against the bars.

"Please, Li Soong, hold on. I'll get us out, I promise," Jeffrey said, painfully aware of his powerlessness.

"How?" Li Soong asked. "I wish my father were here."

"No, you don't," Jeffrey said, feeling his own steam. "You don't need him! I'll think of something by the time the sun comes up."

"Do you mean escape?"

"Yes, if there's no other way."

"Escape," she said with some wonder in her voice. "Have you ever done that before?"

"Yes, yes," Jeffrey said desperately.

"Then, escaping is how we shall leave," she said, regaining her equilibrium. "What is your plan?"

Jeffrey looked at the thick walls and bars that offered no answer. "Shh, don't say anything more," he said, as Clarence turned restlessly on his cot.

"My lips are tight. Let us sleep and refresh ourselves in preparation for the escape. Did you eat dinner? We must keep up our strength."

"Sort of. Did you?"

"No, I couldn't. What was that awful brown paste on the bread?"

"Peanut butter."

"No matter," Li Soong said. "We will be away from here in time for lunch tomorrow. Right?"

"Right," Jeffrey said, with little faith in his own words.

"Now I will sing you to sleep," Li Soong whispered. "Listen to the words of my song. It is very inspirational."

Jeffrey lay on the floor as Li Soong falteringly sang the words of the song in English.

"My father is as steadfast as the pine.
Here I raise the red lantern and let it shine.
Now my aims are high and my way is clear.
Our children take on the cause of our martyrs. "

Her braveness saddened him, and he hated himself for bringing her to this place because of his fantasies. He shifted on the floor, then found himself back at the bars of the cell.

"Li Soong," he called. "I have to tell you something."

"What is it?" she asked. "Why aren't you asleep?"

"Listen to me. I want you to know something about me that I never told anyone else."

"Yes," she said.

Jeffrey took a breath and screwed his eyes tightly shut. "We might be in more trouble than I can get us out of," he began.

"No," Li Soong said staunchly. "We will escape."

"You see, Li Soong, I sometimes exaggerate. What I mean is, I haven't always done all the things I may have said . . ." He waited in the long silence.

"It doesn't matter, Jeffrey," she finally spoke. "No sweat," she said, her voice quivering.

"Thanks, Li Soong. I mean it," he said softly. "You're really a good kid."

Neither of them spoke, and then Jeffrey heard Li Soong walk back to her little cot and lie down.

*

It was near dawn when the Devil's Son-in-Law pushed past the torn screen door of the Red Ace Truck Stop. He walked stiffly to the counter and straddled a leather stool. "Coffee," he said to the waitress, peeling the cowboy hat from his head and raking his fingers through the Vitalized hair.

"Buddy, you look like your truck hauled *you* all the way here," the Devil's countermate said as he swiveled towards the trucker.

"I just got outta jail over in Thicketty last night," he said. The café grew quiet as a dozen men tuned themselves in to the conversation.

"Don't say?" the other trucker spoke. "You're a gearjammer, ain't ya?"

"I sure am, but I'm a sorry excuse for one tonight, 'cause I got my truck but the sheriff over in Thicketty's got my money and my cargo."

"Shame to hear that, buddy," another man at the counter said. "But you ain't alone. That ol' boy has been cracking down like a pistol on any trucker what tries to skirt that scale out on the interstate. He must be richer'n Fort Knox by now with all the hot goods he's helped himself to."

"Have some coffee. It'll put some juice back in you," the waitress said, depositing a steaming cup in front of the Devil's Son-in-Law.

"Your java's Western style, I see." The trucker grimaced after a sip. "Been on the range all day."

The others at the counter laughed, but the counterman spoke up. "There's a lot of funny things goin' on around this town, y'know. Some kinda Chinese or something were snooping around just a little while back, asking all kinds of questions. They say they heard something on the CB radio about some beaver they know."

The Devil's Son-in-Law thought about the ridiculous story the boy and girl had told the Thicketty sheriff.

"Mean-looking bastards, too," the counterman continued. "Wouldn't say exactly what it was they wanted."

"Peculiar," the trucker said, shrugging his shoulders. "Oh, well, they're probably scouting out some land to build a laundrymat."

"You bet." the waitress winked.

"Hey, where's the crapper? This coffee's got me already."

"Outside, to your left," the waitress said.

The Devil's Son-in-Law trotted quickly out to a flimsy outhouse with the word *he* spray-painted on its door. He adjusted himself on the wooden seat and picked up a newspaper that had been abandoned in the corner. He spread the front page on his lap and confronted a foot-tall picture of Jeffrey and Li Soong. "*KIDNAPPED?*" exclaimed the headline.

As the shock of recognition jarred him, the trucker suddenly saw daylight from the corners of the outhouse that seconds before had been firmly planted on the green grass. He grabbed the paper to cover his nakedness as the walls of the wooden shack lifted straight up, revealing to him four sets of black trouser legs, one at each corner of where the outhouse used to be.

"What the . . . ?" He gasped as the wind whistled in around him and the four walls of the outhouse tumbled back towards the truck stop. Glaring down at him were the malevolent faces of the Society of the Four Winds.

*

"On your feet," the deputy sheriff called into the cell, encouraging the prisoners to their feet with the end of his wooden stick. "Outside," he commanded, and they walked single file towards the sheriff's office.

As Jeffrey shook himself out of a dreamless sleep, they passed the cell in which Li Soong had been held. It was empty. "Where's the girl who was in there?" Jeffrey demanded in a panic.

"Shut yer mouth, boy," the deputy called, underlining

his words with a painful rap across Jeffrey's shoulder blades.

Clarence, the older black man, kicked him in the ankle. "Don' make no trouble for us, crazy boy."

They marched past the sheriff's desk into the bright morning, where the deputy announced "Work detail!" and ushered them towards a waiting patrol car.

Li Soong sat in the back seat. Jeffrey squeezed her hand as he was pushed in beside her. "I thought you had run away by yourself . . . or worse," he whispered.

"What sort of friend would do that?" she asked indignantly.

"Damn," Clarence said as he pushed in next to Jeffrey.

"What's the matter?" Jeffrey asked.

"Sheriff and his wife expect us to clean his house all day again."

Jeffrey looked relieved. "That doesn't sound so bad. It's better than sitting in that cell."

"You ain't met the sheriff's wife. You think he's nuts, just wait till you get a load of her," Jesse explained.

"Shut up back there," the deputy called as he tapped the wire cage between the seats with his club.

The Carolina air had grown heavy by the time the car pulled up the driveway of a swaybacked white house surrounded by a picket fence. The sheriff stood on the porch. He stepped forward to supervise the transfer of the prisoners. In contrast to the scraggly lawn, where a few ragged chickens pecked for grain, the sheriff appeared even more meticulously tailored. His uniform shirt seemed so starched that a sudden movement could break it. The bottoms of the man's patent-leather boots were encased in plastic bags to keep dirt from their soles.

The sheriff's wife appeared in the door, circus fat and wearing a housecoat that made her look like a soft monument. She surveyed the prisoners. "I see you got me a girl this time." She addressed her husband as she picked at the cuffs of her rubber house gloves. "She can work in the kitchen unless she's too dirty."

"I am not dirty," Li Soong said haughtily.

"I'll be the judge of that," the woman said, approaching with the gait of a balloon in the Macy's Thanksgiving parade. "Hands!" she barked, grabbing Li Soong's arms roughly by the wrists. She inspected the girl's nails as Jesse rolled his eyes. "Aha," the woman said. "I knew it! Bacteria all over." She moved towards Jeffrey. "At least you're white. You can come inside the house. The rest of you work outdoors."

"I'm as dirty as they are," Jeffrey complained. "Let me work outside too."

"You do as I say," the woman said, catching him with a surprise kick to his behind that knocked him to the ground. The sheriff and deputy laughed as he struggled to his feet.

"I'll be going back to the station now that everything's under control," the deputy said, heading back to the car.

"I'll bring 'em back around dinner time," the sheriff called.

"You stay out here and watch the girl and the niggers," the wife barked. "Let 'em clean the porch good with soap and ammonia. I'll take the blondie one inside with me."

Jeffrey watched the woman waddle into the kitchen ahead of him. He could hear her thighs rub together as she walked. She turned to face him. "Don't take another step," she commanded. "Here, put these on." She handed Jeffrey a pair of plastic bags like the ones she and her husband wore on their feet.

"No," Jeffrey said. "That's crazy."

The woman stepped menacingly towards him. He reached down and slipped the bags over his shoes. Alone in the kitchen with the monumental woman, Jeffrey was handed a fresh sponge and a pail of water.

"You're going to do all the counters and the wood-
work while I cleanse your soul," she said as her voice
rose with inspiration.

"What?" Jeffrey asked, hoping he hadn't heard right.

"Cleanliness is *not* next to godliness. It *is* godliness,"
she proclaimed in a voice eerily similar to her husband's.
"Neatness. Order. Immaculate sanitation. They are the
true commandments."

"What are you talking about?"

"While you sponge, I am going to save your soul. I was
born again when I was mopping the floor. Him too"—
she pointed out towards the porch—"and I know a thor-
ough cleansing can be yours if you do like I say. Dip into
your pail, boy, dip in and find Jesus."

Jeffrey filled the sponge with water from the sink and
started to run it across the window sill, his eyes searching outside for Li Soong.

"You're dripping, you're dripping!" the woman cried,
"Look, a spot!"

"I'm sorry," Jeffrey said, blotting up his error.

"Dip your sponge, boy," the woman's voice mounted.
"In with the fresh water, out with the filth. In with Jesus,
out with Satan."

"Let my girlfriend come in here, please," Jeffrey
asked. "She needs her soul saved too."

"Only whites can ever get clean enough to enter
heaven. All the rest's filth," the woman said.

Jeffrey searched for a way out of the situation. His
mind spun as the woman came closer. "I want to tell you
something I tried to tell your husband," he tried, suddenly spotting a radio perched on a bric-a-brac shelf in
the kitchen.

"Don't be telling tales behind my husband's back," she
warned. "Clean that sill and stop wasting the Lord's
time."

"On the radio, did you hear stories about a girl named

Li Soong and a boy named Jeffrey Hodge? About the Chinese Premier's trip to America?"

"I only listen to gospel. All the rest is the devil's tunes," the woman said angrily. "Will you mop, or do I have to beat Beelzebub out of you?"

"Listen to me," Jeffrey said desperately, inadvertently squeezing dirty water from the sponge onto the floor. "We're them! We don't belong in jail. We're not evil. You have to let me use your phone to call Washington—"

"My floor!!" the woman screeched, ignoring Jeffrey. "My floor! Filth! Dirt! Bacteria! You're dripping, you're dripping!" She grabbed a mop handle that leaned against the sink and raised it up like an avenging angel, smashing Jeffrey across the shoulders. He fell against the kitchen cabinets, and she hit him again. "Dirt worshiper!" she yelled. "Satan's janitor!"

Jeffrey reached out to fend off her blows, and he made contact with the cool rubbery feel of her flesh. He pushed, and to his surprise she seemed to slip as if on ice. Her plastic-bagged foot lost contact on the puddle of soapy water, and like the Titanic, she slid down with a slow, mighty plop, the broomstick flying from her hands.

Jeffrey stood over her and saw the word *help* form like a gassy bubble in her throat, gaining momentum until it burst forth from her lips. "Help!" she screamed louder, and Jeffrey leaped over her, running for the door to the porch.

"Run!" he yelled to Li Soong as he emerged from the house.

The sheriff reached for the silver revolver in his belt, and as he drew it to chest level Clarence heaved a bucket full of ammonia in his face. "Yiii!" the sheriff screamed as the liquid stung his eyes and the gun skidded across the porch into Li Soong's waiting hands.

"Come on, crazy boy!" Clarence shouted, tugging Jeffrey by his sleeve. "Let's move our butts outta here fast. You too, girl. Gimme that gun."

"Where are we going?" Jeffrey panted as the four of them lit off, away from the incapacitated sheriff and his wife.

"Home, brother," Clarence called out, leading the way into the woods behind the house.

"Home?" Li Soong wondered, her feet feeling Mercury-light.

"Where the law ain't never gonna find us." Jesse whooped with joy.

Seven

THEY RAN until each step was a hammer blow to the bones in their feet. They pounded along a path through mossy woods that grew ever darker. Kudo vines reached out and brushed tentacles over their shoulders. Spanish moss caught in their hair like cotton wool. They lost the ability to speak as their lungs screamed for more oxygen.

The morning sun had peaked and angled into afternoon by the time the four ragged escapees drew into a clearing in the trees. Clarence extended a finger towards a small cabin and managed to croak the word "home" as they trotted with their last breaths towards the little house.

A tiny infant girl sat playing on the porch, naked except for a diaper made from a towel. As she saw the two men approaching ahead of Jeffrey and Li Soong, she bounced up and down, bubbles falling from her lips. Clarence stood over her on the porch. His chest heaved. He picked up the little brown form and pressed her face to his. "My baby," he said, turning to Jeffrey and Li Soong.

"Let's go in," Jesse said, and with the baby pressed securely against his damp chest, Clarence led them into the darkened shack.

Jeffrey had never seen anything like this place. The
walls were covered with old newspapers, the print yellowed, rotogravures faded to a monotone sepia. Two
swaybacked beds with ancient quilts lined the walls. A
three-legged stool, an ice box and a worn kitchen table
comprised the rest of the furniture. Instead of closets, a
clothesline ran across one corner of the room, displaying
the occupants' wardrobe like the limp flags of impover-
ished lands. Jeffrey knew not everyone lived as he did,
but even his poorest friends had a TV and more than a
single room. He knew that the shock of their poverty was
showing on his face, so he cleared his throat to end the
discomfort of the moment.

But his hosts were too happy to be concerned with his
perceptions. "Oh, Lord, how good it is to see this place
again," Clarence said.

"Man, you're saying something," his brother agreed.

"Where's Sally at?" Clarence looked around the single
room. "She wouldn't leave Baby alone if she went far."

"Is this a town?" Li Soong interrupted, looking out the
front door to the circle of woods that ringed the house.
"Where are we?"

"You are nowhere," Clarence said. "This place ain't
got a name. It's just a handful of shacks in the middle of
a lot of bugs and brush."

"There's Sally," Jesse said as a young woman appeared
in the clearing. "Must've been over to Terrible Slug's to
borrow something or other."

The woman wore a faded cotton dress, her head
tightly wrapped with a scarf. She was intensely dark,
and in the blazing sun highlights shimmered off her
shinbones as she walked closer.

Clarence moved to the door and the woman saw him.
She hesitated, then broke into a run, skimming across the
sharp stalks of grass until she flung herself into his out-

stretched arms. They clutched at one another, locked together as their tears mixed.

"That's Sally, my sister-in-law," Jesse said in a low voice. "She didn't think she'd ever see him again. She's all shook up."

Li Soong felt like an intruder on this private moment. She turned to Jesse. "Could you show us where your water is? I would like to clean off the dirt from the road."

Jesse drew his eyes away from the reunion and pointed to a pump far behind the cabin.

"Thank you," Li Soong said, pulling Jeffrey's sleeve. "Let's wash. They must want to be alone."

They walked past the cabin to a patch of sunlight around the pump, where Jeffrey summoned his strength and cranked the handle. A rush of clear water spilled over Li Soong's waiting hands. They rinsed their faces and their tired feet; then, cupping their hands, drank deeply until they were refreshed.

In the distance Li Soong heard the crying turn to laughter and the cooing of a happy baby, again in its father's arms. She turned to Jeffrey with a smile on her face, but he looked upset and uncomfortable. "What's wrong?" she asked him. "I would think you would be as elated as they to have escaped."

"It's not that," Jeffrey said. "It's this place. It's the most depressing thing I've ever seen."

Li Soong glanced at the cabin that listed with age, its sloping porch that threatened to collapse, its whitewash chipping and peeling under the sun. "I admit, it is certainly unlike Washington."

"Unlike Washington!" Jeffrey's eyebrows shot up. "How can people live like this?"

"I doubt if they do it by choice," Li Soong said. "But the men seemed quite happy to return here."

Jeffrey shook his head. "What will we do? We can't stay here."

"No?" Li Soong questioned. "Why not?"

"It's obvious, Li Soong. They don't have room. And we certainly can't expect them to feed us. I mean, they probably don't have enough food for themselves."

"Where can we go?" Li Soong asked, surveying the woods that surrounded them, remembering the mazelike trail that brought them here.

"I don't know, but we have to move on," he said uncomfortably.

As they pondered the situation, Clarence and Sally approached. The baby rode her father's shoulders, gurgling blissfully. "Y'all want to help with the garden?" Clarence asked. "We're gonna have a welcome-home party tonight. All the neighbors will be coming."

"Neighbors?" Jeffrey asked.

"Oh, yeah, they all live tucked away in the woods and clearings. Nice folks. You all will like them."

"That's really nice, but . . . my friend and I, we were just thinking it might be better if we wandered on. We're heading for Texas, and—"

"Wandered on?" Clarence cut him off. "Man, you've been running all day. Aren't you tired and hungry?"

"Sure, but—"

"But what? You may be crazy, but think of your girl here. What do you expect her to eat for supper out there in the woods? Leaves?"

Sally spoke up: "We got plenty of food. All the neighbors are bringing a dish, and we'll have a house party."

"But where could we sleep?" Jeffrey asked.

"We'll make do," Sally said. "You're sure a fussy one, ain't ya?"

Li Soong started to giggle, and the others joined in, leaving Jeffrey feeling foolish about his long face. The girl stepped forward, shading her eyes from the sun. "What shall we do in the garden?" she asked.

"I'll fetch the tools," Sally said.

"Fine. We will be glad to work for our supper, won't we, Jeffrey?"

"Whatever you say." He nodded, following behind the girl, who moved with a new determination towards the patch of cultivated land.

*

The sun felt warm against Li Soong's back as she worked the soil with the old hoe Sally had given her. She had secured her braids with a bandana, and she now hummed a tune as she tilled the earth.

Beside the girl, Jeffrey tried to strike a rhythm with the unfamiliar tool he had been given. He moved awkwardly, unlike the others. "Don't do that!" Sally yelled more than once as he accidentally dug up half-ripened vegetables and discarded them as weeds.

"You did a good job in the garden by yourself," Clarence said to his wife as he plucked pole beans from the vine and laid them in a white oak basket.

"Sonny Thomas came around and helped me while you was gone," she said.

"He did, hm? I hope the garden is all he helped you with."

Sally playfully threw a clod of dirt at her husband. "You ask him when he gets here tonight," she teased.

"I'll be too busy with you to mess with him," Clarence said. "Don't you forget how much I missed you while I been in that Thicketty jail."

Jeffrey was listening so intently to the conversation that he hit himself on the foot with his rake. "Ow!" he yelled as he danced on one leg.

"Crazy boy," Jesse said. "You find something else to do before you cut your foot off."

Jeffrey laid his rake against the stump of a tree and watched as the others worked. He was impressed by Li Soong's grace as she stooped to gather the vegetables and moved from row to row. He couldn't remember the last time he had run his hands through soil—probably never. To Jeffrey, flowers and fruits and vegetables were things that automatically appeared in vases and on plates. He stretched lazily in the bright daylight, hearing sounds he had never heard back home. Bees carved lazy arcs in the air overhead.

In the distance he spotted a patch of water, rounded by tall weeds. "Is that pond safe to swim in?" he asked.

"Safe?" Clarence shrugged his shoulders. "I guess it's safe. We ain't never met a shark there yet."

"If you don't have anything else you'd like me to do, maybe I'll take a dip."

"Sure, go ahead," Jesse said. "But if you meet up with anything dangerous, like a frog, you holler and I'll come and rescue you."

"Thanks," Jeffrey said happily, and walked towards the pond.

Sally leaned against her hoe. "He sure is a funny one. Full of the damndest notions."

Li Soong smiled in emphatic agreement. "He is from a different background than we are. He is a member of the moneyed aristocracy."

"Say what?" Clarence asked.

"The rich," Li Soong clarified.

"No kidding," Jesse said, rather impressed. "What was he doin' in the Thicketty jail, then?"

"He tried to run away from his wealth. He wanted to meet real people, like yourself," Li Soong explained.

"Shit," Jesse said, tossing a big rock to the side of the garden. "If I had money, I sure wouldn't wind up in a place like Thicketty. I'd be sittin' in a big easy chair all day, drinking bonded bourbon and watching TV."

Li Soong looked horrified. "But that's awful! How could you trade your productive lives for such meaningless diversion?"

"It would be fun to be rich." Sally grinned. "Ain't nothing noble about being poor."

"But the rich lead lives of futile aquisition," Li Soong said, drawing herself up to her full height. "Having property and the lust to acquire more is a disease poisonous to the individual and to society."

"I don't know what you're saying"—Jesse looked at Li Soong—"but, girl, you must be rich yourself to talk nonsense like that."

"I am *not* rich," Li Soong said, her cheeks coloring.

"You got a big house where you live?" Jesse asked.

Li Soong thought of her father's home, in Peking's Forbidden City, with its many rooms and comfortable furnishings. "It isn't small," she conceded.

"You got a car?" Clarence asked.

She thought of the black limousine that always waited to transport her through the bicycle-filled streets of the city. "It's not really ours . . . but there is one—"

"You got food on the table, you never have to worry about your next meal?" Sally asked.

Li Soong nodded uncomfortably.

"Then you're rich," the three chorused in unison.

Li Soong flushed with embarrassment. She had prided herself on her immediate rapport with these poor people, but none of her teachers had prepared her for their obstinate clinging to the values of the society that she thought oppressed them. She searched for a way to clarify her beliefs, but before the words came they had returned to their chores, and she stood in the center of the vegetable garden, feeling like a foolish scarecrow.

Sally looked up at her. The whites of the woman's eyes shone intensely against her ebony cheeks. "If you're tired, why don't you go on and take a swim in the pond?" she suggested.

"Oh, no, I couldn't do that," Li Soong said. "I must share in the work if I want to eat your food."

"You don't have to be so serious all the time," Sally said, shaking her head. "We won't think poorly if you want to have some fun."

Li Soong looked across the field towards the patch of clear water.

"Go on." Sally pushed her. "Join your boyfriend."

Li Soong turned back to see the three people smiling at her. She reached out for Sally's hand. "Thank you," she said. "I think I would love to take a swim." She laid her hoe against a tree trunk, then ran playfully towards the pond, where Jeffrey floated on his back under the crayola-blue sky.

*

After their swim, Jeffrey and Li Soong collapsed along the mossy bank of the pond.

"Doesn't the sun feel good?" Jeffrey said, looking at Li Soong through a half-opened eyelid.

"Wonderful."

"I love swimming," Jeffrey said lazily.

"Yes, I know."

"You know?"

"Of course. I had to study all about you. I know you better than I do myself."

"I had to study all about you too. Did you know that it is on record in Washington, D.C., that you are allergic to wool and you are afraid of spiders?"

"What! I haven't been afraid of bugs since I was a child. How silly. Is it true that you had a pet dog named Elmer who died last year?"

"You learned *that* in my file?"

"Why did you leave your studies at the University?"

"Because I was sent there to learn to become my father, and that's one course that doesn't interest me."

"What do you mean?"

"Have you ever heard of Princeton?"

"The University you chose to attend?"

"That's just the point. I didn't choose. Do you know that the first thing my father did when I was born was to order a baby bib for me that said 'Property of Princeton University'?"

"And so you were owned by the University since birth? What is the penalty for running away?"

Jeffrey thought a moment, then began to laugh. "Don't take this personally, but the penalty was being your escort."

"What?"

"My father insists that I want to be in politics, like he is. And since I didn't want to learn it at school, he decided that your father's visit would be good on-the-job training. What my parents refuse to see is that I have no interest in that kind of life."

"With me, it is exactly the opposite. I am passionately interested in the politics of my country, but my father does not show any interest in my opinions."

"I guess if either one of us had been allowed to do what we wanted, we wouldn't be sitting here together now."

Li Soong thought about Jeffrey's remark. "If you had your way, what would you be doing?"

"I honestly don't know. But I do know that I won't find the answer back in Washington or at school. Those two months I spent on the road were the only time I ever felt like my own man."

"They did not say that in your résumé."

"I'll bet they left out a lot about you too. What do you do when you're not studying politics or English? You can't be serious all the time."

"I like to draw, and I started to learn the flute last year."

"Maybe someday I can hear you play . . ."

They lay on their backs, eyes closed, feeling a breeze sweep over the pond. In the distance they could hear Sally's baby.

"Do you like being an only child?" Jeffrey asked. "You know, I'm one too."

"I know. When I was young I wanted a brother or sister to play with in the evenings, but instead I had to share my games with one of my father's security men."

"I used to drive our maids crazy when I was a kid. Do you remember your mother?"

Li Soong shook her head. "Not very well."

Jeffrey turned to look at the girl.

"I think I remind my father of her. I have had to be more than just a daughter to him, and sometimes I know when he looks at me he thinks of her and our resemblance makes him uncomfortable."

Jeffrey inched closer to Li Soong so that they only had to whisper to hear each other. "You know, when you came I wasn't supposed to talk about anything personal with you."

"But isn't it better than trying to talk about the weather?"

"It sure is," Jeffrey said. "Now it seems like there is so much to say."

*

The departure of the Premier of China from the United States had been so markedly different than his arrival that no spokesman for either government had officially commented upon it. At Premier Chu's request, the President of the United States had not accompanied him to the air base. Neither the press nor the Division of Protocol had been notified. Even after the jet wrenched itself from the ground, none of the Premier's aides spoke to him; or if they did, it was in a tone suited more to a funeral than to the return of the head of state to his homeland. The crescents of flesh under Premier Chu's eyes were swollen from the tears he had shed in private as he prepared to leave America without his daughter.

As the plane neared Peking, Cheng Wu approached the Premier's seat. "Comrade, we thought you might like to see this."

"What is it?" the man asked, too exhausted to look for himself.

"Look," Cheng insisted. He held a video printout of the New York *Times,* just transmitted to the Chinese jet. A pointillistic rendering of Li Soong appeared over the solid black headlines *"Chu's Daughter Vanishes"*; *"Bromley Vows Nationwide Search"*; *"Premier Returns to Peking."* Smaller and less discernible on the computer page was a portrait of Jeffrey Hodge of the Division of Protocol, also reported missing.

"Good," the Premier said. "Have you any other word?"

"We have received one communication from the Society of the Four Winds. They have already interrogated a truckdriver from Texas who claims to have given her a ride. It seems that she was then detained in a jail, from which, it is believed, she has escaped—"

"'Escaped'?" The Premier looked stiffly at his adviser.

"Yes. The Four Winds believe that Li Soong left the American capital on her own volition. They feel there is little chance that kidnappers are involved."

"That is encouraging," the Premier said, motioning Cheng away, then turning to face the window, alone with the possibility that his daughter had run away from him.

*

Terrible Slug arrived at twilight. She held one infant under a massive upper arm, and two sons followed in tow, each holding a dish of food. Jeffrey and Li Soong watched from the porch steps as she bellowed commands at her boys, who darted around her like minnows about a whale. As the sun descended, people appeared from the tangled brush of the woodland, holding pots and platters, skillets weighted with pork chops and greens, "dirty rice" and giblets, spoon bread and spiced apples. It was better than Sunday food; it was celebration food.

Li Soong and Jeffrey helped Clarence make a table in front of the house out of two sawhorses and planks. The thick dishes felt like water-polished stones. "Looks good, don't it?" Sally said to Li Soong, who was staring at yams and biscuits and meat the color of cinnabar, crusty with a glaze of barbecue sauce. Li Soong had never seen food like this, and she savored a morsel of sweet-potato pie that Sally handed her.

The neighbors gathered at the table to heap their plates, then found places to eat in the open air. Jeffrey chose a spot on the porch stairs, and Li Soong sat at his feet. He watched as she greedily attacked her food. "You never ate like that at the White House," he mused, recalling her stiff demeanor across the fancy pink tablecloth.

"I had no appetite for that life," Li Soong said, biting into a corn dodger. "The fresh air, the work in the garden and our new friends have given me one."

Jeffrey noticed that Li Soong's pale and reserved countenance had become charged with healthy color, her cheeks lustrous from the Southern sun. Jeffrey himself felt revived. His muscles tingled from the long day's run to freedom and the swim in the mossy pond.

"Aren't you glad we stayed here?" Li Soong said, surveying the gathering.

"No kidding, this is great," he agreed, moving closer to the girl.

When the last biscuit had been eaten, an old man took up a three-string guitar and signaled to the guests that he would start to play.

"Who's that?" Jeffrey asked a man seated near him on the porch.

"That's Poppa Jazz. He plays good," another man said.

"Play me a song in a snuff-dippin' key!" Terrible Slug called out, hoisting a lantern near the musician.

Poppa Jazz began to sing:

"Just say I'm a million miles from nowhere
In a dark and dusty shack . . ."

"Tell the truth!" Jesse called out as the old man fixed him with his one good eye, the other shining in the lamp's illumination like a piece of milk glass.

"I got me a good little girl, oh, Lawd!
The law ain't never gonna take me back . . ."

Another man whipped out a harmonica and blew a long, wailing note in agreement. Others laid down a heavy base beat with their work shoes and hands.

A mason jar was passed around, further igniting the magic of the bluesy moment. Jeffrey took a swallow of the clear liquor and felt it hit the back of his head like a cherry bomb. "Be careful," he said breathlessly, handing the jar to Li Soong. She sniffed the contents, her eyes watered, then she gingerly sipped the shine, passing it on to the woman next to her. Jeffrey could smell the vapor on her breath as she smiled at him.

Owls hooted in the trees overhead as Poppa Jazz sang his songs of love and prison and death. Jeffrey put a sheltering arm around Li Soong as the sultry evening gave way to a cool country night.

A bonfire was lit in the clearing, and as Poppa Jazz continued to play, couples got up to dance by the light of the fire and the moon. "Hey, crazy boy, don't you dance?" Jesse called out to Jeffrey as he held a plump young woman in his arms.

"Sure I do," Jeffrey said, taking another long sip of the moonshine that had come his way. Li Soong sipped too;

then Jeffrey stood up on shaky legs and turned to her. "Miss Chu." He bowed deeply in his most formal proto-colic manner. "May I have the honor of this dance?"

"No," she whispered, to his surprise. "I don't know how to dance like that." She pointed to Jesse and the rest, who had started a fast bump-de-bump rhythm. "I only know how to dance in groups."

Undismayed, Jeffrey took Li Soong's hand and pulled her to her feet. "There's nothing to it. I'll teach you." He drank from the mason jar again, then drew Li Soong close to him. "Follow what I do," and he took an awkward step that caused Li Soong to trip over his feet. "That doesn't matter," Jeffrey said, bulldozing her unsteadyness. "Just do this . . . one-two-three, one-two-three." He guided Li Soong in a formal fox trot around the fire.

Her hesitant steps gradually synchronized with Jeffrey's lead, and she threw her head back in a rich laugh as he picked up the pace. They whirled together, oblivious to the funky beat and other dancers, spinning joyously, laughing and drinking as they danced their own invented steps. The night wind swept between them, cooling their bodies by the fire. Li Soong's braids unraveled and her long hair shone violet in the night.

*

They collapsed together, exhausted, on the grass, staring up as the constellations seemed to spin like sparklers. Jeffrey rotated his head on the bristly patch of ground, greedily sucking in the cool air, and rolled over to face Li Soong.

She laughed at the pieces of dead leaves that clung to his face and hair, and at the lopsided grin he wore.

"I'll teach you to laugh at me," he said, reaching out and tickling Li Soong. She shrieked and tried to free herself from his hands.

Sally's voice interrupted them: "Shhh. The baby's asleep."

Jeffrey struggled to his feet. He lurched as he tried to focus his eyes on the party that only moments ago had been in full swing. Or had it? He looked around. The guests had disappeared back into the woods. Poppa Jazz and his guitar were gone. The night had slid by easily as he danced with Li Soong in his arms. "What time is it?" Jeffrey asked.

"Late," Sally said. "Y'all should be getting to bed yourself."

"Bed? Can we sleep here?" he asked.

Sally looked askance at him. "Where else you gonna spend the night! Back there in the Thicketty jailhouse?"

"No, no." Jeffrey waved his hand, trying to keep his dizziness in check. "It would be lovely to stay here. We thank you for your cordial accommodations," he said, punctuating his studied politeness with a hiccup.

"Where can we sleep?" Li Soong was now on her feet.

"It's a nice-enough night. You can sleep out on the sofa," Sally said, pointing to a dilapidated couch on the porch.

"But of course," Jeffrey said, swooping down in a mock bow. "It is the custom for visiting dignitaries to make use of the porch sofa."

Sally looked at Li Soong and shrugged. "He's somethin' else, ain't he?"

Li Soong nodded in agreement. "We'll go to sleep now," she said, leading Jeffrey towards the porch.

They climbed the porch steps together. Sally stood framed in the doorway to the cabin. Inside, a light glowed, and Li Soong could hear the mixed sounds of men's snoring and the baby's gurgles. She saw a peaceful smile form on Sally's face as the woman gestured towards the sofa.

"Goodnight," Sally said. "You all sleep good."

"Thank you," Li Soong said, feeling a rush of tenderness for the woman. "And thank you for your generosity and friendship too."

Sally shyly waved a hand as if to dismiss the statement. "Ah, go to bed. You two have had too much home-brew. See you in the morning." And she disappeared into the cabin, shutting the door behind her.

"Goodnight," Jeffrey called after her.

They lay close on the couch, covered with a quilt and supported by mildewed pillows.

"Do you have enough room?" Jeffrey asked. His body ached from the long day's running and dancing, his head was light from the moonshine.

"I have room," she said sleepily. "Do you?"

"No, but I like it this way." The sleek curve of her body against his arm excited him. He felt her push away. They had touched before, danced, walked hand in hand, but lying here together on the unfamiliar porch seemed more intimate. Jeffrey sensed her discomfort. "What's the matter?" he asked.

"Nothing."

"You can tell me, please." He felt his breath as cool as an icicle.

"This evening," Li Soong began in a soft voice, "it was different than anything I have done before. I feel uncomfortable . . ."

Jeffrey looked at her sympathetically.

"I feel perhaps we have forgotten why we set out on this journey."

"I don't understand," Jeffrey said, snuggling closer.

"We swam, we danced, we drank and we feasted," she enumerated.

"It was great, wasn't it?" Jeffrey yawned. "I'm stuffed."

"No, no," Li Soong said. "What I mean is that we should have spent our time trying to delve into the minds of these oppressed people. Our Institute for Minority Relations would be appreciative of my insights."

"Oh, boy," Jeffrey threw an arm over his head. "You never quit. Can't you ever just enjoy yourself? After last night in jail and this morning, we deserve a party."

"Our time is too precious to waste," she said authoritatively.

"You'll do your work in the morning," Jeffrey said, trying to ease Li Soong away from the topic. The warmth of her body felt too pleasant to argue. He could feel her relax, and he returned his arm to its former spot, so that her cheek rested in the crook of his elbow. It felt good there. A rush of warmth spread through his limbs as he lay beside her. He wanted to be close, but he didn't know if she would let it happen. "I still feel like I don't know anything about you," he said.

"Of course you do." She lay back with her eyes closed, limp as a kitten. "I thought you said you spent six months studying all about my likes and dislikes."

"Sure, I know you like opera better than soccer, but that's not what I mean."

"That is more than most people know about me," Li Soong said, enjoying her mystery.

"I don't even know if you like movies, if you have a boyfriend, if you can drive a car—"

"Why must you know all that?" Li Soong opened her eyes halfway.

"There is a law in America forbidding cohabitation on a sofa by two people who have not been properly introduced," he teased.

"Cohabitation!" Li Soong said, suddenly drawing herself away from him. "We certainly could not be accused of that!"

Jeffrey cursed himself for shattering the mellow mood. "I was just kidding," he said. "You sure get uptight about sex."

"I do not," Li Soong said defensively, pulling back into the folds of the sofa. "We are not like Americans, however. In China we are not promiscuous."

"Who said anything about being promiscuous?" he blurted out as he felt her withdraw. "You know, you're not exactly my type."

"And you are certainly not mine!" Li Soong said huffily. "You are the last person I could imagine marrying."

"Marrying!" Jeffrey said, his voice rising.

"Shhh! You'll wake them," Li Soong motioned to the house.

"Marrying," Jeffrey whispered. "Who said anything about that? You know, Li Soong, sometimes you really act like a creep."

"What is a creep?" she demanded.

"A jerk, a nerd," he clarified. "Uncool. Get it?"

"A *huai tan,*" she translated. "You dare to call me that? You . . . you"—she searched for a word—"you deviant!"

Jeffrey started to laugh, which further angered Li Soong.

"You may think the rampant immorality of American youth is humorous," she lectured, "but it is only a final symptom of your country's moral collapse."

"Oh, knock it off. There's a big difference between what you're talking about and what I am," Jeffrey said. "Anyway, if there's eight hundred million Chinese, somebody's got to be doing something!"

At that Li Soong flipped over on the couch, turning her back to him. "Goodnight," she said curtly.

"Hey, come on," Jeffrey said, putting a hand on her shoulder. "Don't get so mad."

"You insulted my people," she said into the pillow.

"Okay, I apologize," Jeffrey shrugged. "To you and to the People's Republic of China. Do you all forgive me?"

"Perhaps." Li Soong softened slightly as she enjoyed

the warmth of Jeffrey's hand on her arm. She was troubled by this feeling, the way his every touch startled her as if it were an intimate gesture. She imagined her father seeing them lying together on the couch, and somehow the boldness of that thought thrilled her.

They lay quietly together for some time until Li Soong heard Jeffrey's breath fall in regular intervals. Perhaps he had fallen asleep. She rolled over to face him, but his eyes were open. Their faces were hardly inches apart, their breaths flowed into each other's mouths. Beads of moisture appeared on Jeffrey's brow like individual tears. He raised his hand and picked up a long strand of her hair and let it fall through his fingers. He moved his hand to her face, hesitantly touching her with the backs of his fingers.

Li Soong closed her eyes, letting the touch of flesh on flesh send a soft throb of sensation along her nerves. She felt like animals she had seen in pictures—their bellies rubbed until they lay in hypnotized stupor, pure touch driving out all their energies. Jeffrey's hand traveled across her cheek, his fingers moved across her bottom lip, and she responded with her mouth as the fingers moved.

He shifted, drawing close to her, and the movement jarred her out of her languid pleasures. She pulled backwards, rubbing her face with a childlike gesture, as if trying to erase the map he had left with his fingertips.

"No!" she said, shocked at the insistence of her own voice. She pushed back from him.

Jeffrey focused on Li Soong, who looked alone and bewildered by his actions. He wanted to touch her again, to reassure her, but he dared not. He perceived her as he had before—a stranger from the other side of the world. Their tentative intimacy he chalked up to the moonshine and the moonlight.

He shifted on the couch, trying to ignore her presence. "Do you want me to sleep on the floor?" he finally asked in a formal voice.

"Yes," Li Soong said.

Jeffrey eased himself onto the wooden porch and the quilt showered down on top of him. "That will keep you warm," she said, and he thought he detected a seed of concern in her voice.

"Goodnight," he answered gruffly as he pulled the old cover over himself and drifted off to sleep.

*

The managing editor of the Washington *Post* paced his office, staring at the night editor who had okayed Hazleton Brown's mysterious departure. He dragged on the nub of a cigarette and angrily crushed it into a pyramid of other butts that spilled over the sides of his ashtray. "Look at this!" He dug his hands into a mighty stack of newspapers, magazines and wire-service reports. "Look!" He pulled out a Chinese newspaper. "Even the *People's Daily* put out an extra on it. You know, there are about a billion people between here and Peking who are dying for the goods on this story. One third of the world wants to know. So a man—our man—Brown, *of the Post*" —his voice escalated—"walks into your office, tells you he's got a lead on the story, and you send him off without even a clue! For the love of God, Jimmy, you know better than to send our best man out on the biggest story since Lindbergh and Patty Hearst rolled into one without even a hint of where we can hook up with him!"

"He said he would quit on the spot—"

"Aw, shit," the managing editor said. "You should know that's the way Brown operates. He fleeced ya, Jimmy, and now he's gone to who knows where, and we're stuck with the same AP and UPI crap every other paper's running. If we knew what this 'big lead' was, we could have sent photographers, covered him on the trail, played it up right. For all we know, the man's on a beach in Bermuda taking a vacation."

"He wouldn't do that," the night editor said cautiously. "Would he?"

"Aw, you make me sick." His boss cursed, lighting up another smoke. He rubbed the palms of his hands over his face. "Okay, let's think clearly. How can we find him? How can we get a preview of what he's got? Think back. He must have told you something. I mean, you *did* give him a bundle of money and a car!"

"I know, I know." The man flushed. "But he didn't say anything, just that he had to get going right away, and then he left the office, singing like he was happy."

"I'm so glad he was cheered by your management policies," the managing editor said, throwing up his hands. "That's it, I give up. He's gone and we have to sit on our asses until he decides to call us."

"He told me he wouldn't let us down—"

"He told you . . ." The editor trailed off. "Go away, please, I've got a paper to run."

*

"Are you ready to go to Texas?" Li Soong stood over Jeffrey's sleeping form on the couch. He opened his eyes to see a shimmering sky. Li Soong had pulled the quilt off him and was folding it in her arms. "Get up," she said cheerfully. "Our hosts have made plans for our journey."

Jeffrey lifted himself from the wooden planks of the porch. His head ached and his eyes felt bleary. The floor's hardness had left its signature on his stiffened muscles. He squinted his eyes at Li Soong to see if he could detect any remnants of last night's fight. "You're not still mad, are you?" he asked.

"Ridiculous," Li Soong said in a chipper voice. "We have far too much to accomplish to bear grudges."

Jeffrey rubbed his eyes and raked his fingers through

his hair. "Good. Hey, do you suppose they have any coffee around here?"

"They're eating breakfast now." Li Soong pointed Jeffrey to the cabin's door. "They wanted me to wake you up."

"Hi," Jeffrey said as he entered the house. Clarence and Jesse and Sally had crowded around the little table and were eating hunks of last night's cornbread.

"Hungry?" Clarence asked.

"No, thanks." Jeffrey shook his head. "But I sure could use a cup of coffee."

The man poured a mugful and motioned Jeffrey towards a stool. "Your girlfriend said you wanted to be moving along," Clarence said.

Jeffrey nodded his head.

"While you was sleeping, Jesse made a few arrangements with Poppa Jazz to give you a ride out of these heavy woods. He's got a pickup truck, and he goes to town every week."

"That's great," Jeffrey said, waking up quickly. "Say, maybe I will have some of this cornbread if you don't mind."

"Help yourself," Sally said.

"Did you sleep okay out there on the porch?" Jesse asked.

"Oh, yeah, it was fine," Jeffrey said, hoping they wouldn't question why he had spent the night on the floor.

"Sleeping outdoors is good for you," Clarence declared. "When Mama was alive, Jesse here slept inside every night, and I stayed on that sofa outside. That's how come I grew up so strong and my brother's such a puny little sucker." He hissed out a long laugh, causing Jesse to punch him lightly on the shoulder.

Jeffrey looked at the muscularity of both men and was glad he was on their side; and suddenly he was struck by the strangeness of the situation. No one had mentioned the reality of the Thicketty jailhouse, or the crimes of which any of them had been accused. As if it were an unspoken agreement, neither the past nor the future was discussed. For within the magic ring of the Thicketty forest the present, *now,* was all that seemed to matter. And for this moment the Premier's daughter, the Secretary of State's son, two men who might be murderers and a lovely woman with a baby had become friends.

They drank chicory coffee and talked, and after an hour a rattling Chevrolet pickup truck pulled up to the cabin.

"Poppa Jazz," Sally said without looking to the outside.

The old man ascended the steps of the porch. His overalls were bleached white, and a battered straw hat perched atop his almost bald head.

Jeffrey recognized him. "You're the musician from last night."

"That's me." He smiled. "And you're the boy who danced like you was at the governor's ball."

"That's me." Jeffrey laughed.

The baby in Sally's arms started to cry, and she stood and bounced it easily on her hip. "Hush up," she said to her little one.

Jeffrey finally said it: "I guess we're ready to go."

"Did Clarence tell you how we're going to do this?" Poppa Jazz asked.

Jeffrey shook his head.

"Y'all are going to crouch down in the bed of the truck, and cover yourself with the straw that's back there and some old blankets I brought along with. We can't have no one from town see you sneaking out of here."

Clarence took the initiative to say goodbye. He walked towards Jeffrey and offered his hand. "Good luck, man."

"Thanks," Jeffrey said, drawing reassurance as he squeezed Clarence's arm.

Jesse and Sally came up and exchanged hugs of parting. Sally handed Li Soong a small brown bag. "This here's some groceries in case you get hungry . . . for later."

Li Soong smiled sadly and leaned over to kiss the baby on the tiny peppercorns of hair that dotted her head. "We will always remember you," she said tenderly.

"Goodbye," Jeffrey called out as he walked down the ancient cabin steps with Poppa Jazz. He glanced back one last time to set in his mind the image of these new friends he knew he would never see again. Then he and Li Soong stepped forward, ready for the unknown miles that lay ahead.

Eight

A PLAIN gray Plymouth streaked down Route 277 into
Carrizo Springs, Texas. From their base of operations in
nearby Eagle Pass, FBI agents Wright, Hoffman and
McKay were the first to move in on what looked like a
break in the case of Premier Chu's daughter. The manager of the Carrizo Springs Quick Mart had called in to
report that he was holding Jeffrey Hodge and Li Soong
in his locked storage room. He had caught them shoplifting an hour before.

The half-hour drive to the site of the capture was
one of ecstatic tension for the men. How lucky they
were that fate should bring the nation's biggest man-
hunt to a close on their turf. Hoffman yanked the
wheel, and the sedan's tires bent screaming as the car
slammed to a halt in front of the grocery store. They
bounded out of the car and heard a burglar alarm
ringing from within.

"Look. The lights are out," McKay said, slowing his
run to a cautious walk. "Something's up." They approached with guns drawn and saw customers pressing
themselves hysterically against the locked doors of the
grocery, trying to pry them open. They could hear
muffled cries for help.

"What the hell . . . ?" Wright said, looking at the panicked faces inside.

Someone wedged a crowbar into the door and forced it open. A dozen people exploded onto the sidewalk, falling into the dry afternoon air with deep breaths of relief.

McKay's foot slid out from under him as he skidded on a broken jar of applesauce. The three men looked around the store to see the shelves, the vegetable bins and the meat counters raked. Boxes, demolished fruits, canisters, family packs and shrink wraps were strewn across the floor like a cataclysmic cornucopia.

"Looks like a horde of Cossacks ran through here," Hoffman said, scanning the rubble for the manager who had placed the call. They spotted him, propped against a wall, sitting in a collapsed mountain of toilet tissue. A young woman dabbed at a cut across his forehead.

The agents slogged through the mire of edible goods towards him. "FBI," they said in unison. "Where's the two kids?"

The question didn't seem to register. "I think he's in shock," the young woman said. "I'm his daughter."

"Your father placed a call with us half an hour ago. He said he had nabbed the Premier of China's daughter and Jeff Hodge. You know anything about it?"

"Sure," she said, her eyes welling with tears. "That's what started World War Three in here."

"Hold on, let's not get hysterical," Hoffman said, whipping out a handkerchief and handing it to her. "Where are they?"

"It doesn't matter now," the girl said, blowing her nose. "It wasn't them, anyway."

"How do you know that?" McKay asked.

The girl stood up and faced the three men. "I'll tell you, but you probably won't believe it. I don't—and I saw it with my own eyes. About an hour ago we caught this Oriental girl and white guy shoplifting some groceries. My father had the picture that the police have been handing out on that runaway pair. Anyway, the guy was blond, and the girl—well, she looked like that Chinese one. So my father grabbed them and locked them in the storage locker. Then he called you guys."

"And?" McKay hurried her.

"About ten minutes later—I swear it couldn't have been more—these four Chinese men come in and demand to see them. Well, we were sure they weren't the FBI, and they were a pretty creepy-looking bunch, so my father tells them to get lost."

"And then what?" Hoffman asked.

The girl sighed deeply. "And then this." She swept her hand over the rubble. "My father was in the War, and he isn't what you'd call a big fan of Orientals. So he started to pull a GI Joe number with them, told them the FBI was coming, and said the only way they could see the couple was over his dead body."

The man on the floor moaned, and the three agents looked sharply at one another. "I take it they almost complied with his wishes," Hoffman said.

The girl nodded. "Then it turned into a free-for-all. There must have been eight or ten ranchers in here, all real tough guys, and probably a few oil riggers from the fields up north. But these four Orientals cut through them like a dose of salts. I've never seen—"

"And they took the two kids?" Hoffman interrupted.

"No. That's the funny part. Look over there." She pointed to where a metal door had been ripped off its hinges.

McKay picked his way through the debris towards the food locker. Inside huddled a terrified Oriental girl and her Caucasian boyfriend. "Don't hurt us," she pleaded as McKay's flashlight fell across their faces.

"It's not them," he called back.

Hoffman moved towards the front of the store, and as he squeezed ketchup out of his pant cuffs he motioned to the other agents to join him. "I see Bromley laid out the welcome mat for those Four Winds bastards."

"At least somebody ought to tell them to lay off the heavy muscle tactics," McKay said.

Hoffman shot a withering look at the agent. "Do you want that job?"

McKay surveyed the demolished store; then, without another word, the three men trudged out into the daylight and headed back to the FBI branch office at Eagle Pass.

*

A long boat of a Cadillac slowed to look over the hitchhikers outside of Burr Ferry, Louisiana. The old lady at the wheel poked her head towards the windshield as the car drew close to them. She had picked up dozens of hitchhikers over the years, but couldn't recall a stranger looking pair. The girl wore a denim cap pulled low on her head; a pair of purple-framed sunglasses obscured her eyes; and her clothes were so large they threatened to engulf her. The boy was even weirder. His hair was a blue black that nature never produced, and it was slicked down in a Rudolph Valentino fashion. A pair of mirrored sunglasses enabled him to look out but keep the outside world from looking in. Like the girl, his clothes were dusty and worn.

"Git in before I get tail-ended," the old woman commanded as Jeffrey and Li Soong dashed for the car. "You look like you've been standing in the sun all day," she said to Jeffrey. "Your black hair is leaking onto your forehead." He threw up a hand to mop his brow, embarrassed to discover that his disguise was melting away. "That's all right," the woman said as she peeled away. "I used to use that henna rinse when I was young. No shame in helping nature along."

"How far can you take us?" Li Soong asked as the woman headed west.

"Shhh," she said angrily. "Don't talk while the car is in motion. I got to concentrate."

"Sorry," Li Soong said quietly, looking at Jeffrey, who seemed especially buoyant.

"Do you realize we're almost in Texas," he whispered. "We can't be more than fifteen or twenty miles from the line."

Li Soong bounced in her seat and squeezed his hand. "And then we'll get to Balmorhea?"

"Nope. That's still a ways, maybe five hundred miles from here."

"But we will make it there easily," Li Soong said, cheered by the wonderful luck they had enjoyed with rides and good weather.

"Nothing can stop us," Jeffrey said, congratulating himself. He pointed a sly finger at the old lady who maneuvered the car with the ferocious concentration of a battleship captain. "She's something else," he said in a low voice. "Must be eighty-five."

"I ain't eighty-five," the woman snapped. "I'm eighty-eight and I told you to keep quiet when I'm driving."

They suppressed their amusement and rode, watching the swampy lushness of the South turn scruffy and sun-burned as they approached the Texas line.

Jeffrey was the first to spot the sign. Welcome to Texas it said in red and blue letters festooned with a single star. Overcome with excitement, Jeffrey issued forth with the ear-piercing rebel yell he had picked up from the Devil's Son-in-Law. Suddenly the great whale of a car was out of control, fishtailing wildly across the highway, the old woman clutching at the spinning wheel. Li Soong screamed as the Cadillac broke loose like a rodeo pony. Jeffrey reached across the seat, grabbed the wheel, and brought the car back to an even keel as passing vehicles blared their horns.

The old woman picked up her gnarled fist and pounded Jeffrey hard on his shoulder. "Idiot!" she screamed at him. "You're lucky we weren't killed. When I told you not to talk, I didn't mean it was all right for you to howl like a banshee! Get out!"

Li Soong and Jeffrey were promptly dumped on the Texas roadside, where, undismayed, they danced a celebratory jig in honor of reaching the Lone Star State.

Five rides later they arrived at the outskirts of Balmorhea. It was the agreed-upon final point, the place where they would turn back or surrender.

They had been gone only five days, and in that short time they had journeyed as if in a state of grace. Rides had come easily, and with the aid of their disguises they had traveled unnoticed. In the small brown bag Sally had handed them when they left the Thicketty cabin they found a twenty-dollar bill between a piece of cornbread and a plump tomato. When that ran out, Jeffrey had pawned his watch in Alabama, and the small fortune it brought made them feel lightheaded and carefree. They circumnavigated the newspapers and radio broadcasts that told of their escape, and neither had mentioned exactly what they might do when they reached the end of the line.

They climbed the plateau that overlooked the dusty stretch of Texas town. Sahuaro cacti grew randomly in place of trees, and a lonesome dog roamed the single unpaved street. "We're here," Jeffrey proclaimed. He had somehow expected a blare of trumpets to sound as he and Li Soong approached.

"No one would have believed we could come this far," Li Soong agreed, but she couldn't hide the hint of sadness in her voice. In her mind she had imagined herself treading the main street of Balmorhea with the victorious step of an astronaut on a distant planet. Bursting with the knowledge she had gained along the way, she would halt at the town square and declare her identity to the world. But Li Soong felt more depressed than victorious. The dozens of people she and Jeffrey had encountered during the last three days only confused her, and she felt even further from the answer she sought to the riddle of America. She wondered if a hero always felt so down at the end of the quest, ill prepared to return to the daily chores. She turned to Jeffrey, seeking an answer. "You know, it is now time for us to turn back," she said, testing him.

He crouched on his heels, looking towards the horizon. "I know," he said, picking up the pale yellow sand that covered the ground and sifting it through his fingers.

"What's out there?" Li Soong asked.

"New Mexico, Nevada, California, the ocean," Jeffrey recited. "I never thought we would get here quite so fast. I thought it would take us at least another week."

"That would have been nice," Li Soong said. "There is so much more I would like to have seen."

"Yeah, I know what you mean." Jeffrey avoided her gaze. "But this is the goal we set for ourselves, and I guess we better stick to it, not push our luck."

"You're right," Li Soong said. "I imagine both our parents must be terribly upset, not to mention all the inconvenience our disappearance has caused."

Jeffrey detected a slight amusement in her voice, and it annoyed him. He was feeling too glum for her gaiety. "You kind of like that, don't you," he chided. "I mean, causing a big stir."

"I do not!" she replied. "What makes you say such a foolish thing?"

"I saw you sneaking a look at that magazine this morning, the one with the picture of you on the cover."

"Liar," Li Soong said, rising to the provocation. "I did

no such thing. You are the one who enjoys that. My only interest in this trip was to learn of your country, not to become a celebrity like yourself."

"Oh, man," Jeffrey groaned. "Me? A celebrity? I'm here only because I couldn't stand all that fuss you made back in Washington, that's all."

"It doesn't matter now," Li Soong said, dismissing Jeffrey's words with her hands. "Now that we are going to turn ourselves in, we must be prepared for endless interviews and articles."

"Ugh." Jeffrey grimaced. "Now I see what the trucker meant about moving on. After a week of being normal, eating cheap burgers, wearing grungy clothes, who wants to go back to Washington? I'm going to miss traveling."

"Me too," Li Soong said sadly. "I'm sorry I was cross. I guess I don't look forward to what is in store for us. There is so much more to do . . . if only we had the time."

"Look, it's not over yet." Jeffrey tried to be cheerful. "At least we can stake ourselves to a big Mexican dinner and a few more hours of freedom before we place the call."

Li Soong brightened. "That's right. We don't have to do it right away."

"Hell, no." Jeffrey added, "Maybe we could even spend the night here and do it in the morning."

Li Soong spontaneously threw her arms around him, toppling him off his heels onto the sand. He caught her in his arms, and they lay together in an unexpectedly intimate embrace.

Li Soong struggled to her feet and dusted herself off. "Do you know how to speak Spanish?" she asked Jeffrey, breaking the spell of her accidental gesture.

"A few words," Jeffrey said, collecting his thoughts. He looked a long time at Li Soong. *"Señorita, tu es muy especial y bonita."*

"What does that mean?" she asked.

"It means you're a royal pain in the ass," Jeffrey said.

"Stop wasting time," Li Soong ordered. "Let's go to town."

With the possibility of another day together they ran hand in hand down the side of the low mesa towards the town of Balmorhea.

*

"The first thing we want to do," Jeffrey said, "is to see if that old cook I know still works here." They stood outside the town's one café, an adobe roadhouse sheltered by a peeling tin roof. Stepping out of the white blaze of the Texas sun, they entered and were blinded by the darkness. The place smelled of refried beans and chile, and Freddy Fender belted out *"El Rancho Grande"* from the jukebox.

"There's the kitchen," Jeffrey said as his eyes adjusted to the dim light. "You wait here, and I'll go see if my man is still around. Maybe we can get a couple of steaks."

Li Soong planted herself at a small table by the wall under an outsized Mexican hat and serape.

Jeffrey caught Sonny Moon mid-slice in the kitchen, standing with a cleaver poised high over a slab of barbecued brisket. "Hi," Jeffrey said on the downstroke, and he winced as the man severed the meat in two.

"Can I help you," he asked, with no apparent recognition.

"You don't remember me, do you? I hitchhiked through here about two years ago, and you let me spend the night at your ranch house."

"Nope. I sure don't recall." The man squinted at him. "What's the name?"

Quickly Jeffrey realized the foolishness of his push to relive old memories. The danger of his being recognized was more important than impressing Li Soong with his hardbitten Texas friends. "Uhhh," Jeffrey stammered, trying to grab a name. "Pate . . . Lucas Pate."

"Funny, I usually don't forget a man's name. I guess you caught me with my pants down." The man squinted at Jeffrey.

"That's okay," Jeffrey said, moving back towards the kitchen door, anxious to end the discussion. "It's nice to see you, anyway."

"Same here. But wait up . . . did you want something?"

"No. Just thought I'd drop in and say hello," Jeffrey said, treading backwards.

"You sick or something?" The man scrutinized him. "I ain't never seen anyone sweat black before."

Jeffrey ran a hand through his awful dye job. "I, uh, had a case of the flu, left me all messed up."

Sonny Moon scratched the whiskers on his face. "Damn, I never forget a mug. Now that I look at you, there is something that rings a bell . . . Tell ya what, you being sick and all, let me stake you to a meal. If you say we met, pal, I guess maybe we did."

"I'm not here alone," Jeffrey said. "I have a friend with me." Jeffrey looked back towards the dining room and saw Li Soong. A shadowy figure seemed to be approaching her. His pulse quickened.

"I'll make it two dinners, then. Just don't eat no steaks," the man said as Jeffrey disappeared through the door.

He rushed for Li Soong, and moving closer he slowed, trying to figure who the stranger was who was approaching her. The denim jacket didn't look like either FBI garb or the uniform of one of Chu's warriors. There was something in the posture and the smooth auburn hair that was familiar . . . Jeffrey intercepted the figure as it drew up to the table. He grabbed it by the shoulder and pushed it against the wall so he could look it in the face.

"Howdy, pahdna," Hazleton Brown said. "Welcome to Balmorhea."

Jeffrey's jaw fell slack. His first instinct was to grab Li Soong and run, but his old friend's hand held him in place. Hazleton eased himself into a chair and casually tapped the back of another. "Sit down, kid," he said. "Let me buy you a meal."

Jeffrey sat, too dumbstruck to speak.

The waitress appeared. *"Tres biftec, por favor,"* Hazleton ordered.

"No steak," Jeffrey croaked out as the waitress headed for the kitchen.

"That's all you have to say to me?" Hazleton grinned. " 'No steak' ?"

"No!" Jeffrey tried to figure the man's presence. "You can't order that, and you can't be here. We aren't ready to give ourselves up yet."

"Look, Hodge, if you can't afford the steaks, I'll put 'em on my tab. I've been here three days already, waiting for you."

"But how . . . how did you know we would come here?" Jeffrey stammered.

"Who is this person?" Li Soong interrupted. She looked at Jeffrey. "What do we do? Are we caught?"

"Well," Jeffrey said, turning to the reporter, "are we?"

"That all depends." Hazleton leaned back in his chair. "Let me introduce myself." He tipped a salute to Li Soong. "I believe we met at the White House. Hazleton Brown—have typewriter, will travel."

Li Soong sat poised like a cat on the edge of her chair. "What do you want from us?" she demanded.

"Who else knows we're here?" Jeffrey asked tersely.

"You know me, kid. I like exclusives. Nobody knows."

Jeffrey felt slightly relieved. He shared a quick private look with Li Soong. "Are you going to turn us in?"

"Hodge, you sound like Bonnie and Clyde," Hazleton

said, turning to Li Soong. "He always did have a flair for the dramatic."

She emulated her father's best stony glare at the reporter.

"Okay, okay, forget the jokes," Hazleton said. "All I want from you is to find out what the hell you've been up to for the last week. Nothing the whole world doesn't want to hear."

"It's none of your business," Jeffrey said.

Hazleton turned to Li Soong. "How about you? Do you agree it's none of my business, or this country's business, or for that matter your father's business? You know, from what I hear he's pretty upset about this."

He had touched a sensitive nerve, and Li Soong's face mirrored it. Jeffrey interrupted to divert the reporter. "How did you find us?"

"Hodge, you wouldn't stop singing the praises of this dump. 'Balmorhea—Pearl of the Pecos.' Personally, I don't know what you see in it."

"It was fine until you showed up," Jeffrey said grudgingly.

"By the way," Hazleton said, pointing to Jeffrey's hair, "is it true brunettes have more fun? I think you're supposed to end the color at your hairline."

"It's the hot weather," Jeffrey said, his eyes downcast. "It leaks."

The waitress deposited three massive T-bone steaks on their table.

"Dig in," Hazleton said as he lifted his knife and fork. "I ate my way through this menu already, and believe me, the chile is deadly. This is the best bet."

"I'm not hungry," Jeffrey said. "What would you do if we just got up and left?"

"Nothing," Hazleton lied. "I wouldn't let a good steak get cold."

Jeffrey heard Li Soong's stomach rumble. The haphazard meals they had snared on the road had left a big empty place just the right size for a steak to fill. "You wouldn't follow us?" Jeffrey said, relaxing slightly.

"I just thought you'd be happy to see an old pal, Hodge. If you gotta go, you gotta . . ."

Jeffrey and Li Soong looked at each other.

"Come on, eat," Hazleton cajoled them.

"Well, perhaps just a bite," Li Soong said as she sawed a small triangle off the end of hers.

"There ya go," Hazleton said. "She's no fool. It's not every day I offer to spring for the check."

Jeffrey lifted his knife and fork and began hesitantly to eat.

Hazleton let some time pass before he ventured to speak again. The tension had diminished as Jeffrey and Li Soong polished off the T-bones. "So what's new?" the reporter said in a mock casual voice.

Jeffrey looked up from his meal. "Not too much, and you?" he answered in an appropriate parody.

"Okay, let's be straight with each other. I'm your friend, Hodge—if I wasn't I never would have found you here. What I want to know is how you got yourselves here and where you're going."

"We're turning ourselves in," Jeffrey said, to Hazleton's surprise. "This is the end of the line."

Li Soong nodded in grave agreement.

"Well, then, where have you been?"

"You name it," Jeffrey said, unable to check the boastful tone of his voice.

The reporter pushed him: "Name one."

"In jail." The words slipped out of Jeffrey's lips. "Forget I said that," he quickly amended.

"In jail," Hazleton said, acting impressed. "Folsom or Alcatraz?"

"I'm not kidding," Jeffrey said, getting his dander up. "You can't pull that on me anymore, Brown. You're not the only guy around who's seen the inside of a crowbar hotel."

"Crowbar hotel? Who taught you that?" The reporter cocked his eyebrows.

"Just let me tell him about the jail," Jeffrey said to Li Soong.

"No. He will print it," she said.

"Me? Print it? Don't be silly."

"What we have done is for us to know," Li Soong said, looking at Jeffrey, but casting a glance at Hazleton.

"Oh, really?" the reporter said sarcastically. "And when you turn yourselves in, is that what you'll tell them? 'Sorry, guys, we'd rather not talk about the biggest story of the year.' I've got news for you, friends—it won't wash."

Hazleton noticed Jeffrey and Li Soong look to each other for reassurance as he spoke. He began to realize that they felt as though they shared a secret too precious to give the world—even if they did believe that they were ready to voluntarily end their adventure here. "Off the record," he conceded. "What've you two been up to?"

"Off the record?" Jeffrey verified, eager to ease the frustration of keeping his now-truthful boasts from Hazleton.

"Sure," Hazleton agreed. "Cross my heart and hope to die."

But Jeffrey was too thrilled at his own recounting of their story to pay attention to Hazleton's sarcasm. Aided by Li Soong, he leaned over the table and told his friend about the crazy sheriff and their miraculous escape, about Jesse and Clarence and their night in the Thicketty woods. Hazleton's face took on a look of genuine surprise, and as the story drew to a close he whistled under his breath. Jeffrey and Li Soong congratulated each other with their eyes.

"Tell him about the cabbie," Jeffrey nudged Li Soong, "and the trucker . . ."

Li Soong began to recount their adventures to the avid listener. Jeffrey watched Hazleton as the girl talked. "Hodge did that?" he asked as Li Soong told about the rides Jeffrey had flagged down and the roadside places they had found to sleep and eat.

"He is an excellent guide," she said authoritatively. "We ran out of money, and so he pawned his watch, and when that ran out he got a job one morning washing dishes in a . . . what is it called . . . ?"

"Diner," Jeffrey answered.

"And he thought of these disguises, too," Li Soong continued. "He even invented names for us so that if we were asked we would not give ourselves away."

"What are they?" Hazleton asked, his fingers itching to write it all down.

"I'm Lucas Pate and she's Sue Preston."

"Sue Preston?" Hazleton echoed incredulously, looking at Li Soong. "Where did you get that one?"

"My fourth-grade teacher," Jeffrey explained. "I had a crush on her."

"We should tell your friend about the Jercups family," Li Soong suggested.

"Jerkoff?" Hazleton questioned.

"Close." Jeffrey nodded. "They picked us up in their Winnebago a few days ago. There were eight of them, and they had more appliances and furniture in that thing than a department store. They had two microwave ovens and three TVs."

"My God," Hazleton said. "With that many TVs, didn't they recognize you?"

"No. All they watched was game shows. They had been on *Family Feud* once, and they were trying out for *High Rollers.*"

"Is that how they won all the junk?" Hazleton asked.

"I think so . . . Hey, that reminds me of the U-Haul guy," Jeffrey said, and Li Soong started to laugh at the memory.

"Who?"

"We got picked up by a U-Haul vigilante. I swear I'm not kidding. His job was to drive all over the country and look for stolen U-Hauls. He told us that when he caught someone, he made it his business to make sure they never did it again."

"You're putting me on, Hodge."

"No, he's quite serious," Li Soong said. "We were a little frightened of him because he seemed so angry—"

"Frightened!" Jeffrey interjected. "What about the salsa band that picked us up? You would have liked them, Haz. They were like Cheech and Chong. They came from New York, and all they did was smoke dope from the minute we got in until they dropped us. Their van was covered inside with pink angel hair, like on a Christmas tree, and their lead singer looked like a cross between Charro and the Goodyear blimp."

"A real pigboat, huh?"

"Three hundred pounds, easy," Jeffrey said.

Li Soong continued: "And the man with the dinosaur bones in his trunk—"

"Wait a minute!" Hazleton threw up his hands. "This isn't fair. I gotta phone this in to the paper."

"No," Jeffrey said adamantly.

"Hodge, you can't do this to me," Hazleton said, leaning forward with the old look that always managed to intimidate Jeffrey. But the look failed to penetrate, and Hazleton was struck by the difference between the Jeffrey Hodge who sat before him now and the one who had started a fight at the Atomic Bar. "You think you've lived a little bit and it's nobody's business but your own." Hazleton was pushing harder. "Well, you're wrong. You're news. And make no mistake. Somebody is going to tell your story. That could be me, a friend, or . . ."

Jeffrey stared straight at him. "You know, Haz, you sound like an old *Dragnet,* with the nice cop and the tough one taking turns with the suspect. Well, I've got news for you—that stuff went out with Jack Webb."

"Okay, let me tell *you* a little story." Hazleton was turning the pressure screws tighter. "Once upon a time, in a faraway town called Washington, D.C., there lived a nice if not too bright kid named Jeffrey. He met an equally nice but foolish girl, and together they set off across this grand and glorious land to find the other end of the rainbow."

"Get to the point," Jeffrey said uncomfortably.

"The point, my young friend," Hazleton said, lighting a cigarette, "is that this fairy tale doesn't have a happy ending. Because instead of the wicked witch of the North, we've got a head of a country who's scared shitless and the head of another with an edgy trigger finger and a hotel full of American tourists who aren't coming home until she does." He pointed at Li Soong. "Don't you read the papers?"

"No," Li Soong said. "We don't want to know those details."

"Then there's the little matter of the FBI, and the local and state police, and four very angry Chinamen with whom I believe Li Soong is closely acquainted."

"The Society of the Four Winds," Jeffrey said.

"Give the man a cigar," the reporter declared.

"So how come, with all that to worry about, *you* aren't turning us in?" Jeffrey asked.

"Because I'm just a humble reporter . . . and for all I care the world can go to hell in a handcart if I get my story."

"You're so patriotic," Jeffrey said cynically.

"That's me," Hazleton said. "You know, Hodge, I can walk over to that pay phone right now, call in what you just told me and be a hero besides."

"Don't," Jeffrey warned, squeezing Li Soong's hand under the table.

Hazleton Brown had never known Jeffrey Hodge to display this kind of will. He pushed himself away from the table and sat back in his chair, staring at the couple. They sat close together, hands clasped in solidarity. Hazleton compared Li Soong to the baggy-suited girl he had first seen stepping from the Chinese jet. Her once-dour countenance had an energy that radiated a contagious excitement. A look of recognition began to spread across his face as the jukebox belted out *"El Rancho Grande"* for the dozenth time.

"You know something?" Hazleton said, tapping the edge of the table with a fork.

"What?" Jeffrey said guardedly.

"You lied to me."

They looked at him, puzzled.

"You're not going back at all."

"Yes, we are," Li Soong argued. "This is our final destination."

"Like hell it is," Hazleton said, starting to chuckle.

Jeffrey turned to Li Soong with an expectant look on his face. "It is," he said, but the words came out like a question. "You want to go back, don't you?"

Li Soong hesitated. "Of course . . . unless there is still more for us to see."

"Nothing much," Jeffrey said in a voice designed to convince no one. "Only New Mexico, Nevada, California . . ." His words trailed off.

"You got any money?" the reporter asked. "You must've just about run out of watches."

"That's right," Jeffrey said, dropping the pretense of finality. "We're broke."

"But at least we're not hungry," Li Soong said, pointing to the T-bones denuded of meat.

"True," Jeffrey said slowly, daring a level look at Hazleton. "If we wanted to leave right now, would you turn us in?"

"One thing a reporter learns," Hazleton said, looking hard at Jeffrey and Li Soong, whose hands were clasped tightly together, "is to let a story finish telling itself before you write it up."

Jeffrey looked at his friend, considering the meaning of his words.

"I don't have an ending yet, Hodge."

"You don't?"

The reporter shook his head.

"You are a friend," Li Soong said to him. "It would be a wise decision to observe the rest of this land before I return home with my findings."

"Uh huh." Hazleton nodded, amused at Li Soong's reasons for wanting to continue the trip. There were some things, he figured, that even she hadn't come to understand yet.

*

They walked onto the deserted street of Balmorhea at closing time. Sage perfumed the air, and the mountains that ringed the town were a sharp purple against the midnight sky.

"Where are you staying?" Jeffrey asked.

"At the fleabag hotel. How about you?"

Before Jeffrey or Li Soong could answer, Hazleton drew to a sudden stop. A gray sedan was edging its way towards the front of the Balmorhea Hotel.

"What's the matter?" Li Soong asked.

"Something's up," Hazleton said. "Who does that car belong to?"

Jeffrey and Li Soong looked at each other, then all three ducked into a small walkway between two buildings.

"You got trouble," Hazleton said, grabbing Jeffrey by both his shoulders and looking him square in the eye.

"That car—they always use them. They're so plain they stand out like a lavender Cadillac. It's the Feds, boy."

Jeffrey moved close to Li Soong.

"We have to run," she said without hesitation. "We can't let them catch us."

Hazleton looked at the two of them; then, with a long sigh, he spoke. "This isn't going to win me any popularity contests back at the paper . . . but I think I got an idea. Look, they followed *me* here, not you, and I am probably one of a hundred different leads. They're hoping that if they pin me down, they're setting a trap for you." He reached into his pocket and took out a car key. "Behind the inn, a black sedan, Ford. It's the car the *Post* gave me. Take it. Go."

"What will you do?" Li Soong said. "Those men will get you."

"They're not after me. My old man isn't the Premier of China." He pushed the car key into Jeffrey's hand.

"We can't just leave you, Haz."

"Sure you can. Besides, I expect to hear some more great tales from you when you're done . . . And I mean *on* the record."

"Absolutely," Jeffrey said, shaking his head fiercely.

"Now, get going before I regain my senses and change my mind."

They turned towards the car behind the inn.

"One more thing," the reporter called, stopping them in their paces.

"Anything," Jeffrey said.

"Don't forget to write," Hazleton winked, and they turned back towards the car. He stood in the walkway as the car pulled quietly away, heading west. He watched the taillights climb towards the hills, then disappear over a ridge.

Nine

THEY HAD FLED Texas into the eerie purple of Arizona's Little Dragoon mountains. Jeffrey found a news station on the radio dial. "It is rumored that the couple are in the Southwestern United States. A gas-station attendant in Carrizo Springs, Texas, reported spotting them yesterday heading West in a black Ford sedan . . ."

"Turn that off," Li Soong said nervously. "Don't they have anything more important to discuss than two people on vacation?"

Jeffrey stared ahead at the road, deserted except for an occasional speedster whose car whipped past with a shrill howl. There were no signs of life here, only a few armadillo casualties strewn across the highway.

The oasis of calm in which they had wandered as they entered Balmorhea had vanished, replaced now with fears instilled by their near run-in with the FBI. Jeffrey's nerves felt raw as they navigated the hypnotic curves of the mountain range. As night gave way to day, they entered the town of Diablo del Fuego.

The buildings of the small town looked as though they had been swabbed with Clorox and set in the sun to bleach. The street was void of color. Even the black skin of Hazleton Brown's sedan shone a lifeless gray.

"We've got to get rid of this car," Jeffrey said. "Who knows who else saw us. We're too recognizable if we keep it."

"I feel hunted," Li Soong said edgily.

"You are," Jeffrey agreed. "We both are."

"And I'm tired." She turned to Jeffrey and he could see the exhaustion in her face.

"Me too."

"Do you think it would be possible for us to stay in one place for more than just a few hours?" she asked.

"I doubt it," Jeffrey shook his head. "I think it's too dangerous." He watched the portion of Li Soong's face that was reflected in the mirror as he drove. He saw her start to cry. "Hey, what's wrong?" he said, reaching out to touch her arm.

She shook her head, denying she was upset.

"You can tell me," Jeffrey said softly. "We're friends. We've come a long way together."

Li Soong wiped her face and sniffed. "I'm scared," she said, to Jeffrey's amazement. "I'm scared and I'm tired and I have to go to the bathroom."

Jeffrey felt a surge of tenderness for her vulnerability. He reached out with his hand and stroked her damp cheek. "Ah, come on, there's nothing to be scared of."

"Yes, there is," she said sadly. "We are like common criminals. We are forced to run like mongrel dogs and hide in alleyways."

"It hasn't been that bad." Jeffrey tried to soothe her. "We've had a great time—"

"But now it's different. We're running out of places to go, and everywhere we turn we're recognized."

Jeffrey tried to take control of her runaway emotions. "Here's what we're going to do," he said reassuringly. "We'll stop in this town, trade in the car, you'll find a john someplace, and we'll check into a motel."

"Is it safe?" Li Soong asked in a hushed voice. "Oh, if

we could just rest for a while, I would feel so much better."

"We'll make it safe," Jeffrey declared. "Just leave it all to me."

They cruised the center strip of Diablo del Fuego, past a car lot demarcated by four white pillars. Faded plastic pennants hung limply from strings that ran between the pillars to form a square. The square was strewn with a few cars and trucks parked among weeds. In the center was a metallic Quonset hut marked "Uncle Sid's Used Cars."

"All right," Jeffrey proclaimed. "This is where we'll start. "I'm going to sell the car."

"Possibly Uncle Sid might be a sympathetic man," Li Soong suggested. "In China, 'uncle' is a title of honorable endearment."

"Ha," Jeffrey said. "That's a laugh. If he's honorable, it'll be a first. Used-car salesmen are a tough bunch, Li Soong."

"We are just as tough," she said adamantly.

"Right," Jeffrey agreed. "I wonder how much I can get for this car?"

"How much will you ask?"

"Well, it's probably worth about four thousand, but we'll be lucky to get one. It's possible the license plates are on the police bands, and car dealers are the first to be alerted to this sort of thing."

"Perhaps we should abandon it and run?" Li Soong ventured.

"We're broke, it's all we've got. If we can sell it, we'll travel first-class. Won't that be a treat?"

"Certainly not!" Li Soong said, and Jeffrey realized he was about to get lesson number 215 on the benefits of a classless society.

"Hold it," he said. "Can the lecture, and give it to me later when we get to the motel." He drew the brakes near the Quonset hut in the center of the lot. Surrounding them were dying and dead cars, cars with different colored doors and primer-gray panels, cars with smashed front ends that gave them sour expressions. They exited the safety of Hazleton's Ford and walked towards the front door of the metal hut.

The inside was like an airless steel oven. "Uncle Sid here—the poor man's pal," the man hissed through rotting teeth. He looked like a snake, wearing a suit of iridescent green. His cheeks reflected the same foul green cast.

"Did you hear that?" Li Soong nudged Jeffrey. "He is the poor man's pal. How encouraging!"

Jeffrey could think of no way to explain to Li Soong, so he ignored her and extended his hand to the man. "I have a car outside I'd like to sell. Need a little cash."

"Let's have a look-see," the man said, uncoiling from his chair and sauntering towards the dusty vehicle outside. He made a perfunctory tour around the sedan, looking more at its two nervous owners than at the car itself. He seemed to enjoy the way they shifted anxiously, awaiting his decision. Without lifting the hood, he declared flatly, "Three hundred."

"Impossible!" Li Soong threw up her arms. "You are not a friend of the poor if you try to steal our car for that price."

Uncle Sid turned on the heel of his Corfam wing tip and walked back to the office.

"She didn't mean that . . . wait up!" Jeffrey ran after him, casting a look of exasperation back at Li Soong.

"Two hundred, and that's my final offer," Uncle Sid said with a smile that resembled a death's head. "Let's see your title."

Jeffrey froze. His exhaustion had fogged his mind and he had forgotten about such legalities.

The man watched him squirm. "Problem?" He rolled the word out like a pair of loaded dice.

"I don't—" Jeffrey started.

"Let me guess." Uncle Sid grinned unpleasantly. "You don't have the papers. Pity, too, because there's not another dealer around for miles." He walked closer to Jeffrey and draped a skeletal arm around his shoulders. "I like you, kid, honest I do."

Jeffrey could feel the man's acrid breath on his face. He pulled away, trying to put daylight between them. But Sid clung.

"I can see when a guy's in a tight spot. I'll tell you what. I'll give you a hundred dollars flat, and no questions asked."

The man pressed closer, and in the heat of the Arizona morning Jeffrey agreed to the deal.

"You sold it!" Li Soong said excitedly as Jeffrey walked back to her.

"Calm down," he said. "I only got a hundred bucks."

"How could you do that?" Li Soong moaned.

"I forgot about the title papers. It's a good thing he's a crook, or he wouldn't have taken it at all," Jeffrey explained.

"I don't understand." Li Soong shook her head. "But at least we'll get some sleep."

"That's right," Jeffrey said protectively. "And we have a few bucks in our pocket again."

*

Inside his office Uncle Sid looked at the registration papers he had found in the glove box of the Ford. They listed the owner as the Washington *Post.* He reached for the crumpled-up newspaper in his garbage can and flattened its front page out on the desk next to the registration, straining his mind to compare the nervous couple who had just left his lot with the news photos of the runaway pair from Washington.

He dialed the telephone that sat in the dust on his desk. "Get the hell outta bed and get over here," he said to the man who answered. "I got a way to make us rich."

*

The Diablo Motel was a long concrete bunker pressed close to the ground and painted a bilious yellow.

"Uncle Sid said it's the only place in town," Jeffrey explained to Li Soong. "What here and I'll get a room for us."

"Can't I come too?" Li Soong asked as Jeffrey started for the door with the office sign.

"No, stay outside. I wish that Uncle Sid hadn't seen us together. Let's not compound the mistake," he said, looking nervously up and down the highway that ran through town. "If I wasn't so bushed, I'd say we ought to move on now—"

"No." Li Soong groaned. "Please . . ."

Jeffrey nodded in agreement. "Wait here."

A woman sat, facing away from the desk in the motel office, watching television. The place smelled of roach spray. Jeffrey tried not to imagine the rooms as he approached the woman. "Hello," he said, but there was no response. "Room, please," he said louder.

The woman turned to him with an annoyed look on her face. "I hear ya, I hear ya," she shouted, exposing a massive hearing aid in one ear as she turned.

"I'd like a room," Jeffrey enunciated.

"She shoved a key across the desk. "Ten dollars, pay in advance," she blared, her eyes wandering back to the TV.

"Thanks," Jeffrey said as he turned for the door. Outside, Li Soong was shielding her eyes from the sunlight when he emerged, dangling the key in his hand. She did a jump of glee when she saw him with it.

"Don't get too excited," he said. "It's probably the pits."

"But it's ours, at least for a while; and I can take a shower."

"I hope at least there is one," Jeffrey said, turning the

key in the door of room eight. As he peeked inside his spirits lifted slightly. The room was tawdry but reasonably clean. Pink chenille spreads decorated the saggy bed, giant gawky flamingos woven into their surfaces. A round-screened TV in a blond cabinet squatted in the corner. Wallpaper with a homing-pigeon motif patterned the walls. Jeffrey laughed as he watched Li Soong's face register the kitschy decor. "What's the matter, lady, you got something against birds?" he said as he pushed her inside.

She raced into the bathroom. "They're in here, too," she called out. "On the rug and shower curtain, too."

"Yuk," Jeffrey said, walking around the room until he kicked off his shoes and flung himself on the bed. The springs made noises like alley cats in heat. He sighed deeply, trying to let the tension flow from his muscles. "Be it ever so humble, there's no place like home . . ." He yodeled a serenade as Li Soong ran the water in the shower.

*

The motel office door opened again, and Uncle Sid entered. "Hello, ma," he said in a booming voice. "What room they in?"

"Eight. The last one. Like you told me to put them."

He nodded and the woman went back to her television. As Uncle Sid stepped outside, a rusted-out pickup truck rumbled up to the motel and shut off. Three men stepped down, each thick and mountainous, so heavy their feet splayed outwards as they walked, so wide their heads looked like the points on top of three soft-serve ice cream cones.

"Howdy, Sid," one of the men said. "What'd you drag us over here so fast for? Sounded like you struck gold."

"I did, Earl," Uncle Sid said. "You boys ever see TV or look in the papers?"

They grunted yes, and Uncle Sid explained to the three men exactly who was staying in room eight.

*

Jeffrey listened to the shower pelt Li Soong. The sound was reassuring, homelike. He wanted to walk in and watch her, like he had seen so many movie heroes do—so cool, so perfect in their self-assurance. But he was unsure of the feelings he had for her; and even more unsure of how she would react to his imposition.

Li Soong emerged in her jeans and shirt, hair wrapped turban-style in a towel on top of her head.

"You look beautiful," Jeffrey said, appreciating the symmetry of her face.

"Thank you," she said shyly. She was not used to praise like this, especially from Jeffrey, who seemed more at home teasing her. She stood in the center of the room, toweling her hair, as the bed seemed to impose its presence on the two of them. It creaked with every shift of Jeffrey's weight. He moved ever so slightly as he saw Li Soong deposit herself in a chair.

"You can sit here if you want," he said, tapping the side of the bed.

Li Soong felt embarrassed not to, as if her refusal was an accusation against Jeffrey for something she wasn't sure he meant. She wondered if she was only imagining the feelings she sensed between them. She bridled at the thought and stood up, pulling the towel from the long streamers of hair, shaking her head violently as if to cast the demons out of her mind.

"Hey, you're getting me all wet!" Jeffrey yelled. "Who do you think you are—Lassie?"

"And I suppose that is another of your many girl-friends?" Li Soong said archly.

"No, but you're not far off." Jeffrey found himself laughing. He sensed another fight about to start. He had found that whenever the subject of girlfriends or boyfriends came up, they squabbled. "You never had a boyfriend before, did you?"

"I don't know what you mean 'before,'" Li Soong said.

"Well, you've never mentioned any boyfriends from home. I guess you don't date." Jeffrey tried to make the statement sound more casual than it felt.

"No, we do not 'date.' When we are in our mid-twenties, we go about the job of selecting a suitable mate."

Jeffrey replayed the words: "'Suitable mate.' Boy, does that sound awful."

"I can assure you, it is not awful," Li Soong said protectively. "But it is no doubt different from your life. I assume you have many girlfriends."

"It depends on what you mean. I go out pretty much . . . but there's no one special."

"Then why do you go out?" Li Soong asked, trying to sound clinical.

"Because it gets boring sitting around the house on Saturday night. It's not dating, really. Just going to the movies or whatever—"

"Are they pretty? Your girlfriends?"

"Some are." Jeffrey was enjoying her concern.

"Are they intelligent?"

"I don't know, some are, some aren't. Why the cross-examination?"

Li Soong drew in her breath. "Do you engage in sex with them?"

Jeffrey burst out laughing.

"You are always making fun of me," Li Soong said.

"Are you going to start that again?" Jeffrey felt as if a great charge of energy had built up between them, and like lightning between conductors it crackled and flared.

"You are always laughing at me." Li Soong pouted.

"That's because some of the things you say are very funny," Jeffrey explained. "For instance, Lassie is a dog in the movies."

"A dog in the movies!" Li Soong exclaimed. "Americans astound me by their idea of worthwhile amusement."

"Who says it's worthwhile? It's just fun."

Sitting back in the armchair, Li Soong untangled her hair with a comb. " 'Fun,' " she scoffed. "That is how different we are. I have no interest in 'fun' unless it is also politically enriching."

"Bullshit," Jeffrey said. "You don't know yourself very well, do you? I saw the way you danced back in Thicketty, and how you laughed your head off when we were in that Winnebago and those kids told the world's stupidest jokes. I can think of a million times you've cracked up, and there was nothing 'political' in the slightest about any of them."

"Hmmph," Li Soong said, covering the look of amusement on her face with a strand of hair.

"Don't be such a grouch," Jeffrey said. "Come sit here and we'll watch TV."

"Perhaps that would provide some interesting insights," Li Soong said, obstinately refusing to acknowledge the fun implied by his invitation. She walked over to the ancient set and turned the knob. A hail of dots and lines assaulted the screen, finally clearing to a blurry black and white image.

"Great," Jeffrey said, *"The Honeymooners* . . . I love it." He patted the bed, inviting Li Soong to occupy the space next to him. "Sit down and I'll tell you all about Ralph Cramden."

She moved to the side of the swaying bed and sat down, allowing herself to relax against a pile of pillows that Jeffrey had arranged for her.

"There, isn't this fun," he said, gently putting an arm

around her. "That's Norton." He pointed to the flickering screen. A warm glow welled in his chest as he felt Li Soong nestle into the pillows next to him.

The minutes passed comfortably as Jeffrey explained the show to her and Li Soong became involved in the little drama of the bus driver and the sewer worker.

"What's that?" Jeffrey said, breaking the spell.

Li Soong had been too intrigued by *The Honeymooners* to notice the noise.

"There's someone out there. I see silhouettes," Jeffrey said. "Oh, God, I bet the cops tracked the car to the lot . . . Damn!"

The door slammed open, sprung with a key. Li Soong and Jeffrey backed to the wall until they could go no further. The three men with Uncle Sid did not look like federal agents or even local police.

"Uncle Sid?" Jeffrey said cautiously as the four men drew close. "What's the matter? Something wrong with the car?" In one man's hand Jeffrey could see a tabloid that showed his and Li Soong's faces across the front page.

The man looked at them, then at the picture, squinting his eyes into two mean lines. "Ain't no doubt about it— it's them," he said, toothpick wagging from his mouth. "I think ya finally got something worthwhile, Sid. We'll be billionaires by the time this scam is down."

A sick shiver ran the length of Jeffrey's vertebrae. He could tell Li Soong instinctively understood the treacherous nature of their visitors. He prayed that FBI agents were in these men's places. He prayed for anything but the imaginings that were running through his head. "You're going to be in a lot of trouble, mister," Jeffrey said as Uncle Sid walked closer. "You can't get away with this kind of thing. You know, we've got FBI and secret service right behind us."

"Ain't you never heard of Patty Hearst?" the man said.

"It's not the same thing," Jeffrey asserted.

"Or that kid, what's his name, with the ear, Getty?"

"I'm telling you it's not the same. You won't get anything for us," Jeffrey pleaded, knowing that whatever the men asked would be a fair price for their return.

"Or how about that Italian dude, the one they killed anyway?" one of Sid's companions volunteered.

A horrible thought entered Jeffrey's mind. Li Soong's price was without a limit, but was his? He could be the first sacrifice made to up the ante. He felt his teeth chatter.

Two of the men slipped beefy arms around Li Soong.

"Let go of her!" Jeffrey cried, running up behind them, catching one on the back of the neck with an unexpected punch. The man rubbed his neck and snarled.

"Get rid of him. Lock him in the bathroom," Sid commanded. "We gotta write a note."

Jeffrey struggled, but found himself locked in the tiled room. He pounded on the door and flung himself against it until his arm swelled. He could hear the muffled sound of Li Soong crying. He could hear snatches of the men's talk.

"Show 'em we mean business . . . We can send an ear, a finger, like they always do . . . Cut some of her hair, anyway. That'll prove it's her . . . It's her that's worth the dough . . ."

Jeffrey screamed Li Soong's name and flailed in the room like a wild animal. He had to get out. He would not let them do this.

He had seen the window right away, but it was hopelessly small, the frame rusted and stuck. At most he could get a leg through . . . but it was the only chance. He pulled out the screen and tore at the rotting frame. It started to give; then the concrete around it began to crumble. He bloodied his fingers scraping at the hole. He dug at it with all his strength, his breath coming in great gasps as he struggled relentlessly to escape.

He stood on the toilet seat and tried to thread himself through the hole he had torn. Finally, he wedged himself out and tumbled onto the walkway that ran along the back of the building.

He moved catlike around the front until he got to the door, crouching low under the window. The pickup truck was parked in front, a shotgun slung in the hunting rack of the cab. Jeffrey reached into the open window of the truck and removed the long weapon. He pumped the slide gently, feeding a shell into the chamber. He crept closer to the door. He listened.

"The kid stopped his racket," one of the men said. "Musta knocked himself out." He laughed. Jeffrey could still hear Li Soong weeping.

He got as close to the door as possible, then stood to the side. He was working on raw nerve and energy he had never tapped before. His hand went out and knocked.

"Go away," one of the men called out.

He knocked again.

"Ma, go away, we're busy," Sid hollered.

Jeffrey knocked again.

"She's deaf," one of them said. "I'll get the door and shoo her outta here."

Jeffrey took a deep swallow. The door opened—just enough for him to turn and slam it with a mighty kick. It flew back, surprising and toppling the man who stood there.

Jeffrey lifted the shotgun and blasted a lamp. He pumped the slide and blew apart the television, pumped again and took a chunk out of the wall. He pumped the slide now and held the gun at chest level, fanning it between the four men inside, who had scrambled towards the back wall.

"Li Soong," Jeffrey called out. "Move it!" She was by his side so quickly he thought he had seen her fly. "The truck," he called. Li Soong ran for the pickup and turned the key left in the ignition. Jeffrey pulled the room door shut and ran for the idling truck. Before he jumped in, he blasted the motel room window. He wanted to give the men inside second thoughts about trying to follow.

*

By the time they reached Sweetwater, Arizona, the shaking in Jeffrey's hands had subsided and Li Soong had regained the ability to speak. But he kept a heavy foot on the accelerator, not daring to look back for fear of being followed, scared to stop lest they be recognized again.

The gas gauge was on the low side of E and Jeffrey could feel the pickup's engine begin to sputter. He turned to Li Soong, but she still clutched herself tightly as if to protect her from the memory of Uncle Sid. "We're all right," he said.

"We have to call Washington," Li Soong announced as the truck bucked again. "We can't go on like this."

"Damn!" Jeffrey cursed as the truck ran out of gas and died, sliding to a halt in front of a white frame building on the outskirts of town. "You're right, Li Soong, this is it, the end of the line." He and the girl looked sadly at each other, both despising this ignominious conclusion to their journey. "It's a lousy way for it to end, isn't it?" he said. "Broke, tired, scared . . . and out of gas."

"Yes, it is," Li Soong said. "But we must go back."

"I know," Jeffrey conceded. He pushed a hand into his pocket. "I guess we're not broke. I forgot we still have a hundred bucks from selling the car." He shrugged his shoulders. "At least that's more than we had when we started out."

"What does it matter now?"

"Nothing, I guess. How do you want to do it? I mean, turn ourselves in."

"Why don't you call your home. Tell your parents where we are. Or should you call the reporter and tell him?"

Jeffrey pondered the alternatives, and neither seemed right. "I hate to make the call. It seems so . . . final."

"It *is* final," Li Soong said, staring out the window at the desert.

"But it's the right thing to do." Jeffrey looked towards the house in front of which the truck had stopped. "Maybe they would let us use their phone. I bet whoever lives there will sure be surprised at the publicity they get once we make the call. I almost hate to inflict that on anyone."

"True." Li Soong nodded, and for a long while neither of them spoke.

Finally Jeffrey took the initiative. "I'll go in and do it. You wait here." He stepped out of the truck and walked past a picket fence and up the stairs to the shaded porch. He rang twice, finally summoning an elderly lady to the screen door.

She eyed him through thick glasses, then looked at Li Soong in the truck. "C'mon in," she said, opening the door and leading Jeffrey into the hallway. She stood in front of him, mopping her hands on her apron. "You have to excuse me, but you caught me in the middle of baking. Can I help you?"

From where he stood on the hooked rug, Jeffrey surveyed her home. His weary eyes took in the starched white curtains, the violets blooming on the window sill, a Victorian sofa sitting primly in the living room. He could smell the yeasty odor of baking bread from the kitchen.

"Young man!" The woman startled him as she reached out and touched his arm.

"I'm sorry." He started to explain. "I've been on the road for a while, and staying in some pretty grungy places. This place . . . your home . . . is so, so homey."

The old woman chuckled. "Glad you like it. Do you want to see your room?"

"My room?" Jeffrey said with amazement. He felt as if he had just stepped over into the Twilight Zone.

"Certainly. That's why you're here, aren't you?" The woman furrowed her brow. "This *is* a rooming house. Didn't you see the sign?"

"No, I guess I didn't," he apologized. "Like I said, I've been traveling pretty hard—"

"Mrs. Allen's Room and Board," the woman announced.

"And you're Mrs. Allen?"

"What's left of her." She grinned. "Now, do you want to see your room?"

"Actually, I was wondering if I could use your phone," Jeffrey said, turning back to look at Li Soong in the truck.

"That your wife?"

"Um, yeah," Jeffrey agreed.

"Good, I like young couples. But about the phone—we don't have one."

"Oh," Jeffrey said, not as disappointed as he felt he should be. "Is there one nearby?"

"In town, at the drugstore."

Jeffrey remembered the empty gas tank. "How far is town?"

"Fifteen miles," Mrs. Allen said. "Now, do you want to see that room or not? My bread's going to burn while we stand around yakking."

"Sure," he said. "Let's see it."

He walked up the stairs behind the old lady and was let into a room at the end of the hall. It was a small room with a single brass bed. The wallpaper was patterned with dots of blue and white, and a blue and white wash basin sat on the dresser. Another hooked rug curled at the foot of the bed.

"It's clean," Mrs. Allen said as she watched Jeffrey take it in.

He inhaled the smells of the house—a mingling of laundry soap and lavender sachets. "It's very nice," he said, sorry that it would be the end of the line for him and Li Soong.

"Then you'll take it?" Mrs. Allen asked. "I hope so. I like the company, and the house has been empty for weeks."

"Sure," Jeffrey told her. "Why not?"

*

Mrs. Allen watched the young couple through the window as they walked towards the house. She smoothed the bedcovers and ran her hand along the already dustless mantle of the room's fireplace as she waited for them to come upstairs. She could hear them whispering, their voices trailing off as they reached the room.

"Hello," Li Soong said shyly to the woman as she walked through the door.

Mrs. Allen looked at her dirty, oversized clothes and tattered cap. "Hello," she said in a concerned voice. "Don't you have no luggage with you?"

"No," Jeffrey said. "We're heading home tomorrow. It was a short trip." Li Soong nodded in wordless agreement.

"Well, it's none of my business anyway." Mrs. Allen smiled, her wrinkled face dotted with two small circles of rouge. "There's a bathroom down the end of the hall," she said. "It's all yours, since there's no one else here."

"That's nice," Jeffrey said gloomily. The cozy sanctuary only made him sadder that the end of their adventure drew near.

"I'll leave you alone now. Dinner's at six, downstairs."

"Thank you," Jeffrey said as she left, closing the door behind her. "It's a nice place, isn't it?"

Li Soong sat in a little wing chair in the corner. "Very nice," she agreed, taking in the crocheted dresser scarves and spotless clear glass of the window over the bed.

"At least we'll go out in style," Jeffrey said. "It's better than if we had turned ourselves in when we were sleeping out under a tree, or in that Thicketty jail."

"Certainly," she replied.

"What's the matter with you?" he said sharply, seized by a flash of anger.

Li Soong jumped. "Me? What's wrong with you?"

"You act like a zombie, sitting there staring off into space."

"I'm tired and I'm still frightened from before," Li Soong explained.

"Well, you don't have to worry," Jeffrey said curtly. "Tomorrow you'll be safe in the arms of your father's beloved bodyguards . . . where you belong."

Li Soong was hurt by his words. "Why are you acting like this?"

"Like what? Realistic? Look, Li Soong, I'm sick and tired of having to be John Wayne—beating up sheriffs, fighting with a gang of thugs in a cheap motel, protecting you from all the trouble you get us into . . ."

Li Soong felt herself begin to shake. "Jeffrey," she said. "What are you talking about? I didn't make you do those things. We did them together."

"Right," he said sharply. "Well, I'll be damn glad when this whole stupid trip is over and you're back home." Jeffrey began to pace the carpet as he escalated the fight.

The girl sat in the chair with her eyes cast down. "I didn't realize you hated it so much."

"I do, it stinks," he said. "It's no bargain to steal your

best friend's car or sleep on the floor so you can sleep on a couch alone."

Li Soong looked up to see the hurt in Jeffrey's face.

"To be chased from one place to the next, to, to . . ." His voice rose in a crescendo as he thought of all the injustices he could muster, all to counteract the pain he felt at the inevitable phone call they must place.

Li Soong looked at him planted on the floor. The veins in his neck stood out like rigid cords. His hair was dirty from the dust of the road, his work shirt soaked with sweat. He whipped a towel off a hook by the door.

"I'm going to take a shower," Jeffrey said, and he slammed the door behind him.

Li Soong was overwhelmed by his outburst. A dizzying emptiness made her reach out to touch the bedpost as she stood to steady herself. She paced across the floor, trying to clear her vision, but the walls grew closer and there was no place to move. Jeffrey's words rang in her ears, and her own doubts began to close in around her. Was he right? Was the whole journey a terrible, irrevocable mistake? Or was the dreadful void she suddenly felt inside herself a response to feelings about Jeffrey that she constantly pushed from her mind? Why did he have the power to upset her so much? She had sought in him nothing more than a traveling companion, someone who would help her move easily through the land. But now she felt as though the floor had dropped from beneath her feet, for the journey had become secondary to the time they shared together and the devastating finality she knew they had to face.

*

The hot steam of the shower cleared Jeffrey's head. Rivulets of water drew the anger and frustration from his body. As the lilac soap scent billowed around him, he felt tranquil and sad. He knew he had hurt Li Soong. He imagined her sitting in the chair where he had left her.

He wanted to go to her and apologize, to wipe the tears he knew he had caused. He knew he could not walk away from her tomorrow forever, leaving the situation as it was.

He could see the open door of his room as he left the bathroom and walked down the hall. He remembered slamming it loud and hard as he left. The room was empty. He called Li Soong's name. He raced to the stairs and called again.

He ran back to the room for his shirt, and on top of it found a small piece of paper, folded over. He swept it up and read: "My friend Jeffrey, what you said is true. I ask too much of you. I had no right to expect you to undertake this dangerous journey with me. I thank you for taking me this far. I will never forget you. Li Soong."

Jeffrey fiercely crushed the note in his hand. He felt his heart explode and fill his chest with pain. Grabbing the shirt, he raced to the stairs and took them three at a time, almost colliding with Mrs. Allen at the bottom. Wild-eyed, he stammered, "Where is she?"

"Your wife?" the old lady asked, shocked by Jeffrey's crazed look. "I believe I heard her go out."

"Where did she go?" he demanded, placing both hands desperately on the woman's shoulders.

"My dear, I have no idea. What's wrong, what's the matter?"

Jeffrey had no time to answer. He rushed outside and scanned the street, but saw no trace of her. He went for the pickup truck, but remembered it was out of fuel. He saw cars traveling past, and a sinking feeling swept over him as he imagined Li Soong picked up by any of them. He started to run along the road, hoping to spot her.

As he ran he cursed himself, cursed his anger and his inability to tell her all the feelings he had for her. He walked and ran for hours, and the desert spread before him like an empty canvas. He knew she could have gone in any direction, and he shivered as the sun began to set and long shadows fell across the sands.

His steps felt like lead as he came back to the rooming house. Strange night sounds howled in the distance, and he prayed Li Soong had changed her mind and come back to him.

Mrs. Allen's parlor was empty as he entered. An unnatural calm hung in the air. He ascended the steps in the dim glow of a light from the end of the hall. He knew he hadn't left the light on in the room—it had to be Li Soong—and he bounded to the end of the corridor and entered.

There was Mrs. Allen, turning down the corner of the bed. "Hello," she said pleasantly. "I thought you two had deserted me. You missed dinner."

Jeffrey's face was a mask of pain.

"You didn't find your wife?"

"No," he said, slumping onto the bed with his head in his hands. "It's all my fault," he moaned.

"It most always is," Mrs. Allen said. "Men always do start the arguments."

"But you don't understand." He looked up at her. "This is different. She can't just run off . . . You don't understand."

"Of course I understand," Mrs. Allen scoffed. "I was married thirty-eight years before my husband passed away."

Jeffrey tried to explain: "But we're not like other couples."

"You're just like everyone else," the old lady said, fluffing the pillow. "Don't have such a high and mighty idea of yourself. Everyone argues—and everyone makes up. That's what being in love is. Up, down, good, bad. It's a circle that never stops. She'll come back."

"But she ran away. I have to find her. Who will take care of her?"

The old woman smoothed the sheet. "If I told you the number of times I slammed out of here in a huff, madder than hell, I'd bore you to tears. But I always came back. Don't just sit there like a lump," she ordered. "You start thinking about what you're going to say to her when you get her back."

Jeffrey shook his head defeatedly as Mrs. Allen headed for the door. Then she doubled back and stood in front of him, touching him gently on the shoulder. He looked up, and a forelock of hair tumbled in his eye.

"You could use a haircut," she said, then smiled and walked out the door.

*

Jeffrey collapsed and wept, wept until his sobbing was hoarse and painful. He had never felt so alone in his life. He had driven away the person he now knew he wanted most of all, and he mouthed her name as he buried his head in the bed pillows.

It seemed as though hours passed; then Jeffrey sensed the door open. He lifted his head and saw that he was not alone. Silhouetted in the doorway was a form—familiar, slender and lovely. She moved towards him, extending a hand to touch him lightly on the cheek. It was Li Soong, and Jeffrey grabbed her outstretched hand and pressed it to his lips.

"Jeffrey." She said his name, and it was the most beautiful thing she could say to him because it was all that she wanted on her lips.

"Li Soong," he responded, reaching out, drawing her to him, pulling her down on top of him. "I'm sorry," he tried to say, but the words could not escape. His mouth was nuzzled in the warmth of her neck as they lay together on the bed.

"Don't leave me," he said as his rough cheek pressed against her skin, his lips ran across her collarbone, taking in the heady warmth of her skin like hyacinths in the sun. He pulled the cap from her head, releasing streamers of hair that flowed around them like silken cords, binding them until Jeffrey's arms replaced the tenuous dark threads. They reclined onto the smooth linens, caressing and melting curve for curve into each other like perfectly matched ivory spoons.

"I searched for you," Jeffrey whispered as he held her trembling form in his hands. "I was so scared you wouldn't come back, that I'd never see you again."

"Be still," Li Soong whispered back. "It doesn't matter now." And she shivered at the touch of bare flesh on flesh.

"I need you . . ." Jeffrey's words were muffled by her body.

Li Soong surrendered to the new sensations that overwhelmed her. She felt open and vibrant as a flower in first bloom. She ran her fingers up the deep groove between the muscles in Jeffrey's back, and held him tightly.

"I love you," they said in unison, rocking with their newfound rapture.

Ten

AFTER THE smoke cleared in the motel room, Sid and his brothers went to the Diablo Saloon and got mean, angry drunk. It was noon, and except for the four of them the bar was deserted. No one overheard or minded their vociferous argument.

"I still think we shoulda followed them," Earl complained to Sid. "We could've split up and gone separate ways."

"Yeah," another brother beefed. "You let a million bucks wheel outta here just like that." He snapped two stubby fingers in Sid's face.

"You moron," Sid countered. "If you hadn't locked the kid in the room with the window, they woulda still been right here."

"An' who tol' me to lock him there?" The brother leaned towards Sid.

"Ah, you fatheads gimme a pain," brother number three said, sliding off the barstool. "I'm gonna walk over to the lot and pick me out a new truck, since Sid here gave my old one to those kids."

"Like fun you are," Sid said, blocking him from the door. "You ain't layin' a hand on any ve-hickle in that lot unless I tell you to." He stuck an angular jaw out as if it were a weapon.

"I oughta push your face in," the brother said.

"Try and I'll wipe the floor with you," Sid came back.

And so the argument continued relentlessly, without peaking. They needed to vent their frustration at their failure, but had only each other to do it with. "Whaddaya say we go down to Greaserville and bust a couple of tamale asses," Earl suggested, pounding his fist into the snug harbor of his other hand.

"I got work to do," Sid said, although his drunken belch belied his words. "I don't have time to screw around with you palookas all day." He dropped some money on the bar and headed for the door. The three brothers followed. "That Chinese chick was pretty cute, y'know," he grumbled. "We coulda had some fun with her."

They walked into the brightness of the desert day. "Hey, looka there," Sid said, pointing to four blue-suited figures in the used-car lot. "What the hell . . . Chinamen. What do you think they want here?"

"Beats me," Earl said.

"I bet they followed her here. They're on her trail. Say, that gives me an idea. We may be able to get a little cash out of this after all," Sid said.

"What are you gonna do?" one of the brothers asked dully.

"Look at them lookin' at that black car the two of 'em sold me. They want information—and we got it. I'll sell it to 'em . . . and for plenty yen, ha ha. This is gonna be fun," Sid said, walking towards the contingent of Orientals, who now stood in a line with their arms folded uniformly against their chests.

"Howdy, boys. Uncle Sid, the poor man's pal, at your service," he said unctuously. "This here's a beauty—low mileage, a real cream puff. Or"—he lowered his voice— "are you looking for something a little more 'exotic'?" He poked the closest of the Chinese in the ribs.

They closed into a tight circle around him.

"Whaddaya think they're talkin' about?" one of the men asked Earl.

"I bet Sid's got 'em by the balls. Ain't he something? He can sell snow to an Eskimo." They craned their necks to see.

Suddenly Sid's head dipped down as if drawn under by a strong ocean current. His twisted mouth formed a silent scream. "I didn't mean anything by that," he pleaded with the Chinese. "I was kidding, she's fine, she's fine. Honest, we didn't touch her."

"Hey, he's in trouble," Earl shouted, and the brothers rushed forward.

Earl grabbed a length of scrap iron and headed for the nearest of the Four Winds. The agent reached out towards Earl with a raised left hand. The hand grabbed the arm that held the jagged piece of iron as the right hand grasped Earl at the waist. To a passer-by on the main street of Diablo del Fuego, it might have looked as though the two men were greeting each other with a half-embrace. Earl made no sound as the agent gripped him, applying pressure that appeared effortless. Then it looked as though Earl had suddenly become very tired. He crumpled to his knees, his body swaying backwards, and as the agent released him he dropped to the ground.

Under silent physical persuasion by the Chinese, the other brothers drifted onto their backs as if a sudden wave of narcolepsy had swept over Uncle Sid's car lot. The four Chinese turned back to Uncle Sid, who stood watching the collapsed trio of men.

"Go on, knock me out too," he said with a still-drunken bravado. "I ain't gonna tell you a thing."

One agent reached out and put a left hand on Sid's shoulder, a right hand extended as if to shake. It looked like a friendly greeting. But Uncle Sid didn't smile. His spine turned brittle and an icy paralysis clutched his muscles. He realized that until this moment he had never known the meaning of pain. And just as suddenly he was eager to tell the four Chinese everything he knew: "Blue Dodge pickup, heading west."

*

Jeffrey awoke at dawn in Li Soong's arms. Stray beams of light filtered in past the edges of the drawn curtains, illuminating her sleeping form. He raised his hand above her body and lightly grazed the flat plane of her belly, her small breasts and delicate limbs, her lustrous skin that shone in pale tea-rose hues.

She turned in her sleep at his touch, slowly opening her eyes. "Hello," she said softly as he bent forward to kiss her, and in the fog between sleep and wakefulness Li Soong felt Jeffrey cover her with his weight, reconfirming the passions of the night before.

They lay together until the Arizona sun glittered in the sky. They dressed slowly, as if covering their bodies from one another was painful. "Let me," Jeffrey said as Li Soong started to button her flannel shirt. His hands trembled as he closed each button, planting a kiss before he concealed the next piece of her flesh. Li Soong watched him as he bent in front of her, and she caressed the smooth muscular curve of his neck, tracing the pattern of blond curls that fell across his tan skin.

They walked arm in arm down the stairs, at the bottom of which Mrs. Allen stood looking up at them. "You almost missed breakfast, too!" she scolded. "But at least I see you settled your fight."

Jeffrey nodded. "You were right. She did come back."

Li Soong looked puzzled as the old woman guided them into the dining room.

"Are we still the only guests?" Jeffrey said with wonder as he looked at the culinary bounty that seemed enough for twelve.

"Yes, but don't let that concern you," the woman said,

pointing him to a chair. "It's no fault of anyone's but that main highway that stole all my business away from me."

Li Soong watched the tiny woman as she uncovered each platter with a dramatic flourish. "If you don't have guests, then how do you manage to support yourself?" she asked with concern.

Mrs. Allen looked at the girl, choosing to ignore the question. "You're not an Indian," she said like a detective solving a case. "You're Japanese."

"Chinese," Li Soong corrected, suddenly realizing the jeopardy of her admission.

Mrs. Allen saw the troubled look on Li Soong's face. "Don't worry about me, I'm not prejudiced," she said bluntly.

"I'm glad," Li Soong said, relaxing slightly.

"Lots of folks are bad about that kind of thing, and don't I know it, too," the old woman said as she passed a plate of *huevos rancheros* to Jeffrey.

"Why do you say that?" he asked, pouring honey into a warm *sopaipilla*.

"Because my own husband was a Navajo Indian. And we got kicked from pillar to post plenty before we settled here."

"But Allen isn't an Indian name," Jeffrey said.

"His tribal name was Nanombe, but when he married me they forbade him to use it."

"Is your husband dead?" he asked.

"Five years ago. We were married thirty-eight years."

"Wow." Jeffrey whistled under his breath. "Thirty-eight years—that's forever."

"I wish it had been," Mrs. Allen said sadly. "How long have you two been married?"

Li Soong shifted uncomfortably in her chair. "Not long," she said.

Mrs. Allen pursued the question. "How long?"

"Just a few weeks," she lied.

"Newlyweds!" The old woman clapped her hands. "You've got it all ahead of you still."

"I don't know about that," Jeffrey said wistfully.

"Well, of course you do," Mrs. Allen said, choreographing the meal by keeping the platters of food in motion.

Jeffrey sank back in the comfortable chair, trying to absorb the calm shelter of the old woman's house, trying not to think of the phone call they had agreed to make. Just as they had decided to give themselves up they had found each other, and the idea of surrendering to their old lives now seemed impossible. The burden of their false identities and constant vigilance now seemed even more oppressive, and in the peaceful atmosphere of Mrs. Allen's dining room he fought the urge to break out of their covert life, to tell her who they were. He longed for a way to stay forever in the clean sanctuary of the blue and white room at the top of the stairs, to sever all connections with the past that pursued them, to lose himself in the slipstream of Li Soong's arms for time without measure.

He reached out his hand under the fresh linen of the table to touch her.

*

The ticking of the clock cut the morning into tiny slices and swallowed them up. Mrs. Allen and her guests drank the last of the coffee as they sat together around the table.

"It's all right with me if you want to stay an extra night," the old woman said. "I got plenty of room."

"I wish we could," Jeffrey said, sensing the lonliness that undershadowed her offer.

"I'll only charge you half."

"Could we?" Li Soong asked, casting a glance at Jeffrey.

He had become so accustomed to moving on that he

had never considered the possibility of enjoying the luxury of staying. "Why not?" he said happily, the burden of their flight temporarily lifted.

"All right," Mrs. Allen said in a businesslike tone. "If you're going to stay, there's plenty to do. Seeing that you're newlyweds and all, you can work off one night's lodging by doing chores."

"Like what?" Jeffrey asked.

"I need someone who can climb a ladder without getting dizzy. My gutters are all clogged up, and I have a mess of papers in the attic that need to be bundled up and put outside. You look like you could reach the rafters and straighten the shingles I've got up there. Then—"

"Okay," Jeffrey said. "You've got your man. Can my . . . wife help too?"

"I'll find something for her to do, don't you worry."

*

By late afternoon, Jeffrey had cleaned gutters, patched up the roof, regroated the bathtub and more. All the while, Mrs. Allen stood behind him, supervising, helping, making sure that each job was done just so. By the time her house was back to perfect, Jeffrey's clothes were a composite of paint and plaster splotches.

"Is that all?" he asked. He was weary but enjoying the domesticity of the household tasks.

"Unless you want to hold up the house while I dust under the foundation."

"You should have asked me earlier before I got tired."

"You more than paid for your room and board. Why not stay the week free of charge?"

"I'll have to consult with my wife." Jeffrey began to enjoy referring to Li Soong that way. "Where is she, anyway?"

"She had some notion of cooking dinner. I've never let another woman in my kitchen. But you're newlyweds, and she told me she hasn't even cooked you a meal yet, so I let her go ahead."

"Li Soong is cooking? What?"

"She wouldn't tell me. Said it was a surprise."

*

When Jeffrey descended the stairs, scrubbed and refreshed, Li Soong and Mrs. Allen were huddled together in the kitchen.

"You set the table. The plates are in the cupboard." Mrs. Allen directed him.

Li Soong was too engrossed in her activities to even look into the dining room where he stood.

"What smells?" he asked, making a face.

"Cabbage and red peppers," Mrs. Allen called from the kitchen. "She's been in here dicing and stirring all day."

"Cabbage and red peppers," Jeffrey muttered as he took the plates from the cupboard.

"You'll find forks in the drawer," Mrs. Allen called out.

Li Soong turned from the stove. "No, wait," she called to Jeffrey. "Do you have any lengths of wood about twelve by one centimeter?" she asked Mrs. Allen. "Something about the size of a pencil?"

"I have pencils. What for, dear?"

"Yes, pencils will do. I want to make chopsticks."

Jeffrey and Mrs. Allen found six pencils and cut off the points and erasers while Li Soong worked in the kitchen. She banished them both from her work area as the preparation neared completion. Finally, the door to the kitchen opened and Li Soong emerged victorious.

"Tonight," she beamed, "I have cooked for you a Chinese meal. I have been able to use much of what is native to this region, and substituted similar ingredients where necessary."

"Let's see it," Jeffrey said, now intrigued by the spicy smells coming from the kitchen.

"Wait here," she instructed Jeffrey and Mrs. Allen, and she began bringing platters forth into the dining room. "First, we have pork with hot peppers, a Szechuan dish which I was able to recreate with the native Mexican dried peppers in your cupboard."

"What's that?" Mrs. Allen asked, pointing to a crisp-skinned bird sided by thinly sliced cucumbers.

"It is my version of salt roasted chicken; those cucumbers are quite spicy. There are egg shreds and cold stirred vegetables, and steamed pears with honey, also a version of sesame noodle in which I substituted peanut oil and crushed sesame seeds for the correct ingredients."

"Well, let's dig in," Mrs. Allen said adventuresomely. "First, you have to show me how to eat with these pencils."

"Yow!" Jeffrey yelped. He had swallowed a piece of the pork and hot peppers. "I'm on fire." He downed his glass of water.

"I warned you it was hot."

Mrs. Allen took a small taste, chewing it carefully. "Um, that's tasty."

"You don't find it too hot?" Li Soong asked.

"Not too bad. But I was raised on these peppers."

"Good," Li Soong said, passing her the chicken. "Try this."

By the end of the meal, Mrs. Allen had mastered the mock chopsticks, and Jeffrey had been won over by the complex and searingly spicy food. Hardly anything remained on the platters as the three of them fell back into their chairs, stuffed and happy.

"You look pleased with yourself," Jeffrey teased Li Soong as the girl surveyed the empty plates.

"I am," she said. "I am happy you enjoyed my efforts."

"Your efforts were delicious," Jeffrey said, walking to where she sat and kissing her forehead. "I'll do the dishes."

"Leave those where they are," Mrs. Allen commanded. "You both worked enough today. You go on upstairs and I'll finish here."

It took little more than a few words to send Jeffrey and Li Soong arm in arm up the stairs to the blue and white room at the end of the hall.

*

"Are you going to stay the week?" Mrs. Allen asked after breakfast the next morning.

"No, we have decided that we must move on," Li Soong said softly.

"But the next time we pass through . . ." Jeffrey began, wishing he was a character in another life. "Next time, we'll stay longer."

"I hope you do," Mrs. Allen said. "And I hope I'm still around to keep this place going when you get here."

Li Soong attempted her question from earlier. "Then it is hard for you to make a living?"

"Of course it is," Mrs. Allen replied firmly. "Everything's hard when you're old. You can't just pick up and start again. You have to sit and wait for life to come to you."

"And does it?" Li Soong asked tenderly.

"Not often. But that's my problem, not yours."

Li Soong looked surprised by the remark. "Why do you say that?"

A soft look tempered Mrs. Allen's face. "Because I've had it all, and I'm grateful for that. I know when people stop here it's for their convenience, and I don't expect them to take on my problems for the price of a room."

"But that is awful," Li Soong said. "We are all each other's concern."

"You say that now, but when you leave here I don't

expect you will be thinking much of me. You and your husband will be figuring out ways to enjoy each other."

Li Soong looked pained at the truth of her words.

"Don't look so sad," Mrs. Allen said. "I'm a survivor, and that's what you should be too. When I was your age I had a ball, and now it's your turn. When you've lived your life right, it's not so bad to watch other people take their turn at it."

"We would stay on if we could," Jeffrey interjected.

"Of course you would, but you can't," Mrs. Allen said in a mock-businesslike tone. "So how about if we settle up for the room and board before you two start to cry."

"But—" Jeffrey said.

"But nothing, you owe me twelve dollars," she said, enjoying her guests' compassion.

Jeffrey stood up and reached into his pocket. He walked to the head of the table where she sat and handed her twelve dollars.

She pushed his hand back at him, shaking her head. "Take that money away!"

"Why?" Jeffrey questioned, recounting it. "Twelve dollars, like you said."

"And what's it for?" Mrs. Allen said, folding her arms over her narrow chest.

"I don't know. Room and board, I imagine," he said nervously.

"And what did I say to you yesterday?"

"Uh, that the work I did was payment for the room?"

"Then why are you giving me twelve dollars?" the woman asked gleefully.

"Because you asked for it," Jeffrey countered.

"And I suppose you give your money away to anyone who asks for it?" Mrs. Allen clucked her tongue. "You won't get very far with that attitude. "Twelve dollars is a ridiculous amount for room and board."

Li Soong began to smile at Jeffrey's unease.

"And you, young lady." Mrs. Allen focused on the girl through her fish-bowl lenses. "It's your job to make a dollar stretch until it howls for mercy. How do you think my husband and I got this house and car on the little money we had?"

"Please take the twelve dollars," Jeffrey said. "We can afford it—"

"No matter what you might think, this isn't a charity ward." Mrs. Allen looked at the tattered clothes on her two guests. "How can you sit there in those rags and give me money?"

"We're not as poor as we seem," Jeffrey said. "Honestly."

"And I suppose that broken-down heap of a pickup truck outside my house is actually a Cadillac you disguised for the occasion," Mrs. Allen scolded. "That car is in worse shape than me."

"Well . . . we were planning to hitchhike the rest of the way."

" 'Hitchhike,' he says as he gives away his money." Mrs. Allen assumed a look of shocked outrage.

"Actually, the truck's out of gas. That's all that's wrong with it," Jeffrey said.

"And when his car runs out of gas, he discards it," the old woman said with a flourish of indignation.

"It's a long story." Jeffrey tried to extricate himself. "If we could get a ride into town, we could get some gas and then come back and fuel it up."

"I see," Mrs. Allen said imperiously. "And then drive five miles until it breaks down so you can give all your money away to some crooked mechanic."

"I hope not," Jeffrey said. "You don't have a car that we could borrow just to drive into town and get some gas, do you?"

"I don't make a habit of lending my car."

"I see," Jeffrey said politely. "All right."

"All right in a pig's eye!" Mrs. Allen exclaimed. "You need a car or not?"

"Yes, yes, we do," Jeffrey said.

"Then it's not all right for me to have one sitting here when you need it."

"But it's yours," Jeffrey argued against his favor. "I couldn't make you give it to me."

"Why not? You didn't even try. You're not going to get very far in life with that attitude."

"Does this mean you'll lend it to me?"

"You tell me," the old woman said. "Will I?"

Jeffrey looked at Li Soong, who seemed to be enjoying the strange argument. "Yes, you will," he said positively.

"Why would I do a foolish thing like that?" Mrs. Allen said, immensely pleased with herself.

"Because we need it, and it wouldn't hurt you to do us a favor."

"That's better," she said. "Now, if you watch your money and learn to be a mean bastard like I taught you, you'll do all right. There's just one problem."

"Now what?" Li Soong asked, joining the colloquy.

"I won't have anyone dressed like you driving in my car."

"How about if we get undressed," Jeffrey offered.

Mrs. Allen raised her brow. "Not in my car you don't."

Jeffrey looked hard into the woman's face, trying to decipher a clue to the new game. "We can't afford to buy new clothes," he said sternly. "You'll just have to let us drive it the way we are."

"Absolutely not." Mrs. Allen stood and walked away from the table towards the stairway.

"Hey, wait." Jeffrey trailed her. "I'm sorry if I was rude."

Mrs. Allen turned around and glared at him. "I didn't hear that."

Jeffrey and Li Soong followed in her wake until they arrived at her bedroom door. "Wait here," she said, stepping inside to rummage through a closet. She appeared at the door moments later. In each hand she held a clothes hanger draped with a vintage outfit. "This is for you." She held out an immaculate white linen suit towards Jeffrey. "And this is for you." She laid a green gingham dress on Li Soong's outstretched arms. "Hard to believe I had a figure like that once," she said, admiring Li Soong's youthful body.

"You want us to wear these?" Jeffrey asked.

"Of course," Mrs. Allen said, pushing both of them into her bedroom. "You change in here. Look in the closet, and if you see a pair of shoes that fits, take it too."

They heard the woman pad her way back down the hall. Inside her room they slipped out of their worn denims and into the dated outfits. Jeffrey zipped her dress up the back as Li Soong selected a billowy white shirt for him from the small pile that Mrs. Allen had laid out on the bed.

"That must be her husband," Jeffrey said, pointing to an old portrait on the dresser. They walked closer to admire the sepia gravure that showed a strong-featured man in a white linen suit with his arm around a young woman.

"And that must be Mrs. Allen," Li Soong said, staring at the old memento. "Wasn't she pretty."

"Very," Jeffrey mused as he looked from the photo to Li Soong, who was trying on a pair of sea-green shoes with tiny buttons that secured them to her ankles. "How do they fit?" he asked as she took a tentative step on the modest heels.

"Fine." She smiled shyly. "They are a little large, but I can certainly wear them."

"You look beautiful," Jeffrey said. He walked closer and put his arms around her. "It's funny, but I would have thought that wearing someone else's old clothes would give me the creeps . . . but I like it."

"So do I," Li Soong said. "I feel like I have been reborn."

"It reminds me of when I was a kid. I used to lie awake at night and pretend I had a magic suit that made me invisible. I could go anywhere and do anything in it."

"That sounds wonderful," Li Soong said. "Do you think these clothes are magical? Will we be able to do as we like without notice?"

"If they were"—Jeffrey considered—"she'd never tell us. We'd have to find out the hard way."

"Certainly," Li Soong said, feeling giddy in his embrace. "Perhaps we should test them, walk in crowds, go to parties . . . see if we are still flesh and blood."

"I agree," Jeffrey said, whirling her around the room. "I bet I could go anywhere, do anything I wanted to. How about you?"

"Absolutely the same," Li Soong agreed as she waltzed circles with him.

*

Mrs. Allen stood at the bottom of the stairs with a single key in her hand. "That's more like it," she said as her eyes skimmed over Jeffrey and Li Soong. "Now you look respectable."

"Thank you," Li Soong said modestly. "They are lovely clothes."

"The car's in the garage. I'll show you how to start it."

They followed her out of the house and around back to a white garage padlocked with a long chain. "Now this here's an old car, but it's in good shape," Mrs. Allen said, jiggling the lock until the chain slipped from the latch.

"Do you drive it?" Jeffrey asked, worried that they might find a cobweb-covered relic with an engine turned to rust.

"Never do," Mrs. Allen said. "My eyes are too bad. But I have a mechanic come from town to keep it oiled, and he runs it back and forth for me."

"Why do you keep it, then?" Li Soong asked. "And how do you get your groceries?"

"I have friends. You can see I don't starve. And about the car, I know it's worth money, and I'm going to sell it someday—when the right person comes along."

"Have you tried?" Jeffrey asked, pushing the doors of the garage apart.

"Not recently," she said. "But I will. Now, I'll go in and start it up and you pull open these doors for me. They're heavy." She slipped into the blackness of the garage, and Jeffrey heard an engine turn over once, then rev to life.

"Open the doors!" Mrs. Allen commanded as Jeffrey and Li Soong pulled them in opposite directions.

"My God, what is that?" Jeffrey cried as a black bathtublike form emerged into the light.

"It's a Hudson Commodore," Mrs. Allen called from the driver's seat. "Isn't it elegant?"

"It's something," Jeffrey exclaimed. "It looks like a whale."

Li Soong gasped. "How old is it?"

"Nineteen forty-eight," Mrs. Allen proclaimed, bringing it to a halt in front of them. She turned off the engine and stepped outside the car to admire it along with the couple. The Southwestern sun twinkled off the black lacquer paint as if it were an ebony mirror tied with thick ribbons of chrome.

Jeffrey stuck his head inside and admired the maroon velvet of the seats. "This is unbelievable," he said, falling in love with the decades-old luxury of the vehicle.

Mrs. Allen beamed as Jeffrey and Li Soong paced the car, touching it lightly, admiring its design and detail. "It is nice, isn't it?" She beamed as the two young people reflected off its polished skin.

"Get inside, I'll show you how it works," she said, opening a heavy door. Jeffrey climbed behind the steering wheel as Mrs. Allen proceeded to explain each button and dial and glass pod and silver ring across the dashboard. ". . . And this here light comes on if the oil is running low." She pointed to a thick red lens. "Mr. Allen was very fussy about that. He always got the best oil—like Milton Berle used to advertise."

"Milton Berle?" Jeffrey looked puzzled.

"Now, I want you to take good care of this car. It's not like any other," she said, placing the keys in Jeffrey's hand.

"We're only going to town," he said. "We'll be back in an hour, at most."

"That's not why I'm giving you the key," Mrs. Allen said as she sat next to him on the cushioned seat. "I'm giving you the car for good, because I know you can use it."

"I can't accept it," he said. "Not a car!"

"It's not new enough for you!" Mrs. Allen said in a vinegar voice. "It will do until you can afford a fancy one."

"It's not that." Jeffrey flushed. "It's just that a car like this must be worth a fortune. It's a collector's item, and I can't pay for it."

"Did I ask you for money?" Mrs. Allen said feistily. "Funny, I can't recall."

"You didn't," Jeffrey said. "But you should have. Someone will come along and give you a lot of money for it. Have you advertised?"

Mrs. Allen threw up her veined hands and waved them in front of Jeffrey's face. "I want you to have this car, and that's all there is to it! If you get some money sometime, send it to me. If not, I'll know it has a good home with the two of you."

"But why us?" Jeffrey asked, looking into the weathered face.

"Because you're so green, you wouldn't know how to buy a good used car if you had to," she said toughly. "And because I want to. Now, do you want it or not?" "Yes," Jeffrey said emphatically, and he threw his arms around the old woman's neck.

"Save all that for your wife," Mrs. Allen said, untangling herself from him. "Now, get going before I have to feed you dinner."

Jeffrey eased the car along the driveway, then watched Li Soong hug Mrs. Allen before she climbed in.

"Take good care of it." Mrs. Allen pointed a finger at Jeffrey.

"Don't worry, we will," he assured her.

"And change the oil," she called out as he began to pick up speed.

"I will, just like Milton Berle," Jeffrey called.

"And come back and see me sometime," she said. They had already reached the end of the driveway, and were waving excitedly back to her as they pulled onto the road. "You be careful," she said, but her words floated unheard into the dry desert air.

*

The Hudson was parked at the edge of an overhang that looked out on the Hopi nation. Jeffrey and Li Soong had wound their way past miles of scrub brush and grazing sheep to the top of the red mesa.

"It hurts my eyes to look at it," Li Soong said, pointing to the striated rocks that glowed under the desert sun. "Surely this must be the most beautiful place in America."

"We can't judge until we've seen them all," Jeffrey said, spreading a map of the United States across their laps in the front seat. Thousands of tiny red and blue veins that translated as roads offered paths that were theirs for the choosing.

Li Soong surveyed the map, reciting names of towns

like an incantation. "Tehachapi, Zillah, Owatonna, Dinuba . . . Where will we go after this?" she asked, leaning against the velvet cushions of the car.

"Let's pick a place at random." Jeffrey spun his finger and plunked it down on Akron, Ohio.

"Is that as beautiful as this?" Li Soong asked.

"Only if you like tires," Jeffrey said negatively. "Let me do it again." He closed his eyes and dangled a finger above the country, swooping down onto the Atlantic Ocean. "I'm terrible at this. You decide." He pushed the map towards Li Soong.

"I don't like your methods," Li Soong announced. "They are not scientific." She perused the map with great seriousness as Jeffrey leaned over and nuzzled her neck. "Please." She tried to retain her composure. "I am concentrating . . . I have it," she said, pointing a victorious digit to the western part of the country.

"Las Vegas!" Jeffrey exclaimed. "Are you kidding?"

"No," Li Soong assured him. "I would like to see Las Vegas."

"But we can't go there. The streets teem with people, it's more lit up than a Christmas tree. We'll be spotted in a minute."

"We have seen only mountains and goats and the desert. It would be wonderful to be lost in crowds of people for a change."

"Can we risk it?"

"Of course," Li Soong said, snuggling close to him. "Remember, we are wearing our magic outfits. We are invisible."

"How could I forget?" Jeffrey said, turning the key in the ignition. "Next stop—Las Vegas."

*

The Hudson cut across the desert until they came upon the neon city. It was eleven at night, and Jeffrey parked at the edge of the wasteland to gaze at the lights ahead as a desert breeze perfumed the car.

He looked at Li Soong, her image framed by the tubular chrome of the window's edge. The scimitar curves of her cheekbones and the luster of her skin made his heart pound.

"What is it, Jeffrey?" she asked, glancing away from the lights' glow. "Have you changed your mind?"

"No," he said, feeling slightly mad with his runaway passion for the girl.

"Then, let's go. Look how exciting it looks from here, like a comet that fell from the heavens."

"Li Soong . . ." Jeffrey hesitated. "What if something happens, what if we're recognized? I couldn't stand to lose you."

Li Soong played with the collar of her vintage dress, finally turning to look at him. "Please don't say that," she said, and he could see the tears form in her eyes.

"But what if . . ." Jeffrey began, silenced by her small hand on his lips.

She moved closer to him, stroking the sides of his face with her fingers. "I love you," she said. "I never thought it would happen, but it has."

"I love you too," he repeated the words.

"It shouldn't have happened," she said. "It goes against everything I have ever been taught, everything I have wanted for myself."

"I know. It's the last thing I could have believed would happen to me."

"And in our hearts"—Li Soong bit her lip to control her trembling—"in our hearts we know that someday—"

Now it was Jeffrey who stifled her words. "Don't say it," he pleaded.

She looked at him with a profound gaze, nodding her head in agreement. "All right, then, let neither of us mention it again. We will not talk with words like *forever*, or *tomorrow*, or *someday*—"

"Stop," Jeffrey cried as he pulled her close to him so they could hold each other.

"And we will continue fearlessly ahead," Li Soong said.

"Are you ready?" he asked as he drew in a great breath of air.

"Of course," she answered, and the Hudson crested the hill and sailed into Las Vegas.

*

"Let's park the car and walk around," Jeffrey said recklessly as they cruised the light-soaked streets. All around them gamblers, showgirls, nighthawks, whores and tourists milled beneath behemoth signs.

A loudspeaker boomed from the front of a tour bus: "Las Vegas! Glittering mecca of gaiety and gold, where a billion candlepower turns night into day, where Aladdin and Caesar beckon, where the Riviera and Dunes await your whim!"

"Wonderful!" Li Soong clapped her hands as she bounced on the car seat. "Can we gamble?"

"Why not?" Jeffrey said, feeling intoxicated from the surreal commotion that surrounded them.

They parked the car and wandered into Caesar's Palace, gawking like all the other newcomers at the siliconed superwomen who paraded their wares. Li Soong pulled Jeffrey by the arm as a white-wigged Amazon with amethyst lipstick rolled her hips for him.

"How do you work this?" she asked, directing him to a nearby one-armed bandit. Jeffrey deposited a stream of coins into the baroque contraption as Li Soong pulled the handle and sent the cherries and stars spinning in their orbits.

"We've got a winner!" a floor boss said as a siren trilled and a rush of silver coins cascaded into Jeffrey and Li Soong's hands.

"Let's play poker," she said, rushing towards the casino.

Jeffrey started to laugh. "What do you know about poker?"

"Nothing, but you said you always win at it."

Jeffrey thought back to one of his boasts on Air Force One. "You remember that?"

"Certainly," she said. "I remember everything you have told me."

"Oh, oh." He grinned. "I'm in trouble. Let's walk around outside." He steered Li Soong towards the door.

Jeffrey felt euphoric as the two of them walked the streets of the electrified city. They enjoyed the crush of people, all so involved in their own lives and their own hustles that they paid little heed to the young couple. The coins they won jingled in their pockets. "Let's spend some money," Jeffrey said. "We're too rich."

"I like that," Li Soong agreed, pointing to a souvenir store. "Let's go in there."

After investigating the souvenirs, they finally settled on two manically ugly felt hats with ostrich feathers and the legend LAS VEGAS scribbled on their brims. Jeffrey paid the man with their winnings from the slot machine, and they donned their hats and walked for the door.

Two men blocked their way. As Jeffrey's eyes locked on them, he was hit with a shot of adrenalin. He cautiously reached for Li Soong. "This might be trouble," he said under his breath as they continued for the door.

"Hey, you," one of the men said, collaring Jeffrey.

"Get your damn hands off me!" Jeffrey demanded as toughly as he could.

To his surprise, the man broke his grip. He looked almost sheepish.

"You're blocking my way," Jeffrey said, anxious to get on the other side of the door. Li Soong huddled close to him.

"You're that kid," the man said in a hopeful voice.

"I don't know what you're talking about," Jeffrey said, attempting to push through them.

"Sure you do," the man said almost desperately. "The kid, Hodge, the one the whole world's looking for." He took a folded-up newspaper page out of his pocket and showed it gleefully to the man who was with him. "See, I told you."

"They said they ain't," the other man said.

"We're not," Jeffrey said angrily. "Now let us by."

A few people had begun to collect, watching the argument. Jeffrey and Li Soong watched painfully as the men's voices grew louder.

"It is them."

"It isn't them."

"Is."

"Isn't."

Jeffrey shook the man who flapped the newspaper as he argued. He looked at him desperately, then at Li Soong. "It is," he finally yelled. "Now let us by." He grabbed Li Soong and they ran into the street.

"I won, I won!" The man inside the store danced with glee. "You owe me five hundred bucks. I won!"

As they ran, Jeffrey and Li Soong looked back, but to their surprise no one pursued them. They slowed their steps. "I can't believe it," Jeffrey panted. "They didn't want us. They only cared about their bet."

"How amazing," Li Soong said ebulliently. "We *are* touched with magic."

"Let's not strain our powers any more," Jeffrey said. "Where's the car?"

They found the Hudson as they had left it, its finish mirroring rainbows of light.

"Are you tired yet?" Jeffrey asked as they pulled away from the city.

"No," she said breathlessly. "I don't want to sleep at all. Today is a special day for me."

"Special?" Jeffrey echoed. "Why?"

"It's my birthday," she said, rolling down her window and letting the wind toss her hair.

"You're kidding!" Jeffrey said, screeching on the brakes.

"Why would I make that up?"

"Your birthday!"

"It's not that important," Li Soong said. "I hardly celebrate it at home."

"How old are you?"

"Eighteen," Li Soong said with a smile.

Jeffrey whooped a celebratory cry. "It's birthday-party time."

*

They drove for an hour before they got to the speck of a town called Borax Creek. The general store sign had been turned off hours ago, but Jeffrey's pounding on the door finally woke the owner. Seeing Jeffrey was a paying customer, the man checked his rifle on the counter and opened the door.

As Li Soong waited in the car, Jeffrey scanned the shelves of the store, piecing together the makings for his eclectic celebration.

"I've got it," he said, bounding towards the car, balancing two shopping bags in his arms, leaving his casino winnings behind. He laid the bags on the back seat. "Now we have to find a suitable spot."

They drove until Jeffrey settled for a formation of rocks that signaled a natural cave. He insisted Li Soong not leave the car until he called her; then he disappeared into the darkness of the rocks, toting his bags.

Li Soong watched the illuminated clock on the dashboard until finally she heard Jeffrey call. When she arrived at the entrance to the cave, she gasped. Inside, dozens of candles had been secured by their own wax to the rocks. Stones had been draped with pink streamers.

Confetti glittered in the light of sparklers that blazed in random crevices. Jeffrey had cleared a circle on the floor and laid out a sheet of crepe paper, on which he had placed a cake ringed with smaller candles. "It's wondrous!" Li Soong said as she walked inside.

"This is just the beginning." Jeffrey plunked a gold paper crown on her head and blew a pitiful honk from his saggy party horn.

Li Soong's hand reached up to touch the crown. She spun around to see Jeffrey take a bottle of wine from behind another rock.

"I think they've had this bottle since the gold rush," he said, dusting it off. "It's probably worth a fortune." He pulled at the cork with his penknife and emptied its contents into two Dixie cups.

"You haven't forgotten anything," Li Soong said merrily.

"This is your first American birthday. And now, the cake." With the penknife he tapped the icing of the little cake. "I think this has been around since the gold rush, too," he said as he attempted to break the brittle surface. He cut two pieces, and as Li Soong nibbled at the corner of hers Jeffrey waltzed over to another rock.

"And now, the presents," he announced with a flourish. He pulled a box from behind the stone and approached Li Soong. "Something every woman needs," he said, handing her a small package.

She tore at the wrappings until she reached a tiny bottle of perfume inside. "Savage Sin?" Li Soong pondered the scent's strange name. She unscrewed the top and sniffed it, making her eyes tear.

"And here is something no home should be without." Jeffrey handed her another box.

Li Soong lifted a set of plastic dentures from the box, then a key. Mystified, she looked to Jeffrey for an explanation.

"Chattering teeth," he said, winding them up and sending them scooting across the crepe-paper mat. Li Soong's look of disbelief turned to laughter as she shared the ridiculous gag with Jeffrey.

"And this is because you are so sweet." She accepted a large red satin heart filled with candy that had not aged well.

"And now, the *pièce de résistance*," he proclaimed, tooting a fanfare on his party horn: "Ta ta . . ." He handed her a small package. "Open it."

Li Soong removed the gold foil wrapping and found a small hand-tooled picture frame. No more than two inches long, the leather was embossed with saddles and spurs and brands and all things Western. The words *remember me* were burnt into the top of the frame. In the space that allowed for a portrait, Jeffrey had inserted a picture of himself torn from a newspaper.

"Do you like it?" he asked as Li Soong cradled it in her hand.

"Yes, Jeffrey," she said tenderly as she held it. "I like it very much."

"Then let's drink a toast to this special day," he said, raising his Dixie cup in the air and putting his arm around her shoulders.

They drank the wine and with light hearts reclined against the rocks to enjoy the candle-strewn beauty of the cave and their precious time together.

*

The odometer on the Hudson spun like a magic top, as if Mrs. Allen's car were a charmed carriage that let them pass freely through the land. Desert bronze gave way to green, and as they traveled into California, mountains mellowed out to the sea.

The wheels of the car slowed, coming to a stop on a cliff that jutted over the Pacific Ocean. They stood by the car under a low-hanging sky, and felt the chill of the sea mist.

Jeffrey sensed Li Soong's distress. "What is it?" he asked, hoping to rekindle the warmth that had become so familiar.

"The water." She sighed. "And what lies on the other side."

"China." Jeffrey said the word as if confessing a secret. "I think we have run out of land." And the breaking waves offered up a wreath of water that stung like briny tears.

Eleven

THE LACQUER PAINT of the Hudson was beaded with dew, its windows misty from the warmth of the two people who slept inside. Jeffrey's eyes snapped open as if he had been startled into wakefulness. He listened, but heard no close sounds—only the distant foghorns and bells of San Francisco Bay. He unwound himself from Li Soong's arms and climbed over into the front seat, wiping the windshield clear with his hand.

"Li Soong," he said quietly, reaching back and gently touching her shoulder. "Look."

The girl smiled at the face that looked at her. She raised up and gazed with Jeffrey over the hood of the car. The edge of a full moon was beginning to cut into the Pacific. Backlighted by the brilliant lunar white and bathed in the gray haze that signaled dawn, the Farallone Islands jutted across the horizon like pieces of an abstract granite puzzle.

They watched the white disc drop lower. Li Soong spoke: "It is hard to believe that I have lived my whole life on the other side of that moon without ever knowing you were here."

Jeffrey let her words wash over him. "When I was a kid, we used to believe that if you dug straight down into the earth you could reach China. Did you think the same for America?"

"No." Li Soong shook her head. "We were taught only what is logical and real."

"You have no fairy tales?"

"Of course we have fairy tales, but we do not believe in them. They are based on wishes and dreams that can never be." She watched the last of the moon disappear behind the Farallones. "And how did your fairy tales turn out? Did people live happily ever after?"

"Sometimes," Jeffrey said, sensing a question behind the question.

"And what would determine how they were to end?" Li Soong probed.

"Different things," Jeffrey said, intertwining his hand with hers. "If you were pure of heart, if you wished hard enough—"

"Jeffrey, how hard are you wishing?" Li Soong asked, looking deep into his eyes.

"Very hard." He felt the words catch in his throat. "And you?"

She couldn't bring herself to answer.

"You have to want this as much as I do," Jeffrey said, with a desperate edge to his words.

"I do . . . But I cannot believe in magic, Jeffrey, in invisible clothes, in wishing stars, I cannot—"

"Can you believe in me?" he asked, holding her face between his hands. "Can you believe in us?"

Li Soong slowly nodded.

"Then I'll find a happy ending for us. I promise, Li Soong."

She searched for reassurance in their embrace, but found only premonitions of despair.

*

"I wish we hadn't come here," Li Soong said gloomily as they drove up the coast highway towards the city of San Francisco.

236 · *Friendly Relations*

"Why?" Jeffrey asked.

"I hate seeing the Pacific waters. I know that my father might be looking at them the same time we are."

"Your father," Jeffrey repeated. "Do you know it's been days since you've mentioned him?"

"Has it?" Li Soong said distractedly.

"Um hm," Jeffrey said, slowing as the Hudson mounted one of the city's steep hills.

"This car is a mess," Li Soong said, edgily changing the subject.

"You're in a great mood. What's the matter with you?"

"Everything about this place worries me. I feel that we are closed in, that there is no place left to run."

"All right," Jeffrey said, slamming his hands on the wheel. "So we made a mistake. We'll head north and then decide where to go from there. Look at the map and see what you want to do."

"Later," Li Soong said. "I'll do it later."

Jeffrey felt the car buck as he topped a hill. "Damn!" he cursed. "I think the moisture in the air is ruining the engine. Mrs. Allen always kept this car in the desert, and the dampness is going to screw it up."

"We should bring it back to her."

"Too dangerous," Jeffrey said, starting to share Li Soong's free-floating discomfort. "We can't retrace our steps anywhere. Didn't you hear the radio? The FBI is practically in the back seat."

"Then we should sell it and start hitchhiking again."

"Too dangerous," Jeffrey repeated.

"Then what *can* we do?" Li Soong's voice escalated.

"Don't yell at me! What makes you think I have all the answers around here?"

"You always acted like you did," she said, looking more frightened than mad.

"Well, I don't. I'm sorry, Li Soong, if I've let you down."

"I'm sorry too," she said, trying to extinguish the little flare-up. "It's my fault. I just woke up in a funny mood."

"Friends?" Jeffrey reached out his hand to her.

"No sweat," Li Soong replied.

"But we do have to make new plans," Jeffrey said, somewhat wearily. "We can't let our guard down."

"Of course not," Li Soong agreed, but her voice seemed dispirited. "We will persevere."

Jeffrey pulled the car around a steep corner and maneuvered into a narrow alleyway, where he put on the brakes. "The first thing we have to do is clean up our home." He surveyed the litter inside the car. "Mrs. Allen would drop dead if she saw all these candy wrappers and garbage."

"You're right," Li Soong said, stepping out of the car and pulling a garbage can close.

"We'll feel a hundred percent better once we're organized," Jeffrey said as he sorted through the back seat. He extracted one of their Las Vegas hats and put it on his head. "What do you think?" He offered the other to Li Soong.

"Throw them out," she replied, surprised by her own decision. She wanted to soften the harsh words. "They look silly in the light of day. Anyway, we have memories of them, here." She pointed to her forehead.

Jeffrey pulled out Li Soong's birthday presents.

"Don't throw that away!" she said as he held the little frame with his picture in it. She tucked it safely in her dress pocket and found a place for the chattering teeth in the car's glove compartment.

As they sorted through the layers of souvenirs, Jeffrey discovered the pawn ticket for the watch he had traded for cash. "Doesn't this seem like years ago?" he asked.

"We've come many miles since Alabama," she agreed.

He looked at the pawn ticket and read, *"Bi-Rite Pawn, Exmoor, Alabama.* You know, that's Hazleton's home state. I wonder if he knows Exmoor . . . I've got a great idea. I'm going to put this in an envelope and mail it to him. He'll love it."

"I like that." Li Soong smiled. "We promised we'd write."

*

"Now we are set to go on," Li Soong said, surveying the immaculate interior of the Hudson.

"As soon as I mail this, we're on the road," Jeffrey said, easing the car out of the alley and searching the streets for a small post office.

"Is it my imagination, or do people stare at us as we drive?" Li Soong asked.

"It's the car. Driving it in the city, we may as well advertise our presence."

"We are no longer invisible. Our magic is gone," she said.

"Don't say that, Li Soong."

"There's a post office," she said, looking out the window instead of at Jeffrey.

"What's wrong with you today?" Jeffrey hesitated to get out of the car.

"Please, just mail the letter and let's leave."

Jeffrey got out and took two steps towards the building, then hesitated and turned back towards the car. He tapped on the window and she rolled it down. "You know, I think you're scaring me with your weird vibes, but just in case something does happen . . . if I'm recognized in there, I want you to run."

"Run? Run where?" Her voice was agitated.

"Anywhere. I'll get away and find you."

"How?"

"I'll find you, just run."

"Where?" she insisted.

"Chinatown." Jeffrey picked the name at random. "How about there?"

"What?" Li Soong asked. "Did you say 'Chinatown'?"

"Uh huh. It's a famous part of the city—"

"I know about Chinatown. I don't think that is a place I would like to be."

"I'm not asking you to move there, for Pete's sake."

"I have seen pictures of those plastic pagodas and silly decorations. It is a disgrace."

"Okay, okay, sorry I mentioned it." Jeffrey threw up his hands. "Forget it. I'll be out in a flash. Just sit tight." He turned towards the post office again.

Li Soong watched him move away from the car, and even in her nervous state she allowed herself to admire him. He had metamorphosed during their time on the road. The droop of his linen suit accented the hardness of his body underneath, the transformation of his gentle Washington posture to a look of determination. She fretted to have him away from her for even a minute.

As he walked in the revolving door at the top of the steps, Li Soong turned back to the street. A thin, dark-suited figure was staring back and forth between the Hudson and the door of the post office. A dark beard obscured his face, wire-rimmed glasses made his eyes glare. Li Soong wondered, How long had he been watching them?

She slouched low in the front seat. The man walked closer to the car. She wanted to hit the horn to signal Jeffrey. Then the man turned and ran after him up the stairs of the post office.

Standing in the lobby, Jeffrey jumped as a hand grasped his shoulder.

"I didn't mean to startle you," the stranger apologized. The man looked with confusion at Jeffrey's shocked face. "My name is Roscoe Street," he extended his hand. "I'm a collector."

"A collector of what?" Jeffrey stammered, afraid to run, afraid to stay.

"Cars," he said. "I saw you park that Hudson outside. It's a beauty."

"A car collector!" Jeffrey felt a laugh forming, a hysterical bubble of release. "That's all?"

"Well, it may not seem like much to you, but in our little circle I'm regarded as quite—"

"Forgive me." Jeffrey soothed the stranger. "I thought you were . . . someone else."

Jeffrey edged forward in the post office line as the man handed him a business card. "Maybe you've heard of me. I run the Roscoe Street Auto Museum. It's a small one, but well thought of."

"Uh, no, I'm not from around here," Jeffrey said quietly.

"Funny, I thought I had seen you around."

Outside, Li Soong knew it had been too long. Jeffrey should have been out by now. Looking furtively each way, she got out of the parked car and headed towards the doors of the post office.

"You weren't thinking of selling that Hudson by any chance?" Street asked, sensing Jeffrey's edginess. "It never hurts to ask."

"No," Jeffrey said, moving closer in the line. He remembered Uncle Sid and their close call.

"Too bad. I could give you a good price."

"I couldn't." Jeffrey tried to discourage the man. "I don't have the title for it."

"Of course not," Roscoe Street said. "There are no titles for cars that old."

Jeffrey allowed himself to look at the man. He knew that driving the car was becoming impossible. In the desert, its rarity had not been a problem, but here in the city it turned too many heads. "How much?" Jeffrey ventured.

"I couldn't go over fifteen," Roscoe Street said flatly.

"Fifteen?" Jeffrey tilted his head. "Hundred?"

The man smiled. "I wouldn't insult you with an offer like that. Fifteen thousand, of course." He watched the amount register on Jeffrey's face. "I know you could probably get more at Harrah's or one of the larger museums, but we're just a little operation, give the cars the best of care—"

"Sold!" Jeffrey said, straining not to draw attention to his exhilaration.

"Sold? You mean it? It's mine?"

"It's yours," Jeffrey said, handing his envelope and change to the postal clerk.

"Come with me to the bank and I'll get you a cashier's check."

"Great," Jeffrey said, pulling the key out of his pocket. "But there are two conditions."

"Anything," Street agreed, as if mesmerized by the Hudson's key.

"You've got to put a plaque on it that says 'The Allen Special.' "

The man nodded enthusiastically. "It's done."

"And I want you to send the money to Mrs. Allen's Room and Board, Sweetwater, Arizona."

Roscoe Street tilted his head quizzically.

"My mother," Jeffrey explained. Then he held out the key. "You got that?"

"Mrs. Allen's Room and Board, Sweetwater, Arizona," Street repeated.

Jeffrey dropped the key in his hand and took a step towards the door. "Let's go."

"Fantastic!" The man whooped, looking at the key. He blocked Jeffrey's path towards the door and flung his arms around him in a dramatic bear hug that lifted him off the ground.

Li Soong had reached the glass doors of the post office. She looked in and saw what she most feared seeing. The man appeared to be grappling with Jeffrey, holding him, keeping him from leaving. She turned furiously, as if the violent gesture had been a starting gun, and without glancing back she ran.

Jeffrey finally sloughed off the embrace. "That's not necessary, Mr. Street."

"It's really mine," the car collector crooned, trying to compose himself.

As Jeffrey left the post office his glance went immediately to the Hudson. The car was empty. Li Soong was gone. "Gone." The word stuck in his throat. He turned frantically to Roscoe Street. "The girl in the car—"

"Mrs. Allen?"

"Yeah, where is she? Where did she go?"

"I don't know. I saw her sitting there when I chased you inside."

"Chased me?" Jeffrey said, the panic growing. "She saw you chase me?" He started down the steps as fast as he could move.

"Mr. Allen, wait," Street called after him. "About the car . . ." But Jeffrey had broken into a run, leaving the Hudson's newest owner behind. "Mr. Allen," he called out again, but his voice trailed off as he caught the splendid lines of his newest aquisition.

Roscoe Street looked at the Hudson Commodore and then to the key in his hand. He strode over and walked around it once. "What a beauty," he murmered to himself. *"The Allen Special."*

Jeffrey collided with a pedestrian who was lugging a bag of groceries up a steep hill. He scurried to put the things back in her arms, then breathlessly asked, "Which way to Chinatown?"

*

Jeffrey ran desperately through the foreign streets of Chinatown, ducking in and out of small shops that smelled of ginger root and tiger balm, overwhelmed by a mounting fear that he might never find her. He pushed

past people on the street, crazily running after phantom
girls who looked like Li Soong, grabbing their arms to
spin them around—only to be confronted by strange,
uncaring faces. Mumbling apologies, he searched on.

As night fell, hundreds of lanterns illuminated the
crowded streets. He heard shreds of conversation in
other tongues, the spill of atonal music mixing with
rock and roll. Almond-eyed girls walked by him, looking at his pained face, giggling to boyfriends who held
them protectively. Old women in saggy kimonos jostled him with their shopping bags. Tourists bustled by,
giddy and amused at the delights of the Chinese city
within a city.

Jeffrey felt he was spinning backwards in a blue ether
cloud. He covered the same streets in circles, losing track
of where he had been, repeating her name, rolling it on
his tongue like a piece of barley sugar that would fuel his
search. How could it all have ended so quickly? The car,
the maps, the plans and Li Soong, *vanished.* How easily
he had grown accustomed to her beside him. He could
not imagine another way, a day beginning without her
in his arms. Jeffrey knew that what had started for him
as a reckless adventure had now become his whole life.

A hand shot out of a doorway and grasped his shoulder. He froze, his mind shaken from the one-track obses-
sion that had propelled him. He turned to look. It was
Li Soong, her face haloed by the dark doorway in which
she stood. A shudder of relief shook Jeffrey's body, then
exploded in a wail that came from deep within. He
clutched her to him with all the energy he had left.

In the sanctuary of the hallway behind the door they
clung to one another, feeling the heave of each other's
breath like a calming lullabye. They rocked back and
forth, making little sounds of comfort, kissing and stroking each other's faces with trembling hands.

"I was so frightened," Li Soong said. "I thought that

man was trying to kill you. I thought I would never see you again."

"That could never happen," Jeffrey said. "Not to us."

"How did you break away?"

"I didn't have to. He wasn't after me. He only wanted to buy the car."

"The car? Did you sell it?"

Jeffrey nodded. "He's sending a check to Mrs. Allen. It's worth a fortune."

"That will help her . . . But what of us? How will we continue?"

"I don't know." Jeffrey leaned back against the wall. "We'll find a way."

"Maybe in the morning our heads will be clearer," Li Soong said, surveying the small space they occupied. "Do you think it is safe to stay here?"

"I don't know. But we should try to rest; eat something, too. We need to keep our strength up."

"I'm not at all hungry."

"I am," Jeffrey said. "Now that you're with me I feel much more human."

"Do you have any candy bars left?" Li Soong asked, pushing her hands into the pockets of Jeffrey's suit jacket.

"All out. We should eat real food, not that junk. You know, Li Soong," Jeffrey said as he stroked her cheek, "we're like the Owl and the Pussycat."

"Is that another fairy tale?"

"When I was a kid it was my favorite."

"Tell it to me." She let her eyes close.

Jeffrey recited the rhyme to her as she relaxed in his arms:

> *"The Owl and the Pussycat went to sea*
> *In a beautiful pea green boat.*
> *They took some honey and plenty of money*
> *Wrapped up in a five pound note . . ."*

"Is there more?" she purred.

"I don't remember the rest," he said.

"How does it end?"

"I think they danced forever by the light of the moon." He kissed her forehead.

"How nice," she said sleepily, cuddling close.

"I'm going to get some food," Jeffrey declared, straightening up. "You stay here. I'll be back in five minutes."

"Do you have to? Suppose we are separated again?"

"Naw," he scoffed. "I'll just go across the street to the Chow Mein Palace."

"What?" Li Soong looked puzzled.

"You know," Jeffrey said, "chow mein, chop suey, egg rolls—Chinese food."

"That is *not* Chinese," Li Soong insisted.

"You'll love it. We can have a picnic right here in the hall." Jeffrey looked into her plaintive eyes. "Don't worry, it's just across the street."

Li Soong nodded agreement.

Jeffrey touched her cheek. "I love you."

"I love you too," Li Soong said as he slipped out the door and into the street. She stroked her body in the places still warmed by Jeffrey's hands. Her world had quickly reknit itself with him nearby. Now safely cloistered here, she would not allow herself to think of what was or of what would be. She had grown accustomed to living in the trough of a wave about to break. Resting a cheek on the stucco wall, she waited for his return.

From the other side of the door she heard the noises of the street, conversations in her own tongue filtering through the wood and glass partition. How strange it was, she thought, to hear the familiar words, how out of place in the life she and Jeffrey had created.

An eclipse of darkness fell across the glass pane of the

door. Li Soong looked up to see a silhouette moving across the entranceway. The knob on the door turned.

"Jeffrey." She called his name as the door whined open. But the silhouette was quickly joined by three others, and they pushed into the cubicle of space. Their faces were illuminated by a light bulb that swung in a metal cage from the ceiling. Li Soong was sure she would die as she felt her blood and breath roar ferociously at the sight of the Society of the Four Winds.

The Four Winds were around her, appreciating their victory, exchanging satisfied looks before they thought to speak. Li Soong's words cut them off.

"Not yet!" she shot in brittle Chinese that made the warriors halt their movements towards her.

She squared off with Hsieh Tsai-tao, the fiercest of the men and their leader, locking him with her stare as she moved her face directly in front of his. "Not yet!" she reconfirmed.

"You must come with us, Li Soong," Hsieh said. "Now."

Li Soong stepped forward as Hsieh wrapped his hand around her upper arm. She reached up and gripped his hand sharply with her own. "Remove this," she commanded, digging her nails into his callused flesh.

Hsieh Tsai-tao loosened his grip and allowed her to pull her arm free.

She backed off, abruptly hitting the wall behind her. She scanned the four faces. "You must give me five minutes more."

"We cannot," Hsieh said, drawing close again.

"Wait!" she said as they encircled her. As she looked at these mighty warriors, she noticed their faces tempered with a strange gentleness. Hsieh's heavy hand again fell upon her, and his familiar eyes looked into hers; eyes that had watched over her when she was a child playing in the gardens of her father's house, eyes that had followed her in loving protectiveness as she grew up.

"Hsieh . . ." She felt tears well up as she spoke his name. She knew his touch was not that of an enemy, but an old friend who had come to guide her back to the life she couldn't escape any more.

"Please," she said in almost a whisper. "Allow me these few minutes. I promise I will go with you."

Hsieh looked at her intensely, then looked to his comrades. Seeing no potential for her escape, Hsieh granted Li Soong's wish. "We will be outside," he told the girl.

"Thank you," she said almost formally. "Now please go."

The Four Winds rearranged themselves outside the door in the shadows, away from the eyes of Jeffrey Hodge, who was returning from the restaurant across the street. His arms were wrapped around brown paper bags filled with food.

As Li Soong heard his step she rubbed her face hard, trying to banish the tangible shock and sadness that had formed across her features.

"Just wait until you taste this," Jeffrey said as he entered the hallway. He sat and deposited the paper cartons across the floor between them. "Spare ribs, sweet-and-sour shrimp, chop suey . . ." He recited the menu as he went about arranging their feast.

Li Soong watched him, recording each movement, every line and curve of his face as he talked.

"What a treat," he said, pulling apart the tops of the containers. "I even got chopsticks, so you'll feel right at home."

"Jeffrey." Li Soong said his name as if she never would again. A hundred different epitaphs struggled to make the trip from her heart. She moved her lips, but the words did not sound.

Jeffrey opened the last of the containers and settled back against the wall.

"Listen to me," she pleaded.

"Did you say something?" He smiled up at her, then saw the anguished expression on her face. "Hey, are you all right?"

"Give me your hand," she said, her eyes welling with tears. "I don't know what to do without you."

Jeffrey stepped over the food and sat next to her. "That was some close call," he agreed, referring to their earlier separation. He squeezed her hand. "But it's all right now."

Li Soong shook her head, unable to compress the fate that waited outside into words. "It's not all right, Jeffrey."

He looked hard at her.

She bit her tongue. The few seconds she had with him were too precious to try and explain what was inevitable. "I love you," she said instead.

Jeffrey relaxed slightly. "I know." He stroked her cheek and she kissed his fingers as they breezed by.

"What did you bring me?" She forced a smile, pretending for the last time that the world would let them be alone.

"The best part of the meal," he said, shaking a little paper bag, out of which tumbled a handful of fortune cookies.

She looked at his hair, which danced with the multicolored lights from the street outside, at his blue eyes, which turned her words to vapor.

"They're fortune cookies," Jeffrey said merrily. "Here, take one." He thrust the beige pinch of dough into her hand. "You open it like this . . ." He broke the delicate pastry between his fingers. He unfurled the tiny piece of paper, and reached out to guide her fingers with his. "Now, read the pink slip inside: *You Will Travel across the Ocean and Meet Your True Love.*" He looked down at Li Soong's face. "Isn't that wonderful?" He held out her fortune. "Here, you take it."

She pushed away his hand. "I can't." She forced the words out. "Not now."

He put the paper prophecy in his jacket pocket.

She stood.

"What's the matter?" he asked as he also stood and saw her begin to cry. He moved close to her.

Li Soong searched for a way to stop time.

"What is it?" he asked, unable to decipher her expression. "Hello." He held her face between his hands. "Remember me?" he said softly. "Jeffrey Hodge, official escort to the Premier of China's daughter?"

"The Premier of China's daughter will never forget you," she whispered.

He could not understand why Li Soong suddenly seemed so remote. It was as if she was slipping away from him. "Chu Li Soong," he said, pulling her tight against him. "Tell me, what's wrong?"

Li Soong didn't have to turn to feel the four figures who now blocked the light from the street. "Goodbye," she said, standing in the shadow cast by her future.

"What are you saying? What do you mean, 'goodbye'?"

"Our journey has ended. There is nowhere else to go, nothing left to say except . . . I love you, Jeffrey."

She pressed forward to kiss him for the last time. She had to pull herself from their embrace, turning away, squeezing her eyes shut as she pushed through the door.

"Li Soong!" Jeffrey called.

She would not look back. She could not bear to see his face. Blindly she hit the night air, refusing to see, refusing to breathe, refusing to run another step.

Li Soong did not have to run. Like a winged horse, she flew; her feet hardly touched the pavement as two of the Four Winds swept her into the streets of Chinatown.

Jeffrey bolted out of the doorway after her, but was pinned by a fist against his chest. The air whooshed from his lungs as he reeled back, trying to maintain consciousness. His vision telescoped to a small iris of sight, but he refused to surrender to the overwhelming blackness. In front of him stood one of the Premier's bodyguards, holding him to the spot. Beyond, he watched Li Soong disappear into the night like a fragment of a dream.

Twelve

THE PRESIDENT caught the eye of a servant who stood at his service in the President's study. "Please mix me a bourbon and branch water," he instructed the man; then, turning towards Raymond Hodge, he changed the order. "Make that two."

David Bromley downed some of the amber liquid. "Ahh . . . maybe this will poison a few of those bats winging through my stomach. This isn't going to be easy," he said, referring to the news corps now gathering in the Press Room for a hastily called presidential press conference. "I wish your son were back here. He could take some of the heat. He deserves it."

The Secretary of State offered a contrite nod of agreement.

Robin Bettinger, who stood nearby, spoke up: "I'm sure our men will pick him up soon. We know where the Chinese found them, and he couldn't have gotten very far."

"So far as the public knows, Bettinger, your men were right behind them every step of the way."

"We were, sir," the agent replied.

"Too far behind," the President grumbled. "And your son, Ray, he comes out of this like Yankee Doodle

Dandy. We're going to play up his little adventure as an act of unmitigated patriotism. We're going to pretend that he got so carried away by the spirit of showing Chu's daughter this country that he just went a little overboard."

Raymond Hodge tested a cautious grin. "That's good," he ventured. "It's the smart way to position it."

The President stepped close. "I hope you nail his ass to the wall when he gets back here."

"Of course," the Secretary of State said, swirling the liquor in his glass.

"But as far as the press is concerned, he did the right thing. The girl's on her way home now, and everybody's happy."

"Neat and tidy," Ray Hodge affirmed.

"That's the only way," the President said, finishing his drink.

Press Secretary Rosenfeld entered the study. "Mr. President, they are ready for you."

Before he exited, the President turned to the Secretary of State. "Ray, I've been on this planet a long time, and I've seen a lot of people do a lot of ballsy things, but your kid . . ." He slammed his glass down on the table.

Raymond Hodge nodded gravely. "I know," he said. And as the Chief Executive led the way out of the study, the Secretary of State searched for the dregs of liquor at the bottom of his glass in order to stifle the small proud smile that had formed at the thought of his son.

*

"Why the hell are you here?" The managing editor of the Washington *Post* loomed over Hazleton Brown.

The reporter finished pecking at his typewriter, scanned the lines of type that rested on the roller, then, without looking up, replied, "Where else should I be?"

"The presidential press conference started fifteen minutes ago."

"I can't waste the time. Say, I'm pretty busy." Hazleton looked up. "Can you come back later?"

"Pretty busy?" the man repeated, turning a deep crimson. "You come back from the road with nothing more than a smirk on your face, you rehash a bunch of wire stories for us all week, and now you're too busy to follow up on the biggest story of the year—"

"Not necessary," Hazleton said, typing out two more lines as the editor stood rigid with anger. "Here it is now." He pulled the paper from the machine and handed it to the man, along with a sheaf of other pages.

"What's this?" The editor glared.

"Well, it's like this. While all those folks are getting their ears massaged by Bromley's fish story about the circumstances that sent Chu's daughter off on the road with our own native son, I've put together my own version. I think even my friend Li Soong would like this story."

"What do you mean, 'your friend'? You know her?"

"Sure," the reporter said casually. "We had some steaks together down in Texas, all three of us."

"You're putting me on," the man said, scanning the pages.

"Hell, no." Hazleton stretched his arms lazily above his head. "It's all there—the café and close call in Balmorhea, their escape from prison, the hitchhiking— they had a ball."

"What's this about 'the great American love story'?" the editor asked, his eyes focusing on the pages. "I don't believe this."

"You better believe it," Hazleton said. "Bromley might want to use this whole affair to toss out a few cupfuls of patriotic eyewash, but I'm telling it the way I saw it, and it's a love story with a capital L."

"The way you saw it?" the editor echoed, fishing behind himself for a chair into which he could collapse as he read.

"You bet," Hazleton said. He stood up and pulled his corduroy jacket off the back of his chair. "But look, I'm bushed. If it's all right with you, I'm taking the rest of the day off."

The editor did not respond as he sat reading the story. He was engrossed. Finally, he turned the last page and looked up at the reporter. "I can't print this." He slapped the pages. "Who would believe it?"

"Too bad," Hazleton said casually. "It's a hell of a story."

"Didn't you tape it? Don't you have any notes? I've *got* to have proof before I can go with this."

"Sorry, no tape, no notes. Nothing but a pawn ticket." Hazleton pulled a small cardboard stub from his shirt pocket. "It came in the mail this morning."

The editor grabbed it and read, *"Bi-Rite Pawn, Exmoor, Alabama.* What am I supposed to do with this?"

"Read the other side."

Beneath a small hand-drawn caricature of a Chinese girl and an American boy were the words *Thanks for the Texas T-bones* and the signatures of Jeffrey and Li Soong. Beneath the signatures they had written: *P.S.: You can get your car at Uncle Sid's Used Cars in Diablo del Fuego, Ariz.*

"This is fantastic," the editor said. "We'll run this as artwork with the piece. But I want a follow-up. I want your story. How did you get to them? How long have you known the Hodge kid? What's going to happen to them now? Brown, you're going to be famous." He looked up, but the reporter had left for the day.

*

Li Soong sat in the jet, covered by a gray blanket, the hum of supersonic flight droning in the background. "Have some broth," a woman said, handing her a steaming cup, which she grasped with shaky hands. She drank,

watching the assembled knot of people watch her. They
stood around like spectators observing a peculiar animal.

She leveled her eyes at Hsieh Tsai-tao, the leader of the
Society of the Four Winds. "Don't watch me like that.
Go away," she said as she noticed an amused expression
play at the corners of his eyes. "What do you expect me
to do, jump from the windows of this plane?"

The man turned and walked to his seat.

"Has my father been told of our departure?"

"Yes," replied the woman who had given her the
broth. "He will be waiting. We will arrive at ten
o'clock."

"Ten o'clock our time or theirs?" Li Soong asked in
confusion.

The woman looked shocked. "Why, 'their' time, of
course. Their time is our time."

Li Soong watched the woman back off, as if her confusion were the symptom of a contagious disease. "More
broth, please, Comrade," she asked, sending the woman
to the galley.

"May I sit next to you?" Li Soong looked up to see
P'eng Hsi, her father's eldest aide. His avuncular countenance tempered her distress, and she nodded him to a
seat. "You look very tired," he said. "You should try and
sleep before we arrive. Your father will no doubt want
to speak with you at length."

"What is there to say to him?"

"Everything. He has missed you. This has not been
easy for him, Li Soong."

She leaned closer to the old man. "Tell me honestly,
P'eng, how upset is he?"

"Very."

"Is there any way he can understand why I ran away
from all of you?"

"I don't know . . . But let me tell you something about
your father. When he was about your age, he, too, ran

away, and together we walked alongside Chairman Mao on the Long March. To leave his parents and his home as he did was not the easy path to take, but it was something your father felt he must do. He has always acted upon his beliefs, and he could not expect you, his daughter, to do otherwise."

"P'eng, tell me more. Tell me about my father when he was young."

"Later, Li Soong, when we are home. Now you should relax."

Li Soong leaned back against the pillow and thought of Jeffrey. She ached for him, but the searching eyes of the others on the plane were warning flares. She knew she must grow a callous around her heart to keep them from her deepest feelings. Her love for Jeffrey was the one thing she could not—would not—share with her countrymen.

"We have a clean suit of clothes for you on board," the woman said, returning with the broth. She cast a disparaging glance at the fanciful print of Mrs. Allen's dress.

"Of course," Li Soong said as she stood and headed for the lavatory. Even the dress was too precious to parade in front of them. "I'll be out in a moment." She walked on wobbly legs past Hsieh and the others, who pretended to look out the windows.

She locked the door to the small cubicle and faced herself in the mirror. It was strange to see her own reflection, accustomed as she was to watching Jeffrey's face. When she pulled her hair back, the features she saw in the mirror seemed different than before. The planes of her cheeks appeared more angular, her eyes more intense, her expression less childlike.

She braided her hair, securing it with a pin, then slithered out of the dress. She drew a basin full of water, then lathered her face and soaped it until it shone.

Dressed in her familiar garb, she regarded Mrs. Allen's dress. Its magic now gone, it lay limply across her arms like a tired ghost from another lifetime. She began to fold it, then felt a sharp geometric form within one of its pockets. She removed the small leather picture frame that Jeffrey had given her on her birthday. The dress slipped from her hands as she held the frame before her. Li Soong's lips soundlessly mouthed the legend burnt into the leather souvenir: *remember me.*

She was startled by a knock on the door. "Li Soong, will you be out soon?" a voice demanded.

"Yes." She spoke the word hoarsely as she opened the button of her jacket and buried the small picture deep in her undervest.

Her hands still shook as she released the lock on the lavatory door. All faces turned towards her to acknowledge her retransformation back to her former image.

She thought of the look of invulnerability she had seen so many times on her father's face, and tried to emulate it. How strange, she thought, that she had never questioned his confident expression before, she had never considered that he was touched by the same emotions she felt. She imagined him waiting for her at the airport, and the thought warmed her.

Her hand traveled to the space between her breasts, and she felt Jeffrey's picture that was hidden there. The feeling of tenderness grew and spread through her tremulous limbs, steadying her and making her strong. "Now," she said in a commanding voice as she raised her eyes to meet the gaze of those who watched her, "if you have finished staring at me, I would like to hear what has transpired in our homeland since I have been away."

*

Jeffrey had wandered the streets of Chinatown in a fog, plowing aimlessly through the sea-damp air. In the early morning, people began to push past him on their way to work. Under their arms, newspapers confirmed the awful fact that Li Soong was on her way home. He picked up a discarded front page and sat on the edge of a park bench. He stared at her picture.

"No," he said. "No." And he repeated the word over and over again like a heartbeat until the desperate mantra put him back on his feet. He walked quickly, automatically, without direction. He wanted Li Soong's hand to reach out from a doorway again and stop him . . .

This is not the end, he insisted. There was a way to be with her again. It seemed impossible to find the path, but then he thought back to the beginning of their journey out of Washington and he knew that had seemed equally unimaginable.

They had traveled further together than the span of a continent. What they shared was immeasurable; and Jeffrey knew that the magic that had made it happen was still within him. Li Soong had given him the power to see it.

He looked at his image in the panes of glass as he walked—the full white suit, the tousled hair curling below his collar. The determined face and form he saw were his own creation, not the will of those around him. He felt energized by this perception, and he stuffed his hand into his jacket pocket to see what his resources were.

There were a few dollars and coins. Then his fingertips brushed a stiff piece of paper. He pulled it into the daylight, its pinkness shining against his dirty palm. *You Will Travel across the Ocean and Meet Your True Love.* The fortune was all he had left of her.

He moved faster still, his step lightening. He moved with purpose. People on the street were no longer obstacles in his path. They parted as he strode by.

A taxicab screeched to a halt as Jeffrey stepped from the curb. "Hey, watch it!" the driver called out, and

Jeffrey stopped. "Hey, you." The driver leaned out his window. "You in a hurry?"

Jeffrey spun his head towards the man. "What?" He hesitated, the paper fortune still in his fist.

"I said, you need to go some place?"

Jeffrey stood still, then stepped around and seized the door.

"Get in, the light's about to change."

He pulled himself in and the cab spun away. They drove for half a block, and the driver waited for the obligatory directions. Receiving none, he turned around to face his fare.

Jeffrey stared back at the cab driver, an inspired grin spreading across his face as he realized that for him there was only one place to go.

"Where to, buddy?" asked the driver.

"China, please," the passenger replied.

About the Authors

JANE and MICHAEL STERN have spent the last ten years exploring America together and writing about the people and places they have found. Their home is in Connecticut, where, with a bullterrier named Spud, they intend to live happily ever after.

PEOPLES OF THE WORLD
IN COLOUR

PEOPLES
OF THE WORLD
IN COLOUR

FRANCIS HUXLEY

illustrated by
MARY SIMS and MARY CAMIDGE

LONDON

BLANDFORD PRESS

First published in 1964
Reprinted 1971
Reprinted 1975
Copyright © 1964 Blandford Press Ltd.
167 High Holborn, London WC1V 6PH

Colour printed in Holland
by the Ysel Press, Deventer
Text printed and books bound in England
by Richard Clay (The Chaucer Press), Ltd., Bungay, Suffolk

120217
578·3

CONTENTS

North Europeans	**Europe**
Celts	**to North India**
Mediterraneans	**and North Africa**
West Europeans	
East Europeans	
Russians	
Balts, Finns, Lapps	
Armenoids	
Irano-Afghans	
Semites	
East Hamites	
West Hamites	
North Indians	
South Indians, Ceylonese	**South India**
Negritos	**and Pacific**
Australian Aborigines	
Polynesians, Micronesians	
Melanesians	
West Africans	**Africa, south**
The Bantu	**of the Niger**
Nilotes, Nilo-Hamites	
Bushmen, Hottentots, Pygmies	
Mongols	**Asia,**
Turks, Tatars	**East Indies**
The Eskimo	
Chinese, Koreans	
Japanese and the Ainu	
Tribal Chinese	
Assamese, Burmese	
Himalayans	
Southeast Asians	
American Indians	**The Americas**
Emigrants, Mixed Races	**Old world, New world**

Western Hemisphere

Eastern Hemisphere

ICELAND

NORWAY

SWEDEN

FINLAND

IRELAND

SCOTLAND

WALES

ENGLAND

DENMARK

NETHERLANDS

Saxony

POLAND

BELGIUM

GERMANY

LUXEMBOURG

FRANCE

1 Icelandic girl

2/3 Danish man
and girl

4/5 English schoolgirl
and schoolboy

6 Englishman

8 Dutch girl,
Zuider Zee

7 Flemish man
and child, Belgium

10 Man and girl
from Saxony

9 Dutch couple, South Holland

11 Norwegian young man and girl

12 Norwegian girl, Hardanger

13 Swedish woman with baby

14 Swedish man

15 Swedish girl

SCOTLAND

NORTHERN IRELAND

IRELAND

WALES

ENGLAND

Cornwall

Brittany

FRANCE

17 Scots boy

16 Welsh woman

14

18 Scotsman (playing bagpipes)

19 Irishman

20 Irish girl (in Kerry coat)

21 Breton woman (Penmarche costume)

22 Breton man

23/24 Portuguese man and woman

25 Portuguese girl

26 Spanish man

27 Spanish woman

28 Basque man

29 Sardinian woman

30 Girl from Arles

31 Italian boy   32 Italian woman

33 Man from Crete

34 Sicilian man

35/36 Greek youth
and woman

19

DENMARK

NORTH
SEA

GREAT

BRITAIN

NETHERLANDS

BELGIUM

GERMANY

POLAN

Normandy

CZECHO-
SLOVAKIA

Bavaria

FRANCE

Alsace

Black
Forest

AUSTRIA

SWITZERLAND

ITALY

SPAIN

37 German girl from Black Forest

38 Alsatian girl

39/40 Peasant man and girl, Central France

42 Woman from Normandy

41 Bavarian youth

43 Swiss man

POLAND

GERMANY

U. S. S. R

CZECHOSLOVAKIA

AUSTRIA
Tyrol

HUNGARY

RUMANIA

Slovania

ITALY

Croatia

Y
U
GO
S
L
A
V
I
A

Bosnia

Serbia

BULGARIA

ALBANIA

GREECE

44 Serbian man and woman from Yugoslavia

5 Slovene girls from Yugoslavia

46 Croatian man from Yugoslavia

47/48 Bosnian man and
woman from Yugoslavia

49 Gheg man from Albania

23

50/51/52 Tyrolean boy, girl and man

53/54 Hungarian men

55 Northeast Austrian woman

24

56/57 Rumanian girl and man

58 Czech girl

59 Bulgarian man and woman

25

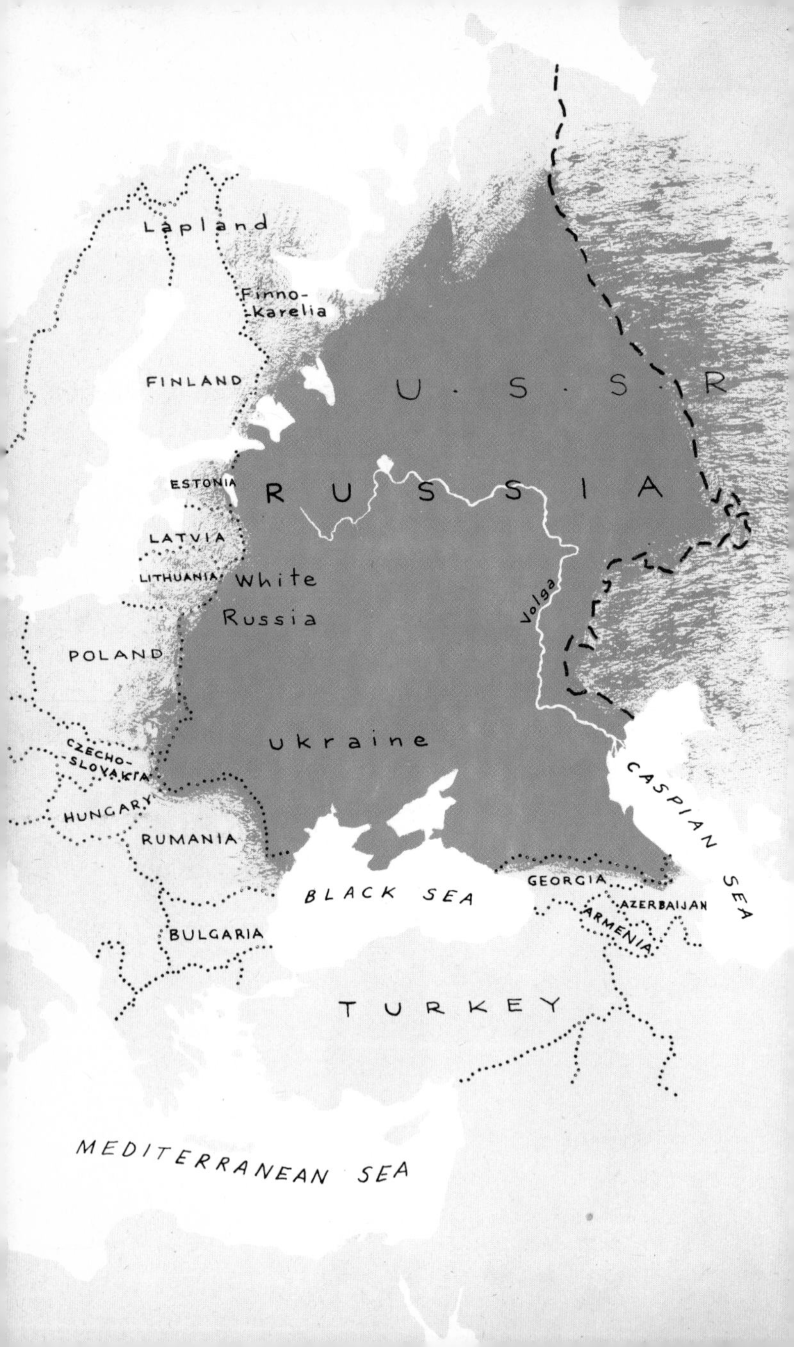
Lapland
Finno-Karelia
FINLAND
U.S.S.R
ESTONIA
RUSSIA
LATVIA
LITHUANIA
White Russia
Volga
POLAND
CZECHO-SLOVAKIA
Ukraine
HUNGARY
RUMANIA
CASPIAN SEA
GEORGIA
BLACK SEA
AZERBAIJAN
ARMENIA
BULGARIA
TURKEY
MEDITERRANEAN SEA

60 Man from
White Russia

61/62 Girl and youth,
Central Russia

63 Ruthenian man

64/65 Ukrainian
girl and woman

NORWAY

SWEDEN

Lapland

FINLAND

BALTIC SEA

ESTONIA

LATVIA

LITHUANIA

POLAND

66 Latvian woman

Balts, Finns, Lapps

67/68 Lapp man, woman and baby

69 Finnish man

70 Latvian girl

71 Estonian girl

72 North Polish girl

29

BLACK SEA

U · S · S · R ·

GEORGIA

ARMENIA

AZERBAIJAN

TURKEY

PERSIA
(IRAN)

SYRIA

IRAQ

73 Georgian man

74/75 Armenian
woman
and man

76 North Turkish man
and woman

U · S · S · R

TURKEY

PERSIA
(IRAN)

AFGHANISTAN

KASHMIR

IRAQ

Baluch-
istan

PAKISTAN

INDIA

SAUDI

ARABIA

78 Persian man and
woman

77 Kurdish woman and boy,
North Persia

81 Afghan-
Baluch
warrior

79 Afghanistan man

80 Pathan man from
Afghanistan

82/83 Man and boy
from
Baluchistan

84 Pushtan
woman

33

TURKEY

SYRIA

LEBANON

ISRAEL

JORDAN

IRAQ

PERSIA
(IRAN)

PERSIAN GULF

RED SEA

AFRICA

SAUDI

ARABIA

OMAN

YEMEN

HADHRAMAUT

85 Druse woman
from Lebanon

86 Iraqi woman

87 Syrian men

35

88 Jewish woman (Israel)

89 Jewish man (Israe

90 Arab boy

91 Syrian Arabian man

92 Arabian man

36

93 Arabian Sheik

94 Arabian woman

96 Yemenite
child

97 South Arabian
warrior

95 Bedouin girl spinning

37

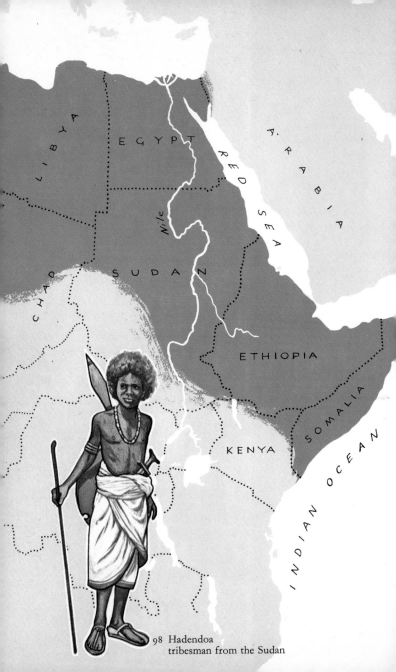

98 Hadendoa
tribesman from the Sudan

East Hamites

99 Egyptian
water carrier

100 Egyptian boy and woman

102 Somali woman

101 Abyssinian
woman

103 Egyptian man
with water pipe

39

Uled-Nail

TUNISIA

MOROCCO

Atlas Mts

Kabyle

B e r b e r

SPANISH WEST AFRICA

ALGERIA

LIBYA

B e r b e r

Tuareg

Tibbu

MAURITANIA

M A L I

NIGER

CHA

L.Chad

104 Tuareg tribesman

40

106 Berber girl

107 Tunisian girl

105 Moorish woman
from
Atlas Mountains

109 Uled-Naïl woman

108 Tibbu girl

110 Kabyle man

41

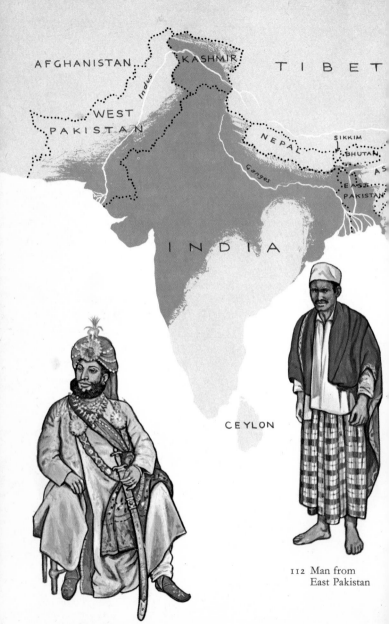

AFGHANISTAN

KASHMIR

TIBET

WEST PAKISTAN

Indus

NEPAL

SIKKIM

BHUTAN

AS

Ganges

EAST PAKISTAN

INDIA

CEYLON

111 Rajah of North India

112 Man from East Pakistan

113 Man from Kashmir

114 Devadasi
or Temple Dancer
(woman)

115 Hindu woman

117 Hindu
woman
in sari

116 Hindu man

118 Sikh man

43

AFGHANISTAN KASHMIR

TIBET

WEST PAKISTAN

NEPAL

Ganges

EAST PAKISTAN

Gujarat

Bihar

Madhya Pradesh

INDIA

Hyderabad

Annamali Hills

CEYLON

119 Tamil man,
Ceylon

121 Sinhalese man,
Ceylon

120 Vedda man, Ceylon

22/123 Kol woman and man,
Bihar

124 Gond woman
and child,
Madhya Pradesh
and Hyderabad

125 Kadar man,
Annamili Hills

126 Chenchu man,
Hyderabad

127 Bhil man, Gujarat

45

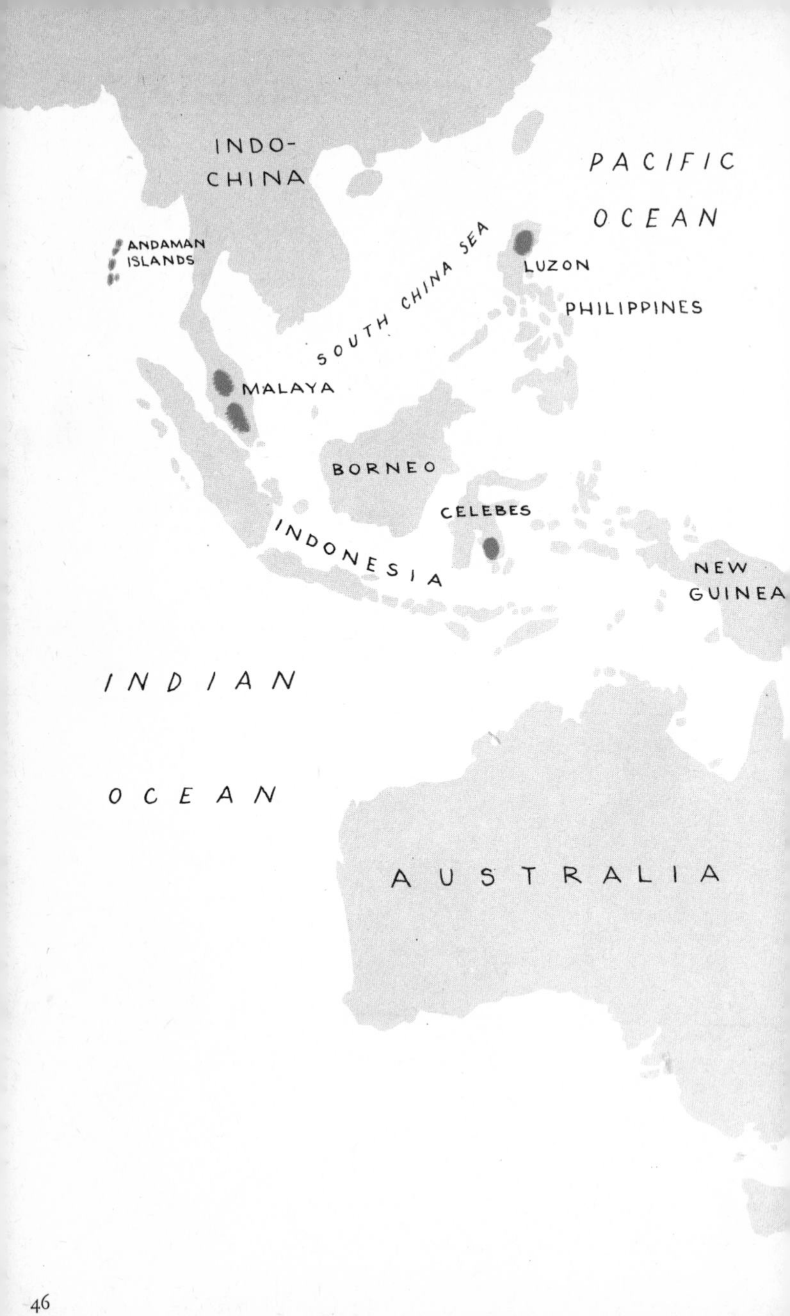

INDO-
CHINA

PACIFIC

OCEAN

ANDAMAN
ISLANDS

SOUTH CHINA SEA

LUZON

PHILIPPINES

MALAYA

BORNEO

CELEBES

INDONESIA

NEW
GUINEA

INDIAN

OCEAN

AUSTRALIA

128 Sakai
woman,
Malaya

129 Aeta man,
Luzon

130 Andamanese
woman and man

131 Semang man, Malaya

47

NEW
GUINEA

MELVILLE I.

ARNHEM
LAND

CORAL
SEA

INDIAN
OCEAN

AUSTRALIA

132 Tiwi man
with throwing sticks

Australian Aborigines

133 Tiwi child

134 Tiwi man

135 Arunta
woman and
child

137 Arunta girl,
with mat woven
from beach grass

136 Arunta man

49

MARIANA
ISLANDS

HAWAIIAN
ISLANDS

MARSHALL
ISLANDS

P A C I F I C

O C E A N

CAROLINE ISLANDS

GILBERT
ISLANDS

NEW
GUINEA

ELLICE
ISLANDS

MARQUESA
ISLANDS

SAMOA
ISLANDS

SOCIETY ISLANDS

FIJI
ISLANDS

TAHITI

TONGA
ISLANDS

COOK
ISLANDS

EASTEI
ISLAI

NEW
ZEALAND

138 Yap woman, Caroline Islands

139 Maori woman,
New Zealand

140 Samoan man in war dress

141 Hawaiian man

142 Tongan woman

CAROLINE ISLANDS

MARSHALL
ISLANDS

PACIFIC

NEW GUINEA

NEW
IRELAND

NEW
BRITAIN

SOLOMON
ISLANDS

OCEAN

GILBERT
ISLANDS

ELLICE
ISLANDS

CORAL
SEA

NEW
HEBRIDES

FIJI
ISLANDS

NEW
CALEDONIA

AUSTRALIA

NEW
ZEALAND

143
Man from
Wahgi Valley,
New Guinea

144
Girl from Waghi
Valley, New Guinea

146 Solomon Islands
chief

145
New Hebrides
woman

147 Papuan girl,
New Guinea

148 Fijian woman

53

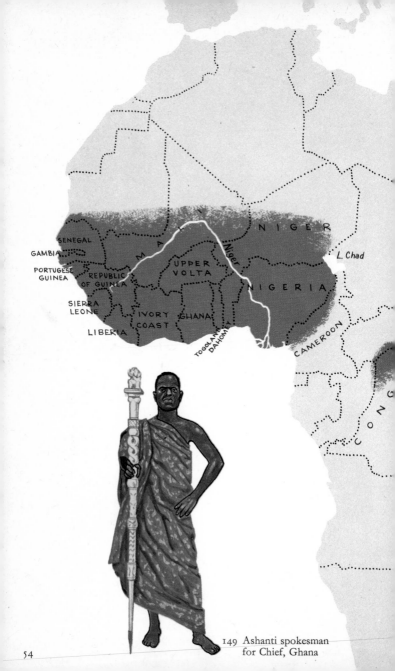

SENEGAL
GAMBIA
PORTUGESE GUINEA
REPUBLIC OF GUINEA
SIERRA LEONE
LIBERIA
IVORY COAST
M A L I
UPPER VOLTA
GHANA
TOGOLAND
DAHOMEY
N I G E R
Niger
NIGERIA
L. Chad
CAMEROON
C O N G O

149 Ashanti spokesman for Chief, Ghana

54

150 Ashanti girl, Ghana

151 Wolof woman, Senegal

152 Ewe man, Dahomey

3 Fanti man, Ivory Coast

154 Mandingo woman and child, Gambia

155 Ibo man,
East Nigeria

156 Mangbetu woman, northeast
Congo

157 Yoruba woman, West Nigeria   158 Fula man, North Niger

159 Hausa horseman, North Nigeria

160 Bornu Peul
dancer, Mali

162 Songhai man,
Mali

161 Nupe man, North Nigeria

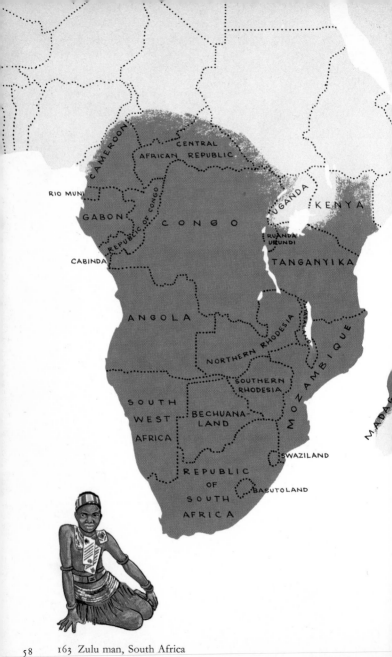

CAMEROON

CENTRAL
AFRICAN REPUBLIC

RIO MUNI

GABON

REPUBLIC OF CONGO

UGANDA

KENYA

CONGO

RUANDA
URUNDI

CABINDA

TANGANYIKA

ANGOLA

NORTHERN RHODESIA

NYASALAND

MOZAMBIQUE

SOUTHERN
RHODESIA

SOUTH
WEST
AFRICA

BECHUANA-
LAND

MADAG

SWAZILAND

REPUBLIC
OF
SOUTH
AFRICA

BASUTOLAND

58   163 Zulu man, South Africa

164 Zulu matron,
South Africa

165 Zulu warrior,
South Africa

166 Xhosa woman,
South Africa

167 Ndebele woman, South Africa

168 Pondo woman
South Africa

169 Herero woman,
southwest Africa

170 Matabele warrior, Rhodesia

172 Batonga woman,
Rhodesia

171 Nguni woman and child,
Nyasaland

60

174 Wakamba man
Kenya

173 Kikuyu man, Kenya

175 Mwili woman, Angola

177 Sakalava woman,
northwest
Madagascar

176 Baluba man, Congo, Angola

61

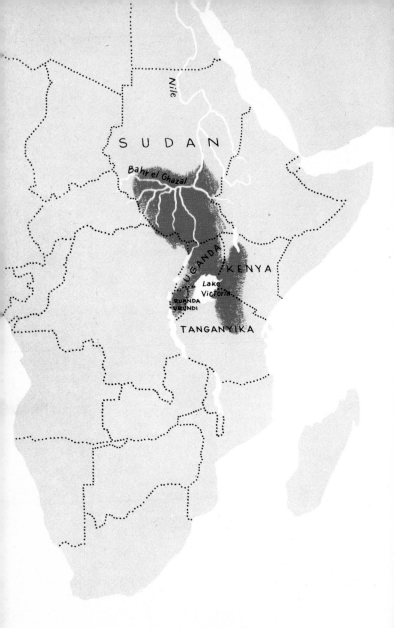

178
Shilluk woman,
Nile Valley,
Sudan

180
Madi woman,
Nile Valley,
North Uganda

179 Shilluk man,
Nile Valley, Sudan

181

182

181/182
Dinka man
and woman,
Bahr el Ghazal
basin, Sudan

63

183 Masai youth,
Kenya and
Tanganyika

184 Masai warrior,
Kenya and Tanganyik

185 Masai girl, Kenya and
Tanganyika

186 Watussi dancer,
Ruanda Urundi

187 Bari woman,
Nile Valley, Sudan

188 Turkana elder,
Sudan
and Kenya

189 Watussi noble,
Ruanda Urundi

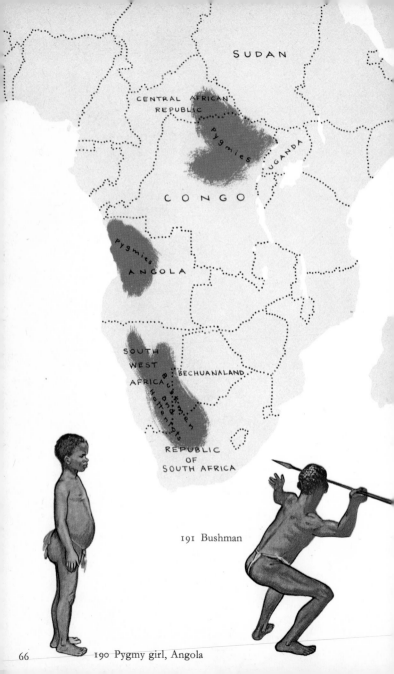

SUDAN

CENTRAL AFRICAN
REPUBLIC

Pygmies

UGANDA

CONGO

Pygmies

ANGOLA

SOUTH
WEST
AFRICA

BECHUANALAND

Bushmen
and
Hottentots

REPUBLIC
OF
SOUTH AFRICA

191 Bushman

66   190 Pygmy girl, Angola

192 Bushman

193 Bushman

194 Hottentot man

196 Congo
Pygmy man

195 Congo Pygmy
woman and child

67

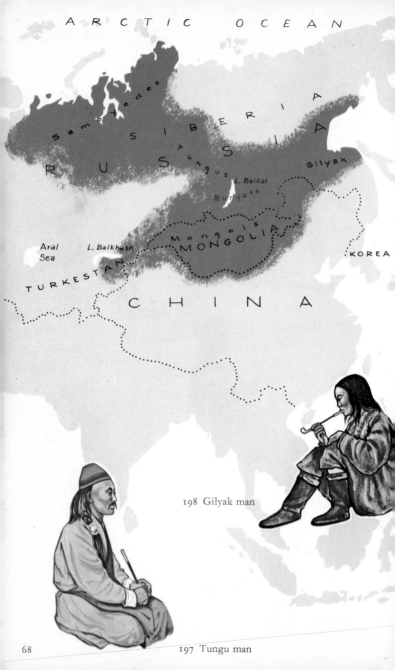

ARCTIC OCEAN

Samoyedes

RUSSIA

SIBERIA

Tungus

L. Baikal

Buryats

Gilyak

Aral
Sea

L. Balkhash

Mongols

MONGOLIA

TURKESTAN

KOREA

CHINA

198 Gilyak man

68

197 Tungu man

200 Samoyed child

201 Kalmuck boy, East Turkestan

199 Samoyed woman

203 Buryat woman

32 Mongolian horseman

U. S.   S.   R.

RUSSIA
IN EUROPE

RUSSIA
IN
ASIA

Tatars

K a z a k h   Kirghiz

ARAL
SEA

CASPIAN SEA

BLACK SEA

TURKEY

MEDITERRANEAN
SEA

Turkomans   Tatars

Kara Kirghiz

Pamir

CHIN

PERSIA

AFGHANISTAN

PAKISTAN

KASHMIR

TI

A F R I C A

205 Turkoman man

204 Kazakh
Kirghiz woman

208 Turkish woman

207 Kara Kirghiz woman

206 Tatar man

209/210 Kirghiz man and boy
from Pamir

RUSSIA
Kamchatka Peninsula
Koryak
SIBERIA
Bering Sea
Yakaghir
Chukchee
ALEUTIAN ISLANDS
ARCTIC
Bering Strait
NORTH POLE
ALASKA
OCEAN
GREENLAND
VICTORIA ISLAND
Central Eskimo
BAFFIN ISLAND
Caribou Eskimo
Hudson Bay
LABRADOR
CANADA

211 Greenland
Eskimo woman
and child

212 Greenland
Eskimo boy

213 Central
Eskimo woman

214 Alaskan man

215 Caribou Eskimo woman

218 Manchurian woman

216/217 Man and woman
from Peking

219 Boy from Loyang

74

220/221 Korean man and boy

222 Fisherman, Formosa

223 Woman from Fukien

224 Cantonese boy

225 Hakka woman

226
Cantonese woman
from Hongkong

75

CHINA

SAKHALIN

PACIFIC
OCEAN

KURIL ISLANDS

HOKKAIDO

JAPAN

SEA OF

JAPAN

KOREA

HONSHU

SHIKOKU

KYUSHU

PACIFIC
OCEAN

227 Ainu man, Hokkaido

228 Japanese woman

229 Japanese man

230 Japanese
girl and
child

231 Ainu children

232 Ainu woman

77

MANCHURIA

MONGOLIA

INNER MONGOLIA

KOREA

• Peking

Hwang Ho

• Loyang

Yangtse

TIBET

SIKANG

SZECHWAN

FUKIEN

FORMO

KWEICHOW

• Canton

YUNNAN

• Hongkong

ASSAM

BURMA

VIETNAM

HAINAN

LAOS

THAILAND

233 Meo woman Laos

34/235 Miao woman
and man
from Kweichow
and Yunnan
Provinces

236 Lolo man from Yunnan,
Kweichow and Sikang
Provinces

237 Ahka woman,
Laos

238 Li woman, Hainan Island

CHINA

ASSAM

Brahmaputra

Kachin
State

EAST
PAKISTAN

INDIA

BURMA

239 Angami Naga man, Assam

240 Angami Naga
woman, Assam

241 Kachin man,
North Burma

242 Abor man, North Assam

243 Shan man, East Burma

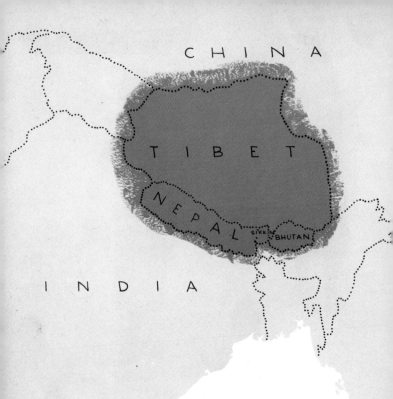

C H I N A

T I B E T

N E P A L

SIKKIM BHUTAN

I N D I A

244 Bhutanese man

245 Tibetan woman

246 Lepcha man, Sikkim

247 Tibetan Lama

248 Gurkha woman, Nepal

CHINA
BURMA
LAOS
VIETNAM
THAILAND
(SIAM)
CAMBODIA
SOUTH CHINA SEA
LUZON
PHILIPPINE
MALAYA
SUMATRA
NORTH
BORNEO
SARAWAK
BORNEO
CELEBES
INDONESIA
JAVA
BALI

249 Malay man

250 Thai man

251 Siamese dancer

252 Vietnamese woman

253 Burmese woman

254 Kha man, Laos

256 Moi man, Vietnam

255 Batak man,
North Sumatra

258 Balinese man

257 Javanese man

260 Ifugao man, North Luzon

259 Sea Dyak woman and man
Sarawak

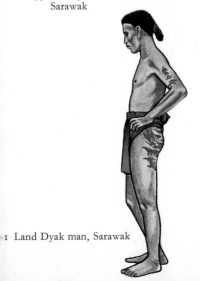

1 Land Dyak man, Sarawak

262 Hova woman, Madagascar

Northwest Coast Indians

Northern Hunters

P A C I F I C

C A N A D A

Plateau Indians

Plains Indians

California Indians

U. S. A.

Pueblo Indians

Eastern Woodland Indians

Southeast Indians

M E X I C O

O C E A N

263 Kwakiutl woman, northwest coast

88

264 Tlingit man, northwest coast

265 Tsimshian man, northwest coast

66 Kutchin man,
Northern Hunter

267 Micmac girl,
eastern woodland

268 Iroquois woman,
eastern woodland

269 Cheyne warrior, Plains

270 Osage woman, Plains

271 Kiowa dancer, male, Plains

272 Dakota sioux man, Plains

273 Oto boy, Plains

274 Pawnee dance male, Plains

90

75 Nez Percé man, Plateau

276 Hopi snake dancer,
male, Pueblo

277 Isleta Pueblo woman

279 Navaho
silversmith, Pueblo

8 Seminole woman, southeast

280 Yuman woman and baby,
California

UNITED STATES OF AMERICA

MEXICO

PACIFIC OCEAN

GULF
OF
MEXICO

YUCATAN

CARIBBEAN
SEA

BRITISH
HONDURAS

GUATEMALA

HONDURAS

SALVADOR

NICARAGUA

COSTA RICA

PANAMA

SOUTH
AMERICA

281 Cuna woman, Panama

82 Quiche woman,
    Guatemala

283 Tzotzil woman,
    Guatemala

284 Zinacantecan
    man, Mexico

285 Chocó girl,
    Panama

286 Lacandón man, Mexico

287 Mixtec hat-
    weaver (woman), Mexico

93

CARIBBEAN SEA

VENEZUELA

COLOMBIA

GUIANA

ECUADOR

Amazon

P E R U

B R A Z I L

Xingu

Araguaia

Bananal Island

BOLIVIA

L. Titicaca

PARAGUAY

PACIFIC OCEAN

C H I L E

ARGENTINA

Pampas

URUGUAY

Patagonian

TIERRA DEL FUEGO

94

288 Aymara water-carrier (man), Peru

289 Quillacinga man,
Columbia

290 Aymara dancer
(woman), Bolivia

291 Araucanian
woman, Chile

92 Quechua woman, Bolivia

293 Cágaba man, Colombia

294 Tehuelche man,
Patagonia

295 Lengua man, Paraguay

297 Yahgan woman,
Tierra del Fuego

296 Ona woman and child,
Tierra del Fuego

298 Suyá man,
Xingu River, Brazil

299 Carajá man,
Bananal Island,
Brazil

300 Jívaro man,
Ecuador and
Peru

301 Bororo man,
Brazil

302 Carib woman,
South Guiana

97

EUROPE

ASIA

AFRICA

AUSTRALASIA

303 A Portuguese-
Indonesian man

304 Orthodox Jews (man and boy), Europe

305 Boer farmer, South Africa

308 Australian farmer

307 Gypsy woman, Europe

306 Lascar seaman

THE NEW WORLD

GREENLAND

U·S·A

CANADA

NORTH AMERICA

U. S. A.

Texas

MEXICO

CENTRAL AMERICA

BRITISH HONDURAS
JAMAICA

SOUTH AMERICA

CHILE

ARGENTINA

309 French-
Canadian man

310 Canadian man

311 American
woman and
man

312 Farmer,
midwest
U.S.A.

313 Cowboy,
Texas,
U.S.A.

314 American
boy

315 American
Negro boy

316
Farmer,
British
Honduras

317
Creole
woman,
Martinique

318 Mexican
man

319
Jamaican
man

320
Chilean
horseman

321 A Gaucho, Argentina

INTRODUCTION

Peoples of the World is at first sight a grandiose title for this small book. After all, there are over 3,700 million people living in the world today, and it would be impossible to show representatives of every nation, province, city or tribe in such a small compass, however different they may be from each other or interesting to look at.

For what is a 'people'? It is not the same as a 'race', which should be a purely biological term: a race having certain definite physical characteristics, such as a particular shade of skin colour, shape of head, or form of nose and eye. We can point to certain peoples as belonging to a definite race, because they all look much the same and are distinct from their neighbours, but certain other peoples may be so racially mixed that, although they have the same culture, a racial definition would not be satisfactory.

Take Britain, for instance. The British are notoriously a mongrel race: the historical Britons have long since given place to Angles, Saxons, Normans, and Vikings, and the term now includes the Scots who are part Celt and part Pict, the Celtic Irish, Welsh and Cornish, and numerous immigrants such as Huguenot weavers, German refugees and members of the Free Polish Army who have since become naturalised. Each of these groups in its time was regarded as being foreign, as they indeed were, since they spoke a different language and had different customs; sometimes they were also regarded as being of a different race, because of some distinctive physical trait, such as red hair, or a hooked nose. However, most of them have now become assimilated by long residence here and by intermarriage, so that their cultural differences have largely disappeared and the physical traits by which they were recognised have either blended into those of their neighbours or perhaps just go unnoticed as part of the enormous variety of physique and facial appearance which we now find in Britain.

Racially, then, the British are a marvellous mixture, and while they may be unique, they are certainly not pure. One could spend pages in an attempt to describe such a mixture, to define the various

104

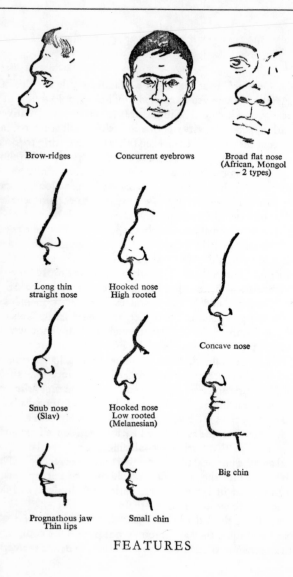

Brow-ridges   Concurrent eyebrows   Broad flat nose
(African, Mongol
– 2 types)

Long thin
straight nose

Hooked nose
High rooted

Concave nose

Snub nose
(Slav)

Hooked nose
Low rooted
(Melanesian)

Big chin

Prognathous jaw
Thin lips

Small chin

FEATURES

racial types which compose it and to show its history. The same holds good for mainland Europe: like Britain, it has had a long and complicated history and has witnessed the movements of many peoples from one region to another, so that the racial basis is confused. If we were given the photographs of a number of Europeans and asked to pick out a Frenchman rather than an Italian, or a German rather than a Pole, we might easily be wrong as often as not, for we use the label of nationality as a convenient way of speaking about people who share the same language and have much the same way of life, regardless of their racial background. If we wished to, we could make an atlas of the various physical types who live in Europe, but we would find little correspondence between the areas in which they are to be found and natural social and historical groupings. In addition, we would find that the physical characteristics of the various types would be mingled by intermarriage – indeed, it is not hard to find people who show traits of three or four different races – and would be left with the conclusion that physical anthropology has certain good ways of classifying individuals, but not peoples.

The inhabitants of Europe, of course, can all be classed as belonging to one great section of mankind, often called Caucasoid or Europiform. It is easy enough to distinguish Europeans from typical Chinese or Negroes, particularly when social distinctions are mixed with racial ones, and this has led to the old belief that there were but three or four original races forming mankind, all of them different in their pure state, whose mixture formed the various subraces. These races were founded mainly on differences of skin colour, and further subdivisions were based on stature, the shape of the skull and the nose, the colour of the eyes and form of the eyelid, and the character of the hair.

Such features were thought to be non-adaptive, that is, unaffected by the environment, and caused by radically different forms of genetic constitution. It may be, however, that differences of skin colour are controlled by only one or two genes, since the skin of all races tans easily in the sun; the same may be true of such things as the typically Mongolian form of eyelid, which appears from time to time in Europeans who apparently have no Mongolian ancestry, perhaps as a mutation. In any case, the more we know of human anatomy, the more we see that nearly every feature has some adaptive significance. If we take adaptation to climate alone, there are many interesting adaptive features. The Nuer, for instance, who live on the upper reaches of the Nile, are tall and thin, and this is the best build for a people habitually living in a hot dry climate since it offers the maximum skin area for heat loss to take place through evaporation. Their skins, besides, are dark, which protects them from ultra-violet burning by the sun. In the Arctic, on the other hand, the optimum physique is thickset, with short limbs, so that the radiation of heat is cut to a minimum. The Eskimo are a good example of this type; in addition they have other physiological ways of protecting themselves against the cold, such as a fatty deposit in the cheeks, the orbits of the eyes and the eyelids, narrow eye-slits, an increased flow of blood to the face and hands to protect them from frost bite, and narrow nostrils which warm and moisten the air before it gets to the lungs.

Many physical features and processes may thus be adaptations to certain definite environmental influences. Even the head may show changes: the skulls of children born to Japanese immigrants in Hawaii, for instance, are already slightly different in shape from those of their parents after only a few generations, for reasons which have not yet been discovered. A race, therefore, may be fairly plastic and may slowly be transformed; and we should think of it, not in terms of an individual type, but as a collection of traits which usually hang together.

Blood groups seem to be an exception. There are a number of these groups, such as the ABO system, the MN system, the Rhesus factor, and others. One can map out the different frequencies to be found in each system as they occur throughout the world, and this was once thought to give a clear indication of racial origins. Thus there is an absence of one of the A blood groups in the Americas, and little of the B; Europe shows a little more B and a great deal more A, while B is commonest in Asia. But exactly why this is so remains a problem, for these frequencies do not correspond at all exactly with other forms of racial classification. They may have some adaptive significance, because we know that there is some association between certain blood groups and certain diseases such as ulcers and stomach cancer, but a lot more work needs to be done before we know just what function blood groups really have. At present, the main use of blood groups is to compare related populations in order to work out their immediate relationships, and they cannot be used to provide a general taxonomy of the human race.

Every system of classification is useful, but it may not tell the whole story. Our results, of course, depend on just what it is we are trying to classify. Classification by physique gives us a kind of guide book to human anatomy; we can measure skulls and see whether they are long and narrow, or short and broad, and this gives a useful indication of the differences existing in a population, and whether neighbouring populations are anatomically similar or not. We can classify by language, or religion, or culture, and these systems give us quite different kinds of information and are guide books to human society. Thus on the one hand we have the methods of physical anthropology, which measure individual human beings and combine these measurements to give a general picture of a definite population, and on the other hand there are the methods of social anthropology which describe social institutions and their history.

We can bring these two categories of information together if we remember that a race, or tribe, or people, is at bottom a breeding population which perpetuates different individual types at the same time as definite social forms. This is indeed the basis for the rather simple classification of the peoples of the world which has been used in this book. These populations correspond sometimes to geographical areas, and sometimes to racial or linguistic ones. All three are important, but one will sometimes be more convenient than another; it is anyhow impossible to keep tags on all the physical and social differences which people display, for in some cases we know so much that the picture becomes confusing, and in others we know too little.

Thus the first section corresponds with what is usually called the Caucasoid division of mankind, and includes Europe, North Africa, the Middle East and northern India. The peoples living in this vast region are subdivided by national boundaries, where racial and historical facts are too complex to be easily demonstrated, and sometimes according to racial type. In the same way Africa south of the Sahara is treated as one region, subdivided into three smaller areas: West Africa, the Bantu speakers of the east and south, and the Hottentots, Bushmen and Pygmies. The Pygmies are not related to the Bushmen, but are brought in here for lack of space. Asia is the home of the Mongolian race, subdivided into the Mongols proper, the Turkic tribes, the Chinese and Japanese, the Tibetans, the inhabitants of the East Indies and tribal groups in southwestern China and northeastern India. In the Pacific we have the Polynesians, the Melanesians and the Micronesians. The Australian Aborigines and the tribes of southern India go together, since they are the representatives of a much mixed but physically primitive race; and we are left with the Americas, which are divided into broad cultural zones, since too little is known of the physical anthropology of the Amerindians for a racial classification to be at all useful.

Maps always pose something of a difficulty. It is often hard to know just where to draw a boundary, since so many factors have to be taken into account, and it can seldom be done with accuracy: the best that can be done is to give a broad indication of the region in which certain related peoples live, which may be a little arbitrary. Another difficulty will be seen in the maps for the Americas and Australia. Since the colonisation of North America, for instance, the American Indian is only found in certain very restricted parts of the country, and one might travel the length and breadth of the Great Plains without ever catching sight of a Plains Indian. Rather than leave them out, however, the map shows where the Indian tribes used to live before the white man settled there, and the same is true of the Australian Aborigines and certain other tribal peoples who have been driven out of their original territories.

The historical problem has also affected the illustrations. Take the Plains Indians, again: the Iroquois have long given up their old way of life, and are now famous for their skill as spidermen in erecting the steel frame-works of skyscrapers in New York. Their typical dress nowadays is a steel helmet and jeans, but since they are not unique in this, and their ancient dress is more interesting, they have been shown in war bonnets and deerskin suits. In the same way the Australian Aborigines nowadays are by no means naked tribesmen living in the desert, for many have become cattle herders in the north and now wear European clothes and drive trucks. Nor do the Scots always wear a kilt, Mexicans a poncho, Norwegians a peasant costume, or Indians a heavily brocaded gown: but these are satisfying images, and serve to bring to mind something that each of these people represent. The last section makes up for this slightly romantic point of view by showing peoples who have left their home countries and have settled in foreign parts: the Dutch in South Africa, Negroes in Brazil, Spaniards in Latin America, the British in Australia. In all, the peoples of the world show a wonderful diversity, and in the end their differences are as interesting as their similarities.

Straight hair

Wavy hair

Peppercorn hair

Curly hair

Woolly hair

Light facial hair

Heavy facial hair

Eyelids padded
top or bottom

Oblique eyes

Straight eyes

Mongoloid eyes

FEATURES

The numbers appearing after
each heading in the text in-
dicate the reference numbers of
the coloured illustrations.

EUROPE TO NORTH INDIA AND NORTH AFRICA

Our survey starts with what is often called the Caucasoid division of
mankind. The term was invented in the late 18th century by Blumen-
bach, who thought that the Caucasus was the original homeland
of many of the present-day European populations, since it contains
an astonishingly complex array of peoples.

'Caucasian', in the passport offices of the world, means white-
skinned. The Caucasoid race, however, is by no means always
white: Arabs, Englishmen, Indians and North Africans all come
under the designation, with skins ranging from pinkish white to
dark brown. We can, however, usually tell a Caucasoid by a number
of features: hair ranges from straight to curly, body hair is often
quite thick; the shape of the head can be anything from long and
narrow (dolichocephalic) to round and broad (brachycephalic);
(mesocephalic is a third term, meaning a shape intermediate to the
others); the lips are usually thin, the nose fairly large and narrow,
the face straight, forehead high, chin prominent.

We can make this description more useful by making a more
detailed classification. Europe itself has nine major divisions of the
Caucasoid race, called Early Mediterranean, Mediterranean proper,
Dinaric, Armenoid, Nordic, Celtic, Alpine, East Baltic and Lapp.
There are two more in North Africa, the Eastern and Western
Hamites; two in the Middle and Near East, the eastern branch of the
Mediterraneans and the Irano-Afghans; and one in India. In the
space of this book, the best we can do is to describe each type somewhat as if we were making a caricature of it: we shall pick on their
distinctive features without paying much regard to the many
variations within each region, unless something of their historical
roots can be traced.

North Europeans (1–15)

If the concept of the 'white race' is a caricature, as it were, of the term Caucasoid, the Nordic race is the most obvious caricature of what we mean by white. Nordics are typically tall, muscular, blond, a long face going with a long head, the nose narrow, the chin large. We can see this type best in Sweden, where the population is more or less homogeneous, for Sweden was where the Nordic tribes settled in the greatest numbers, having arrived there from eastern Europe and the steppes of Russia. There are other strains present, however, notably one with darker hair, sometimes red, and with a rounder head; this may have been the type of the original inhabitants of the country, and it is still to be seen in western Norway along the fjords. Indeed, three different strains are mentioned in Scandinavian myth which tells how Heimdal, one of the early gods, wandered over the country and married three women who each bore a different brood. The children of the first wife were short, dark and ugly – these became the thralls, who were perhaps prisoners brought by the Nordics from central Europe. The second woman bore large, red-faced muscular men, who became craftsmen, the carls; it is these who may represent the original inhabitants. The third woman bore the aristocratic jarls, with blond hair and piercing eyes, who were warriors and the type of the Nordics proper.

After they had been settled about a thousand years, the country became over-populated and the climate worsened. Denmark was at this time the cultural centre for the Nordics, as we may see nowadays from the great number of monuments and graves in the area; and the Nordics emigrated thence to other countries on warlike expeditions. The Goths, Vandals and Huns all came from Sweden, and swarmed into Germany; Jutes from Denmark and Saxons from Schleswig-Holstein invaded England; then came the Vikings from Norway, raiding the coasts of Britain and settling in the north and in Ireland, eventually colonising Iceland with women picked up from Celtic settlements. People looking like the Vikings can still be found in the isolated mountains of Norway, where their way of life has changed little over the centuries.

Before this Nordic invasion, Britain had been settled by Neolithic peoples who came from the Mediterranean, some by sea and some via Spain, and who must have mixed with the more ancient population already there. Others, with round heads and faintly hooked noses, came from France and Germany during the Bronze Age, settling in the northeast and around Wiltshire, where their monuments remain. Later, during the Iron Age, the Celts arrived, and a Germanic group of tribes called the Belgae. In England the Celts retreated in front of the advancing Saxons into Wales and Cornwall, the Saxons in turn being driven from the east coast by Danes and Norwegians.

The Roman and Norman invasions brought further peoples to the country, but they did little to alter the amalgam of physical types which had by then been formed; nor did succeeding movements from the Continent, such as that of the Huguenots, though they brought in technical skills which had much influence.

The same rough-hewn men we found in eastern Norway also lived in the Low Countries, one of the richest parts of Europe and also a natural battlefield for those wishing to control the coast and the hinterland: here the Romans fought the Germanic tribes, the Spaniards and Austrians threatened northern Europe, Napoleon was defeated at Waterloo, and the battle of Flanders was fought in the First World War. But long before these battles, Germanic tribes had been warring here, and the present-day population descends from the old inhabitants of the country, from the Germanic Franks, the Saxons – the Frisians of today – and the Belgae, so that the Nordic type has suffered considerable admixture.

The Belgae, after whom Belgium is named, is divided between the Flemings and the Walloons. Flemish is a Germanic language to which English, Frisian and Dutch are all related; Walloon (the word comes from the same root as 'Welsh', and means a stranger) is an archaic form of French. Even a Latin dialect survives here from early times, known as Langue d'oil. The Walloons are somewhat darker than the Flemings, and have rounder heads, due to racial admixture from the south; but the Nordic strain is still visible, especially in the north.

Celts (16–22)

The Celts, whose main groups were the Milesians, the Goidels and the Cymry, were an Iron Age Nordic people who came from Spain. In Ireland they formed the upper classes, having conquered the original inhabitants; they also invaded western Scotland, pushing back the Picts into the Highlands. Today they are to be found mainly in eastern and central Ireland, the pre-Celtic peoples being in the southwest, the region which has provided most of the immigrants into the United States. Typically the Irish are distinguished by a mesocephalic skull, a nose that turns up at the end, wide cheeks, a long upper chin and lower jaw; freckles are common.

Mediterraneans (23–36)
The Mediterranean peoples stretch from the Iberian peninsula eastwards into India. Slender, long-headed, with sallow complexions, they have always been noted for their intelligence and it was they who in early times created the first civilisations of the Middle East and Egypt. Since they were also a maritime people, they spread their culture throughout the Mediterranean area and into western and northwestern Europe as far as the Baltic.

Spain, however, was originally populated from North Africa during the third millennium B.C., when large numbers of people moved away from the once green Sahara which then was turning into a desert. Mediterraneans from the east came after, taller people with a knowledge of metals, who are sometimes known as Prospectors; they were also builders of megalithic monuments, which can be seen in the north at Stonehenge, and Carnac in Brittany. The Phoenician settlement of Spain continued this movement from the east until the Roman conquest; then Celtic tribes moved in from the north, forming the basic Celto-Iberian nation, with more Nordic blood coming in with the invasions of the Goths and Vandals. Later, Arabs and Berbers from North Africa dominated Spain for eight centuries, and under their rule Andalusia became a centre of civilisation, with traders and artisans coming from many countries, including Persians who made Shiraz wine, the present sherry. The Arabs and Berbers, known as the Moors, were expelled in 1492; this was also a time when Spain lost many of its peoples to the newly founded colonies in the New World, and the inhabitants of the

Christian north filtered down to take the place of Moors and emigrants alike.

The long-headed Moors have not left much trace of their occupation: Spaniards are basically mesocephalic, with some round-headed people in Asturia and Galicia. We can distinguish several general types: the lithe, golden-skinned inhabitants of Andalusia, with their finely modelled faces; a blond type in the north, something like a short Nordic; there are people notable for their hook-noses – of which General Franco is an example – and a coarse Mediterranean type, short, thickset, with a broad face and a nose which is almost snub, is common.

Portugal contains a similar population to that of Spain, though the Lusitanians to the north of the Tagus are much influenced by Celtic and Germanic invasions; the broad-faced type is much in evidence, and is made fun of in Portugal's one-time colony, Brazil.

A small group of Early Mediterranean people live in northern Spain and the south of France: the Basques. They speak an agglutinative language which is not related to Indo-European, and has caused much discussion amongst linguists; their blood groups are also quite atypical of Europe, having a very low incidence of group B and a high frequency of Rhesus negative. This shows their long isolation for, though they are not a nation, they have kept many of their particular customs from early days and are recognisable, whether living in Spain or France, by a typical appearance: a broad forehead, narrow chin and long nose, and a slender build. Their skulls are not uniform, but are usually mesocephalic and approach the Celtic Iron Age type quite closely.

The belt of Mediterranean peoples stretches along the coast of southern France and up the Rhône valley, though here they are much mixed with round-headed peoples from the north and, in recent times, with Italians. More typical are the inhabitants of the islands in the western Mediterranean, especially Sardinia and Corsica which early on were peopled by the Megalith-builders, long-headed people with swarthy skins. Corsicans, with their special style of architecture, their method of farming and their exogamous marriage system, not to mention their passion for their blood feud, have sometimes been compared with the mountain Berbers of

North Africa. The Sardinians, who are the shortest people in Europe, may have got their name from the Shardana, one of the Peoples of the Sea who attacked Egypt at the time of the Middle Kingdom. They still spoke a non-Italic language in late Roman times, in spite of the fact that the island had been settled by Romans and, before that, by Greeks and Carthaginians. Later conquerors were the Saracens, who did not stay long, and the Spaniards, whose language remains in a local dialect.

The history of Italy was much the same as that of Spain in the beginning: tall Megalith-builders and hook-nosed Prospectors followed the short Early Mediterraneans, settling mainly in the Po valley and central Italy. Then Etruscans, also from the east, colonised Tuscany, and Greeks built their cities in the south and in Sicily. During the Bronze Age there was a counter-movement from the north, as Nordic tribes, the Italici and the Illyrians, entered the country: from them the Roman patricians were to emerge. Other Celtic and Germanic invasions were to follow, but it was Roman civilisation which did most to alter the basic population by introducing peoples from outlying parts of the Empire – slaves, traders, soldiers, craftsmen and visitors of all kinds, who were eventually assimilated.

In Italy, stature increases as you go north, where there are more individuals with light or brown hair than in the south. The round-headed Alpine type is much in evidence together with the long-headed Megalith-builder strain, and the Nordic is responsible for the relatively tall and blond physique. In the south, the classic Mediterranean features have been coarsened by Greek and Armenoid intrusions, so that the typical individual there is considerably hairier than is usually found in Europe, thick-limbed, mesocephalic, with a narrow forehead, a big jaw, and a straight nose; Armenoid brow-ridges are also seen with the classic Armenoid nose, high-bridged and with the tip down-turned. Sicilians, on the whole, are like the inhabitants of the toe of Italy: both these regions are noted for their poverty and backwardness, although when the Greeks first colonised them they must have been wealthy enough. Because of its natural strategic position, too, Sicily has been long under foreign rule without benefiting from its various conquerors, who have rather ignored the economic problems there; and this has allowed the Mafia to emerge and dominate the island.

The Greeks originally were of the usual narrow-headed Mediterranean type, as one may see from ancient skulls found there and in Crete. This population was changed by the advent of two northern peoples: first the Achaeans, fairer than the original inhabitants, who doubtless came from the steppes like other Nordic peoples; then the Dorians, a broad-headed people from the north and northwest, who swept away the Achaean civilisation. In the 6th century A.D. the Avars and Slavs entered the country, and there has been a steady infiltration of Slavs ever since, so that a zone of round-headedness exists from Albania to Corinth, and indeed many districts in Greece now speak Albanian. The Turkish invasion also brought changes, though later there was a general repatriation of Greeks from Thrace and Turks back to Turkey.

The Greeks are a short people, though taller in the northeast. There is some Nordic colouring present, but heavy beards and eyebrows meeting over the nose are common, as among Armenoids, and the most important racial type is perhaps that represented by Socrates, being round-headed and snub-nosed. True Mediterraneans are also to be found, however, especially in Crete, though these are taller and blonder than the original Megalith-builders who settled the area; one group, the Sphakiotes, may even be Dorian by descent, resembling the traditional type found in Sparta.

West Europeans (central zone) (37–43)

We now return to France, to start another sweep across Europe from west to east in a survey of the Alpine race. France must have supported a considerable population in early times, as we can see from the numerous sites which have given their names to archaeological phases, and by the palaeolithic cave paintings of the Dordogne. As on the Iberian peninsula, Neolithic food producers entered from the south, and the later Megalithic people settled especially in the west, along the coast, penetrating to the north where their monuments are most in evidence. After the Bronze Age, which had its centre near southern Germany, the Iron Age brought large invasions in the north, first of Celtic peoples, and then of Germanic ones which led to the founding of Charlemagne's empire. Later the Norsemen entered Normandy, giving their typical cast of features to the population which even now have a long face and high thin nose, and Cornish immigrants settled in Brittany, though they have left little trace except for their language.

Thus northern Frenchmen are usually tall, occasionally blond, and mesocephalic. Even taller and blonder are the inhabitants of the northeast, descendants of the Burgundian tribes who settled there with the approval of Rome in the 5th century A.D.: this is an Alpine type, known by its extremely round head. Another zone of brachycephaly is to be found in the great granite plateau of the Massif Central, whose inhabitants are also unusually short; but this seems to be caused by the poor soil of the region, for stature has increased there since living conditions improved.

On the whole we may say that the highlands are occupied by round-headed peoples, the lowlands by mesocephals. The great lowland corridor running from Paris to Bordeaux has been peopled by Nordics and Megalith-builders; the other major corridor, that of the Rhône valley, by Mediterraneans. Another long-headed region is in the Catalan-speaking district of the eastern Pyrenees, where Iberian influence is obvious; and a curious nucleus of dolichocephals is present at the edge of the Massif Central, who are apparently very ancient and may be the remnants of an Upper Palaeolithic stock.

To the east, in Alsace-Lorraine, we are in territory settled by Germanic peoples. Germany itself has never been a racial unit, and has only been a nation since the days of Bismarck; geographically it is divided into two parts, the mountains of the south, and the flat northern area giving on to the vast European plains; and this also delimits the two main populations, Alpine and Nordic.

Starting from ancient times, we find many different peoples in Germany: there must still be Palaeolithic elements in the population, mixed with a more advanced influx from the fertile Danube valley. A few Mediterraneans are to be found on the upper Rhine, having no doubt moved over from the Rhône; but the great movements have always been from the north and east. The Nordics who passed into Scandinavia in the Bronze and Iron Ages returned when the climate worsened, and their type is especially seen on the coast. But

other tribes moved far into the west, as part of the historic Volker-
wanderung: East German tribes, Goths, Vandals, Lombards, the
Gepidi and the Burgundians all passing beyond the confines of
modern Germany in the early days of the Christian era, while
Germany proper was settled by Saxons, Frisians, the Franks, who
went far into the southwest, the Chatti – now the Hessians – the
Bajuvars or Bavarians, the Alemanni and the Thuringians. There
then followed two other movements: first the Slavic migration,
which was stopped by Charlemagne just east of the Elbe, and which
led to the use of Slavic dialects even in Berlin during the Middle
Ages; then an opposing movement, the famous Drang nach Osten,
as Germanic peoples pushed their way west. German villages are to
be found today scattered throughout Czecho-Slovakia, Poland,
Hungary, Yugoslavia, Rumania, and even the Ukraine.

These movements have produced an interesting medley, with
Nordic features predominating in the north and southwest but
mixed with old post-Palaeolithic types; in the south one finds the
Alpine form of skull, which is a legacy of the Slavic invasions, sometimes small as in the southeast where there was Mediterranean
influence, sometimes large as in the northeast where there has been
contact with the Balts. However, it is difficult to say how much this
round-headedness is due to Slavic ancestry and how much to a
general evolutionary broadening of the skull which has taken place
throughout Europe in historic times. Both must have had some
effect: certainly we find the B blood group, typical of the Slavs,
running high east of Berlin. The position of Germany as a typical
Nordic country, therefore, does not hold water: the Nordic
element has been plentifully watered down by peoples from the east
and southeast.

Switzerland is an extension of the area settled by the Alemannic
tribe, who found a round-headed Mesolithic people already *in situ*;
Burgundians settled the west, and the Romanized Rhaetians the
southeast. Thus the northern valleys which open into Germany
have a moderately tall Nordic population, while the southern and
eastern valleys leading into France and Italy are populated by a
darker, more round-headed people. The difference can almost be
translated into language divisions, for Switzerland contains five

languages, German, French, Italian, Romansch and Ladin; or into religious divisions, the Nordic north being Protestant, the south Catholic.

In the Tyrol we again find descendants of the Nordic tribes, settled in north-facing valleys, this region being a highroad for Germanic tribes making their way over the Alps, and of the round-headed Dinaric peoples whom we shall come across again in Yugoslavia. To the east a large plateau overlooks the fertile valley of the upper Danube. This has also been a high road for migration from the east where the old Danubian tribes, later to become one branch of the Nordics, developed; here also the Slavs came, to enter lower Austria. Brachycephaly is everywhere dominant, the index often being very high except in the Tyrol, and while hair is usually dark, light hair and eyes increase as you go west and north into Nordic territory.

East Europeans (44–59, 63–65)

The Slavic movement, so important in the history of Central Europe, originated in the Pripet basin, in southeastern Poland and Russia. The Slavs were originally a Nordic people, given to farming in the forests and swamplands, where they escaped the attentions of their neighbours the nomadic Scythians and Goths and could develop in peace. Between the 2nd and 5th centuries their numbers must have increased hugely, for it was at that time that they began their migrations outwards: first into Germany, where the Wends remain as a distinct Slavic group to this day; then south through Austria and into Italy, and southeast into Albania, where they founded an empire. Eastward they farmed the black earth of the plains where previously the nomads had camped, and they dislodged the Finnish tribes who moved north to the Baltic. Eventually the movement east reached over the Urals, into Siberia and to the Pacific Ocean, the latest of the great Indo-European migrations.

In Czechoslovakia, the Slavic Czechs have been largely westernised, being surrounded by Germans. Originally long-headed, the general head form has continuously become more and more round-headed, a phenomenon which has affected all the Slavs, including the Wends in Germany. Their hair is medium brown, being as fair as most southern Germans; the typical snub-nosed, broad-faced blond type is commoner among the Slovaks to the east.

Czechoslovakia also has a population of Magyars whose ancestors were an Ugrian tribe of Russia and who by the 9th century had penetrated the Carpathians and entered the Hungarian plain. There they found other invaders from the east, the Huns and Avars, whom they displaced, and the Slavs whom they dominated. The Magyars, who are often blue-eyed and with chestnut hair, have more or less lost their Turkic features, though they remain brachycephalic, doubtless through crossing with Slavs and Germans; the typical high cheek-bones of Asiatic nomads, however, are still sometimes seen.

The Magyars also penetrated into Yugoslavia, the southern home of three Slavic peoples: the Serbs, Croats and Slovenes. The Slovenes, the westernmost of the Slavs, arrived there in the 7th century and absorbed various Celtic and Illyrian tribes. Later came the Croats and Serbs, the Serbs founding a kingdom in the 13th century and expanding into Albania, Macedonia and Thessaly, where they came into contact with the Ottoman Turks and had to flee northwards. The history of this area is immensely confused, for great changes have occurred everywhere: not only has the country changed masters many times, but there have been mass evictions of the peasantry, and colonisation on a large scale. The southern Slavs are therefore very variable in type, and the Serbs in particular are darker than the Slovenes, and with a rounder head.

Further south, in Montenegro, we come across the tallest race in Europe living in the barren mountain uplands more or less surrounded by Turks. The Montenegrins have large, brachycephalic heads, with dark brown hair and often reddish beards; they have thick eyebrows, often meeting over the nose, prominent brow-ridges, and a nose which tends to be broad and thick-tipped. Though they speak Serbian, they are related to the Albanians and still preserve their exogamous clan system and love of feuds. The physical type is seen, less markedly, in Bosnia to the north.

The Albanians are descendants of the old Illyrian tribes and are Dinaric in type. The Dinaric race is noted for its large round head, flattened at the back – though this flattening may be due to the custom of cradling infants – and for a typical high-rooted, high-bridged nose coming to a thin tip. In the north there are the Ghegs, somewhat shorter than the Montenegrins, their faces showing less bony relief; the Toscs in the south have a more globular head, and their nose lacks the Dinaric high bridge. The Ghegs are Catholic by religion, the Toscs Orthodox; the rest of the population is Muslim. The language of Albania also reflects the mixed history of this area, being a hybrid between Illyrian, Thracian, Latin, Slavic and Turkish.

To the east is Bulgaria, also a composite nation. Once the home of the Thracians, it was subjugated by Rome, submerged by the Slavs and by Ugrian tribes; the Turkish conquest followed, and sporadic invasions by Tatars and the Muslim Cherkesses. There are two main ethnic types visible: one is tall with dark hair and rufous beards, a nose which is sometimes straight and sometimes concave, reminiscent of the Mongols; the other type is shorter and fairer.

Rumania gets its name from Roman colonists, over 200,000 in number, settled by the emperor Trajan in Dacia. The country was later overrun by Goths and Asiatics, and Germans, Magyars, Hungarians, Serbs, Bulgars, Ottoman Turks, Tatars, Armenians and Kurds are also present. The type is mainly Dinaric, fairly dark, and often with a small nose like the Russians. Also present in this very mixed population are the Vlachs (a word cognate with Welsh and Walloon, and meaning foreigner) who are nomadic shepherds. They live in black tents and are perhaps descended from the Scythians; they have spread now into Greece and Macedonia. Gypsies are also here in force: Rumania seems to be the European centre for this wandering people, who originally came from India.

Going north we again enter the territory of the Slavs. The basic type is fair, with characteristic snub nose, round face and plump cheeks, especially amongst women; this appearance is due to a fatty deposit on the cheek-bones and upper eyelids. The dark mountaineers of the Ukraine, however, are also related to the Turks and Tatars, whom they have absorbed in large numbers, together with Scyths, Sarmatians, the Black Sea Goths and the pre-Scythian Cimmerians. (A Mongolian strain is also present in the Crimea, amongst the Kalmuck.)

The Slavic type is also evident in Poland, where ash-blond hair and grey eyes are common amongst the peasants. Poland, however, being open on all sides except the south, also has a large German and Baltic population. Germans and Jews form the bulk of the middle classes throughout, while the aristocracy is German in the west, Polish in the east, where a thin, long-nosed face is common; the peasantry changes from Polish in the west to Lithuanian, White Russian and Ruthenian in the east.

Russians (60–62)

The White Russians are the fairest of these three last groups, and though they are similar to the Baltic populations they must also be descended from the original Slavic stock which was untouched by the Mongolian invasion of Eastern Prussia. The Great Russians, on the other hand, centred upon Moscow, had continually to fight the Mongols from the days of the Huns to Kublai Khan; they also partly repulsed and partly absorbed the Finnish tribes as they made their way up to the White Sea. They show a diversity of racial traits, from the broad-faced, snub-nosed Moujik once famous for his heavy beard – a cultural rather than a racial element – who has a heavy jaw and curious brown eyes, sometimes called beer-coloured, to Nordics, Dinarics, Balts and every kind of Mongol.

Balts, Finns and Lapps (66–72)

The Finnish tribes, part of the great Finno-Ugrian family, originally lived between the Volga and the Don. Voguls and Ostiaks, the closest linguistic relatives of the Magyars, now live in Siberia; however, the bulk of the Finnish tribes moved north towards the Baltic, leaving small settlements behind them as they went, and eventually taking over what is now Latvia and Estonia, where they absorbed the original Iron Age population. They reached Finland by 700 A.D., and settled the south and centre: they are the present-day Tavastians. Later came the Karelians, now inhabiting eastern Finland. The Tavastians are fairly tall and thickset, often blond, and with a square or oval face; their forehead tends to bulge, and their nose is concave. The Karelians are darker and shorter, and less brachycephalic.

Estonians are somewhat taller and considerably blonder, not surprising seeing the numerous Swedes and early north Germans who have settled here. The Nordic element is also visible in Finland proper.

Further down the coast are the Letts and Lithuanians, whose original homeland was in an area circumscribed by the early Finns, Slavs and Germanic tribes. The Letts moved up first, followed around 1200 A.D. by the Lithuanians, who founded an empire. The Hanseatic cities attracted many immigrants and traders, Germans especially, and Tatars also settled here in the 15th century, to help in the defence of the country; but its independence came to an end in 1561, through the concerted efforts of Poland, Sweden and Russia.

Letts have absorbed much Finnish blood, while the Lithuanians are influenced by the Slavs. They are generally medium tall, mesocephalic, with blond hair and blue eyes.

The Lapps are a quite different race. Typically they are dark-haired, with a yellowish skin and sometimes a Mongolian type of eye; their bony structure is infantile, with short limbs, a bulbous forehead, a small weak jaw and a child-like nose. This is a Palaearctic type, and it is probable that this nomadic people represents a stage in the evolution of both Upper Palaeolithic Europeans and of Mongoloids. Their homeland was perhaps in western Siberia, where they can have learnt the technique of reindeer-herding from the Samoyeds in the first millennium B.C.; thence they slowly spread into northern Scandinavia, acquiring a Finnish language with loan-words from Letts, Lithuanians and Scandinavians. Physically their appearance has been modified by Nordic and Baltic features.

Armenoid (Turkey and the Caucasus) (73–76)

We now start another sweep, from Turkey through the Caucasus and the Middle East as far as Afghanistan. We must leave the main body of the Turkic tribes till later, when we deal with the peoples of the great Russian plains; those who concern us at the moment are the tribes who entered Asia Minor.

The first Turks in this region were the Seljuks, who came from Russian Turkestan and invaded Persia in 1048 A.D.; they dominated Syria and Iraq, and a few went north into Armenia. They were followed by many other Turkish tribes, one of the latest being the Osmanlis who obtained control of the Seljuk empire in 1300 A.D. and founded the Ottoman dynasty. The empire then reached into Egypt, Turkey and eastern Europe, and there are pockets of Turks still remaining throughout the Balkans.

The original Turks were not Mongols, but were a white, tall, dark-haired race; they were probably mesocephalic like the present-day Yuruks, a pastoral people living in Cappadocia who retained their ancient ways until the formation of the Turkish republic. Modern Turks, however, show few of these characteristics, owing to centuries of intermarriage with the inhabitants of the countries which they overran; they differ little from the Balkan peoples we have already described, though we can see some Armenian influence in their brachycephaly, and many have the Dinaric nose with its high root and bridge.

In Asia Minor there are groups of people who have been little influenced by the Turks, and whose heads are notably more brachycephalic: the Armenians are the classic example. We can see the type in sculptures of the Assyrian and Hittite civilisations, which show the typical sloping forehead and the large beaky nose; from its centre, perhaps in the Caucasus itself where the Armenians live, the type may have spread out to the east in Pakistan, into western Europe where its modified form is called Dinaric, and south into Arabia.

The Armenians, who may derive from the Hittites, have been established in the Caucasus since the Iron Age, and ruled a powerful kingdom which reached down to the Mediterranean before the arrival of the Turks. They are now largely endogamous, like many another people in times of adversity, and have thus kept their old characteristics, which remain even among those who have left the country in great numbers as traders and entrepreneurs.

Besides their long, curved noses, they are notable for a broad, pointed skull with an almost vertical back to the head which, as among the Dinarics, may partly be caused by cradling habits. They have plentiful hair, often with a low wave, and their eyebrows are thick, meeting over the nose; their chin is large, with a cleft, and they are remarkably heavy for their height.

Another group of people with extremely broad heads are the Aissores or Assyrians, who came from Mesopotamia at the time of the Mongol conquests. Also present are the Ossetes, a remnant of the Scythian tribes; Kurds, Iranians, some Turks, Tatars and Mongols, and the Caucasians proper, of which 16 physical types have been described.

The Caucasians all speak dialects of one language, the best known two being Georgian and Cherkess, or Circassian. The Cherkesses are mainly Muslim; since the Russian conquest of the area many have moved into Turkish territory, to Turkey proper, Syria and the Balkans; the Georgians, who are Christian, remain. All the inhabitants of the Caucasus, however, have the same basic traits, in spite of their tribal differences: they are tall, with dark hair and white skin (for which the Circassians were famous) and with round heads. Their noses are shorter than those of the Armenians and can even be concave, as amongst the Georgians. This type is thus a local Alpine stock with much Mediterranean admixture, the linguistic complexity of the area pointing up its involved history.

Irano-Afghans (77–84)

Southwards we come across the eastern extension of the white race, the Irano-Afghans, a mixture of Nordic and Mediterranean peoples. At one time their ancestors must have lived on the grassy plains about the Oxus and Jaxartes rivers in what is now Russian Turkestan. The Aryans were the first to move out in about 1400 B.C., taking their cattle into India; some six hundred years later the nomadic, horse-riding Iranians moved into Persia. Those who remained behind apparently mingled with Altaic-speakers, and their culture went west with the Scyths, and eastwards into China.

Nomads still live in the area, such as the Kurds, who may be descendants of the proto-Nordic steppe peoples of Turkestan. Though somewhat mixed with Irano-Afghans, they have kept something of their type and language for three millennia. They once lived in Kurdistan, to the south of Armenia, but their warlike character has caused them to be ousted from country after country, so that they now live in Iran, Iraq and Turkey, and at the time of writing they are once more up in arms, this time against the central government of Iran.

Their Nordic character comes out in the blond hair and blue eyes which quite half of them possess, especially in the west; in the east, as they intermarry with Turks and Armenians, their heads become rounder, their hair darker and their features uglier.

The earliest Iranians proper entered Iran in the 8th century B.C., when there was more rainfall and less desert, and they eventually founded the great empires of the Medes (partly Armenian) and Persians, which at one time covered most of the Middle East, and were only stopped from entering Europe by the Greeks. After the invasions of the Huns, the Arabs formed an empire from 637 to 1029 A.D., and established themselves throughout the country; the Seljuk Turks swarmed in during the 11th century, followed by the two great Mongol invasions under Genghis Khan and Timur; in the 18th century there came the Afghan conquest. Thus, though the Iranians are originally descended from early Nordics, the Nordic strain is hard to find. The northwest is largely peopled by brachycephalic Turkomans, the Tajiks, some with Armenoid features and others, long-faced, with Turki ones. Elsewhere the type is Mediterranean, either with the straight nose of the Arabs or with the convex one of the Afghan. Thus those living near Persepolis, the Farsi, are slender, fair-skinned and with abundant chestnut hair, though a few blonds are present; they have long heads with convex narrow noses. This is a more or less Mediterranean stock, though the jaw is heavier than usual for Arabs. Another large group, the Lurs of eastern Iran, are taller, darker, and more dolichocephalic, with an oval face. The population is especially mixed in the cities, where some brachycephalic types may have come either from the north or from the Baluchis in the south.

The Baluchis, some of whom claim Arab descent, are a cross between Iranians, Arabs, Scythians and the ancient Veddoid strain which is otherwise seen amongst the hill tribes of India. They are tall, fair, broad-headed, with a long and narrow nose. Many of them are sought for as soldiers, being fine horsemen and more tractable than their neighbours, the Pathans.

The Pathans and Afghans to the east are often confused with one another. The western Pathans are the Pathans proper, and extend from within the eastern border of Iran to the head of the Khyber pass; the eastern Pathans, or Afghans proper, who include the Afridi, Mohmand and Waziri tribes, extend from the Khyber south into western Baluchistan, the southern two-thirds of the famous North-West Frontier. All this country is strategically important, as it lies across the main routes from India to the Middle East, and all pretenders to empire have tried to control the Hindu Kush from where an easy passage into India is possible. Here the Aryans and Mauryans entered India; here came Alexander, the tribes of the Yueh Chi, the Mongols, the Huns and the Persians, all of whom have made this country one of great racial admixture.

Amongst the Pathans are the Hazara, a remnant of the Mongolian expansion left there by Genghis Khan in the 14th century; they are endogamous and have hardly affected the racial composition of the area. Northwards is a territory with Dardic-speaking inhabitants: the Kafir, the most primitive of these, are divided into strictly segregated social classes representing conquerors and aboriginals, the latter being said to have a non-Indo-European language. The country is so inaccessible that the Kafir were only converted to Islam at the turn of this century.

Pathans, Afghans and Persians are all similar in appearance; they are dolichocephalic, with long faces and noses, hair usually dark but sometimes fair. Metrically they can only be distinguished from Nordics by their longer foreheads and noses. The facial bones are much heavier than those of Mediterranean Arabs, and the living face shows a surprising amount of bony relief and fine modelling. The Dardic-speaking Kafirs are essentially similar, though they are much blonder: an inheritance from the Nordic invaders of the region. The aboriginal population, however, is smaller and shorter-nosed.

Semites (85–97)
Iraq, which was the site of many of the earliest major civilisations, has also known constant migrations and counter-migrations from the 5th millennium onwards. After the empires of Sumer, Akkad, Assyria and the Hittites, the country was dominated first by Greeks

and then Persians until the 7th century A.D., when its history runs parallel to that of Iran: first the Arab empire, followed by that of the Seljuks, then the Mongol invasion which destroyed the careful irrigation system which had raised the country to affluence; later the dull corrupt government of the Turks, and lastly the Afghan conquest. This history has produced a population taller and heavier than that found in Arabia, with a longer, broader nose, a heavier and deeper jaw, eyebrows meeting over the nose, the skull tending towards mesocephaly; by which one can discern the influence of the mountaineers of Armenia and some infusion of Negro blood. Amongst the Arabs proper, those living in the towns have been most affected by their neighbours, for the Bedouin, who live on the southwestern desert fringe, pride themselves upon their pure blood and marry only amongst themselves.

Since early times Syria, from which many of the Semitic invasions of Mesopotamia started, has been involved with the rest of the Near East in wars between the great empires of Egypt and the Middle East. Originally peopled by Arabs from Arabia, it was invaded by Aryans from the north in the 8th century B.C., and a century later by the Scythians and Cimmerians, before whose onslaught fell both the Assyrians and the Medes; later the land lay under Persian domination, till the time of the Roman conquest and the rise of the Arab empire in the 7th century A.D. All these invasions – including those of the European crusaders – have little modified the basic Bedouin type. The desert-dwellers, however, tend towards mesocephaly, and those living in the mountains are brachycephalic like the Ghegs, though with a shorter and broader nose, with the thick hair and concurrent eyebrows of the Armenians, and with a nose which is Armenoid except for its greater breadth.

Lebanon at first escaped occupation by the Arabs in the early days of their empire, and this mountain area became a refuge for many Christian peoples: Aramaeans, Anatolians and Maronites, who fiercely resisted Islam. Later the Druse and other heretical Muslim sects entered the region, and a bitter hatred has existed between them and the Maronites.

Another bitter feud exists nowadays between Arabs and Jews, though both originally are Semitic peoples. The Jews probably originated as a nomadic tribe from the desert borders of southern Mesopotamia, who moved north and west along the borders of cultivation till they reached Sinai, Egypt, and thence Palestine. Their history has been marked by three tremendous upheavals which scattered them over the world, known as the Diaspora. The first was the captivity in Babylon, where many continued to live after the main body had been returned to their homes. The second was caused by the expansion of Hellenism, when Jews emigrated to Egypt, Syria, Asia Minor, the Balkans and the Black Sea, where they had important colonies. Their Crimea settlement, though broken up by the Goths and the Huns, eventually led to the establishment of a kingdom under the Kazars, who had been partially Judaized, and later to the Slavic state at Kiev, the great centre for East European Jewry.

The third Diaspora, after the destruction of the Temple by the Romans, led to the settlement of Jews in Italy, Spain, France and Germany. France was the first to expel her Jews, in 1384, and they took refuge amongst the Sephardic branch in Spain, and the Ashkenazic branch in Germany. The Spanish Jews, expelled in their turn in 1492, moved to Holland, England, Italy and North Africa, and large numbers to the newly-founded Turkish empire; the Ashkenazim eventually moved east and joined the remnants of the Byzantine and Kazar Jews, from which meeting sprang the formation of the Yiddish language. Before the foundation of Israel as a nation, the Sephardim predominated in the Balkans, the Near East and both sides of the Mediterranean; Oriental Jews are to be found along the coasts of North Africa, and through the Middle East into India and even China; the Ashkenazim have offshoots in the New World, South Africa and the Near East.

These Jews have all undergone change by intermarriage in the countries they settled in, but those who remained in Palestine are of two recognisable types. In one, the very narrow head projects at the back, the forehead sweeping back in a fine curve; there is a long narrow face, a small jaw and a convex nose. In the other, the build is more slender, the face shorter and with a larger jaw, the nose short and straight and the eyebrows thick and concurrent. The Jewish look, which many have remarked on, is perhaps more of a cultural than a racial characteristic, for Jews are hardly distinguishable from other Semites except by the nasal wings, which are attached slightly higher on the cheeks than normal, and a more slanting ear.

The homeland of the Arabs is in Arabia, though in the southwest an aboriginal population which may be Veddoid is also present; besides them, there is a sizeable Negro population brought over from Africa as slaves. The purest Mediterranean features are to be seen amongst the Sleyb, an outcast group who attach themselves as tinkers and leatherworkers to the Bedouin.

The Bedouin must have got their knowledge of cattle and camel breeding from the cattle-cultures of southern Arabia, which in turn are connected with India and East Africa. The Bedouin are generally slight, slender, with a small narrow head and swarthy white skin when untanned; their hair is black or brown with a light wave in it, the nose narrow, convex, and with a high root. The Ruwalla tribe, made famous by Lawrence of Arabia, has a very narrow face, and the hawk nose is less common.

A Nordic strain appears amongst some of the plateau peoples; and the coastal Arabs, always great seafarers, may have got their mixed racial type from Armenoids and even Malays, since they are broader-faced, brachycephalic and with straighter, coarser hair than is usual. The Omani, even greater sailors, have acquired a large Negro population strain from their centuries of dominance in East Africa, and a large Negro population is present amongst them.

East Hamites (98–103)

Arabs have settled most of the East African coast in great numbers, but the basic population in the north is Hamitic. This word properly refers to a family of languages which, with Semitic, spreads over most of Africa north of the equator. There are two main branches, the eastern and western (sometimes called northern), and the Hamites are thought to have originated in south Arabia or even further east, and are closely related to the Semites.

The oldest members of this stock were the pre-Dynastic Egyptians, who were long-headed: we can see something approaching this type today in the Beja tribes of the Sudan, who reach into Eritrea. The Hadendoa, known to British soldiers of the last century as Fuzzy-Wuzzies on account of their frizzy hair, have been much mixed with Sudanese Negroes but are the best known amongst them. A fierce wild people, they are nomads who once reckoned their ancestry by the female line and went almost naked, till the coming of Islam made them amongst the most extreme Muslims of East Africa; they have now taken to clothes and they reckon descent patrilineally according to the Koran. They are pastoralists, with great numbers of camels.

From dynastic times in Egypt there were two main types, the northern being of a heavier build, with a larger jaw and a broader skull than the southern which was dolichocephalic, with a narrow face and jaw, thin lips, a long eye-slit and a narrow aquiline nose. Both types are still to be found in Egypt, but the northern one has spread most. There is also a strong infusion of Arab and Turkish blood, especially in the cities, and there are other types reminding one of Armenians and Circassians; there is also a considerable darkening of the skin brought about through mixture with Negro and Abyssinian slaves, and with the local Negro populations in the south. Some observers have also claimed to be able to distinguish the Muslims from the Christian Copts, who are slightly lighter in colouring and perhaps have a thinner nose.

The language spoken in the Ethiopian highlands is the most ancient form of Semitic known in Africa, and the original domestication of cattle seems to have occurred in the region. There are seven main groups of people present: the Cushites and the Sidamo, both of early Hamitic stock who antedate the Semitic Amhara, or Ethiopians proper; the Galla in the southwest, who invaded the country in the 16th century with their cattle; the Somali and their relatives the Danakil to the northeast, and a number of Negro tribes who came originally from the Sudan.

The Amhara came from the Hadhramaut in southern Arabia some centuries before Christ, and their first state was based on Axum, controlling the trade between Egypt and Arabia. An Arab ruling class was established in the 3rd century B.C.; seven centuries later Axum was converted to Christianity by Syrian missionaries, and the kingdom spread to Yemen and the Nile Valley, but declined soon after. Later the centre moved to the highlands.

The Amhara, who trace their royal line back to the Queen of Sheba, are much like the Beja in appearance, though they are mixed with a Negro strain and their skin ranges from almost white to a deep black. Thick lips are common, as is curly hair which sometimes becomes frizzy; the nose is high-rooted with deep nostrils. There is a rare type with a high, wide, sloping forehead and a long bony face, but the usual features are European, as can be seen in the Emperor Haile Selassie.

The pagan Galla, who now provide the bulk of the cavalry of the imperial army, are scattered throughout the country, mainly as pastoralists, though some have become sedentary and practise agriculture. They are generally darker in colouring and have broader noses.

The Somali are essentially Hamitic, though their early history is obscure, and they claim descent from early Islamic missionaries. Like their relatives the Danakil, they live in semi-desert conditions as pastoral nomads, and as a climatic adaptation they have evolved a long thin body with extremely narrow hands and feet; their noses are frequently European in shape, their features finely cut, and their hair straight. Their women can be amongst the most beautiful of the continent. But here too Negro admixture has been common, and a thick-nosed, thick-lipped type exists. They, the Gallas and the Cushites, being Hamitic, are all considerably taller than more Negroid peoples or even than the Semitic Amharas.

West Hamites (104–110)

At some time in the past, when Europe was in the grip of the Ice Age, the Sahara was still green. North Africa was then inhabited by Upper Palaeolithic food-gatherers whose primitive type is still very occasionally met with in the Atlas mountains. The whole area was soon taken over by Mediterraneans, who crossed over to Europe in mesolithic and neolithic times as the Sahara became drier, while Negroes moved up to the Atlas.

The Berbers must have been present in Libya by the third millennium B.C., for they are spoken of by Egyptians of that time; but it is probable that they did not reach over into the west until some time after Christ. There were in fact three great Berber expansions, the last of which was responsible for bringing the camel into North Africa and, occupying Algeria in the Middle Ages, at last invaded Spain in the 13th century.

The Berbers are often called blond, and while their skin is often whiter than that of a Spaniard, their hair is with few exceptions black, and their eyes brown or hazel. Some have suspected a Nordic ancestry for these people, and others even think it possible that the Mazuza, a sub-tribe of the Riffs, may be descendants of some Altaic tribe from Asia, since like them they once drove chariots, strangled oxen for sacrifice and had a council government. Herodotus indeed said that they were descended from the Persians. In any case, the main bulk of the Berbers came from Arabia: the Senhaja, for instance, claim to have come from the Yemen soon after the birth of Mohammed, and they practise the same kind of terraced agriculture as the Yemeni, build the same kind of high earthen castles, and make their pots and their textiles in the same way.

As the Sahara dried, the old inhabitants of Libya retreated to the mountains, and the North African coast became an extension of Europe, and of Egypt in the east. Romans and Carthaginians settled here, to be followed after the Middle Ages by Spain and France. However, with the introduction of the camel, the desert again became habitable, and the Arabs entered in two waves, in the 7th and 11th centuries. Some of these turned to the Berber way of life and practised agriculture, while others used their camels to raid caravans and get slaves. Their influence has spread considerably, but they themselves are mainly to be found in the east where they also arabised the Nile Valley and the Sudan; the Ulad Naïl of north-eastern Libya being a good example, and one of the purer Arab tribes. The cattle-owning Baggara, who keep further south where there is water, are much mixed with Negro blood.

The Berbers also have intermarried with Negroes; the Tibbu, for example, who now live in the mountains of Tibesti (whence their name, 'Rock People') and were once a powerful people, merge in the south with the Sudanese Negroes. To the west of them, in mountains even drier and more eroded, are their old enemies the Tuareg, divided into nobles, who are quite pure in blood, tribute-payers and negroid slaves. Though notorious raiders, they are extremely chivalrous to their women, which struck the great Arab historian ibn Batuta as a folly, and have a great love of music and poetry. They are the most dolichocephalic of the western Hamites, being lean, long-limbed, with long hands and feet, and having the most astonishing powers of physical endurance, like the Somali whom they resemble; their features are clear-cut, with a long face, high convex nose and pointed chin, though this is difficult to observe because the Tuareg men veil their faces.

Further to the west the purest Berbers live in two groups, in the Kabyle hills and the Aures mountains. These people are the most stable and the oldest of the Berbers, and practise terraced agriculture; others are pastoralists who wander from place to place with their flocks, to catch the new pastures as the rain falls. The Kabyles have noticeably European features and blond skin, and the basic form is Early Mediterranean with a dash of Negro, and some of the old Palaeolithic strain which gives them a measure of brachycephaly. Arabic-speakers who are also nomads live on the barren plains and uplands, and in the oases there is a mixture of Arab and Berber, some of them agriculturalists, others traders.

In Morocco are the Riffs, also agriculturalists, who with the Tuareg are famous for their warlike activities. Though they are the blondest and most Nordic in appearance of all the Berbers, they are of very mixed ancestry, some of them claiming Arab descent, others descending from heathen tribes. Most of them have pinkish-white skins, brown eyes tinged with green or blue, and though all are basically dolichocephalic, some are long-faced and hook-nosed, others typically Mediterranean with a straight nose; some look like typical Englishmen, and a fourth variety tends towards the broad head of the old Palaeolithic stock.

North Indians (111–118)

The last branch of the Caucasoid race to consider is that living in India. India is a large subcontinent, bounded on the north by the Himalayas which only allow access through the North-West Frontier and the ranges of Assam. Successive waves of peoples have come into the country through these two passes, filling up the plains of Hindustan in the north and gradually working their way down to the south, where the land tapers away and the only exit is to Ceylon. As a rule one finds that the later invaders inhabit the north, and have pressed the previous inhabitants into the south and into the mountainous regions of the centre.

The first peoples to inhabit India are variously called Veddoid or pre-Dravidian, an early stock who have left traces on the coasts of southern Arabia and in Iraq. The Dravidian-speaking may have entered next, followed by Aryan tribes at about 1500 B.C. These people were notable warriors who, coming perhaps from the southern Asian plains, despised city life, and it is supposed that the destruction of the Indus civilisation came at their hands. Another group, presumably from the region of Afghanistan and perhaps related to the Scythians, came in perhaps five hundred years later, settled in Peshawar and moved down to Gujerat and even further south to Coorg, three-quarters of the way down the west coast. Greeks entered at the same place after Alexander, and stimulated the formation of the Gandhara culture; then a Bactrian tribe of Turkomans conquered Kabul in A.D. 20 and reached as far as Benares, though their empire came to an end in 178 A.D. The White Huns – a mixture of Turki and Mongol tribes – swept over India in the 5th century A.D., and though they were expelled in 528 A.D. by a confederation of Hindu princes, the Turks later followed in their footsteps, having previously annexed the Hun empire. They conquered the north of India in 1200 A.D. and the south a century later.

One result of these many movements of peoples into the country, which here have been grossly over-simplified, was the formation of castes. A caste in its simplest form is a group whose members only marry amongst themselves. Tribes easily get pressed into becoming castes, and it is possible that the low-class Sudras were once the original inhabitants of India, forced into an inferior category by the Aryan invaders who themselves were divided into four classes. Other castes are occupational; a third type is sometimes formed by intermarriage between castes, and a fourth by religious sects springing up who aim at doing away with the caste system, but who rapidly form new castes of their own. All these inherited castes are thus not necessarily racial in the beginning, as may be seen with the

Rajputs and Jats of the north, respectively nobles and Sudras, who have the same long narrow face, regular features and large well-cut nose. Indeed, some of the Jats differ more amongst themselves than the average type does from the Rajputs, and both are believed to be descendants of the original Aryan invaders, though doubtless inter-marriage with other peoples has occurred.

Besides caste, religion is another great social factor in India. The Turkish conquest brought about the conversion of many millions to Islam, the bulk of whom now reside in Pakistan, though large numbers still exist in India proper; Buddhism has disappeared, but Hinduism, its parent religion, occurs in numerous sects; there are also Jains, the Sikhs of the north, Parsees, Jews, Christians, and pagan tribes.

Other Aryan peoples besides the Rajput inhabit northern India as far as the Punjab and into Kashmir, and as far as Nepal which was settled by the Gurkhas, a broad-chested somewhat Mongoloid people who were driven out of Rajputana by the Muslim invasions. East of the Punjab begins the Hindustani type, which reaches as far as Bihar to the northwest of Calcutta, occupying the plains of the Ganges and the valleys leading up to the hills on both sides. The Aryan branch of this stock is supposed to have entered India through passes to the west of the Karakorams, and to have married Dravidian-speaking women: thus the type is essentially mixed, being short but long-headed, while noses – always an indication of social position in India – are straight and narrow amongst the upper classes, and flatter in the lower. Further to the east, in the plain of Bengal and the delta of the Ganges, heads become broader due to an admixture with Tibeto-Burman peoples, and some Mongoloid traits become visible.

SOUTH INDIA AND PACIFIC

South Indians and Ceylonese (119–127)

The use of the terms Aryan and Dravidian, it should be remembered, is a somewhat lazy way out of a difficult problem, for these define languages rather than race. When we come to the south of India the problem is compounded by the existence of people speaking Munda, a language allied to the Mon-Khmer group of southeast Asia, and by the presence of the Veddoids.

The Veddas themselves live in Ceylon, taking refuge there after having been forced out of southern India by the influx of peoples from the north. As a social group they are now few in number and live most primitive lives, gathering food and hunting small animals; they sleep in rock shelters and leaf huts. The type however is fairly widespread, due to intermarriage with neighbouring tribes. They are very short, sometimes almost black in colour; the head is very small, long and narrow, especially at the forehead, although well-developed browridges are present, giving the face a scowling look. The nose is broad and snub, the hair black, coarse and wavy. In Ceylon they have modified the Sinhalese who speak an Aryan language and have some characteristics in common with the Irano-Afghans; they have also influenced the Tamils somewhat.

The Tamils are found mainly in the southeast, whence they have migrated to Ceylon and Malaya. They speak a Dravidian language, and are Mediterranean in appearance; they are a hard-headed, practical people with a peculiar aptitude for music, mathematics and physics, and have produced physicists whose names are well-known in Europe.

Dravidian-speakers have long been thought to have entered India before the Aryans, though one modern theory sees them as coming by sea or along the west coast around 500 B.C. and creating an iron-using civilisation in the Deccan, though this may have been introduced by Munda-speakers from the east. The problem is still murky, and one can say little about them except that they seem to be a branch of the Caucasoid race, darker than usual, short, and with wavy hair, and that the type can merge imperceptibly with that of the Veddoids amongst the hill tribes of India.

There are many interesting Dravidian tribes, such as the Kallar and Maravar in the south, who have a bull cult strikingly like that found in Crete in Mycenaean times: young men have to jump on the bull's back and retrieve a cloth from its horns. In Central India there are the Bhils who speak an Indo-Aryan tongue which probably replaced a Dravidian one, which in turn may have replaced an original Kolarian one. They are small and swarthy, divided into exogamous and totemic clans, and they venerate the horse; they are now mainly peaceful agriculturalists, but once were famed for their brigandry and lawlessness. Another forest group of central India are the Gonds who use the plough in farming and whose favourite weapon is a light axe with which they are known to have killed tigers in single combat. They too have totemistic clans, and they once formed a dynasty of some importance over all the Gond tribes, the old palaces still being visible.

An intrusive tribe is that of the Todas in the Nilgiri hills, who seem to be of northern Indian stock, and may even be descended from the Hittites; they are cattle herders and practise a complicated ritual of the dairy, and they point to the origin of the sacred cow in India.

The hill tribes are much more primitive, some of them, like the Kadar, existing by hunting and gathering food out of the forest, others practising a crude agriculture and using the digging stick, like the Chenchu. Some of the less primitive use the pellet bow, and the blow-gun is known to one tribe of the Palni Hills. The Urali practise shifting agriculture, and build tree houses fifty or so feet above the ground, where women seclude themselves at adolescence and childbirth. Many chip or file their front teeth to a point, and some of the women dress only in leaf skirts which are renewed several times a day.

Negritos (128–131)

These tribes are generally Veddoid in appearance, but the Kadar have been termed Negritoid on account of their very small size and woolly hair. They also have certain features, such as ornamented combs, which are similar to those of Negritos in Malaya and the Philippines. Negritos may have once been found throughout southern Asia, and they are now represented by the Andaman Islanders, the Semang of Malaya, the Aeta of the Philippines, some dwarf tribes in New Guinea, and a dwarf element in the now extinct Tasmanians.

The Onges of the Andaman Islands are remarkable for having pepper-corn hair and steatopygia, a unique combination otherwise present only amongst the Bushmen in Africa. However, their blood groups are quite dissimilar, and link them rather to the inhabitants of Melanesia; their skulls, too, are of a type common in south-eastern Asia. It is possible that they and the other Negritos are dwarfish representatives of a stock which figured in the ancestry of the Melanesians and, some have thought, of the Burmese and Javanese also. Their small size may be due both to isolation and as an adaptation to life in thick forest: the New Guinea dwarfs, for instance, seem to have evolved their form out of the general Melanesian stock which surrounds them.

The Onges are very short, very dark, with short round heads displaying infantile features, for the jaw is singularly undeveloped. Their hair is woolly like that of other Negritos, and they are brachycephalic. The Aeta also are brachycephalic, but their noses are much flatter and broader, and they often have thick beards and hair on their arms. The Semang are lighter in colour and meso-cephalic, with a slightly protruding jaw; the Sakai are a very mixed people. All these tribes are primitive in their culture, the Andaman Islanders living mainly by fishing, the others by hunting and food-gathering; the bow is their principal weapon, though the Sakai have the blow-gun.

Australian Aborigines (132–137)

The link between the Veddoids and the Australian aborigines has been suspected because of their similar appearance, and they also have a rare combination of blood groups in common. They must have reached Australia from somewhere in southeastern Asia during the late Pleistocene, coming by way of New Guinea which was then attached to Asia. Their culture is mesolithic, for they have neither metals, pottery nor agriculture but use stone and wooden implements: stone axes on wooden hafts, flint knives, small stone flakes or microliths used as barbs; clubs, spears, spear-throwers and the boomerang. They live by hunting and food-gathering, and though their material culture is simple, their social life is complicated: they have exogamous clans, some tribes having as many as eight whose members must intermarry in a pre-determined fashion, and a complex of institutions which goes under the name of totemism. When first discovered there were some 300,000 aborigines, thus forming the largest group of Stone Age people left in the world, but their numbers have since rapidly decreased and only some 50,000 pure-bred natives are left.

Physically, four main types have been distinguished. The Veddoid type, also related to the Melanesians by the occurrence of a high ratio of blood group N, is in the north where it has become adapted to desert conditions by a darkening of the skin and a taller thinner body build, an adaptation we have also seen amongst the Somali. They are called Carpentarian. An example of their type is the Tiwi tribe. The Murrayans inhabit the cooler southwest, where the bulk of the modern Australians now live. Their heads are small, narrow and high, their faces being broader than their skulls; they have browridges, a retreating forehead, deep-sunk eyes, a broad flat nose with a very low bridge. Their build is short and stocky, with plentiful hair. The Barrineans, a Negrito type like the Tasmanians, have been found in the rain forests of Queensland; the fourth type, exemplified by the Arunta, is a cross between the Murrayans and Carpentarians, living in the central desert.

The origin of the Australians has given rise to much discussion. The earliest theory was that they were archaic Caucasoids, but their blood groups and finger-print patterns are quite dissimilar. A second theory sees them as a mixture of Negritos with Murrayans and Carpentarians – the Carpentarians having perhaps come from some hot dry region in India, and later worked their way down through southeast Asia where they met with a Mongoloid race and gave rise to the Indonesians. One can at any rate see the Carpentarian type throughout southeast Asia, in New Guinea, Melanesia and the Philippines. The Murrayans in their turn may represent the survivors, with the Ainu of Japan, of an archaic white stock which at one time seems to have spread over Russia, Siberia and into China and which, by crossing with Mongoloid peoples, may have been the ancestor of the American Indians.

The third theory is that Australoids evolved in the region about Malaya and Australia, as evidenced by fossil finds of Pithecanthropus and other primitive men, spread north up the Malay peninsula into India and beyond, and east and south into Australia and Melanesia. Isolated in Australia, they retained their type, while in Melanesia they were influenced by later immigrants. Of these three theories the first is unlikely, the second ingenious and the third probable.

Polynesians and Micronesians (138–142)

There are three main groups of peoples in the Pacific: Polynesians and their relatives the Micronesians, who are both light-skinned; and the dark-skinned, frizzy-haired Melanesians. The origin of the Polynesians has also been a subject of debate, the early theory being that they came from Indonesia, since their language belongs to the Malayan-Polynesian family; this was opposed by the notion that they came from various places on the Pacific coast of the Americas, and it is indeed probable that some contact with America was made, since among other things the sweet potato is known in Polynesia by an American name. The latest, most likely theory is that they were formed by the cross between a Murrayan-like race, who could either be an archaic Caucasoid or the type developed in the Malaysian-Australian region, and a Mongoloid strain, originating in southern China and emigrating when the Chinese were beginning to push down from the north. Their blood groups certainly differentiate them from other peoples in Asia and the Pacific, and show a resemblance to those of the American Indians, which may mean that they share a common ancestry.

The Neolithic inhabitants of southern China were then forced either into Siam or across the sea into the Philippines. From there, it seems, Polynesians sailed to the Micronesian Islands and thence to Samoa, Tonga and Tahiti.

Radio-carbon measurements date early remains in the Marquesas, to the east of these islands, at about 130 B.C., and it is probable that Tahiti was first occupied by 500 B.C. Hawaii, over two thousand miles to the north, was occupied by the 2nd century A.D., Easter Island by the 4th century, and New Zealand by the 12th. These extraordinary feats of navigation were accomplished in twin-hulled canoes, some of which were as much as a hundred feet long, and which must have carried all the stores and equipment for a colonising expedition.

Pacific islands are either small coral atolls, or of volcanic origin. Taro, sweet potatoes, bananas, sugar cane are all grown, and fishing is very important; for meat the Polynesians ate dogs and domestic fowls, while cannibalism was also practised, especially in the Marquesas where human sacrifice accompanied by ritual debauch was rife. In New Zealand the Maoris also ate the roots of edible brackens.

The Maoris were expert at warfare, each man being trained in hand-to-hand fighting, though ambushes and stratagems were preferred; but when the Europeans arrived they excelled in more extended warfare, and the Maori wars were protracted. The Maoris originally arrived in New Zealand in a 'great fleet' under a famous chief, and the social organisation of the country with its tribes and clans still reflects the order by which the original settlers travelled.

In Hawaii, the Polynesians welcomed the Europeans, their culture apparently having lost something of its vigour; they easily gave up belief in their gods, who had ceased to be important to them, and accepted Christianity with surprising readiness.

In Micronesia, the Yap islanders speak an Indonesian language and show various Malayan influences such as the habit of chewing betel-nut and the existence of large community houses. They are also famous for their pierced stone discs, often of enormous size, which they use as a kind of money.

Physically, Polynesians are tall and very handsome, with a light brown skin which can range from almost white to brown; head form is variable, and the face usually long and narrow, though it can also be short and broad, with soft features and large eyes. This variability no doubt bespeaks their mixed origin. Micronesians, who also speak a language of the Malayan-Polynesian family, are brown-skinned, but are smaller and have finer features; and in the east they have been influenced by the Melanesians.

Melanesians (143–148)

Melanesia includes New Guinea, Fiji, the Solomon Islands and the New Hebrides. The inhabitants of this region must have come from Asia through the Malay peninsula, where skeletal remains of a so-called Palaeo-Melanesian people have been found. Like the Polynesians, one element in their make-up may have been the Murrayan stock, and their apparent Negroid features must have evolved quite independently of the true Negroes in Africa, due to living in a similar tropical climate. Their hair, though frizzy, never grows in a spiral, their blood groups are different, and their lips not so everted nor their noses so broad.

Characteristics are a large jaw, large molar teeth and shovel-shaped incisors, also found amongst Mongoloids and American Indians. Their skin is a very dark brown, the skull long but very broad, with a sloping forehead and brow-ridges; their noses, especially amongst New Guinea tribes, are rather beaky, with a depressed tip, a feature which is emphasised in their art. Those living in the smaller islands tend to be shorter, and in Fiji there is some Polynesian admixture.

They are mainly agricultural, practising slash-and-burn agriculture in the heavy forests, though hunting and fishing are also important. Isolated tribes, still living in a Stone Age culture, have recently been discovered in the highlands and in the Wahgi Valley of New Guinea, living in small warring communities; and an ancient Megalithic religion is still practised in the New Hebrides with remarkable ceremonies in a communal long house, whose immediate origin was Indonesian. The Island Papuans have also created a complicated network of trade and barter, known as the kula, in which not only useful commodities such as food and shells circulate, but also purely social ones in the form of prized objects of prestige, dances and rituals, all of which are traded although the copyright is held by the original owners.

AFRICA, SOUTH OF THE NIGER

West Africans (149–162)

South of the area occupied by Hamitic-speakers, Africa is inhabited by Negro peoples. They are divided into four main groups: those who speak the languages of the Niger-Congo, those who speak Bantu, the Pygmies of the deep forests, and the Bushmen and Hottentots.

The earliest known Negroid skeleton, found near Timbuktu, dates from the early post-Pleistocene: it shows long slender bones, a very dolichocephalic skull almost without brow-ridges and a broad nose with the nasal bones fused together, a typical Negro trait. However, the fully differentiated Negro may only have appeared later, and he is found most characteristically in West Africa, with a narrow head, a prognathous, protruding upper jaw, a rounded forehead and under-developed chin, a very broad nose, dark skin which can be almost black, woolly hair, sparse beard, and large everted lips. He is also distinguishable by means of blood groups, some of which are unknown outside Africa.

The Bantu-speakers have possibly evolved from a cross between early Negroes and the Pygmies, since everything points to their origin in West Africa. They are less typically Negroid in the east, and mixture with Hamitic-speakers or with Nilotic Negroes has been thought to account for this; a less likely cause for their variation in the east is an admixture with an early Caucasoid strain which appeared there during post-Pleistocene times. The Bantu-speakers are in any case hardly distinguishable from those on the west coast, though their skin is normally a dark chocolate brown which becomes yellowish among the Tswana who have intermarried with Bushmen and Hottentots.

West Africa is extremely hot and moist at the coast, where there are forests and swamps; as one goes inland the country becomes more open and eventually turns into parkland, steppe country and eventually desert. Apart from these differences, there are no natural geographical boundaries except rivers, and one result has been the continuous formation of empires and small kingdoms which find it hard to resist outside pressures. The largest kingdoms of which we know were formed in the north, where the country is open to Muslim influence and the impact of the ranging cattle-people has been greatest; we know their history from Muslim historians whose accounts sometimes go back to legendary events of the 9th century A.D.

The Senegal river forms the natural boundary between Hamites and Negroes, and to the south of it live the Wolof, said to be the blackest tribe in Africa – indeed their name is said to mean 'black' – and the most garrulous. They reach a considerable distance inland, and with the slightly taller Serer tribe formed an empire under the Tucolor which lasted until the 18th century. All this region has been Islamised, and the Wolof are no exception, though pagan rites still continue; they are divided also into three hereditary classes.

Further inland, stretching to the upper Niger, live the Mandingo, an important group of tribes who raised an empire here in the 11th century. This took place soon after the collapse of the famous Ghana empire in much the same region, from which the present country of Ghana, the old Gold Coast, ungeographically takes its name. The Mandingo capital at Melle was rich and powerful, and the empire the strongest of which we have record, though it foundered at the turn of the 16th century at the hands of the Songhai.

The Mandingo are primarily agriculturalists, though they fish as well; they live in small huts with conical roofs of straw, and are divided into clans and occupational groups. Islam has affected them but little.

The Mandingo empire was often at odds with that of the Mossi, another agricultural people who came from the east and mixed with the inhabitants of the Volta basin; and also with the Songhai. The Songhai flourished from the 9th century until 1300, and controlled the salt mines of the southern Sahara, which gave them a large revenue; but they were expelled by the Moroccans who stayed there till the 18th century, though the real rulers of the Niger valley by that time were the Tuareg. The Songhai, however, also came into contact with the Hausa confederation. The Hausa speak Hamitic but are essentially Negro, though somewhat less prognathous than usual, and with narrower noses; they are also taller. They are farmers, traders, stock-breeders and artisans, noted for their open and cheerful nature. Early in the 10th century they formed a group of seven states which attained great political power though they never became a conquering empire. Islam predominates, though a few pagan customs still exist. The Hausa came under the Peul empire in the 19th century, and were then organised by means of a highly centralised administration.

The Peuls, also called Fulani or Fulbe, are a Hamitic race who came with their cattle from the east. They stayed awhile near the mountains of the southern Sahara when the desert was still green, and then moved over to Senegal. Pressure from the Muslim Almoravids in the 11th century made some of them move back east, leaving colonies behind them as they went. Another group, much later, moved south to the Fouta Jallon where, after conversion to Islam, they proclaimed a holy war against their neighbours in the 18th century. In Nigeria and Adamawa, Peuls formed a kingdom in the 16th century, conquered the Hausa in 1804 but were held in check by another Sudanese empire, the Bornu, and their empire came to an end soon after.

The tribes further south, on the great bulge of West Africa, are numerous, and the next most important kingdom to be found is that of Ashanti. They, the Dahomey nation, the Yoruba, Benin and Nupe all speak languages belonging to the Kwa family, and their countries were the principal ones visited by slave-traders who spoke in wonder of the barbaric splendour of their courts, and the large-scale practice of human sacrifice which accompanied important ceremonies, though they did not see the complex moral systems behind this. They all had well-developed social institutions, a religious pantheon, a highly evolved legal system and a tight-knit military organisation.

The Ashanti, a fairly homogeneous people except in the north where they are mixed with the Peuls, have, together with the neighbouring Akan, a ritual kingship with remarkable similarities to that of ancient Egypt, and they are associated with the famous Golden Stool over which the war with England was fought in the late 19th century.

Further east is the Dahomey country, where the Adja settled in the 9th century, founding the city of Allada. A dissident fraction later moved north to Abomey where they subdued their relatives, the Fanti. In the 18th century they conquered the neighbouring provinces on the coast but then came under Yoruba domination. The Dahomey king was even more autocratic than the Ashanti one, and his death was the sign for his women to destroy the fittings of the palace and then kill themselves. The 19th-century king Ghezo formed the celebrated corps of female warriors, the Amazons, who were his bodyguard and who took a prominent part in ceremonies and battles; under him the Dahomey once more became free.

The Yoruba, comprising a large number of tribes, first settled in Ife in the 13th century and soon conquered the Edo in the south-east, where a complicated hierarchical government was set up. From there the technique of casting bronze by *cire perdue*, for which Ife was famous and which some think came from Egypt, spread as far as the Ivory Coast and the Cameroons.

On the boundaries of the region inhabited by Bantu-speakers live the Sudanic-speaking Azande, who are almost red in colour, tending to fat, and have round heads. To the south of them are the Mangbetu whose colour varies from light brown to almost olive; they are extremely brachycephalic, and have very thick lips and somewhat slanted eyes. It is possible that they have an Ethiopian strain.

The Bantu (163-177)

The Bantu in the west reach down from the Congo to Angola. The Congo tribes were organised in small kingdoms at the time of their discovery by the Portuguese the largest being the Loango kingdom founded by the Bakongo; inland, the Lunda empire flourished in the 18th and 19th centuries, apparently on the foundation of an early indigenous culture which, it is thought, reached over to the Mozambique channel, where the famous kingdom of Monomotapa existed. Huge ruins dating from between the 9th and 13th centuries have been found there, at Zimbabwe, built by the Bantu to protect the gold mines of the region which for long had attracted Arab and Indian traders.

The Baluba, part of the Lunda empire, formed the states of Katanga, Urua and Uguha. They are an agricultural people whose women till the fields, the men being skilled craftsmen; they dress their hair in fantastic shapes, and practise tooth-filling and circumcision. A curious form of primitive communion arose among them in 1870, based on a cult of hemp-smoking in connection with a secret society.

Around the Great Lakes exists another group of tribal kingdoms, of which the Buganda are well known; their variability of features may be due to Hamitic admixture. The other Bantu of the area fall into two categories: the northeastern, and the true eastern amongst whom are Swahili-speakers whose language has become the lingua franca of East Africa. They arrived in the region as part of the early Bantu migrations from the west.

The northeastern Bantu include the Kikuyu and the Kamba (also known as the Wakamba, for the prefixes A-, Ba- and Wa- are attached to tribal names and mean 'people'). The Kamba are agriculturalists who also keep cattle, though against all the traditions of pastoralism they allow the women to do the milking. Like the Masai and Kikuyu they often bleed their cattle and drink the blood, which is a favourite food containing salt, difficult to obtain inland. They are enemies of the Masai to the south, and are divided into totemic clans without chiefs, government being exercised through a council of elders. The Kikuyu, who stemmed from the Kamba, entered the highlands of Kenya some five hundred years ago and continued their movement till the last century. Though they have cattle, goats are the main units of wealth and agriculture is important.

The tribes of Rhodesia are usually tallish, their lips being thinner than usual for the Bantu, and their noses often narrow, as among the Batonga. Further south we enter the southern division of the Bantu, where the Negro type predominates although another cast of features is noticeable, said to be Hamitic. This is especially prevalent amongst the Zulu and Tsonga groups where five per cent of the population have narrow faces, thin lips and prominent noses.

One of the principal language families of the south is Nguni, to which Zulu, Xhosa, Ndebele and Swazi all belong. The Zulus, one of the famous tribes of Africa, were formed by a unification of several groups under Shaka around 1800. Shaka reorganised the warriors through the existing clan structure and age-groups, introduced military service for women and set out to conquer the neighbourhood. This gave rise to numerous migrations. The Nguni, for instance, fleeing from the Zulu, settled in Nyasaland and have since increased enormously by incorporating the peoples they defeated and marrying their women; another tribe, part of the Zulu state, broke away, began conquests of their own and settled in Rhodesia as the Ndebele and Matabele, segments going as far north as Lake Tanganyika.

These tribes are both agricultural and pastoral, cattle rarely being killed for food – meat is obtained by hunting – while the drinking of their milk, as among the Zulu and Pondo, has the force of pledging blood-brotherhood between members of different clans. The Herero of southwest Africa, however, are much more dependent upon cattle, for they do not raise crops; and, like the Kamba, they allow their women to do the milking.

The Hova of Madagascar came from southeast Asia some four centuries ago and, with the Andrana, formed the Merina kingdom which existed until the occupation of the island by the French. The original inhabitants may well also have come from southeastern Asia since they, unlike the Negroes, are seafarers. Negroes do exist on the island today, however, namely the Mara and the Makoa, who were often brought in as slaves from the mainland, and the Sakalava, who live down the west coast. Another group, the Antemoro, claim descent from the Arabs.

Nilotes and Nilo-Hamites (178–189)

North of the Bantu-speakers are the Nilotes and Nilo-Hamites. The Nliotes are markedly long-headed, and have extremely long and slender legs. Negro features are common, though the Shilluk have the Hamitic thin, high-bridged nose and thin lips. The Shilluk are a cattle people who hardly grow enough grain to keep themselves; the men habitually go naked, and show a marvellous scorn for all things European. The Dinka are a group of independent tribes unlike the Shilluk, who are united under a strong king; like the

Dinka headman, he has the duty of making rain, and is killed when his strength fails.

The Nilotes live in the White Nile district; the Nilo-Hamites extend from the Bari tribe in the Sudan to the Turkana near Lake Rudolf and the Masai in Tanganyika. The Nilo-Hamites, as their name implies, have strong Hamitic elements racially, culturally and in their language. Many of them, like the Watussi, are very tall and slim, with long legs, a narrow face and a Hamitic nose, though the Turkana nose is broad. Like the Nilotes they wear few clothes, and their life centres upon cattle and, among the Masai and Nandi, war. The Masai are notable for wearing their hair in pigtails which they smear with red ochre, and for their curious houses like low tunnels.

Bushmen, Hottentots and Pygmies (190–196)

The Bushmen and Hottentots are related to each other, but not to the Pygmies. The Pygmies are to be found in the deep forests of the equator, in French Equatorial Africa, the Cameroons, the Congo and the Ituri basins. They were once more widespread, apparently as far as Liberia and the Gold Coast, and were well known to the Egyptians of the third millennium B.C. for their dancing and powers of mimicry.

The Pygmies stand from 4 ft 6 in. to 4 ft 8 in. high, but are well proportioned; this physique is often evolved in dense rain forest where small size is at a premium. There are two main types, one of them built small with a round head and face and a concave nose; the other is broader in the body, longer in the face and head, has more hair and a lighter skin, which goes from reddish to dark brown. In both types the eyes tend to bulge, the upper jaw juts out, and the arms are longer than the legs. They hunt with bows and poisoned arrows, and exchange game for vegetables with the surrounding Bantu, who stand to them as protectors and overlords.

The Bushmen and Hottentots are closely related and form the Khoisan race. At one time they must have been more widespread, for Bushman rock paintings are found all over south Africa and Tanganyika. The Bushmen have been linked with the Boskop race whose skulls, 10,000 years old, have been found in South Africa; these skulls are larger than those of present-day Bushmen, but have the same pentagonal shape when viewed from above. The Hottentots have a very long skull, similar to the Caucasoid type of the East African Mesolithic, but they must have intermarried with the Bushmen early on, for both have features in common. They are unique in using clicks as part of their language. They are short in stature, have a small broad face with a flat nose, bulging forehead and pointed chin; their eyes have a somewhat Mongoloid appearance, their ears often lack a lobe, and the buttocks tend to jut out and, amongst women, to accumulate fat and become steatopygous. Their skin is yellowish, and their hair grows in tight 'peppercorn' spirals. The Bushmen are somewhat taller than the Hottentots, however, with a narrower head and more prognathous face.

The Bushmen do not practise agriculture but gather all manner of small animals, roots and plants from the desert, and hunt for game with poisoned arrows. They are nomadic, each group hunting over a special territory and putting up rude branch shelters at the water-holes. Like the Pygmies, the Bushmen are wonderful mimics and at one time used to dress up as animals during the chase, in order to get near their quarry.

The Hottentots keep cattle which are of the East African type, and fat-tailed sheep. They can also smelt iron. Many of the Hottentot tribes were destroyed in the last century by the Basuto and by Europeans; some intermarried with Dutch colonists, giving rise to the Cape Coloureds, the Griqua and the Rehoboth hybrids. The largest surviving group is that of the Namas, divided into numerous clans.

ASIA, EAST INDIES

Mongols (197–203)

The history of Asia is largely that of the Mongoloid peoples, who stretch from Russia to China, and south through Burma and Siam into Indonesia; a further branch developed in the Americas. The Mongoloid as we know him now – with yellowish skin, coarse straight hair, a round head, large cheek-bones, a flat face and nose, and the Mongolian fold to the eyelids – is thought to have evolved in northeastern Asia when the original stock had become isolated during one of the glacial epochs, and were forced to adapt themselves rapidly to the extreme cold. Their characteristic features, as explained in the Introduction, all function to conserve heat and minimise frostbite. The cold itself would have stimulated the storage of fat, and two other factors may have been important: one is the evolutionary mechanism called paedomorphy, by which adults retain some infantile characters, which would explain the lack of beard, body hair and brow-ridges amongst the Mongoloids, their brachycephaly and the small differences of build between the sexes; the other is an absence of iodine in the inland areas of Asia which would have led to a thyroid deficiency, the thyroid being the regulator of growth.

Skulls found in China and belonging to the Upper Pleistocene already show some Mongoloid features, but the pre-Mongoloid stock survived into the Mesolithic and we may relate it to the Murrayan type which provided one element in the ancestry of the Polynesians, Australians and the Ainu.

The Mongols have played a great part in history. Chinese historians mention a number of tribes in 800 B.C. who had herds of sheep and cattle, practised a little agriculture, and came to dominate the entire Mongolian plain. Some centuries later they acquired the horse and wagon, perhaps from Turki and Iranian tribes, and from 400 to 200 B.C. they consistently harried China and conquered Chinese Turkestan. The Chinese decisively defeated these people, whom they called the Hiung-Nu, in the 2nd century A.D.; they then fled west to reappear again in Russia as the Huns some two hundred years later. They ravaged Europe as far as Rome, France and Germany, but withdrew after the death of Attila to the neighbourhood of the Volga. Other Hunnish tribes meanwhile invaded the Middle East and India, and a further incursion by the Avars occurred in the 8th century A.D. They were eventually defeated by a clan of the Hiung-Nu, the Tu-Kue, who gave their name to the present-day Turkish tribes.

The Mongols again expanded in the Middle Ages, and, under Kublai Khan, their immense empire included China. With Kublai's death the empire disintegrated, and the Chinese set about to control the steppe people, though the Khalkas and Kalmucks beyond the Gobi remained outside their influence until the 18th century, a fact which has brought about the distinction between Inner and Outer Mongolia.

The most westernly Mongoloid people are the Samoyed, who wander along the Arctic coasts and flank the Lapps of the Kola peninsula. They originally inhabited southwestern Siberia where they were in contact with early Turki tribes, had underground houses and knew how to cast bronze and forge iron; but the Ostiaks displaced them and they made their way north into the tundra where they learnt to hunt seals and reindeer, to fish, and eventually to herd reindeer. Like all Mongols, they are muscular, short-legged and long-bodied; they also have some Caucasoid features such as fair hair and mixed blue eyes.

To the west are the Tungus, whom the Samoyeds call 'Younger Brothers'; their clothes show Japanese influence, due to contact before they spread west; their territory now ranges from the Yenisei river along the Arctic coast, where it has been split in two by the intrusive Turkic Yakuts, and down towards the borders of China. Some have taken up farming, but for the most part they are forest hunters, trapping fur-bearing animals whose pelts they trade for provisions. They use the reindeer to carry their effects. Typically Mongoloid, their heads are slightly longer than their southern neighbours the Buryats, whose skulls are similar to those found in Avar cemeteries in Hungary. The Buryats, who herd cattle, sheep, horses, goats and some camels, seem to have settled in the area in the

13th century, and absorbed nomadic tribes of the neighbour-hood.

The Mongols, most famous of these nomadic people, live on the great open plains in felt tents or yurts, round which can be seen large piles of dung which are used as fuel in this treeless region. They are magnificent horsemen who think nothing of riding a hundred miles a day; they herd sheep, and make a drink of fermented mare's milk called kumiss. Their small local groups are organised into squadrons called 'arrows', the arrows being grouped under a 'banner', the whole under a ruling khan; it is a potentially powerful military organisation though it tends to fall apart at the death of the khan. Their original religion was shamanism, with a complicated sym-bolism concerning the World Tree and the projection of the spirit as a bird into the upper regions, but Buddhism influenced them even before the days of Genghis Khan and in the 17th century, when they were in close contact with Tibet, Buddhism spread throughout the tribes.

The Kalmucks, who moved west from their homeland in Sinkiang, are now settled mainly west of the Volga, where they raise their herds and breed horses which are sold as far afield as Poland. Others are still to be found on the Chinese border, and a few have migrated to the United States, where they settled in New Jersey.

In eastern Siberia a group of Palaearctic tribes is to be found, such as the Chukelis, the Gilyak and the Baryat. They must originally have lived in central Siberia north of the Gobi till they were pushed east by Tungusic peoples. With their longish heads they seem to be a mixture of the oldest Nordic and Mongolian stocks, though the Gilyak have something in common with the Ainu.

Turks and Tatars (204–210)

The other great Asiatic people are the Turks and Tatars, originally a Caucasian people who have a strong Mongoloid strain. Their face is very broad, with nose and cheek-bones prominent; they have a round head, a full beard and robust frame, and they usually lack the Mongolian eye-fold. These Altaic-speakers are to be found far in the east, in Turkestan; there is a central branch centring on the Pamirs, where the Kirghiz live, and also on the Volga and Caucasus, home of the Tatars; the western branch comprises the Turkomans.

The Turks, under their name of Tu-Kue, ranged over Mongolia to the Black Sea in the 6th century, but were expelled by the Kirghiz in the 9th and passed westward as part of the great Turkish expansion into the country south and east of the Urals, the Middle East and Europe. The first wave was that of the Khazars, whose main centres were around the Caspian and in the Crimea, where their descendants are still to be found; the second was that of the Kipchaks.

The Kazan Tatars live mostly in the Volga region, and other related tribes stretch to the east in the Urals and central Asia. These tribes once formed part of the famous Golden Horde which conquered Kazan in the 15th century, only reconquered by the Russians in 1552. Some of these people are settled, others trap furs and hunt in the forests and mountains; yet others are pastoral nomads.

The Turkomans we have already met in northern Iran. They too are pastoralists, and show a mixture of Caucasoid and Mongoloid features. Some, like the Yomud of Russian Turkestan, are dolicho-cephalic, with a high head, an extraordinary length of face and an Iranian nose; the tribes of Choudir are much rounder-headed, with a round face, the nose having a lower root. There is some fair hair, perhaps from admixture with the Kurds.

The Kirghiz occupied central Mongolia, between Lake Baikal and the Yenisei river, till the 12th century A.D. when they fled from Genghis Khan and occupied the highlands of Tien Shan and the Pamir. In this region, which was neither a caravan nor an invasion route, they lived without being molested till the 18th century when they had to fight the Kalmucks. They never formed a state in this region, but continued as nomads moving from the high pasture in the summer to the lowlands in winter, using horses for riding and yaks as pack-beasts. Few have the Mongoloid eye-fold, and their nose is long and high-bridged; they are probably closely similar to the tribes who invaded Europe in earlier times.

The Eskimo (211–215)

The Eskimo, living in Greenland, along the Arctic coasts of North America, and the extreme northeastern tip of Siberia, are closely related to the Mongoloids, and are clearly differentiated from the American Indians by their possession of the B blood group, practically unknown elsewhere in America. They are late-comers to the continent, having arrived in the Aleutians about 1000 B.C., and they spread gradually over to Greenland, which was occupied by the 12th century A.D. Their culture and language remain fairly consistent over this range, and they have shown remarkable ingenuity in coping with a freezing climate and a winter half a year long. Europeans exploring the Arctic have had to adopt Eskimo clothes in order to survive; they are made of seal and caribou skin, chewed to softness by the women. In the early spring they fish for trout and salmon; they hunt caribou in the summer, when the herds come north, go off to sea to kill whales and walrus, and in winter spear seals through blow-holes in the ice. All their equipment – the composite bow, the harpoon, the dogsledge – is beautifully made out of ivory and small pieces of wood found as jetsam; they live in tents during the summer and igloos throughout the winter, except in the west where the rivers bring down large trees and they are able to build log cabins. They have a minimum of social organisation and are liable to nurse blood feuds for generations, there being no leaders to compose quarrels except the shamans, whose functions are primarily religious and medical.

The Eskimo have a large broad face with very large cheek-bones and a Mongolian eye-fold; they are notable for their thick body, short legs and small hands and feet. Their heads are brachycephalic with a high-keeled vault.

Chinese and Koreans (216–226)

Primitive agriculture had probably entered China by the 2nd millennium B.C. from the oasis area in Kansu in the northwest. From there it spread gradually east, north and south, the agriculturalists displacing the early tribes of the area, many of whom now live in the hills and mountains of the south and southwest. The Chinese proper, whose exact origins are unknown, must have intermarried with these tribes as they did with Mongols, Turks, Tatars and Manchus, all of whom have invaded the country at various times.

The Chinese are divided into four main groups: the Northern Chinese, who live around the Huang Ho basin and to the north; the Central Chinese, settled along the Yangtze Kiang up to Yunnan on the border of Burma; the Southern, occupying the valley and environs of the Sikiang river, whose mouth is at Canton; and the tribal Chinese, in the south and west.

The Northern Chinese are somewhat like European Nordics in being strong, tall and fairly dolichocephalic; they have an oblong, squarish face, oblique eyes, a long and moderately high nose, and yellow-brown skin. To their north is Manchuria, the home of the Tungusic Manchu, who invaded the northeast of China in the 12th century and set up the Chin dynasty, and again in the 17th, their empire then lasting until the revolution of 1912.

The Central Chinese are perhaps somewhat shorter, inclined to be stout except on the coasts, where a more slender build is common, and have a fairish skin, less narrow nose than that of the Northern Chinese, straight eyes, and a face which classically should be shaped like a watermelon seed, that is, a long oval. Cheek-bones are prominent, and the head is mesocephalic.

The south is the region from which most of the emigrants to southwest Asia and other lands have come from. Their skins are dark, being a deep yellow or copper, with lank black hair, flattish noses, a rather thick mouth with a tendency for the jaw to be prognathous; their build is short and thickset. Also in the south are the Hakka, whose name means 'foreigner'. These originally came from north of the Yangtze in the 3rd century B.C. in order to escape the invading Mongols and, being an independent people, have continually been in the position of rebels, somewhat like the Highlanders of Scotland. They also live in Hainan Island to the south, which they share with the Miao and the Li tribes.

Hakkas are also in Formosa, together with Chinese immigrants from the central Fukien region, who fled from the recurrent famines of the 17th century. There are numbers of aboriginals present also, who came from Indonesia.

The Koreans to the north are essentially a branch of the Chinese, who moved into the area in very early times. Their language, however, is of the Ural-Altaic group. Before the Christian era the Chinese occupied the north, and Chinese culture has always been of the highest importance to the whole country; but native kingdoms were formed soon after, and lasted till the Mongol invasions of the 13th century. Another native dynasty was founded in 1392, which lasted till the Japanese occupation in 1910.

Japanese and the Ainu (227–232)

Japan was populated mainly from the mainland of China, and the type present shows little difference from that living in northern China and Korea. The face is broad, the eyes slant, the nose is flat and the mouth fairly wide. Amongst the upper classes the head tends to be narrower, and the nose straighter; they are also taller. This height may be due to an improved diet, for the short stature of the Japanese has shown an increase of three inches to an average of 5 ft 4 in within the last fifty years. The Japanese have also slightly more hair on their faces and bodies than the mainlanders, which is probably caused by admixture with the proverbially hairy Ainu, who originally were settled throughout the country and were pushed into the northern islands of Hokkaido and Sakhalin by the Japanese.

The Ainu seem to be the descendants of that archaic stock which was present throughout Asia in early times, emigrating to the south and east as more advanced peoples came on the scene. They used to be great hunters of bear and deer, and fished with the help of dogs; the bear cult, present in Palaeolithic times in Europe and with traces still existing throughout Asia, was practised, a bear cub being caught, tamed, treated like an honoured guest and finally sacrificed as a messenger to the gods.

Their skulls are mesocephalic, but are otherwise similar to Australian skulls, though the chin is much larger; they have a thickset body, with long arms and short legs, a greyish-white or brownish skin, and a remarkable growth of hair on face and body.

Tribal Chinese (233–238)

In the southwest of China are numerous tribal peoples, some of whom must represent the descendants of the early inhabitants of China. The Black Lolo, or Black Bone tribe, live in the Liang mountains in Yunnan, and are said to have originally come from Burma, though curiously enough they have always been associated with the horse and an Iranian ancestry has been imputed to them. They are very tall, dolichocephalic, oval-faced, with small cheekbones, a straight fine nose, straight eyes with a fiery expression, fair skin inclined to be swarthy, and wavy chestnut hair. These people are the aristocrats amongst the tribes, being a kind of Asiatic Spartan; they have stockaded castles in the hills, grow fine potatoes and poppies for the opium trade, keep herds of goats, yaks and sheep, and raid their neighbours for slaves. The Lolo and other similar peoples on the Tibetan border are immensely independent and have never been controlled by the Chinese.

Their slaves, part Chinese, part tribal, are known as White Lolo and sometimes Miao, the word Miao meaning 'plant' and designating the peoples scattered throughout Yunnan and Kweichow. They are a much more passive and sedentary tribe than the Black Lolo. Also in Yunnan are the Minkia, wonderful masons and carpenters who are said to have come from the neighbourhood of Angkor Thom in the south, the great temple which may have been built by their ancestors; and the Nakhi, a passionate and somewhat choleric people whose women are indefatigable traders and do all the work.

This region of the southwest contains within it a confluence of rivers which rise in the Tibetan plateau. Here the Yangtze Kiang flows, first south and then east; then the Mekong, watering the great plains of Indo-China; the Salween, running down the eastern borders of Burma, the Chindwin and Irrawaddy going down its centre; and running along the south of Tibet, reversing direction in Assam to parallel the course of the Ganges with its mouth near Calcutta, is the Brahmaputra. These river courses are the natural ways of entry into southeastern Asia, and it is likely that after the settlement of the region by Negritos and Veddoids, an early Malayan type of people made their way down them. These people, with longer heads, broader noses and a more stocky build than present-day Malays, already possessed some traits of the southern Chinese, and of the archaic Asiatic stock; they must also have mixed with the aborigines to some extent. We can perhaps see their descendants in some of the Naga tribes of Assam, the Karen of Burma and various tribes along the southern Tibetan border; also, it may be, amongst the Igorot and Ifugao of Luzon.

They were followed by a steady infiltration of southern Mongoloids, and the crossing of these two strains produced the Malayans of today. Thus in this area we must consider a number of different groupings: the Tibetans, the hill tribes of Assam and Burma, and the Malays; the Lao who are called Shan in Burma and Thai in Siam, who are of Southern Chinese stock; and the Annamese, who came down the coast on the west from China later.

Assamese and Burmese (239–243, 253)

Assam is full of ancient Hindu sites, but there is a much stronger Mongoloid strain in the population than further west in India. In the north there are the Abors and Mishmis, related to the Tibetans, who used to raid the lowlands from out of their wet forests; there are also the Apo Tani, who have terraced agriculture with irrigation. Mingled with the Hindus of the plains are the Ahom, remnants of the Shans from Burma who conquered the province in the 13th century; in the highlands of the south, in Manipur, is a region influenced by Shan or perhaps Chinese culture, where the British first learnt the sport of polo.

In this area also are the Naga, the Abors of Assam, the Chin of Burma and the Kachin who reach to the borders of Yunnan. These tribes speak a total of forty different languages, and in some Naga villages two different languages will be spoken on opposite sides of the same village street. Their culture is almost as mixed, and some tribes practise slash-and-burn farming, others terrace and irrigate their fields, building long canals to lead water to their rice; some are governed by a council of elders, or by sacred chiefs whose feet must never touch the ground, or by a form of democracy. All Nagas are head-hunters, the head thought to contain the life essence which can be imparted to crops and to the family and village of the

head-hunter; they also erect large stones as part of an ancient megalithic cult. Though they speak languages of the Tibeto-Burman
family, they are also related distantly to peoples in the south and the
Pacific; like Formosan tribes, for instance, who have some similar
institutions such as age-grades. The Kachin group, more mongoloid
in appearance, are clannish, organised under a hereditary chief, and
are slave-raiders rather than head-hunters; as are the Abors, who
practise polyandry.

Himalayas (244–248)

Tibet is divided into innumerable tribes, clans, petty kingdoms and
lamaseries, organised on a feudal basis under the central government. Some of these are quite remote from Lhasa; the province of
Kham, for example, the Holy Land, filled with forests and rivers, is
something of a land of mystery even to the average Tibetan who
lives in gaunt mountains full of dust and howling winds. The
Khamba, who are a gigantic good-looking people, whose women
have fair skins, frequently turn bandit, banditry being a time-
honoured profession.

Tibet is isolated from the main trade routes which connect China
with western Asia, and has been able to develop its own curious
culture with little interference from outside. The Tibetans were
originally pastoralists living near Koko Nor, who united in the 4th
century B.C. and became so powerful that they contributed to the
downfall of the Tsin dynasty in China. Later Buddhist missionaries
from Nepal entered the country, and in the 7th century the ruling
king was converted to Buddhism by the princesses of upper Burma
and western China, whom he had married after his conquest of those
regions. Many native shamanistic practices have been incorporated
into Tibetan Buddhism, and the spiritual leadership is invested in a
succession of Dalai Lamas, each held to be the reincarnation of his
predecessor and originating with the Buddha himself. The Chinese
sacked Lhasa in the 8th century, but soon after the Tibetan empire
recovered and reached the borders of the Arab and Turkish empires
over the Pamirs; Turkestan and Nepal were subject to it, and China
as far as Chang-An. One of their incursions south reached the Bay of
Bengal. Kublai Khan adopted lamaism as the religion for his empire,

and after its hey-day Tibet has been under Chinese influence, and was indeed occupied by China recently.

There are two main types in the country: the representatives of one, dolichocephalic, are like the Northern Chinese except that they are more ruggedly built and hairier; the others, brachycephalic, are somewhat like the Southern Chinese. In general the face is narrower than the typical Mongoloid one, less padded with fat, and sporting a prominent nose.

The kingdom of Bhutan is organised on similar lines to Tibet, with a secular and a spiritual head who is recognised by his ability to pick out the cooking utensils and personal belongings of his predecessor; culturally and commercially it is part of Tibet rather than of India, and the terraced agriculture of northern Assam is practised here. In Sikkim to the west live the Lepchas, a casteless tribe divided into nine clans, whose literature was completely destroyed by the Tibetans; they are now the poorest peoples living in the country, making up the coolie class and farming with hoes in slash-and-burn style. Nepal, finally, has a basic Tibeto-Burman population, overlaid by Hindu influences caused by the Moham-medan invasions of the 8th and 14th centuries, the Gurkha kingdom of the 18th century becoming so powerful that it managed to invade Tibet, and was only repelled by Chinese troops.

Southeast Asians (249–262)

The main aboriginal element in southeastern Asia are called Nesiot, and must have entered the territory about 2,000 B.C. with a know-ledge of irrigation and with cattle. Nowadays this stock is largely submerged, though it can still be seen in the hill tribes of Indo-China – nowadays the two nations of Laos and Vietnam – amongst the Batak of Sumatra, the Dyaks of Borneo, the Toraja of Celebes, and tribes in the Philippines.

The culture of Burma comes largely from India, and the old Burmese kingdom, which flowered after the 11th century, claimed descent from Indian kings. It was destroyed by the Mongols in the 13th century. After a short period when it was subject to the Shan states it regained its freedom and a new native dynasty was set up.

Some representatives of the Nesiots are still present, but the main bulk of the population is formed by the Mon-Khmer people, to the west of the Shan states, some of whom are remnants of the once powerful Pegu kingdom which for long strove with the Burmese for mastery of the kingdom.

The Mon-Khmer settled in Siam, the present-day Thailand, and in the 8th century colonised the north, which later became part of the Khmer empire. The south, which is a distinct region, came under Cambodian influence. Later the Thai entered from southern China where they had a flourishing empire between the 6th and 9th centuries, becoming variously known as Lao, Thai and Shan. They drove out the wild Kha tribes into the hills, sending out expeditions from time to time to capture slaves from them. Some of the Lao at the present time are tattooed from waist to knee, and called the Black Paunch Lao.

The same movement from the north was repeated in Indo-China, where the Chinese have had great influence. The Annamites, who make up 75 per cent of the population, are Confucian and have accepted much Chinese culture, including forms of administrative government; they are slight in build, have pale yellow skins, high cheek-bones and oblique eyes. In the central highlands are the Moi tribes, small, copper-coloured, with wavy hair and a broad nose. To the south are the Cambodians, Buddhist by religion, darker than the Annamites, with almost aquiline noses and no Mongolian fold to the eye.

In the Malay peninsula we find the Negrito Semang, the much mixed Sakai and the pagan Jakun people, who must have entered the region about 1600 B.C. The Jakun were pushed into the interior by other Malaysian peoples from Sumatra, Celebes and Thailand, and later by Chinese traders and Tamil labourers. Like many peoples of this area, they practise slash-and-burn agriculture, using the digging stick; they have the blowpipe, like the Sakai, and file their teeth to a point. Their skin is darker than that of the true Malay, but they have the typical brachycephalic skull, broad but flat face with a prominent chin, and a straight eye-slit with a Mongolian fold.

The Malays exist in small pockets throughout the continent, though they are in force only in the peninsula. Being notable seafarers they have spread to Formosa, the Philippines, Borneo, New Guinea and even to Madagascar.

The true Malays originally came from Sumatra. The East Indies, at about the beginning of the Christian era, were strongly influenced by India and two important states arose later, one in Sumatra from the 3rd to the 13th centuries, and one in Java at the end of the 13th. In the fourteenth century the Malays established a trading post at Malacca which, though paying tribute at first to the Thai, soon became independent and rich. Arab traders brought over the Muslim faith, which spread rapidly after the 14th century, and caused the downfall of the old Hindu-type empires. However, the heritage of this period is still preserved in Bali, which never became Mohammedan and which still has a caste system, and traditional music and dances; although the greatest religious monuments are the ruins of Borobudur in Java.

In Borneo there are two main types of Malaysian peoples: the Land Dyaks, who are more Indonesian, and the Sea Dyaks, such as the Iban of Sarawak, who are more mongoloid. Some Land Dyaks are forest nomads in the depths of the interior, still in the hunting and gathering stage; most of them, however, live on the rivers in their famous long houses which can contain a group of several hundred related people. They grow hill rice, fish, hunt and have highly developed religions. The blowpipe is used, and formerly there was much warfare and head-hunting.

More primitive are the Batak of Sumatra, coarser in feature than the surrounding Malays, who grow rice in terraces, use the blowpipe and were once addicted to war and cannibalism; and the Ifugao and Igorot of Luzon in the Philippines. Both these people practise agriculture, the Ifugao building the most remarkable system of walls, terraces and irrigation ditches which extend a thousand and more feet up the hillsides, the whole being a gigantic piece of engineering done with the most primitive tools. Blood feuds and head-hunting were common until recently.

THE AMERICAS

North American Indians (263–280)

The American Indian, or Amerindian as he is known for short, originally came from Asia. The earliest archaeological finds in the New World date from before 10,000 B.C.: these consist of flint points, some of which were discovered in the bones of extinct mammoths, and we must assume that the early hunters came via the Bering Straits soon after the last glaciation, when a land-bridge connected Asia and Alaska.

The Amerindians, then, are an Asiatic stock, and though they show much diversity a basic Mongoloid appearance is discernible: they have yellow brown skin, sometimes reddish, the hair is black, coarse and usually straight, the cheek-bones can be prominent, and the eye has something of a mongoloid look although the typical eye-fold is rare except in women and children. Noses, however, are not mongoloid, being rarely flat, but are hooked, straight and sometimes concave; and brow ridges are sometimes present. Blood groups also show non-Mongoloid distribution: the B group is absent in America, whereas it is common in Asia; and other groups, such as M and a Rhesus gene, link Amerindians with Polynesians rather than with Mongoloids.

To account for this variability we can suppose that the first comers to the New World were an archaic long-headed stock, the descendants of late Pleistocene peoples whose remains have been found in China and its surrounds. Representatives of this type have been found in California and in an ancient skull found at Lagoa Santa in Brazil; probably all the marginal peoples of America, such as the Yahgan and Alacaluf of Tierra del Fuego, primitive seed-eaters around San Francisco and scattered tribes in the South American jungles, owe something to this first migration. However, brachycephalic peoples must also have been entering the continent. The first indication we have is of a skull dating from 9,000 B.C. at Tepexpán, Mexico; the main migration no doubt came later, around 6,000 B.C. This came down the west coast, groups detaching themselves to settle in the southeast of North America, the Pueblo region, the Isthmus, and down the Andes to Patagonia. Early agriculture began in some of these areas in the third millennium B.C., practised by members of this stock who were responsible for all the great civilisations of central America and the Andes; their early cultures were already flourishing in the first half-millennium B.C., and reached a peak in the next thousand years.

Much work remains to be done both on the racial characteristics of Amerindians and their historical movements, and rather than attempt a description in these terms it is more satisfactory to take them by cultural areas. Many tribes, of course, have now disappeared both in North and South America, after their contact with European culture, and this is especially true of more primitive groups; but even amongst the others much of their traditional way of life has been lost.

The Kwakiutl, the Tlingit and the Tsimshian are amongst the tribes of the Canadian northwest. Before they were affected by European contact they had no agriculture but used nets, harpoons and weirs to catch salmon, which they dried for winter eating, or hunted deer, otters and mountain goats for food, skins and wool. Warfare was so common that they had slatted armour; their society was strongly hierarchical, with hereditary chiefs who ruled over the commoners and slaves, everyone being divided into clans whose totem poles were raised at the side of their plank houses. Masked dances took place in winter, at which cannibalism occurred; and the chiefs competed with each other in the celebrated potlatches, where great quantities of goods were exchanged in order to show the giver's wealth and power.

In the interior, stretching over the continent to the east, were the Northern Hunters, exemplified by the Kutchin of the upper Yukon. The climate here varies from that of the frozen tundra to that of the southern forests, and caribou were the main food, caught in the open or stampeded into gullies. Their flesh, dried or frozen, was cached for the winter. In many respects they are similar to the Eskimo: the tribes were divided into small bands, with leaders but no chiefs; blood feuds were common, dogs were used to draw sledges, tailored clothes were made of skins, cooking was done by dropping hot stones into containers, and hospitality was shown by exchanging wives.

When the Plains were first discovered the few tribes living there hunted the bison on foot and practised agriculture. However, the Indians stole horses soon after the Spanish entered the south, and guns were acquired from trappers in the north: the Kiowa and Comanche burst in from the northwest and the Sioux, Pawnee, Oto and many others from the east, evolving a new type of culture which was based on the horse. Large-scale bison-hunting was started, and raiding for horses amongst neighbouring tribes and settlements; there were male secret societies associated with the sun dance and prowess in war, initiation was a matter of endurance, fasting and self-torture, and solitary vigils were held to obtain visions of a guardian spirit. It was amongst these tribes that the Indian war-bonnet was found, though it has since been copied as a typical and picturesque adornment by many others who did not possess it.

During the late 19th century Europeans began moving into the Plains, first as bison hunters and then as cattle rangers and farmers; the bison were all but exterminated by 1890, the Indians herded into reservations. At this time large-scale revolts based on mythological themes arose, in the belief that the whites would disappear and the bison return, but after a further series of Indian wars the revolts were suppressed and many tribes took up agriculture. The memory of the old days is still strong, however, and many Indians belong to the Native American Church, a part-native and part-Christian religion in which peyote is eaten to induce visions.

To the west of the Plains is a fertile plateau full of deer and salmon rivers, with numerous groups whose culture was influenced both by the Northwest Indians and by the Plains: the Nez Percé, for instance, who used the traditional semi-underground hut as a bachelor's lodge, having the Plains tepee as a dwelling; they cooked by dropping hot stones into pits lined with basketry, had clothes of sewn deerskin, and used the dog as a pack animal.

In California live a number of primitive groups, eating acorn flour whose tannin had been leached out with water, grass seeds, fish and small game. Like many other tribes they had the sweat bath and an underground lodge for ceremonies; their houses were of brush or, in the north, of planks. They had no pottery, except for the Yuman to the south, but made excellent baskets, and fished from rafts made of reed bundles.

Down the Rio Grande and in Arizona lived the Pueblo tribes, the word meaning village in Spanish. Some of these villages in the past were very large, and sited inside cliff caves for defence; others were built in a circle, like the present-day village of Taos, rising several stories high. The villagers are divided into clans, of which sixty are known amongst the Hopi, each divided into twelve segments with their own rites. There are also numerous secret societies who have masked dances in honour of the gods in underground kivas, or in the mountains; public dances are also held, one of which, the snake dance, has attracted much attention. They do some hunting but live mainly by agriculture, planting their crops in terraces along the hillsides.

Athabaskan-speakers from the northwest have also colonised the area, namely the southern Utes, Apaches and Navahos. The Navaho, who farm and herd sheep, are famous for their sand paintings which inaugurate long and complicated ceremonies; they are also silversmiths, an art they learnt from the Spanish.

Small chiefdoms once existed amongst Indians in the southeast, the tribes forming confederacies, society being organised into clans and classes. Their villages were surrounded by palisades and their temples were built on mounds; some, like the Pawnee, practised human sacrifice. Muskogean-speakers, such as the Seminole, seem to be the descendants of the tribes who created the Mississippi culture which flourished in that area between 900 and 1300 A.D., leaving behind large numbers of earthen mounds as monuments.

In the east are the woodland tribes: the Iroquois in the centre amongst Algonquin-speakers such as the Shawnee to the west, the Micmac and Delaware to the east. They lived by farming, gathered wild rice, acorns and maple juice; the men hunted for deer and fished in the rivers, the typically South American use of poison being known in the south. The Algonquins lived in bark- or mat-covered lodges, wore woven feather cloaks and made receptacles out of birch bark; the Iroquois, who during the 17th and 18th centuries banded together in a military federation known as the Five Nations (later six) and whose chiefs were elected by the women, had fortified bark-covered long houses and made pottery.

Central American Indians (281–287)

Central America has seen the rise of many cultures and civilisations, the Maya in the south and the Toltec in the north who were followed by Nahuatl-speaking Aztecs, originally a warrior tribe, who took over the main elements of Toltec civilisation and evolved various refinements in the way of military government, and large-scale ritual sacrifice. They were all fully developed cultures with a great knowledge of metallurgy and astronomy; they evolved complicated calendars, a script, had a considerable literature, built imposing temples and pyramids, wove fine textiles and made pottery, and they only lacked some form of domesticated animal to use as a draught beast and the use of the wheel in transport to bring them on a par with comparable civilisations in the Old World.

With the advent of the Spaniards, however, the superstructure of this complicated way of life was destroyed and what survives is a medley of traditional Indian and Spanish practices. The Spanish influence is greatest in the north, in the old Aztec area, while tribes in the centre who live off the main high roads, and in the south, are less touched. They are governed through a number of offices, secular and religious, based upon a Spanish pattern, which frequently impoverishes the office-holders who must pay for great quantities of liquor which is more or less ceremonially drunk; there are great numbers of fiestas, celebrating saints' days, at which fireworks are let off, and dancers, both masked and unmasked, perform. Groups are often divided by locality, though amongst the Tzeltal and Lacandón there are clans; and a number of old religious practices remains. The Indians of Chiapas in the south, such as the Zinacantecan and Tzotzil-speaking Chamula, still make offerings to the sacred caves, hold half-pagan ceremonies in their churches, regard springs as sacred and erect crosses, which were known in the area before the Conquest; the Mixtecs use the teonanactl mushroom to induce visions in traditional style, and amongst the Quiche systematic Mayan beliefs are still to be seen in their worship and their calendrical farming rites. The Lacandón, moreover, still make offerings of copal incense to the old gods in the ruined temples amongst the forests.

On the isthmus there are other representatives of old cultures: the Cuna, for instance, descendants of the old Coclé, a warlike confederacy of tribes who worked metals, made fine carvings in shell and bone, and practised human sacrifice. Both men and women now hunt game, fish, and use the digging stick in slash-and-burn agriculture. They have lost many of their old traditions though they still are divided into nobles, commoners and slaves, with three sub-chiefs and one head chief in each village or island. The Cuna living in San Blas are noted for the occasional appearance of white skin amongst them, this being the effect of albinism.

South American Indians (285, 288–302)

Further south, in Colombia, are the Chocó (originally from Panama where some are still to be found) and Cágaba. The Chocó fish and farm, and produce large numbers of bananas for export; they have no chiefs or villages, but live scattered along the river banks in circular huts raised on piles. The Cágaba, however, have villages of conical huts, and they practise agriculture sometimes with the help of irrigation.

The great Inca civilisation of the Andes was based on numerous previous cultures, principally that of Tiahuanaco, and subjugated many neighbouring peoples. It was noted especially for its immense irrigation works and network of roads; for a bureaucratic form of government under a divine king whose records were kept by means of knotted strings; for massive public buildings in stone, metallurgy, fine fabrics and the domestication of llamas, alpaca, guinea pigs, etc. The Inca themselves were Quechua-speakers, and by colonising many districts and shifting the native population elsewhere managed to give a general Quechua cast to the whole area. After the Spanish conquest much of the Inca heritage was lost and, as in Mexico, present-day villages are organised on the pattern of Spanish officialdom of the 16th and 17th centuries, and their religion is largely Catholic with numerous fiestas. Quechuas are basically agricultural, growing potatoes, tubers and grain, but have to make do without the irrigation systems of the Inca which were neglected by the Spaniards and whose loss has hastened the movement of Indians to the towns and silver mines. The hacienda system prevails in the lowlands, but in isolated parts many old ways still continue, and llama herding takes place in the uplands; the old Indian Inca ayllus, or local endogamous groups, and the aine, or co-operative labour system, still exist. The narcotic coca is chewed universally, to take the edge off hunger and exhaustion, and offerings of coca are made to the earth before planting.

To the south are the Aymara, another highland people, who before Inca times were divided into a number of warring groups, with a complex system of social classes. Wars were for loot and slaves, and some cannibalism occurred, the blood of captives being drunk to assimilate their courage: the blood of pumas is sometimes taken this way nowadays, to the same end. There is a hierarchy of spirits inhabiting lakes and mountains, to which sacrifice is made in shrines. Like the Quechua, they practise agriculture, their fields often being terraced and irrigated, and those living near lakes fish from reed canoes.

On the coasts and highlands of Chile are the remnants of the Araucanians, influenced by the Inca but never subdued by them, and only losing their independence to the Spaniards in the late 19th century. They are mainly agricultural and until the introduction of the plough used the digging stick, though irrigation was common. Their daub and wattle huts were organised in hamlets under local headmen, who in turn were under a paramount chief. Since Spanish times they have become expert horsemen and workers in silver.

At the tip of the continent live the Yahgan and Ona, in one of the most desolate countries imaginable. Since Europeans have settled here and sheep farms have spread over the region, few remain, many having been purposefully hunted down and killed. The Yahgan had canoes of birch-bark strips, from which they speared sea-urchins, gathered molluscs, fished, caught sea-birds and sea-lions; they dressed exiguously in skin capes, and sheltered in wind-breaks. There were originally five local groups with no very definite organisation, though a chief was necessary several months a year to officiate at initiations.

The Ona were primarily hunters, killing guanaco and rodents, and fishing when near the coasts; they dressed in skin capes and leggings, though the men frequently went naked when hunting, even in the depths of winter, and built huts covered with sods or skins. They had no chiefs.

Their relatives the Tehuelche roamed to the north of them in migratory bands, living in caves and wind-breaks. In the early 18th century they acquired horses and hunted guanaco, rheas and wild cattle with the lance and bolas, small groups uniting for a while under a chief.

Horses were also important to the Chaco tribes, some of them like the Toba becoming robber nomads. They hunted in large groups, setting fire to the grass to stampede the game. The country is very rich in fruit, nuts and roots, and collecting these foods largely took the place of agriculture, though the Lengua had small gardens. Fishing was also important, and many tribes now herd sheep. The Mbayá tribes, unlike the Lengua, had hereditary chiefs and nobles, so aristocratic that even the Spaniards addressed them with respect; they kept slaves, and raided other tribes for children whom they adopted.

In the huge interior of South America are numerous other peoples, divided for ease of reference into agricultural Forest tribes and Marginal tribes. The Marginal tribes live mainly by fishing, hunting and food-gathering, though the Bororo have gardens; many of them, like the Suyá, wear labrets or lip-plugs, whence their general appellation of Botocudo. The Bororo have circular villages, divided into moieties and clans with a man's house in the centre; their funeral rites are complicated, and are linked with initiation.

The Forest tribes practise agriculture often on a large scale, growing manioc, potatoes, yams, cotton and tobacco, and unlike the Marginal tribes who sleep on raised platforms or on the ground, they use the hammock. They live on or near the rivers, like the Carajá whose gardens are along the watercourses and can be reached by canoe; they fish with the bow and arrow, the spear and with poison. The villages are quite large, either of small huts grouped together or as a single very large house, organised under a chief, a shaman and sometimes, as with the Carajá, a priest who officiates at the cult of the dead. Warfare is frequent, and so is cannibalism, the word cannibal coming from the name of the Carib tribes, who in the old days came out of the highlands of the north and swept over the Caribbean islands, taking captives from the Arawak tribes whom they tortured, killed and ate, though they kept the women for wives. The Jivaro in the northwest mountain regions, one of the largest tribes existing whom neither the Inca nor the Spanish could conquer, still war amongst themselves, hunting heads and shrinking the heads as trophies.

OLD WORLD, NEW WORLD

Emigrants and Mixed Races (303-321)

The foregoing account will make it clear that truly aboriginal tribes who have lived in one area for any length of time are rare, and that the history of mankind has been full of wars, invasions and movements of people from one part of the world to another. These movements are not at an end: we can find Caucasians in many parts of the globe, as colonists of the immense tracts of land opened up in the last few hundred years at the expense of native peoples. French, Scots, English and Ukrainians are in Canada; people of every European nationality in the United States, plus large numbers of Africans brought over during the slave days; Africans are also present throughout the Caribbean area, in Brazil and in parts of Mexico. Spaniards and Portuguese have changed the complexion of Latin America, both racially and culturally, and even the apartheid-conscious South African Boers were once responsible for the creation of the Cape Coloureds, through intermarriage with Hottentot women. Syrians and Indians live as traders throughout Africa and South America, Japanese are in Brazil and Hawaii, the Chinese all over southeast Asia, Tamils in Ceylon and Malaya, and Lascar seamen work in many ports and ships throughout the world.

Everywhere there is change, bringing in its train many difficult social problems; for differences of race, though by no means pointing to differences of intelligence, capacity or will-power, are still connected popularly with differences of history and social development. As formerly colonial countries become nations, and industrialism spreads, many of these problems may be solved; but there will always be new ones, as the balance of power shifts, new countries become wealthy, and further movements of peoples take place.

INDEX

References in **bold type** are to illustration numbers and
NOT to pages. Other references are to text pages.